The Inheritance

KATE HORAN

FICTION

The Inheritance
© 2025 by Kate Horan
ISBN 9781038940322

First published on Gadigal Country in Australia in 2025
by HQ Fiction
an imprint of HQBooks (ABN 47 001 180 918), a subsidiary of HarperCollins Publishers
Australia Pty Limited (ABN 36 009 913 517).

HarperCollins acknowledges the Traditional Custodians of the lands upon which we
live and work, and pays respect to Elders past and present.

Author photo credit: Erin Masters

A catalogue record for this book is available from the National Library of Australia
www.librariesaustralia.nla.gov.au

Printed and bound in Australia by McPherson's Printing Group

For my mum, the strongest, funniest person I know.

And my dad. I wish you were here to see this.

DNA Sleuths Facebook Group

Anonymous: Has anyone here gifted DNA kits to expose a family secret? I'm thinking this Christmas might be time for the truth to come out. Finally. Interested to hear your experiences, good, bad or otherwise. No judgment please.

Top comments

Mary Louise: Be careful anonymous. You never know which secrets the DNA will reveal. My innocent curiosity about our family history revealed a case of NPE. My elderly mother hasn't spoken to me since.

> **Anonymous:** Thanks **Mary Louise.** What is NPE? Sorry, I'm new around here.

> **Mary Louise:** NPE is a Non-Paternity Event. Get what I'm saying? More common than you think. Turns out my mum was a bit too friendly with my dad's best man …

> **Anonymous:** Oh, wow, sorry to hear that.

Fergus Schmidt: I agree with **Mary Louise**. You sound very sure what the tests will reveal. Problem is DNA isn't selective. What if you blow the top off something else altogether?

Sara Power: WTF??? This borders on manipulation. It's morally questionable to say the least.

Karen Finn: Rubbish!!! She's just thinking of giving them the test, it's up to them if they do it or not. She's not planning to steal their saliva in their sleep!!!

Sara Power: Okay Karen

Karen Finn: Very mature! Also she said no judgment.

Tracey Dunn: Admin here, just a reminder about our Code of Conduct. Be kind, ladies.

Wendy Turner: Wouldn't it be best to have a robust conversation with the people involved? IMO DNA shouldn't be used for this purpose, real relationships are involved. Do you really want to be responsible for destroying the family?

Karen Finn: SECRETS destroy families!! It's not her fault if people have lied!

Tracey Dunn: Ok I'm closing the comments on this post because I need to go to bed.

* * * **Comments are closed** * * *

Chapter 1

Meg pressed the buzzer and drummed her fingers on her thighs as she waited for a voice on the intercom.

'Come on,' she muttered, fanning her denim shirt, wishing she'd worn something more appropriate for the early December heat.

She had an urge to buzz again, but resisted. The Rosedale nursing staff were stretched enough as it was. Instead, she focused on the sound of water bubbling over smooth pebbles in the water feature by the door. She closed her eyes, imagining she was standing in the shade of a willow tree beside a cool creek. She opened her eyes. No such luck. She was still at a care facility in Sydney's outskirts, too far from the coast to feel a sea breeze. With a looming deadline. She buzzed again.

'Yes?' an impatient voice said through the intercom.

'Sorry, it's Meg Hunter. Jenny's daughter.'

'Oh, good.' The tone softened. 'Come in.'

Stale air filled her nostrils as Meg stepped into the foyer, an acrid cocktail of stewed meat and disinfectant. A large woman got up from behind her computer screen. Doreen, according to her name tag. Meg hadn't seen her before.

Doreen gave Meg a pained smile. 'Thanks for coming down.'

'That's fine,' Meg said. Although it wasn't really fine. Pete would be going crazy. He'd already called twice.

'She's quite agitated, she's—'

A beep came from Doreen's pocket and she reached for her phone, shaking her head at the interruption. 'You know where you're going, don't you?' She was already walking back into the office.

Meg nodded. 'Of course.'

Patterson Wing. Room 422. She'd find it eventually. She'd only visited once since her mother had moved rooms. How long ago was that? A month ago? Six weeks?

She moved through the labyrinth of dark corridors, following signs with arrows and room numbers, until she reached an open area that was vaguely familiar. A small group of silver-haired ladies, decades older than her mum, sat on upholstered chairs, exercising with large elastic bands. Meg gave them a smile as she passed through to the opposite corridor. Yes, Jenny's room was down here on the right.

The first room looked empty. She stepped tentatively towards the door of the second room and met the gaze of a stooped man in navy pyjamas, standing behind a walking frame. His face lit up, clearly thrilled to have an unexpected visitor.

'Hello, there!'

'Oh, sorry,' Meg said. 'Wrong room.'

His face dropped slightly. 'Who are you looking for, love?'

'My mum, Jenny.'

'Ah, Jenny. Next door,' he said, jerking his head in that direction.

Meg thanked him and stopped outside the next room, watching her mother through the open door. Jenny stood at the window looking towards the garden, where the sun was starting to sink in the sky. The only sound was the distant shriek of cockatoos. She was still. Her blonde ponytail almost reached the waistband of her skirt. Meg had suggested a haircut a year or so ago, back when self-care was becoming too hard. Nothing too short, just shoulder length. A long bob. But Jenny had protested, and Meg had given up. She was glad now. Jenny still looked like Jenny. Beautiful. Slightly fragile. Young, despite the streaks of grey.

There had been no grey in her mother's hair when the first signs of this terrible disease had made themselves known. At first, it was just little things. A forgotten name. A mixed-up plan. An overdue bill. Silly little things, easy to ignore or explain away. Her mother was only forty-six then. Who would suspect it? But when Jenny stopped getting book-keeping work from her longest, most-loyal client, Meg started to wonder.

At the first appointment with the neurologist, as they recounted all these little things in one heartbreaking conversation, it was obvious that something was wrong. Their worst fears were confirmed when Jenny failed a memory test, a test so simple that she had laughed when the doctor had given her three words to remember: pumpkin, train, chair. But when she was asked for the words just five minutes later, her brow had furrowed and she'd looked at Meg, glassy-eyed.

'Mum?' Meg said softly.

Jenny spun around and her face broke out into a smile. 'I thought you would never come. Where have you been?'

Meg bristled. 'I've been working.'

Jenny's smile fell just a fraction. 'Yes, of course.' There was a crease now between her eyes as she looked past Meg into the hallway as though she'd been expecting someone else. She looked down at her hands.

'Is everything okay?' Meg asked. 'The nurse rang me this afternoon, she said you were upset.'

'She did?'

'You don't remember?'

Jenny frowned and looked out the window. She shook her head.

'It's okay.' Meg tried to keep her irritation out of her voice. She'd already missed one deadline this week. She felt her phone vibrate and looked at the screen. *Pete Garcia.* Damn. 'I've gotta take this.'

Jenny sat down in the armchair by the window as Meg stepped into the corridor.

'Pete, sorry I had to—'

'I'm getting a bit sick of the excuses, Meg. There are plenty of freelancers who would kill for the work. I need your story—'

'I know, it's nearly done. You'll have it in half an hour.'

'I was meant to have it an hour ago!' He sighed. 'Honestly, if it was anyone else, I'd tell them to forget it.'

'I know, I'm sorry.' Meg glanced in at Jenny. Her eyes were closed. Was she sleeping?

'Just make sure I've got it by six.'

He hung up.

The room was darker when Meg returned. Jenny's forehead was smooth, her mouth slack. The tension in her shoulders was gone and her hands lay motionless in her lap. Peace.

Meg took her laptop from her bag and sat on the bed, tapping softly at the keys.

She was doing a final read through half an hour later when a white-haired orderly appeared at the door, pushing a trolley. The smell of overcooked vegetables filled the room. He gave Meg a warm smile, then looked at Jenny.

'Dinner's here!' he called out.

Jenny stirred as he placed a plastic tray on the little table beside her. She didn't even glance at the plate with grey vegetables and some sort of meat, Meg assumed, under a pool of gravy. Her mother was somewhere else entirely, miles and decades from this small garden-view room. Meg could see the veil.

That's how Jenny had described it when Meg first broached the subject. A veil, between herself and the world. By then, they'd been avoiding it for months, carefully sidestepping it in conversations, both working hard to convince themselves that it was easy to think it was April rather than March, or accidentally put the kettle in the fridge. But then Meg saw the post-it notes on the cupboards and drawers in Jenny's kitchen. *Cutlery. Plates. Water glasses. Wine glasses.* God forbid Jenny couldn't find a wine glass. And then Meg couldn't pretend anymore.

'I knew you'd come,' her mother said, pulling Meg back to the present with a jolt.

'Of course I'd come, Mum,' she said, feeling like a fraud. It had definitely been more than six weeks since Jenny had moved into this room. How had Meg only visited once? But her guilt was pushed aside by the prickle of resentment that always followed.

'Did you drive from Hartwell,' Jenny asked, 'or did you get the train?'

'Where?' Meg said, unable to keep the frustration from her voice. The orderly reappeared with a cup of tea.

'Hartwell!' Jenny exclaimed. 'Do you still live in Hartwell?'

'I live in Marrickville, Mum.'

'Just play along, love,' the orderly whispered to Meg. 'It's better that way.'

Meg tried to meet Jenny's gaze, but she was staring now, just over Meg's shoulder. She studied her mother's striking eyes. Two concentric circles, golden-brown surrounding the pupil, the outer ring a dark blue, the markings of central heterochromia, which Meg had inherited from her. It was like looking at herself in the mirror, although Meg's markings were more pronounced.

And then, the veil lifted.

Jenny frowned. 'Meg,' she said, her voice lighter now. 'How long have you been here?'

Tears prickled behind Meg's eyes. 'Not long.'

'Will you stay?'

Meg looked at her laptop.

'Please?' Jenny's voice was reedy. Thin. 'We can watch *The Princess Bride*.' She reached out her hand, but her bony fingers could only brush against Meg's arm from where she sat. She dropped her hand again, staring into Meg's eyes.

Meg sighed. She reached for her laptop and hit send on her story. 'Yes, I'll stay for a while.'

The flat was dark when Meg arrived home. She took a tub of honeycomb ice cream from the freezer, which she kept hidden under a packet of peas and something unidentifiable in a Tupperware container, and slumped onto the couch, eating it with a spoon in the semi-darkness.

Then she messaged Pete: *Sorry for the delay on my story. Long day with Mum.*

She watched, bracing herself for his reaction. Three dots appeared. *Pulsing. Pulsing. Pulsing.*

God, how long was his reply?

Then they disappeared.

She took another spoonful of ice cream, then looked back at the phone. Nothing. Oh God, this was bad. She needed Pete. He was keeping her afloat since the redundancy.

Her stomach churned and she put the tub on the coffee table. She rubbed her face. Tomorrow she needed to put in a very good day.

Chapter 2

Isobel Ashworth stood by the window on the thirty-second floor of Ashworth Tower, looking east, where the rising sun shimmered across Sydney Harbour like sequins on a dress. She gasped at the sheer beauty of it and reached for her phone, already conceptualising her Instagram story. *Sydney sunrise! Perks of getting to the office early!* she typed, then added a filter to make the colours even more spectacular.

She uploaded it quickly, then turned her back to the window. It was time to get organised. The journalist would be here any minute. She glanced around the expansive office and reached for a photo of Spencer, Helen and the girls, which sat beside the monitor on the terrazzo desk. She stashed it in a drawer, then went to reception and retrieved a large vase of lilies, which she placed on the coffee table by the window where the interview would take place. Perfect. She rummaged through her Birkin until she found the card that had been attached to a bouquet Hugh had sent her last week and placed it beside the vase, then she took out her MacBook, Moleskine and a Montblanc pen, arranging them casually on the desk.

She checked her makeup in her phone camera then flicked to her notes app to run through her key messages one last time.

At 6:08 there was a ding from the lift and Geoff Patterson emerged, wearing a suit jacket with chinos and three-day stubble,

9

his grey hair in need of a cut. A step behind him was a younger man with a camera bag over his shoulder.

'Hello, Geoff,' she said, extending her hand and beaming her warmest smile.

'Issy? My God, look at you!' He pulled her towards him, kissing her cheek, then stood back and studied her. She smiled, feeling mildly uncomfortable. 'You've certainly grown up! Lesley and I were trying to think when we last saw you. Was it at that lunch in the Hunter Valley? What was the occasion? We couldn't remember.'

'Mum and Dad's thirty-fifth wedding anniversary. Gosh, that must be fourteen years ago, at least. I was still at school.'

'This is Marco,' Geoff said, gesturing to the photographer.

'Pleasure to meet you, Isobel,' Marco said, his accent thick. Spanish, she guessed.

'You too.' Issy shook his hand. 'Come through to my office.'

'Thanks for coming, we really appreciate it,' she said, as Marco started unpacking camera equipment.

She'd been working on Geoff for six months, pitching various story ideas designed to credentialise her as a serious player in the family business. Journalists were so lazy these days, you almost had to write the article for them! It was 'the next generation of Australia's wealthiest families' which got him over the line. She'd made the story irresistible by arranging for him to meet with Avery Hart, the daughter of a Western Australian mining magnate, and Fraser Fox, whose father had made his fortune in packaging. Who knew there was so much money in cardboard boxes?

She gestured to an armchair. 'Have a seat.'

Instead, Geoff walked to the window and let out a low whistle. 'Look at this view.'

'Stunning,' she agreed, joining him.

Geoff's gaze travelled from the horizon over the opulent waterfronts in the exclusive Eastern Suburbs to the high rise of the city centre. 'You lot must feel like you own this town. How many Ashworth Hotels can you see from here?'

Issy laughed. 'Four, if you look carefully enough. And six housing developments. In fact, I can even see my apartment.' She pointed to their most recent project in Point Piper, an architecturally designed, luxury development inspired by the sandstone cliffs of the coastline. 'Maybe I should get a pair of binoculars to check if Hugh's out of bed!'

Marco cleared his throat. 'Okay, I am ready to shoot.'

'Oh, I thought we would do the interview first?' Issy said.

'Either way,' Geoff said, with a toss of his hand.

'This light is just incredible,' Marco said. 'Too good to waste!'

By the time they sat down for the interview, it was seven thirty. Geoff opened an app on his phone, hit record and put it on the table by the flowers.

'Let me move these out of the way! We can barely see past them!' Issy said, relocating the vase to the desk. 'Hugh spoils me!'

'I heard about you and John Thorburn's boy. Going well?'

'Boy? Geoff, he's forty-eight.'

'Is he?' Geoff scratched his head as though he was doing the maths. 'He must be a fair bit older than you then?'

'Eighteen years,' she said with a shrug. 'I'm used to that, being so much younger than my brothers.'

Geoff nodded, thoughtful. 'What's it like growing up as the youngest—and the only girl—in a family like yours?'

'Honestly, it's wonderful,' she said, pleased to have the chance to share her first key message. 'I feel so grateful for the opportunities I've had in my life and continue to have. The thing about money is that it's an enabler. It means we can make a difference.'

'What sort of difference do you want to make?'

'Great question.' She squinted slightly, as though contemplating it, keeping her tone casual as she recalled her next point. 'Our vision for the next phase of the Ashworth Group is to invest in the vibrant fabric of our cities and communities by creating innovative, sustainable spaces where people can connect and thrive. I know I speak for Spencer and Felix when I say we want to build on the extraordinary achievements of our father to leave a lasting legacy for the Australian people. In fact, we believe we have a *responsibility* to do that.'

A smile played on Geoff's lips. He was probably surprised to hear her talking like this. She was still in high school last time he saw her! He was used to thinking of her as the baby sister, not as a competent—let's be honest: impressive—executive. What was it with Boomers? They seemed incapable of recalibrating their perceptions of the younger generation. Her father was the same.

'And how do you and your brothers plan to manage the company into the future? Sibling relationships can be tricky when it comes to succession planning.'

'So we hear, Geoff—' she leaned forward in her chair, '—but we have strong relationships built on mutual respect. We each bring something different to the table and we have enormous admiration for each other's strengths. Spencer's very committed to the property business, Felix prefers to manage investments, and my skillset is well suited to Operations. We make a great team. Having said that, Dad has no plans to step back at this sta—'

There was a ding from the lift then footsteps in the foyer.

Crap. Issy looked out the door to see Spencer approaching, immaculately dressed in an Armani suit as always, his red silk tie Windsor-knotted to perfection. His black leather shoes were shinier than his bald patch, which was visible because he was looking down at his phone.

'Spencer!' Geoff said. 'My good man.'

Spencer's head snapped up. 'Geoff!' They shook hands, Geoff adding a back slap for good measure. Spencer glanced over at Marco's equipment, frowning slightly as his eyes flicked to the camera bag, then to Issy's belongings strewn across his desk. 'Issy,' he said, meeting her eyes, a question rather than a greeting.

'Geoff and I are just finishing,' she said, standing.

'Finishing what?' Spencer held her gaze for slightly longer than usual.

'An interview,' Geoff said. 'For the weekend's magazine supplement.'

'Excellent, excellent,' Spencer said.

Issy nodded and cleared her throat. 'Don't let us hold you up, Geoff.' She gestured towards the door.

'We should play a round of golf soon,' Spencer said. 'You, me, Dad, Hugh.'

'That'd be great, mate.' They shook hands again.

Issy led the way to the lift. Once Geoff and Marco were gone, she went back to Spencer's office.

'What was that about?' he said.

She rolled her eyes. 'He's been hassling me for an interview. I've put him off for months, but I figured I had to say yes eventually. Keep him onside.' She gathered her belongings from his desk. 'Let me get these out of your way. I hope you don't mind me using your office.'

There was a long pause. 'We have a media strategy and a PR firm to manage it. We don't go organising interviews outside of that.' ,

'Relax, Spencer, it's Geoff. He's a family friend!'

He shook his head. 'Your naivety is breathtaking.'

'Keep your knickers on. It's just a puff piece. It'll be good PR for the Ashworth Group.'

He held her gaze.

'What?' she asked, putting her MacBook in her bag.

He smirked. 'Good PR for Isobel Ashworth.'

'Oh my God, you must be joking.'

He shrugged.

She hauled her bag onto her shoulder. 'See you tonight.'

'Tonight?'

Was he serious? 'My birthday party.'

'Oh, right.' He frowned. 'I thought it was meant to be a surprise.'

'It is. But I planned it.'

Spencer scoffed.

She turned towards the door.

'One more thing,' he said. 'Before you go, would you mind returning the photo that was on my desk?' He pointed to the empty space where the frame usually sat.

She sighed heavily, then retrieved the photo from the drawer, put it back beside the monitor and left before she said something she regretted.

Instead of getting an Uber, Issy walked up Castlereagh Street towards the mall. The sun was still low in the sky, obscured behind office blocks. The shops weren't open yet, but even window shopping would improve her mood.

The interaction with Spencer had left her feeling bewildered. She played it over in her mind. 'Good PR for Isobel Ashworth,' he'd said. What did he mean? That the interview was driven by … what? Vanity? Self-promotion? Her chest felt tight. All she ever did was the right thing by the family. Hadn't she just been saying how much they all respected each other?

She stopped outside Prada, admiring a crimson silk dress in the window. Fit and flare with a plunging neckline. Not a colour she would wear, but stunning all the same. Feminine, but powerful.

She sighed, thinking of Spencer again. Maybe the interview was a stupid idea. He was probably on the phone to their father already, saying that she 'stormed out'. She couldn't look sideways without it getting back to her father, who would inevitably use it as evidence that she was still young and irresponsible. Her partying phase still loomed large in her parents' minds. It didn't seem to matter what she did, no one ever took her seriously. Why couldn't they see she'd changed?

She looked back at the dress in the window, thinking of her party that night. She'd bought a whimsical Oscar de la Renta strapless dress in a pink floral print, but Hugh had been far from effusive when she'd modelled it for him. 'It's just a little … matronly,' he'd said. She was hurt at the time—matronly!—but maybe he was right. Maybe it made her look like a pushover. Pretty, but pointless, like the tinsel in the shop window. This dress—the Prada one— demanded attention. She reached for her phone to call her stylist. She would have it by lunchtime.

Chapter 3

Meg woke as the first luminous blue tones of daybreak crept around the edges of the curtains and slipped out of bed. She'd always worked best in the morning, but this was especially true since she'd rented out the tiny third bedroom of her apartment to a gamer who spent his days playing *Call of Duty* in the lounge room. On a good day, he'd sleep till eleven. She made a strong coffee—two pods— and sat down at her laptop still wearing her pyjamas.

She opened a new document and sighed. Why had she pitched a story about twin sisters who were dating the same man? Stories like this made her question why she'd become a journalist in the first place, although she was hardly in a position to be picky. Especially after yesterday.

She exhaled loudly then started typing. *When 26-year-old Brisbane-based identical twins Gabbi and Holli saw Steve Jackson's photo on Tinder it was love at first swipe—*

A groan came from the direction of the lounge, then a shuffling sound. Meg froze, looking at the back of the sofa. Was someone sleeping there? There was some throat clearing, then a man sat up, his back to her, and coughed into his fist.

'Who the hell are you?' she said, staring at the back of his head.

He had tattoos on his neck and dirty blond hair which sat up at a weird angle.

He spun around. 'Sorry. Didn't see you there,' he said. 'I'm Salty.'

'Your name's Salty?'

He gave her a disinterested shrug. 'I'm always in a crap mood.'

Meg raised her eyebrows. 'Why are you sleeping on my sofa, Salty?'

'I work at the restaurant with Jay.'

Jay was the gamer. It didn't really answer the question, but she could piece it together. Bloody hell. It was only Wednesday. She was getting too old for this.

'Well, Salty, now I'm in a crap mood too, cos I'm trying to work and you're here, interrupting me. You need to go.'

He coughed again.

'Sounds like you need to see a doctor, too,' she added.

'Nah.' He rubbed his face. 'It's just from smoking cones.'

Meg shook her head and looked back to the screen as Salty pulled on his trainers.

She reread her first sentence and typed on. *The threesome has been inseparable since—*

'See ya,' Salty said to her. As he disappeared into the hall, Gav entered, her long-term flatmate who was permanently dressed in lycra cycling gear that made him look like he was training for the Tour de France, rather than commuting to the CBD.

'You're at it early,' he said.

Meg nodded and resumed typing. *—since their first date eighteen months ago—*

'What are you writing?' he asked, pouring milk onto his cereal.

Meg looked up again, trying to conceal her irritation. She'd chosen Gav three years ago because he had a full-time job in IT that required him to work from the office—she figured he could afford the rent and would hardly be there—but somehow they'd become friends and he was always up for a chat. 'Ah, it's a story exploring unconventional relationships in the age of dating apps.'

'Yeah, interesting.' He swallowed a mouthful. 'You still on the apps?'

She shook her head. 'I lasted a week. I only went on one date, with a guy who asked me back to his place. Turned out he still lived with his parents. He made me hide behind his bedroom door for half an hour when his mum came home unexpectedly.' She shook her head, trying to shake off the awkward memory, and looked back to the screen, hoping Gav would get the message.

'Jeez, when was that?'

Meg sighed. 'I don't know, maybe a month ago.'

'I've got a mate who—'

'Gav, sorry, I'm on a deadline.'

He shrugged. 'Yeah, no worries, that's cool.' He dumped his cereal bowl in the sink and clip-clopped down the hallway in his cycling shoes.

'Oh, Gav?' she called after him. 'Rent's due today.'

'Yep!' he said. The front door slammed.

The lease was in her name, which meant she spent her life chasing rent payments. Gav was pretty reliable, but Jay was hopeless. She opened online banking to see if he'd transferred his rent yet. No. She checked the list of recent transactions, looking for Jay's name. It was over a month since he'd paid her. She opened the to-do list on her phone and added, *Chase Jay's outstanding rent.*

A wave of tiredness washed over her. She yawned. She'd tossed and turned last night, Jenny's confused comments playing on her mind. More coffee, that's what she needed.

She dropped a pod into the machine and opened the fridge, but her space in the door was empty. Where was her milk? She'd just put it back, right there. Did Gav …?

She looked in the bin. There it was. Her empty milk carton. Bloody hell. He hadn't even put it in the recycling! She moved it into the plastics section, then picked up the mug from the coffee machine.

She sat back down and took a sip, recoiling at the bitter taste. How did anyone drink it like this? It was like battery acid. She thought of her mum, who'd always had her coffee black. It was yet another thing about her that Meg found baffling.

She looked back at the screen, reread what she'd written, then stared, letting the words blur. What was it that Jenny had said? 'Have you travelled down from Hart—' Something. Hartley? Hartford? Who did her mother think she was speaking to? Who did she think had travelled from some place she'd never mentioned?

Meg opened a new window and typed *NSW town Hart*, reading the drop-down list of suggested endings. There it was. Hartwell. It rang a bell. She had a vague idea of it as a weekend destination for newlyweds. Beyond that, she was blank.

The top result took her to a tourist site. *Nestled in the lush rolling hills of the Southern Highlands just 90 minutes from Sydney, the exclusive enclave of Hartwell is one of the oldest settlements in New South Wales.* There was a photo of a sandstone church covered in ivy.

She clicked back and scanned the other search results. Real estate listings of mansions on acreage. An article on property magnate Malcolm Ashworth, silver-haired and unsmiling in the accompanying photo. A local news article about the redevelopment of a historic jail built during colonial times, which was set to become boutique apartments and an entertainment precinct.

She skimmed the article about the redevelopment of the jail, then she flicked over to Facebook. She checked that she was logged in to her second account—the one with an alias and a stock photo—although even her real profile was vague and impersonal; she'd inherited her mother's distrust of social media. For Meg, social media was a research tool, a way to find stories and connect with potential sources. Nothing more. Nothing less.

She searched *Hartwell*. A few different groups appeared in the list below the search bar. *Save Hartwell* caught her eye. She read the pinned post at the top of the page, which questioned the local government's integrity around development applications, then skimmed the comments. From what she could piece together, police had arrested a couple of protesters a few months before. She felt the flutter that always came when she sensed a story and sent a request to join the group.

She inhaled sharply as she noticed the time. It was almost eleven. How was that possible? She'd got almost nothing done. What was wrong with her? She'd never missed a deadline when she was full time. Never. She prided herself on that.

Was it working from home? It was virtually impossible to concentrate in this flat, with constant interruptions. Random strangers sleeping on the couch. Talkative flatmates who finished your milk. Soon Jay would be up and she'd be subjected to the traumatising sound of a massacre. No one could work productively in conditions like this! And even when she *did* have peace and quiet, it was so dull, so lacking in the buzz of the newsroom, that she couldn't get any momentum.

She flicked back to her article and reread what she'd written. It was the journalistic equivalent of a McDonald's cheeseburger: cheap, tasteless and deeply unsatisfying. She slumped forward, resting her head on her hands. It was freelancing. That was the problem. It was soul destroying. How much longer could she sit in these four walls, writing churn-and-burn clickbait for *News Day Online*?

Her phone lit up with a text notification: *Deborah Jenkins*. Deb was chief of staff at *The Times* and Meg's greatest ally. After the cutbacks, she'd called in a favour and asked Pete to keep Meg busy with freelancing work. Begrudgingly, he'd complied. Meg's thoughts spiralled back through the last month. Yesterday wasn't the first time she'd missed a deadline. Pete must have told Deb.

Meg winced as she opened the message.

We need to talk. Lunch at Denny's?

Chapter 4

Isobel flipped down the sun visor above the passenger seat of the Range Rover and opened the mirror, scrutinising her makeup with the concentration of a fine arts collector inspecting a precious antique. She'd requested a smoky eye, which was heavier than her usual look, but with a nude lip and the shock of the red silk dress, it was perfect. She took a tube of concealer from the makeup bag on her lap and dotted her inner eye. She dabbed it in with her ring fingers, appreciating the way the light bounced off the diamonds in her tennis bracelet, a gift from Hugh. She glanced at him in the driver's seat to check he wasn't watching, then smiled at herself in the mirror and raised her eyebrows, a coy hand over her mouth. She grimaced. No, that didn't look genuine at all. She tried again, this time with more subtlety.

'What are you doing?' Hugh asked, as they pulled into the private car park of The Ashworth Double Bay.

'What? Nothing.'

He gave her a lopsided smile, her favourite dimple appearing in his stubbled cheek, and raised an eyebrow.

'I was … practising.' She felt her cheeks flush. 'Do I look surprised?' As she repeated the performance, she got the giggles.

'It'll have to do,' he said, straightening his bowtie in the rear-vision mirror. He turned to face her. 'How do I look?'

She studied his chiselled cheekbones, his strong jaw. He was almost too handsome, if there was such a thing, and he was getting even better looking with age. The grey hair at his temples gave him a distinguished look that she found almost unbearably sexy.

'Prettier than me,' she said, then leaned in and kissed him, careful not to smudge her lipstick. She inhaled deeply, enjoying the smoky scent of his aftershave.

'Impossible.' He touched the hem of her skirt. 'I thought you were wearing the pink one with the flowers?'

'Changed my mind. You like it?'

He studied her. 'I do. I like it a lot.'

The dimple danced on his cheek as he ran his hand under the crimson silk and up her thigh, brushing his fingertips lightly over her underwear. A tingle ran through her.

She shifted so that his hand moved away. 'We better get in there.'

He slumped back against the seat. 'Do we have to?'

'Come on. They'll all be waiting for me.'

Issy heard a peal of laughter and a soft clinking of glasses followed by loud shushing as she and Hugh approached the double doors of the ballroom, hand in hand. She took a deep breath as Hugh pushed open the door.

'Happy birthday, Issy!' voices shouted in unison as they stepped into the room, which had been decorated with candles, pink balloons and cascades of peonies in gold vases.

'Oh my God!' she exclaimed, wide-eyed, hand to chest, just like she had rehearsed in the car, looking at the crowd of beaming faces. 'What? How …? You guys!'

A live band started playing as Felix stepped forward and slapped a kiss on her cheek. 'Happy birthday, baby sister!' He wore a tux shirt, but his sleeves were rolled up and his bowtie hung untied around his neck as though he was on his way home from an all-nighter. His long blond hair was tied back in a ponytail. Somehow, he pulled it off. He pushed a glass of bubbles into her hand.

'Thanks, Felix.' She clinked her glass against his, then turned to the friends who were waiting to greet her.

'Darling!' Nadia Westerway air-kissed Issy's cheeks then took her hand to twirl her around. 'Stunning! Prada?' She put an arm around Issy's tiny waist and pulled her in close, holding her phone aloft. 'Smile!' she said, snapping a series of selfies in rapid succession.

Released from Nadia's hold, Issy spotted her father's head above the crowd by the bar and squeezed her way through, nodding to acknowledge the birthday wishes bestowed as she passed.

'Look at this gorgeous creature!' Malcolm said as she reached him.

She dipped her head coyly. 'Hi, Daddy.' Even in heels, she had to stretch up on her tiptoes to kiss him.

Her mother stood beside him, impeccably dressed in emerald-green Carolina Herrera. 'Happy birthday, Isobel,' Heather said, aloof as always. She leaned in for a quick embrace with a waft of hairspray and Chanel No. 5. 'Although there must have been some sort of mistake. You can't possibly be thirty!'

Issy's birthday was always confronting for her mother, who had been almost forty when Issy was born. Heather seemed to view it as an annual insult, reminding her of her encroaching age. She would be seventy in the new year, although she looked a decade younger, thanks to exceptional cheekbones and subtle three-monthly cosmetic procedures.

Spencer stood behind them, with Helen by his side. 'Isobel,' he said with a businesslike nod. Still pissed, clearly. Helen wore a navy suit and sensible mid-rise heels, as though she was going to court rather than a party.

'Did the girls come?' Issy asked Helen, deciding to ignore Spencer altogether.

Helen shook her head. 'Daisy's still out celebrating the end of her HSC, although given she barely opened a textbook, I'm not convinced such protracted celebrations are justified.' Issy's oldest niece aspired to a career as an influencer. She'd already used the Ashworth name to amass a strong following on TikTok, so she didn't see the need for a university degree, much to her mother's horror. 'And Olivia's on an immersion program in Vanuatu, building mud huts for poor people. Honestly, the things these schools do these days. It's just fabulous.'

'Avruga caviar and crème fraîche?' A rotund waiter offered a tray of tiny spoons to the group. Spencer and Helen took one as Felix and Hugh joined them.

'I'm good, thanks,' Felix said, glancing at the tray with one eyebrow raised. 'Can you send over the real food?'

'It's quite a party,' Heather said. 'Are you sure you had nothing to do with it, Isobel? It's got your stamp all over it.'

'Who me?' Issy said. 'Of course not! It was all Hugh. I knew nothing about it.'

The look in Heather's eyes suggested she didn't believe a word.

Felix spotted a waitress with a tray of arancini. 'Ah, this is the good stuff!' He waved her over and put one in his mouth, then took another. 'Keep it coming,' he said with a wink.

Malcolm gestured for a middle-aged man to join them. 'Derek! Come and meet my daughter.'

Issy recognised the man's jowly face but couldn't place him.

He extended a hand. 'Derek Palmer. Happy birthday.'

'Lovely to meet you,' Issy said.

'Congratulations on the election,' Spencer said, shaking Derek's hand. 'It was a landslide!'

Ah, a politician. Invited by Malcolm. Or Spencer. They never missed an opportunity to leverage a family event for business purposes.

It must have been about nine o'clock when the music stopped and the ding, ding, ding of a knife on a wine glass cut through the room. Issy looked up to see Hugh standing at the lead singer's microphone. A chill went down her spine. Speeches were not part of her plan.

Hugh tapped the microphone and cleared his throat as the last of the chatter dwindled to silence.

'Can I ask the beautiful Isobel Ashworth to join me?' he said, eyes scanning the room for her.

Heads swung in Issy's direction. She swallowed, suddenly nervous.

'Come on, baby,' Hugh said. 'I have something I need to ask you.'

'Wooo hooo!' someone hooted.

'Iss-y! Iss-y! Iss-y!' Felix chanted.

Others joined in. 'Iss-y! Iss-y! Iss-y!'

Soon the whole room was chanting like a crazed mob.

A sense of deep trepidation took hold of her, but she forced a demure smile onto her face and weaved her way to the front of the room. Faces blurred and the sound of voices warped in her ears. Her heart pounded as Hugh pulled her up onto the stage.

'Thank you all for coming to celebrate the birthday of this wonderful woman.' He waited as people clapped and cheered. 'But—' he turned to her, putting a hand into his pocket, '—this is not *just* a birthday party.' He pulled out a small box. Issy felt hot. Someone hooted again. 'Issy, some people might think three months is a short time to be with someone, but when you know, you know. And I've never been more certain of anything when I say … I want to spend forever with you.' He got down on one knee. Excited whispers rippled through the room as he flipped open the box to reveal an enormous solitaire. 'Isobel Iris Ashworth, will you marry me?'

A wave of nausea rose up in her throat as she looked at the ring. It had to be five carats, at least. Hugh's eyes bored into her, waiting for an answer. She looked over at her parents. Did they know about this? He must have asked her father, surely. The hushed voices of the catering staff in the next room were the only sounds.

She looked back at Hugh. His smile had dropped a fraction. What on earth was he thinking? This was too soon! Panic rose in her chest but she pushed it down, thinking of the Party Talk column in the *Sun Times*. There were plenty of people here who had that bitchy columnist on speed dial. What would the column say this Sunday?

She had no choice.

'Yes,' she murmured. 'Yes, of course I'll marry you.'

The room erupted in applause as Hugh put the ring on her finger, his hands shaking slightly. He pulled her into a tight embrace as their guests closed in. Her parents pushed through the throng.

'Congratulations, you two!' Malcolm stepped between them, putting a fatherly arm around each shoulder. 'Well done, son!' he said to Hugh. 'She had no idea! No easy feat, pulling off a surprise where my daughter is concerned.'

She beamed her brightest smile back at her father and her … fiancé. She felt light-headed. Fiancé. She had a fiancé.

Chapter 5

The lunch crowd at Denny's was an eclectic mix of locals with dogs, workers with laptops and mums in activewear meeting for a quick bite before school pick-up. Meg and Deb had started meeting there for a takeaway coffee during the lockdowns and it had been a favourite ever since, on days when they were both working from home.

She searched the tables for Deb and found her sitting in the far corner, typing quickly, brow furrowed. Meg's heart sank slightly. She'd been hoping to beat her there. If she couldn't meet a deadline, at least she could be on time for lunch.

'Deb, I'm so sorry,' she said when she arrived at the table. 'I couldn't find a bloody park. I ended up in a thirty-minute zone. Do you think I can claim a parking fine as a tax deduction?'

She was joking, but Deb shook her head. 'I think you'd be pushing your luck.' She closed her laptop screen and took off her tortoiseshell glasses, knocking over the pepper grinder as she placed them on the table. It clattered onto the floor, drawing the attention of diners at nearby tables. 'Bloody hell,' she said, shaking her head as she bent down to retrieve it.

Meg laughed, feeling a surge of affection for her friend and mentor. If it wasn't for Deb's uncanny ability to spill things, they wouldn't have met on a wet Monday morning eight years before, when Meg was hiding in the ladies' loos in the foyer of the Park Street office on her first day as an intern at *The Times*.

Meg had arrived early that day, riddled with nervous excitement, so she was sitting in a stall, scrolling mindlessly, when someone entered the bathroom, swearing under her breath. She'd opened the door of the stall to see Deborah Jenkins splashing water onto a large, brown stain on her cream, silk shirt. Meg recognised her from the authoritative black-and-white photo that accompanied her articles. She was already a high-profile investigative reporter by then, although at that moment, swearing and dabbing at the stain with a paper towel, she looked anything but authoritative.

'Um … are you … okay?' Meg had asked, glancing sideways as she washed her hands at the next basin.

Deb stopped dabbing and looked at the stain in the mirror. It was even worse now. 'Not really, unless you happen to have a spare shirt in your handbag.' She threw the paper towel in the bin and put a hand to her forehead. 'I'm doing a panel presentation at the Hilton in half an hour with Leigh Sales and Kate McClymont.'

Meg thought for a moment. They looked about the same size. 'Swap shirts with me.'

Deb eyed Meg's navy blouse. She'd bought it the week before on a special outing to add some more conservative, corporate pieces to her wardrobe, which was mainly full of frayed denim and faded T-shirts.

'Seriously?'

Meg nodded. 'If this is okay?'

Deb was already unbuttoning her shirt. 'You're an absolute lifesaver.'

Meg unzipped hers at the back and slipped it off, wishing she'd worn a better bra.

'What's your name?' Deb asked, as she tucked the blouse into her trousers.

'Meg Hunter. It's my first day. I'm just an intern.'

'Hey,' Deb said, looking up. 'No justs. It's not easy getting an internship here. That's something to be proud of.'

'Okay.' Meg smiled. 'I'm an intern,' she said again, this time with more conviction.

Six months later, Deb had helped Meg get a permanent role as a staff reporter.

Now, Deb's unruly hair fell over her face as she crossed her arms and leaned forward on the table, meeting Meg's gaze. She exhaled loudly.

Meg raised a hand to get in first. 'Before you say anything, I assume Pete told you I missed my deadline yesterday and I want to apologise. It was absolutely unacceptable for me to submit so late. You've gone out on a limb for me. I know that. It won't happen again.'

'Won't it? Pete said this isn't the first time.'

'Honestly, Deb, I promise.'

Deb sighed. 'When you got laid off, I told you I'd look after you—'

'And you have, and I really appreciate it.' It was true. Like a protective big sister, Deb had promised to keep Meg busy, and she was true to her word. Meg swallowed a lump in her throat. 'It's just … I'm not sure how much more of the online stuff I can write. I want to do more than just pay the bills. I—'

A waiter appeared by their table. 'What can I get you?'

'Smashed avo and feta on sourdough for me, thanks,' Meg said.

Deb ordered a club sandwich.

'It's just,' Meg said, 'I'm finding it hard to keep motivated when all I'm writing is "The babies who were swapped at birth" and "My twin and I are dating the same man". It's not that I'm not grateful, I am, I know I'm lucky to get—'

'I thought you wanted work!' Deb said, throwing up her hands.

'I do—'

'If you keep pitching clickbait, that's what you'll get.' She leaned back in her chair. 'Have you reached out to Harry?' Harry was the editor of *The Times*. Deb had suggested Meg get in touch regarding editorial work.

'I sent him an email, but I haven't heard anything back.'

'How long ago was that?'

Meg shrugged. 'Two weeks? Three, maybe?'

'Can I give you some advice?'

'I guess.'

'If you want a steady income as a freelancer, online's your bread and butter. That's just the way it is. You're a great journo, Meg, but the industry's changed. Twenty years ago, you'd never have been made redundant. You'd have a career like mine. Investigative journalism, breaking some big stories, then into an editorial role if you wanted one.'

'So you're saying I'm too late. Journalism's stuffed.'

'No, but it is different. Print journalism isn't what it was. These days a big story has more chance of being a bloody podcast than a long form article in the Saturday paper.'

Meg sighed.

'What I'm saying—' Deb's voice softened, '—is that if you want a real career in this game, you have to go after it. It won't fall in your lap. If you want to work on a real story, you need to pitch a real story. A good one.'

Meg looked out the window at the crawling traffic on Enmore Road. Where were all those people going?

'Well?'

She looked back at Deb. 'Well, what?'

'Pitch me something.'

'Now?'

'Yeah, now. You must have ideas. Obviously I don't commission stories, but if you've got something good, I'll have a word to Harry.'

'Um, yeah, I do.' Meg scrambled, trying to think. She used to keep a list when she worked full time. The ideas came thick and fast back then. 'What about ...' Hartwell! Yes! 'What about the controversy around the redevelopment of Hartwell Gaol?' She watched Deb's face for recognition. 'Hartwell's a town in—'

'Yeah, my brother got married down there. Pretty town. What's the deal with the jail?'

'It's the oldest prison in the state. It was used for convicts originally, then as a processing centre for immigrants after the Second World War. It sat empty for decades after that, but a few years ago it was sold to Ashworth Property.'

Deb scowled. 'I hate those bastards.'

'Really? Why?'

'Years ago, *The Times* had to settle a suit the Ashworths brought against me and publish a retraction, even though everything I wrote in my story was true. What do they want the old jail for?'

'They're redeveloping it, putting in restaurants, an outdoor theatre and boutique apartments. The locals think there was an under-the-table deal done. Judging by the vitriol towards the family in the *Save Hartwell* Facebook group, things are heating up down there.'

Deb shrugged, unconvinced, as the waiter reappeared, plates in hand. 'Why now?'

'It's meant to open early next year. I think some of the grievances of the locals might come to a head. What do you think?'

'Sounds interesting. You could frame it as a David and Goliath story.' She took a bite of her sandwich.

Meg watched her as she mulled over the idea and realised she was hoping Deb would dismiss the idea entirely. Her mother's past was a carefully guarded secret. There must be a reason for that.

'Why don't you do some basic digging, see what you find?' Deb said, eventually. 'But it would have to be very strong for us to go after the Ashworths.'

Meg spent the afternoon at the library, finishing the threesome article and one other that she'd been putting off writing for a parenting website: I'M A MOTHER OF THREE AND I REGRET HAVING CHILDREN. It was guaranteed to get guilt-riddled mums breaking their fingers to click.

It was late afternoon when she got home. She stepped into the hall, surprised to hear the rat-tat-tat of bullets coming from the lounge room. She stood for a moment watching Jay from behind, the Southern Cross tattoo visible on his bare back. On the screen, enemy soldiers clad in SWAT gear and holding assault rifles attacked through thick smoke as Blackhawk helicopters swarmed overhead. She dumped her bag on the floor and slumped into the armchair. Jay gave no indication he knew she was there.

'Aren't you meant to be at work?' she asked. He was a chef at a burger joint and worked nights.

'Called in sick,' he said, his eyes still on the screen.

She shook her head, thinking of the rent he owed her.

'Damn it! You distracted me.' He tossed the controller onto the table, reached for a Carlton stubbie and took a sip.

'Sorry,' she said.

He scratched his bare chest, dark hair bristling under his fingers. He was still wearing his boxer shorts.

'*Are* you sick?' Meg asked.

'Nah, hungover. I ended up at the RSL club after my shift, playing the pokies.'

Meg remembered the stranger who had spent the night on her couch. 'I met your mate Salty this morning.'

'Yeah, he said you kicked him out.'

'You can't bring randoms back here, Jay. It's not part of the deal. And you owe me rent, by the way. Five weeks.'

'Yeah, no worries,' he said, draining his beer. He took another one from the fridge and disappeared to his room.

Meg was pouring a glass of wine when Gav entered, carrying groceries.

'Hey.' He dumped the bags onto the bench. 'What's happening?'

Meg sighed heavily. 'I met Deb for lunch.'

'Nice.'

'Not really. She's pissed off with me because I keep missing deadlines. I told her I was sick of writing crap and she basically said it's my fault because that's what I keep pitching.'

'Well, is it?'

'I don't know. Maybe.' She shrugged. 'Anyway, I pitched her a story about suspected corruption in a town in the Southern Highlands. You know that Ashworth family?'

'The hotel people?'

'Yeah. Hotels and property development. The locals in Hartwell are unhappy about a deal done with them. Might be nothing, but Deb thinks it's worth looking into it.'

Gav frowned. 'Isn't that good?'

She sat down on a barstool at the kitchen bench and took a sip of her wine. Was it good? She wasn't sure. There had been a strange feeling niggling at her ever since her conversation with Deb. 'I stumbled across it because Mum mentioned Hartwell the other day.

She thought I was someone else, asked me if I'd travelled down from Hartwell. I didn't even know where Hartwell was until I googled it later. It must have something to do with her past, don't you think?' Meg had told Gav all about her strange upbringing, alone with her secretive mother, moving every six months or so.

'Dunno,' he said, stacking microwave meals in the fridge. 'Might mean nothing.'

'Maybe.'

But Meg wasn't so sure. She thought of the Indian neurologist with the musical lilt in her soft, accented voice. 'Imagine that memories are organised on a tall bookshelf,' she'd said, helping them understand the diagnosis. 'As we make memories, we store them on the shelves, filling them up from the bottom, so the shelves at the top are filled with our most recent memories. Now imagine that someone starts to shake the bookshelf. The books on the top shelf, the newest ones, will tumble first. The memories at the bottom will barely move. Once the books at the top have fallen, the ones on the lower shelves will feel more recent.'

That night, after the appointment, Meg had scoured the internet for everything she could find on early-onset Alzheimer's disease, searching for a glimmer of hope. Something she could hold on to, like a life raft. But the prognosis got worse with every click of her mouse. The bullet-pointed lists of early symptoms resonated with dreadful familiarity, her thoughts skidding back through all the little things which had gone mostly unnoticed over the past six months or more. She'd slammed her laptop shut halfway through the list of late-stage symptoms.

Jenny's memory books were tumbling off the top shelves now. Meg pictured a pile of them on the floor. Soon the book of Meg would be on the pile too. It was already teetering. Some days it was as though it had already fallen, along with the ones about

Jenny's tabby cat, the apartment she'd bought six years ago and her neighbour Lynne, who had managed to befriend Jenny, despite her rebuffs. Already her mum had no memory of any of them. Maybe one day soon, Meg would need to wear a post-it note on her forehead: *Daughter.*

Was it possible that Hartwell meant nothing? Could it really be random? She ran her hands through her short hair.

'Why do you think Mum won't talk about her past?' she asked Gav.

'She must have run from something.'

Meg nodded and took another sip. What though? She reached for her phone and searched for Hartwell on Google Maps—104 kilometres. That was all. She could be there in one hour and twenty-two minutes. Was it possible that her mother's past, the past she'd concealed for almost thirty years, could be so close?

She closed the app and rested her head on her hands. Her mother had been resolute in her refusal to discuss her past. There had to be a good reason for that, surely. Best to let sleeping dogs lie. That was the expression Jenny used, whenever Meg asked a question she didn't want to answer.

She picked her phone up again and messaged Deb.

Been googling. Looks like Hartwell's a dead end.

Chapter 6

The morning after the party, Issy woke late, her head pounding with a Veuve-induced hangover. She opened her eyes, baulking at the sunshine that assaulted her through the open curtains, then rolled over, putting her back to the window. Beside her, Hugh stirred and reached out a hand, feeling for her under the covers. He stroked her thigh and gave her a sleepy smile, then closed his eyes again.

Her mouth felt like sandpaper. She put her hands to her temples, trying to ease her thumping headache. How much did she drink? She closed her eyes again, trying to recall the night before. It was all a bit hazy. Very hazy, in fact. She remembered snatches of the night. Arriving with Hugh. The 'surprise' part. Spencer giving her the cold shoulder. Helen, boring as usual. Nadia telling her about doing ayahuasca in Palm Springs. Someone talking about Taormina. She had a vague memory of agreeing to go there in July with whoever she was talking to. Who was that? Then Hugh was dinging a glass—

Oh God.

He didn't.

Did he?

The nauseous churning in her stomach intensified as she lifted her left hand. She braced herself and opened her eyes.

Golden light hit the princess-cut diamond and bile rose in her throat, bitter and burning. She scrambled to the ensuite, flung up the toilet lid and heaved over the bowl. Her skin prickled, eyes watering, as she slumped down in front of the toilet. The Prada dress lay discarded on the floor beside her. Shuddering, she pulled it towards her and wiped her mouth on the hem.

'You okay?' Hugh called from the bedroom.

'Yep.' Her voice was shaky.

How had this happened? They'd only been dating since September, when they both found themselves staying at the Ashworth Southbank in Melbourne for work, and one drink became three, then dinner at Nobu. He'd told her he loved her a week later and the three months since had been a whirlwind of romantic dinners, lazy Sunday mornings and oversized bouquets of flowers. Issy had been unable to believe that she was actually with Hugh Thorburn, who she'd first developed a crush on at the age of ten, when Spencer had invited him to tag along on their family ski holiday. Hugh was twenty-eight then—gosh, it did make the age gap seem a lot, when she thought about it like that—but he was flirtatious and funny, not to mention dazzlingly handsome, and ten-year-old Issy had been besotted.

She lay down on the cold tiles. What was she going to do? What *could* she do? Two hundred people had witnessed the proposal. Someone had probably already told that Party Talk columnist. She was probably writing a snappy summary of the whole debacle right now, for tomorrow's paper. Freaking parasite.

'Issy?'

She took a steadying breath, pushed herself up and brushed her teeth, relishing the minty freshness of the toothpaste. She splashed her face, then patted it dry, looking at her reflection. At least she looked better than she felt. She glanced at the ring again, lifting her hand to her face to admire it in the mirror.

She sighed and dropped her hand. It wasn't that she *didn't* want to marry Hugh, it was just so much sooner than she'd imagined. But it was done. And it couldn't be undone.

'Everything okay, babe?' Hugh said, as she slipped back into their super king bed.

'Everything's perfect,' she said.

He curled into her, closing his eyes again as she reached for her phone to post to her socials.

She positioned her left hand on the crisp white linen, moving it slightly until the brilliant sunshine hit the solitaire, creating a rainbow of light. It was magnificent. Intoxicating.

The caption was simple: *YES!*

She might as well beat the papers to it.

The next twenty-four hours were an anxiety-riddled frenzy. Her Instagram post had over sixty thousand likes. Her DMs were out of control. She'd had calls from three different women's magazines, offering money for exclusive coverage of the engagement and wedding. She let them go to voicemail.

She was right about Party Talk. The proposal was covered in the column the following day. Someone at the party must have spoken to the columnist and given them the inside story. She suspected Nadia, who had sold her own wedding coverage to *Hello* magazine, although, to be honest, there were plenty of others who constantly leaked to the press. It could have been anyone.

Hugh read the column out loud as they lay in bed. '*The stunning heiress was left speechless upon sighting the extraordinary five-carat solitaire selected by her dashing prince.* That's me, your dashing prince.' Hugh gave her a playful smile, the dimple making an appearance. He put a strong hand behind her neck and pulled her in, kissing her deeply.

So far the article wasn't too bad, she thought, as she kissed him back. 'Stunning' was good. 'Speechless' was neutral.

'What else does it say?' she asked.

Hugh sighed and rolled back, lifting the newspaper again. '*The match seals the long-time bond between the Ashworth and Thorburn families, forged by their fathers, who attended Dalton Grammar together before working closely at the Ashworth Group. Guests at the surprise engagement party included a literal who's who of Sydney's elite, politicians rubbing shoulders with morning TV hosts and the offspring of Australia's uber rich.* Blah blah blah, names in bold type. *Well-lubricated with French Champagne, the loved-up couple danced the night away before disappearing into the night and their happily ever after.*'

'Is that it?'

He nodded.

She sighed, relieved at the favourable interpretation of her shocked reaction. It felt like minutes that she'd stood on that stage with Hugh on his knee waiting for her response. She was imagining something like HEIRESS AMBUSHED BY UNWELCOME PROPOSAL, but whoever spoke to the journalist clearly thought she'd merely been overwhelmed by the moment. Which she had been. That's all it was.

'Are there photos?'

Hugh passed her the paper. They'd used a photo taken at Derby Day a month before. Her face was half-obscured by an asymmetrical hat her stylist had described as avant-garde. Hugh wore a grey suit, black shirt unbuttoned at the neck, and had one arm around her waist, a smile playing on his face. There was also a smaller picture of her parents, dredged from the archives.

She put the paper aside. Why did she still feel sick? She thought her trepidation about the gossip column was the source of her anxiety, but she couldn't seem to shake the nausea. She lay back on the pillow, staring at the ceiling, and took a deep breath like her therapist had taught her: in through the nose, out through the mouth. Hugh glanced sideways but said nothing.

She ran her fingers through her hair, then held up her hand, studying the ring. Her stomach lurched. That was natural, though, wasn't it? It had all happened so fast. One minute, she was enjoying a new romance—and, let's be honest, mind-blowing sex—the next minute, she had a fiancé.

It had all just got too serious, too quickly. Everyone was rushing them. Her father had barely been able to conceal his delight when she'd told him she was seeing Hugh, and just last week, her mother had interrogated her about 'their plans' over lunch.

'He was a little … loose … in his younger years,' Heather had said, waving a manicured hand, 'but he seems to have got that out of his system now. He's clearly besotted with you, Isobel, and he's excellent marriage material.'

Issy had laughed. 'Marriage? Who said anything about marriage? We've only been together for a few months, Mum.'

'Yes, but you've known him your whole life, Isobel!'

Issy sighed. 'Let's not get ahead of ourselves.'

'There's little chance of that, darling,' Heather said, looking up from her burrata salad. 'The boys were eight and four when I was your age. Your fertility won't last forever.'

'For God's sake, Mum, I'm twenty-nine.'

Heather had pursed her lips. 'Exactly, Isobel. Female fertility falls off a cliff after thirty. Everyone knows that.'

'Yours didn't,' Issy muttered, but she gave up. She'd never won an argument with her mother.

Anyway, Heather hadn't even asked her if she *wanted* marriage and kids, although that was probably a good thing. What would her answer be? Issy thought her maternal instincts would have kicked in by now, but so far babies were still just snotty, demanding inconveniences that meant she rarely saw her best friend anymore. The last time she'd met Lara was for a highly unfulfilling conversation over bad coffee at a dreadful 'pram-friendly' café, which had ended prematurely when it was nap time. Lara had sent her a text explaining she was unable to make it to the party, citing teething as the reason, which seemed utterly ridiculous to Issy, but it was no great loss. Lara was no fun these days, anyway.

Without warning, a memory flashed in Issy's mind, powerful, visceral. She was riding a bolting horse. How old was she, she wondered? Eight? Nine? She could almost feel its wide back under her legs, her terror, heart racing, as she clung to the reins, the saddle, to stop herself being thrown off.

How bizarre! She shook her head, shaking off the sensation of the memory, and looked back at the photo.

'We do make an exceptionally good-looking couple,' she said.

Hugh murmured agreement, reaching a sleepy hand under the covers again to find her. A pleasant tingling sensation rippled through her as he stroked her bare thigh.

It wasn't that she *didn't* want to marry him. It was just so … unexpected. It had taken her by surprise, that was all. It was totally normal to feel overwhelmed. Once she got used to the idea, everything would be fine. She tossed the paper onto the floor and straddled him, determined to ignore the queasiness in her stomach.

'Good morning, my dashing prince,' she said, looking into his dark brown eyes. She felt him harden beneath her as he pushed up her pink silk camisole and tossed it aside, his eyes travelling over her bare breasts. She leaned down and kissed him deeply.

Chapter 7

Jenny was sitting in the armchair when Meg arrived with the Sunday papers under her arm and a takeaway coffee in each hand. A book lay in her mum's lap, but her gaze was out the window.

'Mum?' Meg held her breath. It was hard to tell what sort of day her mother was having until she spoke.

Jenny looked over. 'Meg, what a nice surprise. Two visits in one week.'

Meg smiled, impressed that her mum remembered she'd come on Tuesday but bristling at the subtext.

'I got you a cappuccino, extra chocolate,' she said, deciphering the writing on the lids and passing Jenny one of the cups.

'What are you reading?' Meg asked, putting the papers down and pulling over the spare chair.

'Reading?'

Meg gestured to the book in her lap. Jenny gave a tiny shrug and lifted the book to show the cover.

'*Gone Girl*,' Meg read. 'I've seen the movie. Ben Affleck. Any good?'

'I don't know.' Jenny laughed, but her eyes were sad. 'I think my novel-reading days are over. I can't remember anything I read.'

She put the book aside and reached for one of the papers. She looked at the front page, then she let it drop into her lap and sat back, closing her eyes. Even the briefest conversation sapped her energy. Sometimes Meg wondered if her visits were worth it. If Jenny wasn't asleep, she was staring at a wall or out a window. On a good day, like today, the best they managed was a few short exchanges. Most of the time, Jenny didn't even remember that Meg had come. What was the point?

Meg flipped the pages, reading the headlines. RETAIL SECTOR HOPING FOR RECORD CHRISTMAS SPENDING. EX-OLYMPIAN IN COURT OVER DRUGS CHARGE. TELCO FACES CYBER-ATTACK. She turned the page and inhaled sharply at the sight of Isobel Ashworth staring back at her. How was it that she'd given barely a moment's thought to these people until she googled Hartwell, and now they seemed to be everywhere? Isobel was dressed in black and white and wore a lopsided hat that sat on her head like a flying saucer. At her side was a smug-looking man who looked like a middle-aged Ken doll.

HOTEL HEIRESS OFF THE MARKET AFTER WHIRLWIND ROMANCE, the headline read. Meg skimmed the article. Apparently it was a surprise engagement. Why did men do that? Ambush women with one of the biggest decisions of their lives? She looked back at his face. Hugh Thorburn. She knew his type. She'd spent her years at Sydney Uni avoiding men like him. The binge-drinking, rugby-playing, private school boys who would no doubt go on to become respected politicians and business leaders with the help of Daddy's mates.

Meg shifted her focus to the inset photo of Malcolm and Heather Ashworth. His was the expression of a man who considered posing for a photo a waste of his time. Power oozed out of every pore. Beside him, his wife was undeniably stunning—in a Stepford kind of way—her vibrant blonde hair and gold silk blouse contrasting against her husband's serious grey suit. If he was the gravitas, Heather was the charisma.

Hearing Jenny stir, Meg glanced up.

Her mother's face lit up, her eyes wide. 'I thought you'd never come.'

Meg huffed audibly. This again. It would be nice if just once she could see her mother without the barbed comments. No wonder she avoided these visits.

Jenny didn't seem to hear her. 'You've cut your hair,' she said, reaching out and gently touching Meg's cropped hair.

'I've had it short for years, Mum. Remember? I cut it ages ago after we watched *Orange is the New Black*. I copied that actress ...' She let her words trail off, sensing the futility of correcting her. Who did Jenny think Meg was?

Tears pooled in her mother's eyes. 'You've grown up so much.' Her eyes flicked over Meg's face as though she was trying to take everything in, then she looked down over her denim vest to the tattoo on the inside of her wrist. 'You have a tattoo?'

Meg nodded, forcing back the threat of tears. She held out her arm so Jenny could see it properly.

'A question mark?' Jenny asked. 'Why?'

'Because I have a lot of questions and not a lot of answers.'

Jenny frowned, then she leaned back and closed her eyes again. 'I'm so glad you came,' she said, her eyes still closed.

'Me too.'

'Can you stay for a while or do you have to get back to Hartwell?'

Meg slipped out of the room when she was certain Jenny was asleep. When she reached her car, she sat for a moment, thinking. Where was she going? Not home. Sunday afternoon—Jay and Gav would probably both be there. She shuddered at the thought. Denny's would be closing soon, as would the library.

The bay. It would be busy down there on a day like this, but the sea air would clear her head. Help her make sense of things. She turned the key in the ignition, thinking of her favourite bench by the water's edge, the cool sea breeze.

Hartwell, she thought, as she pulled into the traffic on Parramatta Road. *Who was in Hartwell?*

The question reverberated in her head as she sat at the lights. It plagued her as she changed lanes, crossed busy intersections and navigated the city streets until she reached the car park.

Who was in Hartwell?

It hounded her as she weaved a path between dog walkers, joggers with prams and sprawling family groups with picnic baskets, until the bench came into view. It was taken by an elderly couple with a fat Labrador.

She sighed and sat on the sea wall instead, dangling her legs over the water. The harbour was dotted with yachts. Voices from a cruiser anchored nearby carried on the breeze. Ripples of laughter, the clink of glasses. Carefree rich people wearing collared shirts, sipping chardonnay in the afternoon sun. The boat was almost as big as her apartment.

Hartwell.

The name elbowed its way to the front of her mind again, bringing with it a sense of dread. Her whole life, she'd wanted to know more about her mother's past, but the conversation was off limits. She learnt that at fourteen, when her mother had smashed a wine glass to emphasise the point. After that, Jenny's past was bricked up. Sealed. Never to be discussed again.

But now, cracks were forming in that wall.

What else might break, Meg wondered, if that wall came down?

Chapter 8

Issy pressed the button for the penthouse, entered the security code and took a deep breath as the lift doors slid closed. She reached for her phone to reread her father's message, her stomach fluttering with nervous anticipation.

Meet me at the apartment at 8am, his message read. *We need to talk business.*

He must have seen Geoff's interview, which had come out that morning. Finally, her father was taking her seriously! Would he offer her the AsiaPac Head of Operations role? When she'd found out Elliot Blackburn was moving back to the States, she'd made it clear she wanted it. There was another flip-flop in her tummy. Why couldn't her father give her a little more notice though? Did he do it deliberately? She'd had to cancel her personal trainer at the last minute.

The lift came to a stop and the doors opened directly into the apartment, the Harbour Bridge looming impossibly close beyond the open balcony doors. This was her parent's Sydney bolthole. It took up the entire top floor of The Brick, an infamous building located almost on the Opera House forecourt that had inspired countless protests twenty years before, when it was in the development phase. The Brick was Malcolm's first foray into property development and it turned out to be a baptism by fire. He'd persevered, as he always did, and won. As he always did. The residents of Sydney got over it eventually, which was exactly what her father had said would happen. The sub-penthouse—which was half the size of this one—had just sold for seventeen million dollars.

'Isobel?' Her father's voice came from the direction of the kitchen. 'I'm in here!'

Malcolm sat at the dining table, the magazine open in front of him. She could hardly bear to think of his surprise when he'd seen her on the cover. She'd approved the photo—sitting, chin on hand—but she hadn't seen the interview yet.

'Hi, Daddy.' She kissed his rough cheek.

'Sit down.' His tone was gruff, although it often was. He prided himself on being difficult to read.

She sat.

'Explain this to me.' He gestured towards the magazine.

She swallowed hard. The excitement she felt a moment ago was now tinged with doubt. 'It's an interview.'

'Yes, Isobel, I know that. How did it happen?'

'It … I … Geoff asked me—'

'Don't lie to me. I've just been on the phone to him. He said you've been pestering him for months. "I assumed she had your blessing," he said.'

'I don't—' She bit her lip. 'I don't see what the problem is. Isn't it … isn't it good for the brand?'

Malcolm picked up the magazine and started reading. '*Isobel Ashworth stands at the window, looking down at Sydney like Cersei Lannister gazing over King's Landing. Unlike the infamous* Game of Thrones *queen, she's not planning to blow anything up. Instead, she's counting how many Ashworth hotels and property developments she can see from the palatial head office. "Four hotels and six apartment complexes," she says, with the carefree laugh of someone who's never given a moment's thought to their next mortgage repayment.* Jesus Christ!' He threw the magazine across the table. 'This is not good for the brand, Isobel!'

The magazine skidded off the edge of the table and fell at her feet. She didn't move.

'Sorry, I thought Geoff would—' She stopped, realising how stupid she would sound if she said what she was expecting.

'Thought he would what? I'm a little unclear what you were expecting by talking like this to a veteran journalist. You thought you could play Geoff Patterson?' He scoffed. 'The man has won Walkley Awards, for Christ's sake!'

'I just want to be taken seriously. I thought maybe it would get your attention.'

Malcolm scoffed again. 'You definitely have my attention!'

She took a deep breath. 'I want you to consider me for Elliot's role. I've tried to tell you that already, but you've just brushed me off.'

'You think you can do Elliot's job?'

'I think so.'

He shook his head. 'Based on what?'

'I've been working in the business for six years.'

'Yes. And you've moved from one role to another the moment you've got bored or things have become difficult. If you see yourself as a serious player in this business, you need to earn it. It won't just fall in your lap.'

'I know that.'

'Do you?' He held her gaze.

'I do. I promise I do.'

He leaned forward. 'Okay, then I've got a job for you.'

Her stomach fluttered again. She knew it! He *was* going to offer her the Ops role. He was just toying with her, making sure she really wanted it.

He cleared his throat. 'The Hartwell Entertainment Precinct is due to open in just over a month, but the contractors are running behind schedule. The project manager just quit. Sounds like chaos, frankly. I need you to go down there until completion, to keep an eye on things. An Ashworth presence usually gets things back on track.'

'You want me to oversee a project? In Hartwell?'

'It'll be a chance for you to prove your commitment to the business.'

'But—'

'Let me guess.' He narrowed his eyes. 'You don't want the job.'

'It's not that I don't want it! I do! It's just relocating to Hartwell isn't—'

Malcolm raised a hand to stop her. 'And you wonder why I don't take you seriously.'

*

Issy's favourite instructor, Abby Joy, beamed from the Peloton screen, her tight curls in a perky bunch on top of her head, rippling abdominals gleaming with just the right amount of sweat.

'Okay, squad! Let's conquer this mountain together!'

Issy pumped the pedals. This was exactly what she needed after the disastrous meeting with her father. Her quads burned as his words reverberated in her head. *Moved from one role to another the minute things got hard.* Was that true? Was he right? She did get bored quickly, that part was true, but she wasn't shy of a challenge, was she? She just hadn't had to deal with very many. Besides, wasn't it *good* to have a broad knowledge of the business?

'Let's give it everything you've got!' Abby implored, as the image of Spencer's smug face flashed in Issy's mind. Was he behind this?

Had he been in her father's ear? She'd been half-expecting him to dob on her about the interview and have it pulled before it could even be published. If only he had! For once, he would have been doing her a favour.

'Feel that burn, Joy Squad!'

Issy responded with a surge of power. Sweat dripped off her forehead as her name—Dizzy_Issy—moved into third place on the leader board. She stood up on the pedals so she could push even harder. Her heart rate hit one seventy. Her mind flicked back to the conversation and she prickled with fury. A construction project! What was her father thinking? She didn't know the first thing about project management. Or construction sites. And Hartwell, of all places! She'd barely spent a week in the place since she'd been packed off to boarding school at twelve. What on earth would she do there?

'Come on, squad! You can go harder than that!' Abby preached. 'Success is a state of mind!'

Issy's singlet was drenched in sweat. A tsunami of rage rose up in her as she moved into second place. It was a test. He'd set her up! Blindsided her! God. Her father was a genius. He knew she wanted that COO role. He'd tricked her. If she said no, she would never get another role in the family business. She would basically be handing it all over to her brothers. Spencer, in particular; Felix was too busy with fringe investments to care.

She knew this feeling. It was the sense of being trapped. It reminded her of playing chess with her father as a child. Other dads went easy on their kids, letting them win now and then. Building their self-esteem. Not Malcolm Ashworth, though. Not even once.

'We're nearly there! Thirty seconds to go!'

Crap. She was still in second place. Her heart pounded as she chased Spin_King69. Her heart rate hit one ninety. Sweat droplets fell on the screen where Abby bounced on the pedals with endless energy. She had her hands in the air, standing up at full height on her bike.

'Ten seconds!' Abby shrieked. 'Give it everything you have left!' She was nearly climaxing with excitement. It was always around this point in the workout that Issy started to hate her.

She passed Spin_King69 to claim first place.

'Woo hoo! We are DONE!'

Issy slumped forward over the handlebars, gasping for air, as the realisation dawned, crystal clear in her mind.

She had no choice.

She was going back to Hartwell.

Checkmate.

Chapter 9

Meg waited until after five to return home, when the day was starting to cool down.

She dumped her bag, ran a bath and went into the kitchen to pour a glass of wine; her standard Sunday evening ritual. She'd been doing it since she was in high school—without the wine back then, obviously. When she was looking at rentals, she'd put 'bathtub' on her list of non-negotiables and every Sunday night she thanked herself for it.

She tipped in some shampoo, which she'd been using since she'd finished the lavender bubble bath Jenny had given her a few Christmases ago. She figured it was all just soap. The stream of water hit the amber liquid, transforming it into frothy bubbles.

She positioned the wine on the ledge beside the bath, along with her phone, undressed and gingerly dipped a toe in. Just right. She eased herself in and lay back against the end of the tub, exhaling loudly, closing her eyes, letting the tension seep out of her body. Bliss.

Beep beep.

She sighed, wishing she'd put her phone on silent, and looked at the screen. It was from Facebook: *Your request to join* Save Hartwell *has been approved.*

Hartwell again. She scanned the posts, then she tapped on the list of members. There were two hundred and seven. The admin was Chris Baxter. Brave man, Meg thought, to take on the Ashworths. His profile picture was a long shot of a middle-aged woman standing between two pre-teen girls. Their faces were in shadow, but she could tell they were smiling.

Her phone rang. Pete.

She sighed and swiped to answer. 'Hi, Pete.'

'Hunter! Have you got a minute?' He sounded breathless, as though he was walking up a hill.

Meg raised her left hand out of the water and studied her wrinkled fingers. 'Yeah, I guess.'

'Have you spoken to Deb?'

'Not since yesterday.'

'Good. You're gonna love this. I just had an intriguing conversation.'

'Okay.'

'I bumped into a mate at the pub. He told me a really interesting story about a guy he used to work with.'

'Yeah?' This was classic Pete. She never knew where his stories were going until he got there.

'He's a partner at Bartlett Brown, one of the top-tier law firms, started there as a grad. Anyway, years ago one of the senior associates was fired abruptly. The whole thing was hushed up, but the rumour is that he was working on a big property deal with one of the senior partners, and he was feeding confidential information to a mate at a construction company about a rezoning that was on the cards. His friend made a fortune out of it, apparently, and the senior partner suspected this guy was clipping the ticket. They couldn't prove it, but he was "invited to leave". My mate reckoned he'd be lucky to work as a lawyer again, but guess where he popped up?'

'Where?'

'Ashworth Property.'

Meg frowned, suddenly paying attention.

'Turned out this guy's father was a good friend of Malcolm Ashworth,' Pete went on, 'who was only too happy to take on a malleable, ethically challenged young lawyer.'

'This is all very interesting, Pete, but why are you telling me this?'

'Because Deb told me about your story idea, the Hartwell thing. I reckon it's a goer. Have you guessed who this guy is yet?'

'No idea. Are you going to tell me?'

'Hugh Thorburn.'

'Isobel Ashworth's new fiancé?' Meg felt her heartbeat pick up.

'Bingo. And Ashworth Property's General Counsel. He's been working there ever since. Apparently, he works on a lot of their property deals. Deb spoke to Harry Madden. He's keen for us to investigate it.'

'Us?' Meg and Pete didn't work on stories together. Pete had been a leading reporter for *The Times*, but he stopped writing a few years back when he took the job in digital.

'Yeah, I suggested we put both our names on it, so he would give it the go ahead. You can run the investigation in Hartwell, I'll dig around up here. He's agreed to put you on a retainer to go down there.'

'He has? When?'

'Tomorrow. Spend a week or two there talking to people, see what you can find out.'

'But—'

'But what? Isn't this what you wanted?'

'Yeah, it is, it's just … sudden, that's all. But it's fine. It's good.'

'It might end up being nothing, Meg, but it could be massive.' A beat. 'It could be the story that defines your career.'

*

Meg spent the following hour throwing clothes, shoes and toiletries into an overnight bag, buzzing with the promise of a big story. Something real. Something that mattered. Something possibly career-defining, according to Pete, who knew a thing or two about career-defining stories. He'd made his own career by blowing open a money-laundering racket, an exposé that sent a high-profile politician to jail. She'd aspired to a similar trajectory and her plan had been working out well until the major shake-up that saw half the editorial staff made redundant and many of the major roles 'streamlined', which was corporate jargon for making one person do two jobs.

She reached for a Zimmermann dress she'd found at Vinnies and chucked it in, then glanced at a pair of heels, debating whether she'd need them. Hard to say. Probably not, but she chucked them in anyway, then sat on the bed to check through what she'd packed.

Whenever the funny feeling she'd had ever since she saw Jenny rippled up beneath the excitement, she dismissed it. None of this had anything to do with her mother. It was serendipitous, that's all. If her mum hadn't mentioned Hartwell, Meg wouldn't have stumbled across the Hartwell Gaol redevelopment controversy, which was the best chance—the only chance—she'd had to get her career back on track since the redundancy.

After one final check of the contents, she zipped up the bag.

'It's you again,' Jenny whispered, eyes wide. She was still in bed. Soft yellow morning light illuminated the garden beyond the window, but the room was dark.

'I just dropped in to say goodbye, Mum. I'm going out of town for a week or so for work.'

Jenny shook her head, agitation rising. At first Meg thought her mother was upset that she was leaving town, but then Jenny sat up, her eyes flicking around as though she was looking for someone else.

'Mum, it's okay, I can't stay.'

Jenny stared intensely, her brow creased. 'Why do you keep coming here?'

'I don't know,' Meg murmured, truthfully.

'It's not safe.'

'Why's that?' Meg asked, wishing she hadn't come. She could be halfway to Hartwell by now.

'Because …' Jenny's voice trailed off. She looked around again. 'They'll know where I am.'

'Who?' Meg could hear the shortness in her tone. The judgment.

Jenny leaned forward abruptly and pressed the call button by her bed. Meg thought of the kind orderly who'd advised her to play along. Maybe he was right. It felt wrong though, patronising or something. She couldn't bring herself to do it.

Meg pressed her lips together, inhaling deeply. She knew that paranoia was a common symptom, but until now, Jenny had just been confused. How did other people handle this? It would be so much easier if there was someone else to share this with. A sister or brother. After everything Jenny had put her through, it was so deeply unfair that she was burdened with this alone. The ultimate injustice.

A young nurse appeared at the door with a cheerful smile, glossy dark hair in a high ponytail. 'Everything okay, Jenny?'

'Brooke,' Jenny said, breathless, pointing to Meg. 'She has to go.'

Brooke frowned. 'Don't be silly, Jenny, she just arrived!' She had the sing-song tone people used when they spoke to toddlers. It rankled Meg.

'She's just confused,' Meg said quietly, by way of explanation.

Brooke ignored her. 'Let's make you more comfortable,' she said to Jenny, reaching for the remote control to reposition the bed.

'No!' Jenny yelled. Meg and Brooke startled. 'She has to stop coming here!'

'Okay, it's okay, Jenny.' Brooke put a firm, reassuring hand on Jenny's arm. She looked at Meg. 'Might be best if you go.'

Meg nodded and walked out the door. She stood in the hall, her heart racing, listening as Brooke attempted to placate her mother.

'It's okay, Jenny. Everything's okay.'

Just as she was about to walk away, Meg heard her mother speak again.

'Has Tina gone?'

Chapter 10

Issy glanced out the window as she approached the sandstone suspension bridge on the outskirts of Hartwell, surprised how quick the drive was. And how small the bridge seemed. She tried to remember the last time she'd driven into town. It must have been years.

She usually bypassed the town entirely by taking the helicopter and landing at the Ashworth Park Hotel, or Kilmore, her parents' place just outside town. This time, though, she was staying for a while, so she'd packed up her tiny Mercedes and driven the ninety minutes from Point Piper. Once she'd got her head around the whole Hartwell thing, she'd decided her father was right. It *was* a chance to show him what she was capable of. If she succeeded here, he'd have no choice but to move her into a more strategic role. And it was only for a month.

She'd be missing all the usual Christmas parties that typically filled her Instagram at this time of year, so she'd spent hours the night before scheduling generic posts to drop while she was away. Close-ups of shoes and handbags, throwback pics from recent social events, a photo taken when Nathan blow-dried her hair last week, tagging his salon. With any luck, her followers wouldn't even notice that anything had changed. And she consoled herself with the thought that Sydney was just a short drive up the freeway. She could go back and forth if the small-town situation got too much for her.

The road wound past the old church and a bed and breakfast towards the main street of Hartwell. She glanced at the shops. All vaguely familiar, except for a little café, which was new. Or newish. It was hard to say. She barely went into town when she was here for Christmas or family events.

Hartwell Gaol was on the other side of the shopping strip. She pulled into the driveway and pressed a buzzer at the boom gate. Nothing. While she waited, she studied some graffiti on the wall to her right, trying to work out what it said. Why did graffiti artists (if you could call them that) use such illegible writing? Why go to the effort of breaking the law to write something in the first place, if no one could read it? It seemed illogical. She made a mental note to ask someone to have it removed and pressed the buzzer again.

'Yes?' a gruff male voice said.

'Hello, it's Isobel.' She watched the gate, waiting for it to open.

'Who?'

'Isobel Ashworth,' she said slowly. The intercom must be fuzzy. They would be expecting her. Her father said he would ask the relevant people to arrange accommodation for her in the new luxury apartments above the original building.

There was a long pause and some shuffling, then the gate started to rise.

'Where do I go once I'm inside?' she asked.

'Ah, just pull into the waiting bay by the site office.'

She drove in and pulled up outside a shed, grateful for a sign by its screen door that said SITE OFFICE. It had more in common with a shipping container. A fat man in a yellow high-vis shirt hauled himself up from a seat and came out, pulling up his trousers. He knocked on her window and gestured for her to open it.

'Sorry, love, it's all a bit disorganised down here since Paul left. Ah …' He rubbed his ginger beard. 'Were we meant to know you were coming? Visitors are usually logged on the system but there's no note of it.'

'Yes,' she said. This all seemed quite unprofessional. 'I'm here to oversee the final stage of the project.'

Warwick frowned. 'To oversee the project?'

'Yes. My father sent me down here to get things back on track.'

'Righto,' he said slowly. 'All good. I'm Warwick. Acting project manager.' He wiped his hand on his shirt and held it out.

Issy shook it despite her hygiene concerns. 'Isobel.'

'Yeah, I know.'

'So, Warwick, next question. There's meant to be a suite organised for me to stay in while I'm down here. One of these?' She pointed to the upper floors of the development. 'I don't suppose there's a note about that in the system somewhere, is there?'

He looked up at the apartments overhead, scratching his greasy hair. 'One of these?'

She nodded. 'That's what I was told.'

'Unlikely,' he said. 'They're not finished yet.' He must have read something on her face, because he started back-pedalling. 'Although don't take my word for that. Sit tight while I try and sort this out.'

He stepped away from the car and made a call, gesticulating as he explained her unexpected arrival to whoever was on the other end of the phone. She tried to eavesdrop, but it was difficult to hear over the cacophony of construction. When a high-pitched drilling sound started, she gave up entirely and looked over at a group of sweaty-looking workmen standing around doing very little, as far as she could tell. They all wore high-vis vests, like Warwick, and she wondered vaguely if she would be expected to wear one. Did they come in other colours? Or just that specific shade of yellow? She massaged her temples, trying to relieve the dull throb of a headache, and looked back at Warwick. Surely he'd sorted this out by now.

After a moment, he hung up and returned to the window. Unfortunately, he was still frowning.

'Ah, no one seems to know anything about this.'

She sighed.

He went on. 'Why don't you leave the car here and go grab a coffee while I sort this out?'

Chapter 11

Meg fiddled with the air-conditioning as she turned off the freeway onto a smaller road. It was on the lowest setting, but warm air blew from the vents. One more thing that was broken in her old Mazda, which she'd bought from a colleague at the paper a couple of years ago.

She'd hardly noticed the heat until now. She'd been distracted, plagued with irritation at how Jenny had treated her that morning. It was silly to be offended, she knew that. It was just the disease. But it was hard not to take it personally when your own mother demanded that you leave and ordered you not to come back. It was only mildly reassuring to hear Jenny call her by the wrong name. Tina. Another crack in the wall. Was there a book of Tina?

She shook off the thought. So what if there was? If she was honest with herself, jostling alongside her offence at her mother's behaviour was a distinct sense of relief. If her mum didn't want her there, that was just fine. She wouldn't go. And she wouldn't feel guilty about it either.

She blew air up over her face and wound down her window. The landscape outside had changed. Luminous green hills rolled into the distance, dotted with black-and-white cattle and topped with old homesteads surrounded by trees. The road dipped down into a

valley and followed a fast-flowing river. When it turned a corner, a
spectacular suspension bridge came into view. She inhaled sharply
at its unexpectedness, its magnificence, as she passed under a stone
archway between two turrets. It belonged in a fairytale. On the
other side of the bridge, a sign on her left heralded the entrance to
the town. *Welcome to Historic Hartwell. Established 1834.*

She sat up taller in her seat, her eyes darting left and right, as
she followed the winding road. It was lined with fertile gardens
beyond wrought-iron fences and pretty sandstone cottages with
tin roofs. She rounded a corner past an ivy-covered church and
a quaint bed and breakfast with a sign advertising free wi-fi, then
found herself in the town centre: one wide street with the tall jail
walls on one side and a dozen shops on the other. At least half of the
shops were boutiques, the kind that sold candles and jam and loose
linen clothing in various shades of beige. Tourist shops.

It wasn't hard to find the Red Lion Hotel, where she'd booked
a room. It was a sandstone building at the top of the street, with
a long veranda under a rusty corrugated-iron roof. She pushed
the heavy door, half-expecting it to be locked, but it swung open
and she stepped into the cool, dark, empty space. It was a typical
country pub, with wood panelling, tartan carpet and a fireplace
that probably made the atmosphere cosy in winter. Today, the grate
was empty.

'Hello?' she called out.

Nothing.

After a moment, she wandered over to the far wall, which
displayed black-and-white historical photographs. The first one
showed the exterior of the Red Lion Hotel in 1845. A group of
expressionless, bearded men in suits stood on the veranda. *Albert
Ashworth*, the caption read, *owner and licensee 1838-55 (third from left).*
It had been typed on an old-fashioned typewriter.

The next showed a small group of convicts standing in front of a squat building with a towering door. *Convicts take a well-earned break from their work on Hartwell Gaol, circa 1830.*

There was a clink of glasses and a woman with long grey hair and heavy eyeliner emerged from a room behind the bar.

'How can I help you?'

'Hi, I'm Meg Hunter.'

No recognition of the name.

'I've got a room booked here tonight. I just wondered if I could leave my bags here until I check in later.'

'Ah, yes. Hello, love.' The woman smiled now, her tough edge replaced with a motherly warmth. 'I'm Sue, I spoke with you on the phone. You can check in now if you like.'

Once they'd done the paperwork, Sue led the way up a steep wooden staircase, then down a long corridor.

'Bathroom,' she said, gesturing to a room with a *Ladies* sign hanging over the doorway. 'Three showers. Excellent water pressure. We had a new system put in last year.'

'Great,' Meg said brightly, trying not to convey her surprise at the shared bathroom situation, which she hadn't realised when she booked the room.

They stopped outside room thirteen. 'This is you.'

Sue kicked the bottom of the door as she turned the handle. 'Gets a bit stuck when we've had a lot of rain,' she explained. 'You just need to give it a good kick.'

She flicked a switch and a cane pendant light came on, casting a dim light over the room. Meg peered inside. It was simple but stylish, with white walls, high ceilings and a double bed against one wall. In a corner under a large sash window, a wicker armchair sat next to a pedestal fan.

Meg could feel Sue watching her as she looked at the room.

'All good?'

'It's perfect.'

'Bistro is open twelve till two and five till eight. No need to book at this time of year. Too hot for most of the tourists. What brings you down here?'

'This and that,' Meg said, deciding to keep things vague. 'I'm studying historic jail sites.' She'd planned her story in the car on the way down.

Sue nodded. 'Not much to see of this one at the moment, I'm afraid. God knows if there'll be anything left of it once the redevelopment's done.' Her eyes lit up. 'There are a few other historical buildings around town, though. I can take you on a tour, if you like.'

'Oh, thanks, Sue, but I've got a few things I need to do today.'

Sue's face fell. 'Of course.'

'Maybe another day,' Meg added, feeling like she'd offended her.

'I'll leave you to it.' She handed Meg the room key and started back down the hall.

'Oh, Sue?' Meg called after her. 'Do you know anyone called Tina who lives around here?'

Sue shook her head. 'Nope, no Tinas around here.'

Meg squinted in the bright sunshine as she walked out of the pub, rummaging in her bag for her Aviators as she crossed the parking area towards Hartwell Gaol, gravel crunching underfoot.

She would have a look around, she decided, see what she could find out from workers on the site, then get lunch while she trawled the *Save Hartwell* Facebook group for people who might help her. She crossed a narrow laneway to the footpath that passed the old courthouse then ran along the prison wall that towered overhead, casting an imposing shadow.

There was something written on the wall. White letters outlined in red, contrasting against the sandy-brown wall. She stood back, trying to read it. The font was blocky, stylised, like the graffiti murals she barely noticed in her Inner West neighbourhood. Here, it demanded attention. *Ashworth* ... something. *Ashworth scum*. That was it. Interesting. She took a photo and walked on to the boom gate guarding the entrance to the compound.

The open space beyond the gate was a chaotic scene. Bobcats beeped, dodging piles of gravel, building supplies and workmen smoking cigarettes. A young woman with long dark hair and long fake eyelashes held a stop-go sign. Somewhere nearby, a jack hammer competed with a drill, making an ear-splitting metallic sound. The heritage-listed building, which she'd seen in the photo on the pub wall, was completely obscured by scaffolding. On the left of the driveway, a vintage convertible Mercedes looked jarringly out of place in the midst of the construction zone.

'You right?'

She whirled around and came face to face with a large, middle-aged man with shaggy red hair, holding a paper bag and a can of Coke. Morning tea.

He eyed her suspiciously. 'You're not one of those bloody protesters, are you?'

'Oh, no, sorry, I was just passing and I stopped to have a look.'

He frowned as though he wasn't buying it.

'I'm doing a PhD on historic buildings,' she added.

He shrugged, relaxing slightly. 'Each to their own, I guess.'

'How's the redevelopment going?' she asked. She might as well see if he'd tell her anything.

He shrugged again. 'Slowly.'

She looked up at the modern apartments above the original building. They seemed high for an old town like this. She was about to ask if he'd show her around when his phone rang. He tucked the Coke can under his arm and pulled the phone out of his pocket.

'Yep?' he said into the phone.

As she stood watching him walk away, her stomach growled.

The Apple Tree Café was on the other side of the main street, halfway down, nestled between Stevenson's Sweet Shoppe (Established 1911) and an art gallery selling mostly pottery, from what Meg could tell.

A bell jingled overhead as she pushed the door of the café open. Behind the red-tiled counter, a middle-aged woman with dark hair in a messy bun looked up from where she was arranging muffins on a tray.

'Morning,' she said, with a welcoming smile. 'Have a seat anywhere you like.'

It was after breakfast and too early for lunch, so the café was quiet. An elderly couple sat at a table by the wall, sharing a piece of carrot cake. A long communal wooden table with red bentwood chairs ran through the centre of the small room. It was the sort of place that made you want to order pumpkin soup. Meg went to a far corner and sat at a table that would have a good view of the room and the street beyond the glass windows.

'Can I get you a coffee?' the waitress asked, handing her a menu.

'Cappuccino, thanks,' Meg said, studying the woman's face. Her skin had the weathered look of someone who'd spent too much time in the sun. A few locks of dark hair fell loose around her face, giving her a harried look.

The bells over the door jingled again as a young mum manoeuvred a bulky pram through the doorway.

'I'll give you a minute.' The waitress went to hold the door open. A preschooler dressed as Elsa entered a few steps behind her mum and handed the waitress a white flower she must have picked along the way.

'Thank you, sweetheart,' the waitress said, tucking the flower into the hair tie holding up her bun.

Meg smiled. The waitress looked over, catching her eye and smiling back.

Meg opened her laptop, shifting her attention to the reason she was in Hartwell: the story. It was time to find some leads. She went to the *Save Hartwell* Facebook page and read the list of members, then she clicked on the name of the group admin and typed a message.

> **Thanks for adding me to the group. I'd like to have a chat about the Hartwell Gaol development. I'm in town for a short time. Please let me know if you're happy to meet with me.**

She hovered her mouse over the send icon, checking she was on her fake account.

'Sorry about the wait, can I get you something to eat?' the waitress asked, putting Meg's coffee on the table.

Meg looked up. 'I'll have a cheese and tomato toastie, thanks.'

The waitress gave her a nod and turned away. The café was filling up with the start of the lunch rush. Meg watched as the waitress handed menus to a table of three who had just seated themselves, then she moved to the elderly couple, who had finished their cake. As she picked up their plate, she laughed at something the old man said, deep lines creasing the corners of her eyes. The elderly couple stood to leave and the waitress followed them to the door, then she raised a hand at a passing pedestrian and said something. As she turned back, she looked in Meg's direction and their eyes met. For a moment it was as though a thread connected them.

Meg looked away quickly, back at the screen in front of her. She sent the message, then took out her notebook and started writing a list of things to do: *visit Hartwell Gaol site*; *council chambers*; *contact protesters*.

'Here you go.' The waitress put her toasted sandwich in front of her.

'Thanks,' Meg said. Maybe this waitress could help her. 'I read about the protests at the old jail—'

The bells jingled again and they both looked towards the door.

Meg inhaled sharply. The oversized sunglasses did little to disguise the flawless face of Isobel Ashworth, who looked around, then sashayed between the tables to the counter.

Meg sensed the waitress stiffen. 'I'll be back in a minute,' she said, her warm smile replaced with a steely glare.

Chapter 12

Issy pretended not to notice the hush that came over the little café as she weaved a path between the tables. It was no wonder they never came into town. Being an Ashworth around here was like being a Kennedy in Cape Cod: the locals seemed to hold them up as gods of some sort.

She drummed her fingers on the unattended counter, looking for a member of staff. She didn't have long before the site meeting she'd asked Warwick to arrange for twelve thirty. She caught the eye of a waitress in the far corner and reached for a takeaway menu.

'I'll have an oat milk latte and a green Buddha bowl, please, dressing on the side. To take away,' Issy said, as the waitress approached, stony-faced. Honestly, service in Australia was a disgrace. How hard was it to greet a customer with a smile?

The woman shook her head. 'No, you won't.'

Issy frowned. 'I beg your pardon?'

'You're not welcome here,' the waitress said.

The diners at the nearest table stopped their conversation and looked at them.

Issy let out a strange little laugh. 'What? What do you mean? You can't—'

'Yes, I can.'

Issy's chest tightened. She looked around, aware of more eyes on her now, then turned back to the waitress. 'I'd like to speak to the manager.'

'You're speaking to her.'

'The owner, then,' Issy said, flustered.

'Also me.'

Issy swallowed hard. A boy at a nearby table sniggered. A young couple exchanged whispers behind their hands. A woman in the corner with short dark hair watched intently from behind a laptop.

The waitress pointed at the door. 'You need to leave.'

Issy took a steadying breath, then walked out, her face burning.

As the door swung closed behind her, she heard people clapping.

Issy kept her head down as she walked briskly back to the construction site. She hurried past the site office, keen to avoid Warwick, and went straight to the bathroom—another temporary shed, which had been installed behind the old building.

Her hands trembled as she turned on the tap, trying to make sense of what had happened at the café. Was it possible that woman didn't know who she was? Surely not. In fact, maybe the opposite was true, she realised, recalling the expression on the woman's face as she'd entered the café. The set of her jaw. Her cold glare. No. That woman knew exactly who she was refusing service.

As she splashed her face with water, she had another thought. Was it *because* of her name that she was kicked out so unceremoniously? She was accustomed to her family name opening doors, not slamming them in her face. She was an Ashworth! Ashworths were practically royalty around here. This town would be nowhere without them. Just last year, they'd funded a complete overhaul of Hartwell Cricket Ground, including a state-of-the-art scoreboard, lights and a new grandstand, a gift to the people of Hartwell. And this was the thanks they got!

She patted her face dry with a sheet of paper towel, trying not to smudge her makeup. She must be missing something. Maybe that woman was mad! Anyway, there was nothing she could do about it now. Best to put it to one side and focus on the site meeting.

At exactly twelve thirty, Issy stood in front of the office, ready to start the meeting. A few minutes later, Warwick slunk out of the office and joined her. She looked at her watch, for rhetorical rather than practical purposes.

'Where is everyone?' she asked.

'Lunch, probably.'

'But I scheduled a meeting.'

Warwick shrugged. It seemed his primary means of communication. 'Twelve till one is when the subbies knock off for lunch.'

'Subbies?'

'Subcontractors.'

'Right, of course. Maybe you could have mentioned that when I asked you to schedule the meeting?' She was starting to wonder about this man. Was he being deliberately obtuse? She sighed. 'Why don't you take me on a tour. We can push the meeting back half an hour.'

Warwick went into the office and returned with a high-vis vest (yellow, unfortunately) and a hard hat. Issy put them on, reluctantly—the hat would flatten her hair terribly—and followed him through a gate in the makeshift fence.

Over the course of the next twenty minutes, she got a status update from Warwick. The restaurant spaces were all leased, with fit-outs currently underway. The luxury apartments were a few weeks behind schedule, and the outdoor theatre and entertainment space was delayed even further. Reading between the lines, it was clear that the previous project manager was utterly useless. The fact that every worker on site disappeared for a full hour between twelve and one was just the tip of that iceberg of incompetence. They were probably at the pub!

As they made their way back to the office, a nauseous feeling took hold in her stomach. How on earth was she meant to fix this mess and meet the launch deadline? It was less than a month away, and Christmas was between now and then! Did her father know the extent of the mismanagement? She inhaled deeply, wondering if there was flexibility to push the launch back. It would be the most sensible decision, given the state of things.

Although, on second thoughts, her father was not one to admit defeat easily. If she suggested moving the launch back, he would think she was making excuses before she even got started. She huffed audibly.

Warwick turned around, eyebrows raised. 'What?'

'Nothing, sorry,' she mumbled, pulling at the strap of her hard hat, which was rubbing on her neck.

The situation was lose-lose. If she *didn't* tell her father how bad things were down here, he would blame her for it when the project was delivered late. But if she *did* tell him, he'd accuse her of shying away from a challenge.

She thought of her therapist. 'You're catastrophising again,' she would say, before telling Issy to refocus on the positives in the situation. What *were* the positives of the situation? At least her father trusted her enough to send her down here. That was a good sign. He'd given her a real challenge to handle, all on her own. He must believe she was capable of handling it. That was something.

As they reached the site office, a white Prius pulled up at the boom gate.

'Ah good, that's Cathy,' Warwick said.

'Cathy?' Issy bristled as an arm emerged and punched in a code. 'Cathy Stone?' Surely he wasn't talking about her father's long-term personal assistant. *Former* personal assistant.

Warwick nodded as the gate opened and the car rolled into the space next to her own.

'Didn't she retire?' Issy asked. After thirty-plus years as Malcolm's assistant, he'd gently suggested it was time for her to move on and given her a very generous bonus on the way out the door. There had even been a dinner at the new Neil Perry restaurant in Double Bay to send her off. Issy had sent her apologies.

The door opened and Cathy appeared, wearing a clingy wrap dress in one of the garish patterns she'd been inexplicably fond of since the mid-nineties. She'd aged since Issy had seen her last, but her grey hair was still styled into a bob so sharp the corners looked hazardous.

'Hello, sweetheart,' Cathy said.

Issy stiffened at the term of endearment. Two words. That was all it took for this woman to make her feel like a child. 'Cathy! What a lovely surprise!'

Issy's phone beeped.

It was her father: *From what I hear you've got your work cut out for you. I've sent Cathy down to help.*

She shook her head in disbelief, then looked up at Cathy. 'You're just in time for our first site meeting. Would you mind taking minutes?'

Cathy gave her a curt nod.

'Okay, everyone, gather round please,' Issy called out.

A group of workers standing in a circle by the office glanced in her direction, then continued their conversation. The stop-go girl kept scrolling on her phone, ignoring her completely. Maybe she couldn't hear over the sound of a passing bobcat.

'Excuse me!' Issy made her voice louder this time. 'I need everyone to come together for a quick meeting.'

Again, nothing happened.

Warwick walked out of the office pulling up his pants and used his thumb and forefinger to whistle. It was the ear-splitting sound more commonly used to call a dog. Faces snapped to attention. The bobcat stopped in its tracks. Even the stop-go girl looked over, putting her phone in her pocket.

'Get your arses here now!'

Issy straightened her hard hat as the workers crowded around. She didn't approve of the language but at least it was effective. By the time everyone was assembled, roughly thirty sweaty, grimy men stood in a loose huddle. The only other women were the stop-go girl (What *was* the official term?) and Cathy, who stood by her side, holding an iPad.

Issy rose up to her full height, grateful for the extra inch she got from her platform trainers, and stared into the sea of faces. Was she imagining the hard edge she saw there? The steely stares? Hopefully it was in her head; a hangover from the bizarre incident in the café, perhaps. Or maybe they were just wary of newcomers.

She cleared her throat, but the low rumble of voices continued. She looked at Warwick.

'Oi!' he shouted. There was a hush as everyone fell quiet. Warwick looked at her. 'Over to you.'

'Thanks, Warwick.' Her face felt hot. 'Hello, everyone. I'm Isobel Ashworth. I'm down here to—'

'Speak up!' someone called out. 'We can't hear you!'

'Sorry.' Issy projected her voice as loudly as possible without shouting. 'I was saying, I'm down here to oversee the final stage of the project on behalf of Ashworth Property.' There were murmurs across the group. She tried to ignore them and went on. 'I've had a tour just now—'

'What's your experience, if you don't mind me asking?' The question came from a skinny man with an eyebrow ring.

'Of course. I've been working for the Ashworth Group for six years in various roles. Most recently I've been in the marketing team—'

'Marketing?' someone scoffed. 'Jesus Christ.'

'What about construction projects?' someone else interjected.

'I've worked on a number of our residential developments in Sydney,' Issy said, striving for an authoritative tone. It was technically true. Obviously she didn't tell them that the number was one and her role had been purely administrative. She'd never even been on site. There was more chat now, especially from the men at the back.

'Okay! Guys!' Issy called out, trying to restore order. 'Can I have everyone's attention, please?'

God. What a nightmare. It was a total free-for-all. No wonder the project wasn't meeting milestones. Clearly this whole site was out of hand. She tried again. 'Hello? Hello! I need a bit of quiet!' A bit of quiet? She sounded like her high school music teacher, who'd had to take medical leave after a nervous breakdown and was never seen again. 'Please!'

No one was listening.

Cathy stepped forward. 'Thank you!' she snapped.

The voices stopped.

'Like it or not, Isobel is here to work with Warwick to get this project delivered.'

No one spoke. Some of the more vocal tradies looked at the ground in front of them.

'You will show her respect. You will listen when she speaks. Do you understand?'

There were some nods, mumbles of agreement.

Issy swallowed, her face burning. 'Thank you, Cathy.' Right. It was time to assert some control. 'I've just had a tour of the site and I'm more than a little concerned about some of the things I'm seeing. At this rate, the project is at risk of missing the deadline. Things need to change around here. The work rate needs to increase. Pub lunches will have to wait until after the launch, when we can celebrate delivering the project on time.'

Warwick cleared his throat. 'Yeah nah, you can't actually say that.'

'Pardon?'

'Breaks are legislated in the industrial agreement. They can go to the pub if they want to, they just can't drink grog if they're coming back to the site.'

'Right, of course.' Her face felt like it was on fire. 'That's what I meant.'

How dare he undermine her like that in front of the team! She would need to have a conversation with him about this later.

She turned back to address the group. 'Obviously you can take the breaks you're entitled to, but when you're on site, I expect to see people working hard, not standing around having a chat. You can save that for the pub, over your lemonade.'

DNA Sleuths Facebook Group

Bec McKenna: Im on a quest to find my biological father but I think Ive found a half-sibling instead! I was born in Brisbane in 1986 and put up for adoption at birth. I got my mothers name from my birth records but sadly she died in 2014 :(My father wasnt listed. So Ive just got my DNA results thru and I have a strong match in the range of half-sibling! Im literally shaking. What do I do now?

Top comments

Fergus Schmidt: That is such great news, **Bec**. I've been searching for my BF for five years and the best match I've found is a seventh cousin. I think I'll give up soon.

> **Bec McKenna:** Sorry to hear that. Sending u the strength to keep going. U never know when u will get a break thru!

Karen Finn: Screen shot EVERYTHING asap!!!!!

> **Bec McKenna:** U mean the results?

> **Karen Finn:** YES!!! Every bit of information about the match!! They might not know you exist! They might know you exist and not want to open an old wound!! I found a half-sibling through DNA and reached out on Facebook, but they blocked me.

> **Bec McKenna:** Oh no so sorry to hear that. Hopefully theyll come round. Thanks for the advice, will do that now.

Zelda Merlino: This is an excellent match. To find your BF, you will need to work out which side the match is on. You can use your mother's name to help you with this, as well as your other matches, even if they are only weak. I'm a Search Angel, I help people find their family members using DNA tests and family trees. I'm happy to help, I'll DM you.

Bec McKenna: Thank u all for your support. Ive got a search angel helping me now. Please cross yr fingers and toes for me. Hopefully Ill have good news to report back to u all!

Chapter 13

'Beer, please,' Meg said to the surly blonde barmaid.

'What sort?' the barmaid asked, chewing gum.

Meg checked the taps for a craft beer she recognised. 'Stone and Wood, thanks.' She glanced up at the screen above the bar that showed *Deal or No Deal*.

'Six ninety,' the barmaid said, plonking down the glass. Froth ran down one side as it hit the bar.

Meg sat at the nearest table and took a sip of her beer, enjoying the cold sensation. What a waste of a day. She'd achieved absolutely nothing. Her only hope of rectifying that at this stage was to strike up a chat with a local over a drink. Unfortunately, the place was almost empty except for an old couple with a bushwalking map spread out on their table and a few old blokes at the far end of the bar who were busy flirting with the teenage barmaid.

Meg opened the to-do list on her phone. It hadn't been a particularly ambitious plan for day one, but she'd made no tangible progress at all. She'd been just about to ask the café owner about the protests when Isobel Ashworth walked in. Poor woman. Such a public humiliation!

Meg had waited for half an hour after the confrontation for the chance to speak with the café owner again, but she was rushed off

83

her feet. Eventually, Meg gave up. *Follow up with owner of Apple Tree Café*, she wrote on her list for tomorrow.

After she left the café she'd gone back past Hartwell Gaol, but they were having a meeting—every worker on site appeared to be standing in a huddle in the open space inside the compound walls. She'd taken a few steps inside the gate, straining to hear, but she couldn't get close enough. When the group eventually disbanded, she'd tried to catch someone's eye. The only person who'd noticed her was a formidable-looking woman with a sharp haircut and red glasses that matched the eye-catching print on her dress.

The woman had walked over and met Meg's eyes, frowning. 'Can I help you?'

'No, sorry. I was just looking.'

The woman held her gaze until Meg turned to go.

The council chambers were even more unwelcoming. How anyone managed to work in a place like that, Meg would never know. She stood at the counter for a few minutes while a balding man with pallid skin pretended not to notice her.

'Excuse me?' she'd asked eventually.

He'd glanced at her with raised eyebrows in lieu of a greeting.

'I'm wondering if I can see the records about the Hartwell Gaol development. I submitted a request online but I haven't had a reply.'

He clicked his tongue and sighed. 'You'll have to speak to Adrian.'

'Adrian who?'

'Gorecki. He's in the Strategic Planning Team, they approved the development.'

'Okay great, thanks.'

He turned back to his screen.

She cleared her throat. 'Is he here? Can I speak with him now?'

'He's not in on a Monday.'

'Right, when is he in, then?'

'Hard to say.'

At that point, Meg took a deep breath to avoid losing her temper. 'How about tomorrow?'

In the end, the man wrote Adrian Gorecki's email address on a piece of paper. Meg suspected it was only so he could get rid of her. She'd emailed Adrian while still sitting in the car park.

That was a few hours ago. She took a sip of her beer and checked her email. Nothing. She opened Messenger to check she hadn't missed a reply from the admin of *Save Hartwell*. Also nothing. She sighed.

'G'day, love.' Meg looked up to see Sue, a stack of glasses in one hand and a cloth in the other. 'How'd you go with your meetings?'

'Not great, actually.'

'Ah, that's no good, love.' Sue leaned back, resting her bottom on a stool. 'Why was that?'

'One of those days where nothing quite went to plan.'

'What did you say you were doing here again?'

'Oh, I'm just having a look at the old jail. Fascinating history.'

'You're an academic or the like, are you?'

'Yeah, something like that. Is there some controversy around the development? I saw the graffiti on the wall and I noticed there's a Facebook group opposing it.'

'*Some* controversy?' Sue threw her head back and let out a throaty laugh.

Meg laughed along. 'I'll take that as a yes, then.'

'I don't know why they're still at it.'

'So you're not a member of the Facebook group?'

Sue shook her head. 'I don't like to take sides. It's bad for business. Besides, I've only been down here eight years. It's the real locals who are most fired up.'

Meg paused, wondering if she could trust Sue. Her easy conversation put Meg at ease, but that didn't mean she was trustworthy. She would go slowly. 'I saw something a bit strange today, actually.'

'Yeah?'

Meg nodded. 'I was having lunch at the Apple Tree Café and Isobel Ashworth walked in—'

'Well, that *is* strange!' Sue said.

Meg frowned. 'Why's that?'

'Reckon I could count on one hand the number of times I've seen anyone from that family in town.'

'The owner of the café refused to serve her. She told her to leave. It made quite a scene.'

Sue laughed again. 'Ah, good on her. She hates those Ashworths. Can't say I blame her, given what they've been through.'

'Really? What have they been through?' Meg asked, hoping her tone was curious and casual, rather than nosy.

'Long story, love.' Sue stood up, wiped the table over and glanced around. 'Better get back to it.'

Meg tried to conceal her frustration at Sue's discretion.

'Can I get you another one?' Sue gestured to Meg's almost empty glass.

The door swung open and a couple of young guys walked in. They had the toughened, sunbaked look of labourers. They must be working at Hartwell Gaol.

'I'm fine, thanks,' Meg said. A well-timed trip to the bar would be the best way to strike up a conversation, see what they might tell her.

She looked back at the to-do list. Her number one priority tomorrow was following up with the owner of the café. There was obviously a story there. If she hated the Ashworths, maybe she'd be willing to talk. She clearly didn't care about losing their business.

The phone vibrated in her hand with a Facebook Message.

It was from Chris Baxter: *Meet me at the Red Lion tomorrow at three.*

Chapter 14

Issy stood on the dusty balcony outside the display suite, waiting as Warwick fumbled with an enormous set of keys. She yawned as she looked out over the construction zone below, silent and still in the blue evening light. Her feet hurt. In ten minutes, she told herself, she would be sitting down with a glass of chilled white wine with her feet up, and the disastrous afternoon would be a distant memory. If Warwick ever found the key.

'Jesus Christ,' he muttered, as the handle failed to turn yet again. After two more keys, the door clicked open. He grinned, excessively pleased with himself, and gestured for her to enter. She wheeled her suitcase inside and looked around. It was a large open-plan space with high ceilings and herringbone floors. A curved cream lounge circled a marble coffee table, artfully styled with interior design books, a clam shell and an artificial succulent. It had the staged appearance of a showroom.

'This okay?' Warwick asked, redundantly. He'd already explained that the other apartments were still unfinished. This one had been fast-tracked and furnished for publicity purposes.

'It looks fine. Thanks, Warwick.'

He twisted the key off the ring and passed it to her. 'I'll leave you to get settled in.'

'Warwick, before you go …' She waited for him to look up. 'How do you think the meeting went earlier?'

He paused, appearing to think carefully about his answer. 'As good as could be expected. They're a tough crowd.' He gave her a smile. 'They'll warm up once you settle in.'

'Oh, yes, of course.' He'd obviously misunderstood the question. 'But how do you think it made me look, when you corrected me in front of them?'

He frowned. 'Better me than one of them, wouldn't you say?'

She paused. 'Let's present a united front in future.'

She thought she saw him raise his eyebrows a fraction. 'Sure thing.'

He left, the door thudding quietly closed behind him.

She pushed off her trainers, suddenly aware of how stuffy the room was. It had the stale feel of a space that hadn't been disturbed for some time. She pushed open the sliding door to the balcony, hoping to get some air flowing, but outside, the night was warm and still. She gazed out over the twinkling lights of the houses below, stretching towards the rolling hills of the horizon. How strange it was to be back in this town that was both familiar and foreign.

She rubbed her face and sighed. Shower first, then wine.

She took the bottle of Western Australian chardonnay from her suitcase—it could chill while she had a long, hot shower—but when she opened the fridge, the light didn't come on. She put a hand inside. It was warm. She opened the freezer. It wasn't cold either. Great. She put the wine inside anyway, wondering where the plug was. Probably right at the back of the cavity where it would be impossible to reach.

She debated calling Warwick but decided against it. He'd seemed a little put out when he left. Her eyes landed on a cheeseboard that sat on the island bench. Fake grapes and a plastic wedge of brie beside a bottle of warm Champagne in an empty ice bucket, styled to encourage potential buyers to picture themselves popping open a bottle. She laughed out loud at the irony.

Shower then. She dragged the suitcase off the lounge and into the hall, glancing into doorways to get a sense of the layout. Two bedrooms, two bathrooms. The main suite was a little on the small side, but perfectly comfortable. She took out her toiletries bag and went into the ensuite bathroom. She turned the tap, half-expecting no water to flow after the fridge experience, but there was a gurgling noise and a few spurts, then a strong, steady stream.

She held her hand under the water, waiting for it to get hot. It didn't. In fact, it got colder as the water that had been sitting in the pipes flowed through. Fine. A cold shower then. It wasn't the end of the world. People did ice baths, after all! Mad people, in her opinion, but it was obviously possible. Raphael, her trainer, was positively evangelistic about the benefits.

Bracing herself, she stepped in, shuddering as the freezing water hit her skin. Bloody hell. She soaped herself up quickly, cursing Wim Hof—or whatever his name was—for making her feel like a wimp for hating every second of it.

When she was dressed, she poured herself a glass of warm wine and reached for the remote. Had anyone bothered to hook up the television yet? Or was it purely for display purposes, like the cheese plate? She pressed buttons but nothing happened.

She tossed the remote and it hit the clamshell on the coffee table. This was ridiculous. Malcolm wanted her on site to be across what was going on here, but this was just unfeasible. She needed to eat. She needed wi-fi. There was no chance that would be set up yet, if they didn't even have the TV working. She picked up her phone.

'Good evening, the Ashworth Park Hotel and Spa,' said the sing-song voice of a young woman. 'How can I help you?'

'Ah, hello, it's Isobel Ashworth speaking. I need a room tonight. One of the suites, if possible.' The hotel was just a few kilometres out of town. She would stay there. If only they'd avoided this nonsense altogether, she would currently be in a bubble bath perusing the room service menu!

'Oh, Isobel, hello. Um, let me see what I can do … hmm … we have a conference here today and tomorrow and all the rooms—'

'There must be something. Could you put Jeffrey on?' Jeffrey was a delightful gay man who treated her like a goddess. He'd been the manager at the hotel for fifteen years. He'd sort this out.

There was some shuffling, muffled talking, then a deeper voice. 'Isobel?'

'Jeffrey! I'm in desperate need of a room! Please tell me you can help?'

He clicked his tongue. 'Darling, I'm so sorry, but we have nothing.'

'Nothing at all? It doesn't have to be fancy. Anything would be better than the alternative, let me assure you!'

'We have the entire finance team of Macquarie Bank here. Every room is taken, even the two cottages. I wish I could—'

She sighed. 'Forget it. Thanks, anyway. I'll work something out.'

She thought of Kilmore, the sprawling estate where she grew up, just ten minutes down the road. Issy had suggested she stay there to her father, but he insisted that she must be on site. He wouldn't expect her to stay in conditions like this, though, would he?

Her mother went back and forth between Sydney and Hartwell, but she preferred the country. Was she at Kilmore at the moment? Issy couldn't recall. She pulled the elastic out of her hair, letting it fall over her shoulders, and slumped back against the cushions, rubbing her tired eyes, thinking it through. If Heather was there,

Issy would be subjected to an inquisition about her first day in Hartwell. She didn't have the energy for that. On the other hand, if her mother was in Sydney, the house would be locked up. She'd have to call Rosa and ask her to meet her there to open it. She thought warmly of her former nanny, now the housekeeper at Kilmore. It was getting late. That wouldn't be fair.

Instead, she rang Warwick.

'Isobel,' he said, a statement rather than a greeting.

'Warwick, hi. Sorry to bother you, but nothing works in this apartment. The fridge is dead. There's no hot water. I don't think I can stay here.'

'Ah, maybe try the Red Lion?'

'The Red Lion? You mean the pub?'

'Yeah, they've got rooms. Pretty basic, but—'

'Oh, no, I'm not staying at a pub. Is there anywhere else? What about that little bed and breakfast on the way into town?' She tried to recall if the sign said vacancy or no vacancy.

'Nah, that's Pammy Ward's place. They're in the UK for Christmas, visiting the grandkids.'

'Somewhere else, then?'

'I don't like your chances of finding something at this time of night.' A pause. 'You can stay at my place if you want? We've got a spare room. Dani won't mind.'

'Oh, thank you, Warwick, that's very kind, but no, I wouldn't feel comfortable with that.' It was sweet of him to offer, but she couldn't think of anything worse.

'Righto, then. Looks like you're staying put for tonight.'

'Fine. Let's work on it tomorrow.' She hung up.

The phone was still in her hand when Hugh rang.

She swiped to answer and burst into tears.

'What's wrong?' he said.

'Everything! The project's a disaster. It'll be a miracle if it's done by the launch date. The workers think I'm a joke. The project manager made me look like an idiot. I can't even get a coffee in this town! And I'm staying in a display suite where nothing works!' She inhaled a deep shaky breath and exhaled, trying to regain her composure.

'Babe, I'm sure it's not that bad.'

She sighed and took a sip of warm wine, recoiling. At room temperature, the buttery taste she usually loved was nauseating.

'Your parents own a five-star hotel down the road,' he said, as if the thought wouldn't have already occurred to her. 'Why don't you move up there?'

'I tried that. It's fully booked!'

'I suppose now's not a great time to tell you that I, ah … I can't get down there as soon as I thought.'

'What? When, then?' He was meant to be arriving tomorrow, or Wednesday, at the latest.

'Ah, not sure at this stage. I'll see what I can do.'

She filled the kettle and flicked it on. Nothing. Bloody hell. She couldn't even make a cup of tea! 'Fine. I've got to go.'

'Iss—'

'No, honestly, it's fine. I've just got work to do.'

She hung up and threw the phone across the room. It hit the corner of the island bench and fell to the ground. When she picked it up, there was a large crack across the screen.

Chapter 15

The Lindsay Shire Council offices, which included Hartwell, opened at nine o'clock. Meg pulled into the car park at five past. She'd heard nothing back from Adrian Gorecki, but she figured he had to turn up at the office eventually.

The automatic doors hummed open and she stepped into the cool foyer, glancing around. It felt closed even though it was officially open. Behind the counter, cubicles sat empty. She stood at the reception desk, waiting for a sign of life.

She felt herself brighten as a door swung open at the back of the room, but her expectations dropped again as the useless guy from yesterday entered. In his hand he held a steaming mug that said, *Instant human. Just add coffee.* Maybe yesterday he hadn't had his morning coffee.

He frowned slightly upon seeing her. 'Back again,' he said, without an upward inflection.

'Yes, hello. Thanks for your help yesterday. I really appreciate it. Thing is, though, I haven't heard back from Adrian. I'm only in town for a few days. Will he be in today?'

He sat down at his desk. 'Your guess is as good as mine,' he said, looking at the monitor.

Meg suppressed a sigh of frustration. 'Can *you* answer any questions for me?'

He looked over at her, as though he was surprised she was still there. 'Not about specific developments. Adrian's very particular about that.'

'Right.' A pause. 'What about general questions?'

'If it's about parking permits or rubbish removal, I'm your man.' He raised his eyebrows, somehow conveying deep existential disappointment through that one fleeting expression.

'Zoning?'

He shook his head. 'Sorry.'

'No worries. Thanks anyway.'

When she reached the car, she googled *Adrian Gorecki*. It would be easier to track him down if she knew who she was looking for. His LinkedIn page came up. The photo was black and white. He had a long thin face and a receding hairline and wore round glasses.

There was the soft purr of an engine and she looked up to see a silver hatchback pulling into the car park. She looked back at her phone, then realised she'd seen a long face, round glasses. Was it Adrian Gorecki? She tried to get a better look at the driver, but she could only see the small part of his face reflected in his rear-vision mirror. She zoomed in on the photo and took a screenshot, then looked back at the man who was now standing by the car, reaching into the back seat for something.

It was him. She was sure of it. He was older. The hairline had receded further, the cheeks were hollower, but it was the same long face. She got out, slamming the door too hard in her rush to intercept him before he went into the abyss of the council chambers.

'Adrian?'

He looked over, squinting as though he was struggling to see her properly in the bright morning sunshine. 'Yes?'

'Adrian Gorecki? I'm Meg Hunter.' She extended her hand. 'I wanted to ask you some questions about the redevelopment of Hartwell Gaol.'

'Oh, right, yes, you sent me an email. You're doing research …?'

'That's right.' She'd been deliberately vague about what sort of research. 'Sorry to drop in unannounced, but I'm just here until—'

'Look, now's not a good time. I'm late for a meeting.'

'Even just fifteen minutes.'

'I really can't talk—'

'When is a good time?'

Adrian pulled at his tie, loosening it a little, and glanced towards the building.

'Please? Even just a phone call would be fine.'

He got his phone out of the side pocket of his laptop bag. 'Possibly this afternoon,' he said, looking at his calendar. 'I have a window at three.'

Damn. That was when she was meeting Chris. She couldn't risk rescheduling that. 'Sorry, I can't do three. What about later this afternoon?'

He shook his head.

'Please?' She winced at the pleading tone in her voice.

He hesitated. 'Tomorrow morning?'

'Great! Fantastic. Thank you.'

'Where are you staying?'

'Hartwell, but I'm happy to come down here.'

He shook his head. 'No, that's fine. I'll meet you at the service station on the road from Hartwell. There's a coffee shop and a few tables in there. It's always empty.'

'Okay,' Meg said slowly. She'd stopped there yesterday to fill up her tank. It seemed like a weird place to meet.

'Eight thirty okay?'

Meg nodded. 'Sure.'

He gave her a brusque nod. She was about to ask for his mobile number when he said, 'I've really got to go now,' and hurried away.

She watched him walk towards the building. Had he seemed nervous? It was hard to say without any benchmark to go on. Maybe he was always a little flustered, a little awkward. But a roadhouse on a backroad did seem like an odd place to meet. It seemed like the kind of place you'd choose if you were hoping no one would see you.

Chapter 16

A skinny body, slumped and still. An ear-splitting siren piercing the dark night as blue light flashed on the slick wet road. Her own voice then, thin and reedy.

'Stella? Stella!'

Issy stirred. Stella? She was half-awake now, aware she was stuck in a dream but still under its dark spell.

Stella. She hadn't thought of her for years. Her old school friend had moved away after the accident and their paths had never crossed since. Where even *was* she these days? Last Issy heard, Stella was living in Port Macquarie with her parents, but that was ages ago.

It didn't matter.

She took a deep breath, trying to shake off the sense of panic which lingered, tightening her chest, leaving a heavy feeling in her stomach. Her neck hurt. She put a hand up to the sore spot, pressing it, enjoying the pain, as the last fragments of the dream fell away.

She opened her eyes a little, giving up on sleep. A large, over-exposed print hung on the wall by the bed where there was meant to be a window; a generic beach track. Suddenly, she was wide awake. She sat up, looking around the foreign bedroom. Of course! She was in Hartwell, in the ridiculous display apartment where nothing worked.

She yawned and rubbed her face. It was after one o'clock when she'd finally gone to bed. She'd spent hours reading project documents, studying the timeline, poring over site plans, trying to work out how they could meet the launch deadline. There was a loud growl from her stomach and she realised she was ravenous. Dinner last night was a protein bar she'd found in her bag and the rest of the wine. She needed to find some breakfast. Where though? She couldn't go back to the Apple Tree, for obvious reasons. She shuddered. All those eyes on her!

She reached for her phone, self-hatred rippling through her at the sight of the cracked screen, and typed a message.

Morning Warwick, just wondering if there's somewhere you could suggest for a quick breakfast, not too far?

The reply came quickly. *Apple Tree, best café in town.*

Issy sighed. *Yes, I went there for lunch yesterday. I'm keen to try somewhere new.*

Maybe she should go up to the Ashworth Park. They would have a buffet. Yes, that's what she'd do. Best not to complicate things further. Interactions with the locals were fraught, clearly, and she couldn't face another confrontation before she'd even had an oat milk latte.

All good, she typed. *I'll go to the Ashworth.*

She showered in ten seconds flat and flicked through her limited selection of clothes for her most low-key outfit. Why had she packed so many dresses? She was working on a construction site, for Christ's sake. What was she thinking? She made a mental note to ask Hugh to bring some more casual separates when he came down, and selected a pair of black linen shorts and a Camilla and Marc T-shirt. White. Not ideal.

Her phone beeped again as she was pulling on her platform trainers.

Spencer: *Everything okay down there?*

She frowned. Spencer was not the type for welfare checks.

Yes, fine. Why?

I heard you got off to a bad start.

She stared at the phone. Who the hell had he been talking to?

Three dots, then: *Warwick is a mate, we went to primary school together.*

Issy shook her head with disbelief, although it was typical of Spencer to stack the deck with old mates. Allies. He was the one who had hired Hugh! They'd been best friends at Dalton. She just didn't think his network would extend to the acting project manager in Hartwell. She thought carefully, crafting the perfect response.

Really! she wrote eventually. *What a coincidence. He seems like an absolute sweetheart. No one knew I was coming (weird!) which made my first day slightly tricky, but all good.*

Spencer took his time replying. *Any hope of meeting the deadline? Warwick reckons it's impossible.*

It's looking unlik— She stopped abruptly, then started again, imagining every word getting back to their father. *I'm confident we can get there.*

Three dots. *So you're saying Warwick is wrong?*

Issy scoffed. 'Bloody Spencer.'

I'm saying I'm confident we can work together to meet the deadline. The launch is going ahead as planned. She hit send and watched the screen, but there was nothing else.

Right. She sent Warwick a message: *Can you meet me on site in half an hour?*

Breakfast would have to be a yogurt from the convenience store.

She was looking around for her bag when her phone rang. *Dad.* Crap. Spencer couldn't have already spoken to him, could he?

'Hi, Dad—'

'Isobel! Cathy told me things aren't going very well down there.'

Jesus Christ! 'What? Everything's fine, although it would have been nice if Warwick knew I was coming. Have you spoken to Spencer?'

'Spencer? No.'

'You said they knew I was coming down?'

'Yes, they should have. But according to Cathy—'

'Well, it put me in a difficult position. What's Cathy even doing here?'

'She's had her nose out of joint since I suggested she retire. I thought she might enjoy being down there, give her something to do.'

'I don't need someone here checking up on me.'

'Oh for God's sake, Isobel, I thought you could use some support. From the sound of it you should be saying thank you, rather than complaining—'

Her phone beeped. She moved it away from her ear to read Warwick's message: *Sure, see you then.*

'Issy? Are you even listening?' Malcolm said, as she put the phone back to her ear. 'You're not going to let me down, are you?'

'Of course not. It'll be fine.'

'Will the launch—'

'Yes! The launch is going ahead as planned!' She was almost shouting, she realised suddenly, stopping to take a breath. Her father detested shouting, unless he was the one doing it. 'Sorry, Dad, it's just … don't you trust me?'

The question rang in her ears while she waited for him to answer.

Malcolm cleared his throat. 'Of course I trust you.'

'Okay,' she said slowly, not sure she believed him. She sighed. 'I've got to go. I've got a site meeting.'

'Keep me updated.'

'I will.' A pause. 'Dad?'

But he'd hung up.

She sat, motionless, reflecting on the conversation. Something niggled at her. It felt as though they were ganging up on her. As though they wanted her to admit defeat, to accept that she was in over her head, that she couldn't pull off the launch.

She swallowed. No. She was being ridiculous. Catastrophising, her therapist would say. Imagining subtext that wasn't there.

They'd never been an especially close family, despite what people might think, but who was? Spencer in particular had always felt more like an irritating uncle than a brother, a natural consequence of the age gap, perhaps. Eighteen years was a long time. He had just finished his senior year at Dalton Grammar when she was born.

Growing up, it was mostly just her and Heather in the big empty house. And Rosa, of course. Issy would mark the days off on a calendar until Felix came home to visit. He would spin her around until she was giddy, then she'd walk and fall over and they would collapse, weak with laughter. 'Now aeroplanes, Feelie!' she would beg him. He would lie on his back, feet in the air, and she would clasp his hands, her tummy balancing on his feet, soaring over him until she tumbled to the ground, where he would tickle her until she begged him to stop.

She tried to conjure a memory of Spencer. She was a flower girl at his wedding to Helen when she was eleven, but she suspected she was just piecing a recollection together from photos. A lilac dress. Little ballet shoes. A flower garland and a basket of rose petals. Helen in a white dress with an enormous skirt. Men in tails. Spencer was among them, presumably, along with Felix and Malcolm, but they were a blur. An amalgamation. She tried to find another memory, an earlier one, but came up blank.

He mustn't have come home very often, she supposed. He'd lived at St Paul's College at Sydney Uni while he was studying commerce and business, where three generations of Ashworths had been before him, then he moved into a flat in Elizabeth Bay, a twenty-first present from their parents. Spencer apparently charged rent, pocketing his roommates' money to fund lavish holidays. Heather had told Issy that once, her tone admonishing, implying that it was evidence of something but expecting Issy to join the dots herself. At the time, Issy hadn't been able to draw whatever conclusion her mother intended, but the story had stayed with her.

When Issy was in primary school, he sent them photos from a trip to Europe: Spencer and his mates posed with artful nonchalance in front of rented Aston Martins on a twisty alpine pass, snow-capped mountains in the distance. Her mother had pursed her lips and clicked her tongue—her own upbringing had been famously frugal—but Malcolm had waved away the extravagance. 'You're only young once,' he'd said.

Issy reread the text messages, the niggling feeling now stronger. More unsettling. A sense of doubt. Of what, though? Was he encouraging her to push out the deadline? Why would he do that? Unless he *wanted* her to fail—

There was a beep from her phone. Warwick: *Ready when you are.*

Damn. She'd lost track of time. She stood too quickly, feeling light-headed, and steadied herself with one hand on the arm of the sofa. It was as though something had shifted beneath her feet, leaving her footing precarious. As though nothing was quite as solid, as certain, as she thought.

Chapter 17

Meg walked into the bar at the Red Lion and glanced around for someone who might be Chris, but the place was deserted except for the regulars sitting on the same barstools as yesterday. She had no idea who she was looking for. His Facebook profile was full of photos of his wife and daughters.

She ordered a Coke and found herself drawn back to the photo wall she'd looked at the day before. Her eyes travelled over the images, snapshots of moments captured long ago, like time capsules. Ghosts, frozen in black-and-white markings on photographic paper. How strange to think these people were once as vivid and real as she was.

Her eye was drawn to a photo of a spectacular house, where a man and woman posed on a sweeping staircase leading up to a wide veranda under a slate roof. She glanced at the caption. *Built in the Victorian style*, she read, *the estate was the home of George Ashworth and family until 1932, when it was repurposed as a hotel. It is now considered the best regional hotel in Australia.* There was that name again.

She looked back at the photo. So that was the famous Ashworth Park Hotel and Spa. She'd seen it online when she was looking for somewhere to stay. It was way beyond her budget, but she'd clicked on the link and allowed herself to briefly imagine a parallel universe where she would enjoy a massage and order room service, which she would eat while nestled in downy pillows. She'd even put in the dates, to satisfy her curiosity, baulking at the outrageous cost of a four-night stay. Twenty-four hundred dollars! How could anyone justify—

'Catching up on your local history, are you?'

She turned to see the owner of the Apple Tree Café giving her a wry smile.

Meg shrugged. 'Something like that.'

The woman gestured to a high table nearby. 'Shall we sit?'

Meg shook her head. 'Oh, I'm … um …' she stammered. 'Sorry, I'm meeting someone here.' Was she meant to know this woman? She'd had a funny feeling yesterday that she knew her somehow.

The woman laughed and extended a hand. 'You're meeting me, Chrissy Baxter.'

Meg had the strange sensation of recalibrating. Chris was the *woman* in the photos.

Meg felt her face flush. 'Sorry, I was expecting a man.'

Chrissy laughed again. 'It's not the first time that's happened. Maybe I should change my Facebook name to Chrissy.' She had one of those faces that transformed when she smiled. Her eyes crinkled at the corners and came alive with a mischievous sparkle.

'Can I get you a drink?' Meg asked, gesturing to her Coke.

'No, thanks.' Chrissy looked around, selecting a table. One of the regulars raised his beer to greet her from a distance. Chrissy nodded in response and moved to a high table in the corner, as far from the bar as possible. She looked at her watch. 'I've only got half an hour.'

'How did you know who I was?' Meg asked.

'Sue told me there was someone staying here who was interested in Hartwell Gaol. I put two and two together. What's your interest in the development? She said you're doing research?'

Meg nodded. 'I'm studying redevelopments of historic sites,' she said, sticking with her story. 'What made you start the *Save Hartwell* group?'

Chrissy took a deep breath, then sighed and stayed silent for a long time. 'Actually, I think I am going to need a drink for this,' she said eventually. 'You want another one?'

'I'm good, thanks,' Meg said. 'I'll get it, though. It's the least I can do.'

'No need, it'll be on the house.' Chrissy tipped her head towards the bar. 'I know the barmaid.'

'Seems like you know everyone around here.'

'Small town.'

Meg watched from a distance as she chatted to the barmaid.

'You asked why I started the Facebook group,' Chrissy said when she returned.

Meg nodded as Chrissy took a sip of her drink. Bourbon and Coke, Meg guessed.

'I've watched that family rule this town my whole life,' Chrissy said. 'The decision to sell off the jail to them was the final straw for me. The local historical society wanted to make it a museum, keep it in public hands. Next thing, the state government's sold it off to the Ashworths, and then, what do you know? Somehow they have approval to build apartments above it.'

Meg's heartbeat picked up. Her suspicions about the apartments were correct. 'How did that happen, though? Wouldn't they need the local council to approve any development?'

Chrissy scoffed. 'The Ashworths have been careful to look after Lindsay councillors over the years, if you get my drift.'

'Look after? How?'

Chrissy shrugged. 'A school reference here, a donation to a kid's soccer club there … Look, everything I know is based on rumours, but where there's smoke …' She twirled the ice cubes with her straw. 'If you've got enough money, you can do whatever the hell you like and get away with it.'

'So that's why you started the group?'

Chrissy met her gaze. 'I decided enough was enough, not that it's made any difference.'

'I was in the café yesterday when Isobel Ashworth came in.'

Chrissy nodded but said nothing, so Meg went on.

'It's pretty brave, going up against a family like that.'

'Maybe I've just reached the stage where I don't give a crap.' She laughed and the lightness returned to her tired eyes.

The strange feeling came over Meg again, a little like déjà vu. The sense that she knew this stranger, somehow. She took a sip of her Coke, which was mostly melted ice now, waiting for the unsettling sensation to dissipate.

She looked up. 'Do you know of someone called Tina, by any chance?'

'Tina?' Chrissy repeated, a crease appearing between her brows. She picked up a cardboard coaster and folded it in half then shook her head, slowly. 'No, I don't think so.'

'What about when you were growing up? She might have moved away.'

'Tenile? There's a woman called Tenile who works in the office at Hartwell Primary.'

'No.' Meg shook her head, studying Chrissy's face as she played with the coaster, tearing it into smaller pieces. 'It's definitely a Tina I'm looking for.'

Chrissy shrugged and looked at her watch. 'I've got to go.' She drained her drink and reached for her bag.

'Can you stay five more minutes? I just had a few more—'

'No, sorry.' She was looking at her phone now, as though something urgent had come up. 'Good luck with your research.'

'Thanks,' Meg said, but Chrissy was already walking away.

Meg watched her disappear out the swinging doors, her mind racing. There'd been a shift in Chrissy when she asked about Tina. One minute she was relaxed, laughing, the next she was twitchy and distracted. Then she suddenly needed to leave.

'What was that all about?'

'Pardon?' Meg looked up to see the barmaid. Light reflected off the fine gold ring through the septum of her tiny, perfect nose. She was beautiful in the same way a blue-ringed octopus was beautiful.

'Looked serious,' she said, scooping the fragments of the torn coaster into the empty beer glass.

'Oh, it was just—' Meg stopped, prickling with irritation. Why was she explaining herself to the barmaid? 'It's actually none of your business,' she said, then instantly regretted it. Small towns and all that.

The barmaid raised her eyebrows and wiped the table, then gave her a long look. 'Well, it sort of is my business,' she said. 'She's my mum and she seemed a bit shaken when she left.'

'Chrissy's your mum?' Meg thought of the gangly pre-teen girls in Chrissy's profile photo. Was this barmaid really one of them?

The barmaid narrowed her sky-blue eyes and tilted her head to one side, chewing gum. 'She didn't mention that?'

Meg shook her head.

'Well, she is. I'm Georgie.'

Meg gave her an apologetic smile. 'I'm Meg. Sorry, I didn't mean to be rude.'

'It's cool,' Georgie said with the couldn't-give-a-damn nonchalance of a teenager. She turned to go.

'Hey, Georgie?'

She turned back, waited for Meg to go on.

'Do you happen to know those two guys who got arrested protesting at Hartwell Gaol?'

'Oh God—' Georgie rolled her eyes, '—not you, too.'

Meg frowned.

'I'm sick of hearing about that stupid jail. I mean, who gives a crap?' Georgie pulled a couple of fresh coasters out of her apron pocket and placed them on the next table. 'My mum's obsessed. It's not healthy.'

'Fair enough. I wonder, though, do you think it's the jail that your mum's fighting?' Meg hesitated, second-guessing Georgie's reaction. 'Or the Ashworths?'

Georgie smirked. 'I reckon you're onto something there. I do know one of those guys actually, the ones who got arrested at the jail.'

'You do? Would you introduce me? I'd love to ask him a few questions.'

Georgie pulled a pen out of her apron and wrote a name on the back of a coaster. 'You'll find him on Instagram. I can't guarantee he'll be willing to talk, but send him a DM and say you met me.'

Her eyes flicked over to a lanky guy standing at the bar, wearing an AC/DC T-shirt.

'I got a customer,' she said.

Meg watched Georgie greet him and pull a beer, a silent pantomime which she knew well from her own bar days. Georgie twirled a lock of her hair as they spoke. He tossed his change into her tip jar.

Meg looked at the name on the coaster. Dan James. At least she had a lead. He'd been arrested in the early stages of the redevelopment, but the charges had been dropped abruptly, according to what she'd read online. She was intrigued to know why. She pulled out her phone and searched the name but there were dozens, so she searched for Georgie instead.

Georgie's profile was public, thankfully. Meg barely looked at it, instead tapping on the list of people Georgie was following and typing in the name she'd given her. Bingo. Dan James had a goatee and a topknot. In his profile picture, he was holding a complicated yoga pose in front of an orange sunset. His bio read, *Be the change*. She typed a quick message, then flicked back to Georgie's grid.

Meg glanced up to check Georgie wasn't nearby—she was behind the bar, chatting to the regulars—then looked back at her phone. The profile was mostly bikini shots, coquettish poses with intense eye contact. There was no one else pictured. No friends, no family.

She clicked on one of Georgie laughing, tousled dirty-blonde hair falling over a tanned shoulder. In another she sat back, pensive, staring into the lens with a serious intensity, T-shirt tied at her midriff, a smattering of tiny freckles across her nose. It was as though she was balanced precariously on the cliff's edge between childhood and adulthood. A sexy girl or a girlish woman. Take your pick.

As she scrolled back up, Meg's eye was drawn to the follower tally at the top of the screen: *32.2K*, it said. Thirty-two thousand? She frowned and looked back over at Georgie. That seemed like a lot for a small-town barmaid. *Get to know me better*, her bio read. It included a link. Meg clicked on it and a new window opened an OnlyFans profile. In a banner photo, Georgie lay on her side, one hand suggestively close to her crotch, the other on her breast. She was braless, her nipples clearly visible through the thin fabric of her white T-shirt.

Poor Georgie. Why was she doing this?

Meg frowned, wondering why her default response was pity. It wasn't very progressive of her to assume that sex workers were victims. Maybe Georgie liked it. Maybe she found it empowering. How would Meg know?

Still. She couldn't help thinking it was a shame. A subscription was five dollars a month. Five! Five bucks was nothing. You could barely buy a coffee for five bucks. It made it even worse, somehow, although Meg was unsure what logic she was using to reach that conclusion.

Meg searched Georgie's friends list for Chrissy's Instagram profile. Christina Baxter. Her profile was sparse. Six posts, the first dating back to Georgie's first day of school. Tiny Georgie wore an enormous uniform that came down to her mid-shin, one parent on either side. Meg studied Georgie's father, wondering if he was still around. He was salt-of-the-earth handsome, with sandy hair and pride in his glassy-eyed smile. Chrissy looked the same as she did now, but younger and less weathered. Meg chided herself for focusing on how much the woman had aged. What did she expect? The photo was taken, what, fifteen years ago? Georgie was now working behind a bar. And selling naked photos of herself online—

Meg inhaled sharply as a thought struck her.

Chrissy was Christina.

Christina.

Meg's heart raced. Was Chrissy Jenny's Tina?

She took a deep breath, trying to slow her racing thoughts. In her mind, she replayed the moment when she'd asked Chrissy about Tina. At the mention of the name, Chrissy's walls had gone up. She'd become fixated on the coaster, avoiding eye contact. And then she was gone.

Chrissy. Christina. Tina.

Meg was right. She was sure of it. She was bloody right. Chrissy was Tina.

But who *was* Tina?

Frenetic adrenalin pulsed through her. She stood up, pacing. A balding man at a nearby table gave her a curious look, so she pretended to study a family tree on the wall. That feeling she'd had when she first saw Chrissy in the café—and again at the pub—it was the feeling of knowing, the sense that she knew her. Not that she'd *met* her, but that she *knew* her. Somehow.

Could Chrissy be her mother's ... sister? Meg's aunt? She could hardly bear to let the question form in her mind. She'd been here before, giddy with hope, and it had only ever led to disappointment.

Families belonged to other people. It was just how things were. She'd learnt that time and time again, when well-meaning people asked simple questions she struggled to answer. School was a minefield. Even something as simple as Grandparents' Day had stirred up a feeling of being somehow deficient. Inadequate. As though she was missing something simple yet wonderful, that everyone else took for granted, like eyelashes.

It was always just Meg and her mum. No father. No brothers or sisters. No aunts or uncles or grandparents or cousins. It was just the two of them, eating chops and mashed potato, at their Formica table, which they moved from one thin-walled, two-bedroom rental house to another, up and down the east coast. Meg had been to eight schools by the time she finished year six. It felt like the moment she made a friend, a real friend, they would be packing boxes into their station wagon and leaving town.

She looked back at the long-dead family tree. They were all Ashworths, she realised, as she looked more closely. A sepia-toned photo sat alongside each name. The men bore bushy moustaches. The women wore elaborate hats. They all had the blank facial expression common in old photos: a creepy, empty glare. It felt like they were mocking her. *Families belong to other people,* they seemed to say. *Not to you.*

She'd made a family tree once. When was that? She could picture the classroom. It had green carpet and low ceilings. Bangalow Primary School? She must have been in year two.

'We're going to start working on a new project!' Mrs Holly had said, with the sparkle-eyed excitement of an entertainer at a children's birthday party. It was early in term one and Meg had only been there since the start of that year, but she was already a little bit in love with Mrs Holly, a plump, motherly type with a warm smile and a laugh that sounded like honey. 'We're going to make family trees!'

Meg had felt a twinge of something she didn't quite understand. 'Who knows what a family tree is?'

Meg wasn't sure but she didn't like the sound of it. She avoided Mrs Holly's gaze by pulling at the loose stitching on her shoe. The hand of a serious, studious boy shot up. He informed them all that a family tree was 'a way of naming all the people in a family and showing how they are all connected', and even stood up to draw a diagram on the whiteboard. He wrote his own name, then drew a vertical line up to his parents, who he connected to each other with a nice, neat, horizontal line. Then he added his two brothers, and he was about to add his grandmother when Mrs Holly stepped up. 'Thank you, Darcy!' she said, taking the whiteboard marker.

Mrs Holly handed out large pieces of paper and sent them back to their tables to get started. Meg stared at the blank page. Her chest felt tight. Beside her, Sophie Stevens was making speedy progress, her brow furrowed in concentration as she wrote the names of her older siblings. Opposite, Oscar Wells had already connected himself to his mother and father, and two other people too, next to his dad. Meg wasn't sure who they were. Aunts or uncles, maybe.

She looked back at her page. *Meg Hunter*, she wrote in the centre. Above her name she wrote *Jenny Hunter, mum*. The tightness in her chest felt heavy now, like a big stone was making it hard to breathe. She looked over at Mrs Holly, who was crouching beside the next table. 'Good job,' she said to Meg's classmate as she stood. Meg looked back at her page, with all its empty white space. She traced over the letters of her own name so it looked like she was working.

'Good work, Oscar!' Mrs Holly had appeared beside their table to check on their progress. 'I remember your big brothers!' She looked at Meg. 'Come on, Meg. Who are you going to add now?'

Meg shrugged. 'There isn't anyone else,' she said, quietly.

'Pardon?' Mrs Holly knelt by Meg's side, enveloping her in a cloud of sweet perfume. 'I didn't catch that, sweetheart?'

Meg spoke a little louder now, but not loud enough to be overheard by Sophie or Oscar. 'There isn't anyone else.'

'Of course there is!' Mrs Holly said, with the confidence of someone who'd grown up with a tribe of siblings and cousins.

Meg didn't want to disappoint her. She drew a line sideways next to her name. She'd always wanted an older sister. What would she call her? She shuffled through her favourite girls' names. Josie. A warm feeling spread through her. This must be what it feels like, she thought, to have a proper family instead of just a mother.

She looked sideways at Sophie's diagram. 'Who's that?' she asked, pointing to where Sophie had written 'Wendy' on the page.

'That's my auntie Wendy, she lives in London. Last time she came, she brought me a money box in the shape of a red double decker bus.'

Sophie looked at Meg's page. 'You haven't even done your daddy, silly billy!'

'I'm just writing him down now,' Meg said. She hovered her pencil over the white space next to Jenny's name.

Sophie's dad's name was Luke. His name was written carefully next to her mum's. Luke and Alison. Meg sat up higher in her chair, craning her neck to see Oscar's diagram. Sarah and James. Mum and Dad. Just as it should be.

Meg wrote 'Tim' in the space where her dad's name should go. Tim 'The Toolman' Taylor. He was the only dad she could think of—they watched *Home Improvement* on Sunday nights—and Mrs Holly needed her to write down a dad. She sat back and looked at her page. It looked much better. She thought about aunts now.

By the time Mrs Holly announced it was packing-up time, Meg had a father who played the guitar, two aunties who spoiled her when she visited them during the school holidays, and a grandmother called Mary, who would read her Roald Dahl stories. It was sort of like creative writing. She loved stories. Mrs Holly had told her she might be an author one day. Yes. It was just like that.

'You'll probably have some blanks on your family tree,' Mrs Holly said. 'Have a chat to Mum and Dad tonight to fill them in. Tomorrow you will present your family tree to the class.'

Obviously Meg didn't mention the family tree to her mum that night. Jenny was not in the mood—Meg had seen her put the empty wine bottle in the bin before dinner was ready—so that was lucky. And anyway, it was surprisingly easy for Meg to present her family tree to the class. Mrs Holly seemed pleased.

The following week was the Learning Showcase. Meg wasn't sure what that meant, they hadn't done that at her last school. It turned out it meant the parents were invited into the classroom to hear about their learning. Mrs Holly had created displays on the pinboards with examples of their work.

Meg's family tree had prime position, front and centre, directly under a sign which proudly proclaimed these were OUR FAMILIES.

'You have a lovely family, Mrs Hunter. Meg speaks so highly of all her aunties and uncles and cousins,' Mrs Holly said, stopping to stand beside Jenny, who was studying the diagram. Meg felt like she might cry. What would Mrs Holly think, when she found out Meg had made them all up?

She looked up at her mum's face. Jenny's lips were pressed together in a thin line. Then she said, 'Yes, we do. We're very lucky—' she put a hand on Meg's shoulder, '—aren't we, Meg?'

Meg nodded.

'Is Dad coming tonight?' Mrs Holly asked.

Meg frowned and shook her head.

'He's working late, unfortunately,' Jenny said.

Mrs Holly made a sad face. 'Shame,' she said, before moving on to greet Oscar's mum, who had a chubby baby on her hip.

In the car on the way home, Meg waited for Jenny to ask her why she'd lied, but she didn't. She just reached over and held Meg's little hand all the way home. They never spoke about it, then or ever. They moved again a few months later.

Meg went back to the table and picked up her phone, studying the photo of Chrissy. Was she Jenny's sister? Or was Meg getting ahead of herself? She had a tendency to do that, to run headlong down one track. She needed to slow down. These were all just thoughts. Mere speculation. She needed proof.

DNA. A ripple ran up Meg's spine as the idea struck her. She had done a DNA test a few years before, but it had been a disappointing exercise. Her only matches had been distant cousins, but that might change if Chrissy did one. A DNA test would turn Meg's suspicions into facts. A DNA test would prove she was right. Or wrong.

How would she get Chrissy to do one, though? She couldn't even finish a conversation once Meg said Tina's name. Meg could hardly turn up at the café, DNA test in hand, and announce, 'I think you might be related to my reclusive mother, would you mind spitting into this tube?'

That wasn't an option, clearly. She looked at the screen. As she clicked back to Georgie's profile, a thought crystallised in her head: *Georgie and Chrissy would share the same DNA.*

DNA Sleuths Facebook Group

Mel Hunt: Hi all, I have a question I'm hoping someone here can answer. I think I may have found my mum's sister, but she's not convinced. I need DNA proof, but she's unlikely to agree to do a test. I get the sense she would prefer me to leave her alone altogether. Her daughter might agree to do one though. She would be my cousin if I'm right about this. If I can persuade the daughter to do a test, will that give me the proof I need?

Top comments

Patricia Pine: A DNA test will prove you are related, if you actually are. It won't prove she's definitely your cousin though, you need to work that out based on the centimorgans shared and your family tree.

> **Mel Hunt:** Centimorgans?

> **Patricia Pine:** It's the unit used to measure how much DNA you share with your relatives. You will share roughly the same amount of your DNA with your great-grandmother as you will with your cousin or your half-niece. How old is the daughter? How old are you?

> **Mel Hunt:** Thanks **Patricia**. She's 18, I'm 29. If she's my great-granny she looks great for her age ...

Zelda Merlino: Hello, Search Angel here. I think some commenters are over-complicating this and confusing you! The simple answer is yes, a DNA test will confirm if you have found family members. If you and the daughter share between 550 and 1200 centimorgans, she is most likely your cousin.

> **Mel Hunt:** So if the result came back in that range, I could confidently say her mother is my aunt?

> **Zelda Merlino:** Well, yes, given what you know about their ages and the likely family relationships.

> **Mel Hunt:** Great, that makes sense. Thanks **Zelda**.

> **Zelda Merlino:** Pleasure, reach out if I can help.

Chapter 18

'Sorry, Warwick,' Issy said as she entered the site office. 'I was on the phone to my dad. He was keen to get an update on the project.' She watched him, curious to see what he made of that, but she could read nothing. She went on. 'Spencer messaged too. I didn't know you two were old friends.'

Warwick shrugged. 'Wouldn't say friends, exactly.'

'He said you went to primary school together.'

'Primary school was a long time ago.'

'But you stayed in touch, I hear?'

Warwick nodded. He was a man of few words, Issy was learning. She sighed. If she was going to pull this off, she needed his help.

'Warwick, I want to apologise for yesterday.' She swallowed hard, almost unable to form the words. It felt distasteful, shameful almost, to admit she was even slightly wrong. Attack was the best form of defence, in her opinion. It was a basic survival strategy in the Ashworth family, but something told her it wouldn't work with this man sitting in front of her, eyeing her warily.

The corners of his mouth turned down as though he wasn't sure what she meant. He wasn't going to make this easy for her, clearly.

'I think we got off on the wrong foot,' she said. 'A message was meant to be sent from the corporate office, to let you know I was coming down to oversee the final stage of the project. It was obviously an inconvenience to have me turn up without warning. To be honest, it put me in a tricky position too. The team seemed thrown by it.'

He rubbed his stubbled cheek. 'If you don't mind me saying, I think it might have been your approach that threw them.'

Her heart rate picked up. 'My approach?'

He cleared his throat, shifted in his seat. 'Can I give you a bit of feedback?'

She bristled, sensing criticism was about to follow. *No, thank you, I'm fine,* she imagined saying, as though he was offering her an unwanted cup of tea. She didn't want feedback. No one ever wanted feedback. She was positive about that, despite what they might say. Instead, she arranged her face into an expression designed to look open and attentive. 'Of course.'

'You know that old saying, "You don't need to be liked, you need to be respected"?'

'Yes, of course,' she said, feeling patronised. It was one of her father's guiding principles. She could hear his commanding voice in her head: *You can't build an empire by being everyone's friend.*

'Well, in my experience, that's rubbish.'

She must have looked confused, because Warwick went on. 'Issy—is it okay if I call you Issy?'

She nodded.

'Blokes like this don't give a damn what your last name is. If you pretend to be someone you're not, they'll see right through you. If you're out of your depth, but you're pretending you're not, they won't save you from drowning.'

Issy straightened, frowning. 'I'm not out of my depth.'

'I'm not saying you are.' He gave her a reassuring smile. 'I'm just saying, be honest with them. They're good blokes, but they can smell crap a mile away.'

'Right, okay,' she said, not sure what to make of this advice. 'Thank you, Warwick. That's very helpful.' She reached for her bag and took out her laptop, signalling the end of his little feedback session. 'Warwick, my father is adamant that the launch must go ahead as planned. From what I saw yesterday, that will be a tall order, but not impossible. I suggest we redirect all efforts to finishing the entertainment space, and leave the residential development to open at a later stage. I've checked the contracts and there was some leeway built into the completion dates for the apartments.'

She waited for him to respond.

When he said nothing, she sighed. 'Do you think that will work?'

He shrugged. 'It's doable, I guess. You sure it's okay for us to launch without the apartments being ready?'

She nodded. 'Yes, it's fine.' It would have to be. 'You know, Spencer has enormous respect for you, Warwick. He said you're a gun. That if anyone can get this project back on track, it's you.'

He leaned forward, a slight smile playing on his face. 'He said that?'

'He did.' She lowered her voice. 'I probably shouldn't tell you this, but he said he thinks you have a lot to offer Ashworth Property.'

He sat up a little straighter. 'He did?'

She nodded. 'If we can deliver this, I suspect there will be some great opportunities ahead for you.' She opened the project plan document and turned the laptop so they could both see the screen. 'As far as I can tell, this plan is basically a fairytale. Let's get on the same page, then we can work out what we need to do to salvage the project and meet the launch deadline.'

Chapter 19

Adrian Gorecki was right. The cafeteria at the service station between Hartwell and Lindsay was deserted at eight thirty in the morning. Meg sat at a table with her back to the wall, sipping a flat white that was too weak and too milky. It barely tasted like coffee. Every time a beep announced the arrival of a new customer, she would look towards the automatic doors, hoping to see the bespectacled face of the council planner. Instead, it was a succession of tradesmen paying for petrol and takeaway sausage rolls.

She monitored the time on a clock behind the counter, wondering how long she should wait before accepting that Adrian wasn't coming. She didn't have a mobile number for him, so she couldn't ring him. After twenty minutes, she sent him a message through LinkedIn.

Hi Adrian, I'm at the Roadhouse Cafe. Are you on your way?

Who knew if he would even get it.

A few minutes later, there was a ping from her phone, but it was an Instagram notification, not Adrian. Still, she felt a little flutter of adrenalin, remembering the message she'd sent to Dan James the day before.

The hopeful buzz subsided as she read his response.

I moved away from Hartwell after the protest. I got sick of having my tyres slashed. I have no interest in talking about it further. I'm at a place of peace in my life.

She tapped out a reply, an attempt to change his mind, but it felt futile. She added a second message: *Would you be able to put me in touch with the other protester who was arrested?*

The reply came quickly. *He had a motorcycle accident which left him with a severe brain injury. He won't be willing or able to talk to you.*

The door beeped again and she looked up. Not Adrian. It was nine fifteen. He wasn't coming. What a waste of time this was panning out to be. She was running out of leads.

Remembering Chrissy's comments about the local councillors, she googled Lindsay council and studied their faces. Seven out of nine were grey-haired men in suits and ties. Pale, stale and male, Deb would say. The mayor had a moustache and a smirk that made him look more like a seventies porn star than a politician.

Still no Adrian. She rested her head in her hands, her elbows on the table. What now? She didn't want to give up too easily, but she was starting to suspect there was no story here after all. She should probably go to the jail, see if she could get someone talking, but it felt pointless.

She exhaled loudly. She was rapidly losing interest in the story altogether. Nothing she'd found so far seemed particularly newsworthy. There were rich arseholes all over the country bending the rules to increase their already obscene fortunes and the Ashworths didn't seem any different. The only story here seemed to be the one about Jenny and her past.

A pink-haired waitress reached for her cup and saucer. 'Can I get you anything else?'

'No, thanks.'

Meg put her laptop back in her bag. It was time to talk to Chrissy again.

'She's not working till later today,' a bearded man behind the café counter said when Meg asked for Chrissy. 'What's your name? I'll tell her you stopped by.'

'No worries,' Meg said. 'Thanks anyway.'

She got back in the car and checked Facebook, searching for clues to Chrissy's address. A few minutes later, she found an old photo of Georgie and an older girl posing on bikes in front of a neat, bland, beige-brick house. Meg could see a house number on the front fence behind them. She tapped to enlarge the photo, squinting at the blurry number. Thirty ... seven? Yes, thirty-seven. How many streets were there in this town, she wondered, turning the key in the ignition.

She started on the south side of town, where the houses didn't look like the ones in the glossy real estate magazine in the Saturday papers. Ten minutes and fourteen streets later, there it was in real life. Thirty-seven Barton Drive. It was just as dull and nondescript as it was in the photo, but now the paint was peeling above the front door and the gate hung crooked on its hinges.

It squealed as Meg pushed it open. Her heartbeat picked up as she reached the front door, which was propped open behind a flyscreen door. The lounge room beyond was dark and still, except for a fan whirring overhead. Meg pressed the doorbell, but didn't hear it ring.

While she waited, she pulled up a photo of Jenny, which she'd taken on her mother's fiftieth birthday. Jenny hated having her picture taken. She usually managed to turn away or shield herself with a hand, but that day her guard was down and Meg had been able to capture her, long hair flowing over her shoulders, bewitching eyes sparkling behind tortoiseshell frames. It was just over a year ago, but already she looked different. Less like herself than the disease that was gradually taking her.

Meg looked back into the darkness behind the door, straining to hear some sign of life from inside the house. Nothing. She knocked on the screen door, which made a tinny rattle.

'Chrissy!' a man's voice called from somewhere inside. 'There's someone at the door!'

There were footsteps, then Chrissy appeared from a back room. She wore a shapeless cotton dress, her dark hair bundled up on her head. She looked at Meg from behind the screen, then she opened it and exhaled loudly.

'You again.'

'Sorry.' Meg swallowed. 'I hope you don't mind me coming here.'

Chrissy said nothing, so Meg went on.

'I just wondered if you recognise this woman.' She held out the phone.

Chrissy glanced at it quickly, then shook her head. 'No. Why? Should I?'

Meg took a deep breath. 'Do you have a sister?'

'I did.'

Meg's heart raced. 'Would you mind if I asked … what happened to her?'

Chrissy frowned. Meg could almost see her thinking.

'Please?' she said, her voice cracking slightly.

'She got involved with a cult and cut off all contact with us.' Chrissy's voice was sharp. 'Then she died suddenly, a few years after she left.'

Meg's mind raced. 'This is my mother.' She gestured towards the photo. 'I think she might be your sister.'

A flash of emotion crossed Chrissy's face, then her expression hardened. 'Why?' Her tone was wary now.

'Because … Because she's never told me anything about her past, or her family, until now. She has dementia and she's started to say things, about Hartwell and about … Tina.'

There was a twitch of recognition in Chrissy's eyes.

Meg held out the phone. 'Do you want to have another look?' she asked, her voice soft, trying not to startle the woman. She sensed that if she made one wrong move, the conversation would be over, like what had happened at the pub.

Chrissy didn't move to take the phone. Her dark eyes searched Meg's face as though she was looking for something familiar. She put a hand to her head, pushing her hair back off her glistening forehead, then, exhaling heavily, took the phone and stared at the image for a long time. Meg felt hope fading. If only she had an older photo, one which might more closely resemble Jenny as she was when Chrissy knew her. *If* she knew her.

'Could it be her?' Meg whispered.

Chrissy shook her head very slowly. 'I don't think so.'

'But it could be?'

Chrissy gave a slight shrug. 'I haven't seen her since the day before my seventeenth birthday,' she said, dark eyes flashing. It still hurt.

'How do you know that she joined a cult?' Meg's voice was gentle.

'She was seeing this guy who was a bit older. Late twenties, maybe? I don't know. He got her involved with a weird church up in Lindsay. They were supposed to recruit people, so she took me to one of the meetings.'

'What did they do there?'

'Chanting, babbling, weird nonsense words, which they believed was God speaking through them.' Chrissy snorted. 'It was really wacko. Even at sixteen I could see that.' She looked out at a passing car and waved to the driver.

'What happened next?'

'She became really distant.' Chrissy shrugged. 'I can't remember it that clearly, to be honest. It was a long time ago. I was in year eleven, I was busy with friends, boys, you know. She was twenty-one by then. She was studying nursing up in Lindsay, going to the cult meetings, spending all her spare time working or with her boyfriend. Then one day, she left.'

'She didn't tell you where she was going? She didn't say goodbye?'

Chrissy shook her head. 'About a month later, we got a letter from her saying that she wasn't coming back, cutting off all contact.' She paused for a long time. When she spoke again there was a harder edge in her voice. 'It destroyed my parents, especially my mum. It was as though I'd lost her too after that.'

'I'm sorry,' Meg said. It felt inadequate. How could someone do that to their family? Cause them so much pain? She wanted to say something more, something which would capture the enormity of Chrissy's loss, but she couldn't find the words.

They stood, silent, as a hot breeze rustled the leaves in a nearby gum tree.

'I'm so sorry to ask, but how do you know she—' Meg faltered. It felt like she was pressing a bruise, but she had to know. 'How do you know she died?'

'A couple of years later, we were visited by someone from the church. A man. It was a brain aneurysm. She was twenty-three.'

Meg's thoughts raced as she tried to reconcile Chrissy's story with what she knew about her mother. Did the timing work? Without pressing for more details, she couldn't be sure, but maybe it did. Meg was twenty-nine. She could have been born after Chrissy's sister left Hartwell.

'Did this man, the one who visited, did he say anything about her having a daughter?'

'No, he just told us about the aneurysm. They'd already had a funeral by then. He just gave us a box of some of her things.'

'He did? Where would that box be now?'

'Probably somewhere in my garage. That's where we put everything after Mum and Dad sold up a few months back.'

Meg wanted to ask if she could look through the box, but she could sense Chrissy putting her walls up again. 'I really appreciate you talking to me about this. I know it must be difficult.'

'All this happened a really long time ago. It's not something I think about much these days.'

Meg looked back at the photo. 'Do you think there's any chance this could be her? Any chance at all? The timing would work, I think.'

Chrissy looked at the photo again. 'No,' she said, more certainty in her voice now. 'No, I don't think so.'

'Chrissy?' the man's voice called out.

'Just a sec!' She turned back to Meg. 'I've gotta go. Good luck. I hope you find the answers you're looking for.'

She went to shut the screen door.

'Chrissy? Can I ask you one last question?'

She gave her a weary smile. 'Sure.'

'What was your sister's name?'

'Anna.' Her voice was little more than a whisper. 'I called her Annie.' She held Meg's gaze for a long time before she closed the door.

Meg stood on the doorstep, her mind racing. Anna? Anna was her own middle name. Megan Anna Hunter.

Chapter 20

Issy returned to the apartment that afternoon with renewed optimism. The meeting had gone well. They'd developed a new timeline, one they had some hope in hell of delivering on, and Warwick was totally on board, thanks to her little white lie about promotion opportunities at Ashworth Property. That was a stroke of genius. She would have to manage it carefully—hopefully he wouldn't tell Spencer—but if he did pull this off, surely she could find him something satisfactory.

She'd had a moment of brilliance at the end of the meeting and suggested team drinks on Friday afternoon. She told Warwick she would book a function space at the Ashworth Park, but he'd pulled a funny face and suggested the Red Lion instead. She'd arranged it as soon as the meeting was over. They would have their own space off the main room, so she could do a little speech, and she would put money on a bar tab. If beer didn't win them over, nothing would.

Towards the end of the meeting, it had occurred to her that moving to the Ashworth Park might not be a good look—especially in light of Warwick's lecture—so she'd asked him (very politely) if he could sort out the issues with the display apartment. He assured her it would all be fixed before the end of the day. He even sent

Paola, the traffic controller, to the grocery store at the bottom of the main street for some 'bits and pieces'. Whatever that meant.

Now she dumped her Birkin on the bench—noting that the plastic cheese had disappeared—and opened the fridge, curious about what 'bits and pieces' she would find. She was pleasantly surprised. It was stocked with fresh fruit and veggies, yogurt, and some little microwave meals in plastic boxes. She reached for one— red Thai curry and green beans—and read the nutrition panel. The sodium content was high, but otherwise it wasn't a complete disaster. She put it back and ran the hot tap. The water got hot under her hand, steam rising. A ripple of relief ran through her at the thought of a long, hot shower.

Her phone rang. *Hugh. FaceTime.*

Quickly, she took off her cap and pulled the elastic out of her hair—Hugh hated it when she wore her hair back; it made her face too long, he said—then she answered the call.

'Hey, there,' she said, as his face filled the screen, tanned against his white collar.

'Good news!' he said. 'Just had an email from Cecily Morgan-Phillips, she's had a cancellation tomorrow.'

Issy frowned. 'Cecily who?'

'Morgan-Phillips. The wedding planner. The one Nadia recommended. I emailed her the other day. She's usually booked up for weeks apparently, but now she can do a Zoom with us tomorrow at eleven.'

'Tomorrow?' Issy swallowed. What was the rush?

'I'm thinking September,' Hugh went on.

'September? For the wedding?' Issy felt her heartbeat quicken.

Hugh laughed. 'Yes, for the wedding!'

'But that—that only gives us nine months. You can't organise a wedding in nine months.'

'Of course you can. Nine months is plenty of time. Nadia said Cecily's vendors move heaven and earth to accommodate her clients. I figure, why wait?' He gave her a lopsided smile. 'I want you to be Mrs Thorburn as soon as possible.'

Issy's chest tightened. Mrs Thorburn. Isobel Thorburn. Isobel Ashworth-Thorburn? She hadn't even considered any of this yet, but it struck her as something they should discuss, rather than assume. It was her name, after all! Why did men think nothing of expecting women to change their names? There'd be rioting in the streets if someone suggested they should change theirs! She took a steadying breath. 'It's just ... I don't think I can do tomorrow, actually. There's a lot going on down here—'

Hugh's eyes narrowed. 'It's just an hour, Issy. If I can manage to clear an hour, I'm sure you can.'

'Well, maybe ... I don't know ... I need to be onsite to—'

'What's the problem, Issy?' His tone was sharp. 'I thought you'd be pleased about this!'

'I am! I *am* pleased, I'm just—'

'Do you not want to marry me?'

'Of course I want to marry you!'

He sighed and sat back on the lounge, away from the camera, running his hands through his hair.

'I just need to focus on the project right now.' She spoke softly, choosing her words carefully. 'I *do* want to marry you, Hugh. Of course I do!' She swallowed. 'Can we ... can we just put a hold on the wedding plans until the new year? Do you mind?'

He shrugged and sighed heavily. 'Okay.'

'Thank you,' she said. 'I miss you.'

'I miss you, too.'

'When are you coming down?'

'Not sure.' He rubbed his face and yawned. 'Work's bonkers. We're doing a big deal on the Gold Coast so I'm flying up there tomorrow. Maybe Saturday.'

'Okay. I need you to bring me down some things. I'll text you a list.'

He leaned closer to the camera. 'Speaking of the deal, I've got a call coming through. I've got to take this.'

'Okay—'

Suddenly he was gone and it was just her own face, taking up the whole screen. She frowned, noticing a dark smudge on her forehead, and leaned closer to the camera. What the hell was that? Dirt? She licked her finger and rubbed at it. Yes, dirt. She closed her eyes, mortified. She'd had dirt on her face throughout the whole phone call.

Chapter 21

'What were you talking to Mum about?'

Meg spun around to see Georgie leaning against the side of the house, vape in hand. She wore cut-off denim shorts and a cropped bra top, showing off her tanned midriff.

Georgie raised a finger to her lips. 'Let's walk.'

Meg followed her across the driveway and onto the road. Heat rose from the bitumen underfoot as cicadas chanted their shrill song.

'So?' Georgie asked, as they walked slowly. 'What was that about?'

'Someone from her past. Does she talk much about her sister?'

'The one who died?' Georgie shook her head. 'They don't talk about her at all.'

'They?'

'Mum and my grandparents.' She took a drag on her vape, exhaled a cloud of white smoke. She held it out to Meg, an offer. 'Blueberry,' she added.

'No, thanks.'

Meg looked at the houses as they passed. The front garden of number twenty-seven was wild and unkempt, its letterbox stuffed full of junk mail, its blinds down. The number seven had fallen off, leaving a mark where it once was. Hadn't they just passed another derelict house? Meg turned to look back up the street where they'd come from. The shack a few blocks back was clearly uninhabited too, with waist-high weeds threatening to engulf the driveway. One of the front windows was broken.

Meg frowned. 'What's with all the empty houses?'

'Dunno,' Georgie said, bored. 'A few have sold recently around here, but no one's moved in.'

'That's weird.'

Georgie shrugged, as though she hadn't given it much thought and didn't plan to. 'It worked out well for my nan and pop. Mum couldn't believe how lucky they were when someone made an offer on their place. They were too old to be living alone. Now they're living their best lives in a retirement community in Queensland. "Independent living for the over sixties."' She made quote marks with her fingers.

'The house wasn't on the market?' Meg asked. 'They just got an offer? Out of the blue?'

'Yep.' Georgie inhaled on the vape.

'And that was surprising, that they sold so easily?'

Georgie nodded. 'Our old neighbours took over a year to sell a while back.'

Meg frowned. 'Isn't property in Hartwell in high demand? I thought everyone in the Eastern Suburbs of Sydney had a country house down here.' She raised an eyebrow to distance herself from the Sydney elite.

Georgie exhaled. 'Not on this street. The houses are junk and they all back onto the industrial estate. There's a dairy factory just behind those back fences.' She looked in the general direction.

They stopped walking and sat on the kerb in the shade. For a few minutes, they sat listening to the cicadas chant, their lazy pace gathering momentum until it reached a deafening cacophony, then stopped abruptly. Silence crackled in the air momentarily before the slow chant began again.

'What's this stuff about Mum's past got to do with you, anyway?' Georgie asked.

'I think Chrissy's sister is my mum.'

'So we would be …'

'Cousins.'

Georgie frowned. 'I didn't know Mum's sister had a baby before she died.'

'If I'm right, she didn't die.'

Georgie looked at Meg. 'You think she just … left?' A crease formed between her brows that made Meg think of Jenny.

'Yeah.'

Georgie looked down at her purple toenails. 'But why?'

'That's what I want to know. Your mum said there's a box of her sister's things somewhere in your garage.'

Georgie looked up. 'She did?'

Meg nodded. 'Apparently some guy came here to tell them she'd passed away and gave them a box of her stuff.' A long silence. 'Do you reckon you could help me find it?'

Georgie bit her lip, considering the request. 'Nah, I don't think I should. If Mum didn't want to …'

'I'd pay you, obviously, for your time and effort.' Out of the corner of her eye, Meg saw Georgie's eyes light up. 'A hundred bucks?'

'Two hundred,' Georgie said.

'Done.'

'Come around on Saturday morning. Mum'll be at the café.'

When Meg got back to her room, she called Pete.

'Hunter!' he said, over background noise. 'Hang on a tick.'

'Where are you?'

'The pub.'

'Are you ever *not* at the pub?'

'I do my best work here.'

Meg scoffed. 'I stumbled across something interesting today.' She recapped her conversation with Georgie about the empty houses on Barton Drive. 'Weird, don't you think?'

'I dunno, maybe.'

'It'll be easy enough to find out who's bought them, won't it?'

'I'll do a title search,' he said. 'It might turn up a name.' A beat. 'So have you made any progress on the story?'

'Not really.' She sighed, heavily. 'Every lead ends up going nowhere. The Ashworths are probably buttering up the local councillors to get approvals, but that doesn't sound like much of a story to me. The protesters have left town. No one seems very willing to talk. I think I'll head home on Sunday, if nothing changes.' If she was honest, the only thing keeping her in Hartwell was the promise of going through the Baxters' garage.

'Have you managed to talk to anyone at the jail?'

'Not yet.' She wasn't easily intimidated generally, but the truth was, the older woman in the wrap dress had put her off. There was something unsettling about the way she'd glared at Meg that first day. 'I'll go back tomorrow.'

Chapter 22

The following morning, Issy sat at the desk Warwick had cleared for her in the site office. She'd had a productive few hours. Since they'd made the decision to put the apartments on hold, the whole site felt different. With major construction halted, the bobcats and piles of timber and steel were gone for now and it felt a lot less like a building site. She'd had to negotiate a temporary rent reduction with the retail tenants, given there would be some inconvenience when construction upstairs resumed, but they'd all been more than happy with what she'd suggested.

She should feel pleased, but irritation thrummed in her chest. She reached for her phone, even though she'd checked it only five minutes ago, if that. Still nothing from Hugh. She exhaled loudly and tossed it onto a pile of papers.

'Everything okay, Is?'

Warwick had started calling her 'Is' now, as though 'Issy' was too much of a mouthful. She usually disliked it when people took the liberty of inventing their own names for her, but from Warwick, it was strangely endearing.

She smiled. 'Yeah, it's fine. It's just ... Hugh's meant to be coming down this weekend, but I haven't heard from him.'

Warwick frowned. 'He'll just be caught up with work. I'm sure you'll hear from him soon.'

'You're probably right,' Issy said, but she'd felt troubled ever since their conversation the night before. Maybe she should have just gone ahead with the meeting with Cecily whatshername. It would probably have been easier than upsetting Hugh. She wanted to spend the weekend with him to get everything back on an even keel. She'd told him that in a text message last night, but he hadn't replied. Was he giving her the silent treatment?

'Why don't you go ahead and make some plans?' Warwick suggested, as though he was reading her thoughts. 'You can always cancel them if he doesn't come down. Or take someone else.'

There wasn't anyone else, but she didn't tell him that. Instead, she smiled. 'Good idea, I think I will. I've heard good things about the Asian fusion restaurant on the road to Windsor Falls. It has a chef's hat. Apparently the sommelier is amazing. Have you been?'

He looked at her as though she was speaking another language. 'Can't say I have. I'm more a chicken parma kind of guy, myself.'

Issy laughed. 'Fair enough.'

He was right. She should book something. She searched for the restaurant and clicked the *Book Now* button, but there was nothing available. *I'll see about that*, she thought, picking up her phone.

'Ah, hello, I wonder if you can help me,' she said, when someone answered. 'It's Isobel Ashworth. I'd like to book a table for two on Saturday night, but it looks like everything's booked?'

The receptionist cleared her throat. 'Did you say Isobel *Ashworth*?'

'That's right, yes. I wanted to come with my fiancé to celebrate our recent engagement.'

'Let me see what I can do,' the woman said slowly, clicking her tongue a few times. 'Yes, I've got you a window table at seven thirty. We'll see you then, Ms Ashworth.'

Issy hung up. She was about to message Hugh and tell him—it might incentivise him to get his arse into gear and come down—when her phone rang. *Heather.*

'Hi, Mum.'

'Darling, how are you going in Hartwell? Is it dreadful?'

Bloody hell. 'No, it's fine. It's actually going really well. I'm loving it.'

There was a long pause. 'Hmm, well, that's lovely, darling. Listen, about Christmas …' They always had Christmas at Kilmore, which was usually punishing, but this year was very convenient. 'I've decided we won't be doing a lot of presents. It's just excessive and wasteful. Think of the landfill!' Her mother had only recently become aware that the planet was doomed and was taking it upon herself to single-handedly avert disaster through minor household initiatives. She seemed to think recycling her soft plastics was akin to volunteering for Sea Shepherd.

'Fine with me,' Issy said, who hadn't given a moment's thought to Christmas shopping.

'Instead we're doing a Kris Kringle.' She pronounced the words as though Issy would be unfamiliar with the concept. 'We each get one person to buy for, one hundred-dollar limit. Cathy says there's an app you can use so no one knows who got who. I've delegated that to her. You'll get an email soon, apparently.'

'Cathy's coming to Christmas?' Issy asked, irritated at the thought.

'What else is she meant to do? Sit alone in her hotel room? Oh, and I need you to do something for me.'

Issy felt the sense of dread she always felt when her mother said those words.

'You'll have to step in for me at the fundraiser on Saturday night.'

Issy closed her eyes. The annual Ashworth Christmas Gala was held every December at the Ashworth Park Hotel to raise money for children with rare diseases. The guest list was loaded with wealthy Sydney socialites and politicians.

'*This* Saturday?' she said.

'Yes, darling. You'll do it, won't you? I think I have long covid—'

Issy suppressed a snort. Long covid was Heather's most recent explanation for the depression she'd been pretending not to have since Issy was born.

'I just can't seem to get myself into the zone for it. I might still attend, depending on how I feel on Saturday, but I can't face the hosting role. I've lost my dazzle just now.'

Issy swallowed. 'I can't, Mum. I already have plans.'

'Plans? You mean you're going out for dinner or something?' Heather replied, disdainfully. 'Isobel, think of the sick children. Honestly, it's the least you could do!'

No, Issy thought, *the least I could do is go out with Hugh for the degustation meal I literally just booked.*

She sighed. There was no point arguing with her mother. It never ended well. 'Okay.'

'Wonderful! I think you'll really enjoy it, darling. It's a lovely feeling, giving back.'

Issy bristled. How did her mother make it seem as though she was the one doing Issy the favour?

'So do you think you'll come down?' Issy asked.

'Down? To Hartwell? I'm already here. I've been here since yesterday.'

'Oh.' Issy frowned. 'Nice of you to let me know.'

'Don't be silly, Isobel. You're far too busy to have your mother getting in your way.'

'I suppose so,' Issy said, wondering what she would wear to the fundraiser. She'd have to get her stylist to courier her some evening options.

Chapter 23

It was late morning when Meg arrived at Hartwell Gaol and slipped behind the temporary fence that blocked access to the site. She glanced around, surprised by the lack of activity. It looked so different to the chaos that had greeted her on Monday. The rumbling, beeping thrum of heavy machinery was all but gone. She could see now what the finished space would look like, with a stage at the far end and restaurants opening onto the large, rectangular space where she stood. The old exercise yard, she supposed. She imagined it full of people dining al fresco, live music in the night air. Above the original building, a stationary crane loomed over the unfinished modern addition.

She walked towards the site office, which reminded her of the demountable classrooms of primary school, and stuck her head in the open door. Cool air blew from an air conditioner mounted on the wall above a man sitting with his back to her, browsing second-hand motorbikes on Gumtree. She watched him scroll down the listings, then click on one he must have liked the look of.

'Hello?'

He spun around, startled. It was the man who'd mistaken her for a protester a few days before.

'Sorry,' she said. 'I didn't mean to give you a fright.'

'No worries.' He swivelled in his chair to face her, frowning. 'What can I do you for?'

'My name's Meg … Megan Hunter … Bainbridge,' she said slowly, realising mid-sentence that she hadn't thought of an alternative name. She cleared her throat. 'Megan Hunter-Bainbridge,' she said again, more confidently. Short e, like the duchess. Bainbridge was the name of a precocious intern she'd supervised at *The Times*. 'I'm doing a PhD on historic jail sites and I wondered if you had time for a quick chat. The redevelopment you're doing here is really amazing.'

'Ah, right. I'm just in the middle of something …'

'Oh.' Meg glanced at the bright green motorbike on his monitor. He followed her gaze, then clicked the browser window shut.

'Even just five minutes?' She gave him a pleading smile.

He held her gaze, as though he was sizing her up. 'What do you want to know?'

'My work is on the privatisation and redevelopment of historic sites. From what I can see, this development is the gold standard for preserving the integrity of the building and its historical significance, while repurposing it for future generations to enjoy.' Inwardly she cringed, feeling like it was too much.

'Yeah, yeah, I agree,' he said tentatively.

'My thesis is essentially that privatising buildings like this and reinventing the spaces is the key to preserving them. There's always a lot of controversy around this sort of thing, but ultimately it's in the best interest of the local community. I mean, what's the point of having a magnificent building like this sitting here empty, becoming more rundown year after year?'

'Couldn't agree more, love. Jeez, honestly, the way some people talk, you'd think we were bulldozing the place.'

'Did you have a lot of pushback from the locals then?' Meg asked, keeping her tone casual.

'You wouldn't know the half of it.'

'That must have been annoying. What were the main objections?'

He frowned. 'Oh, you know … this and that,' he said, frustratingly vague.

'Like?'

He shrugged. 'Some people wanted it to be a museum, others wanted it to remain untouched. I don't think it helped that it was the Ashworths doing the development.'

'People don't like them?'

He scoffed. 'You could say that.'

'But they do a lot for the local community, don't they? I heard they funded some upgrades to the cricket ground.'

Hartwell Cricket Ground was a picturesque, picket-fenced oval with a brand-new grandstand, lights and state-of-the-art electronic scoreboard—two million dollars' worth of infrastructure upgrades funded by the Ashworths, according to an article Meg had found. Malcolm was quoted as saying it was 'a chance to give back to the town that made him'.

He let out a cynical laugh. 'Yeah, yeah, they did.'

Meg frowned, waiting for him to go on.

There was a voice behind her. 'Excuse me.'

Meg turned to see the austere woman with the sharp grey bob.

'Sorry.' Meg stepped aside.

The woman didn't move. She met Meg's gaze and held it.

'I was just talking to …' Meg looked at the man, realising he hadn't introduced himself.

'Warwick,' he said.

Meg nodded. She swallowed, feeling the need to explain herself to this woman. 'I'm doing a PhD on historical buildings—' God, this story was starting to sound stupid now, '—and how privatisation and repurposing is the best way to ensure the conservation of the sites for future generations ...'

The woman glared at her as though she'd never heard such nonsense. 'Fascinating,' she said eventually, with a deadpan expression and a quick raise of her eyebrows.

'Anyway, I'm just leaving now,' Meg said.

The woman gave her a tight-lipped smile.

'Thanks, Warwick,' Meg added. 'I appreciate your time.'

At that moment, a black Mercedes came through the boom gate and rolled to a stop beside them. Behind the wheel, Meg could see the ice-blonde hair and oversized sunglasses of Isobel Ashworth.

Chapter 24

'Morning, Cathy,' Issy said as she got out of the car, but she was studying the petite woman who stood next to her. Short dark hair, delicate pixie-like face and flawless honey skin, which she'd defaced with tattoos just visible beneath the sleeve of her shirt. 'Hello, I'm Isobel,' she said, extending her hand.

'Megan Hunter-Bainbridge.' Her handshake was firmer than expected. Issy strongly believed you could judge a person's grit by the strength of their handshake, a belief she'd inherited from her father, who would line his children up and critique them before they went anywhere important. Little Issy, last in line, would watch with trepidation as he'd ridicule the efforts of her older brothers. 'Not bad for a girl,' he'd say to her. She was never sure if it was a compliment or not.

Something about this woman was familiar. 'Have we met?' Issy asked, realising as the words came out that she'd been in the café when that awful woman had refused her service. How mortifying!

'I don't think so. I'm doing a PhD on historical buildings in Australia, and the best ways of preserving them for future generations—'

Crap, Issy thought, biting her lip. The last thing she needed was some earnest academic criticising the development. She would have to ask her to leave.

'This is really impressive, what you're doing here.'

Issy smiled, pleasantly surprised. 'It's very important to us that the development respects the history of the site. We've made a real effort to be sensitive to the original building,' she said, although she had no idea if the architects gave two hoots about the original building. In her peripheral vision, she could see the three additional storeys looming above the old building. How had it been approved? It towered over everything else in Hartwell.

'There's something so reassuring about imagining this courtyard full of people, and your development will give them a reason to come,' the woman was saying when Issy tuned back in. What did she say her name was? Megan something something?

Issy smiled. She liked this woman. She was talking sense. Maybe she could write something about the development for the Ashworth PR team to supply to the media.

'Thank you,' Issy said. 'It's so nice to talk to someone who *gets* what we're trying to achieve here. Why don't I take you for a tour? Just let me put my bag down.'

Cathy, who had been tapping away on her phone while they spoke, looked up. 'Before you do,' she said. 'Have you emailed me a copy of the revised project plan? I don't think I've seen it.'

Issy clicked her tongue and put a hand to her head. 'Oh, sorry, Cathy. I haven't got to it. Mum threw a spanner in things yesterday. She's got me hosting the gala on Saturday night, so I had to have a call with Jeffrey at Ashworth Park and go through the run sheet. He's taking an annual leave day tomorrow! The day before one of their biggest functions of the year!' Honestly, staff in these regional places were hopeless. And Jeffrey was one of the good ones! 'Did she manage to rope you into coming, Cathy?'

Cathy nodded. 'It's a wonderful event. I go every year.'

Issy bristled, feeling schooled for her flippant tone. 'Yes, you're right. It's an honour to host it.'

Cathy turned to Megan, who was patiently waiting for her tour. 'Will you still be in town on the weekend?'

'Yes,' Megan said, frowning as though she didn't follow. Issy couldn't blame her. She wasn't following either. 'I'm here until Sunday.'

'Why don't you come along to the gala?' Cathy suggested. Turning to Issy, she added, 'They can always fit in one more.'

'Me?' Megan said, surprised.

'Why not?' Issy shrugged. 'Only if you want to.'

Meg smiled. 'Sure, okay, I'd love to come, thank you.'

Chapter 25

'Isobel Ashworth invited *you* to the gala?' Georgie asked.

'You don't have to say it like that!' Meg said, pretending to be offended. She watched as Georgie filled a schooner with amber liquid and flicked off the tap with a thud. She walked down the far end of the bar and placed the glass in front of a local in a grease-covered work shirt.

'You just don't look like their type,' Georgie said when she returned. 'You gonna go?'

'I guess so, why not?'

'Oh, I don't know,' Georgie said. 'Because she's an arsehole?' She went to serve an old guy standing at the bar.

Meg picked up her phone and scrolled Instagram, clicking on Isobel's most recent post. A sunset shot over Hartwell, which must have been taken from the new apartments above the jail. She'd cleverly cropped out the construction site below.

'She seemed quite nice, actually,' Meg said, when Georgie came back.

'Nah, they're all arseholes.'

'Why, though?' Meg suspected it was because they were rich. Maybe the controversy over the redevelopment was mostly sour grapes. Tall poppy syndrome.

Georgie shrugged. 'They act like they own the place.'

'They kind of *do* own the place,' Meg pointed out. 'They've got the Ashworth Park Hotel and now the Hartwell Gaol Entertainment Precinct and Apartments. Didn't they also fund the cricket ground upgrade?'

Georgie snorted. 'You've been here for, what, like five minutes?' There was a sharper edge in her voice now. 'I've seen them rule this town my whole life. Trust me, they're arseholes.'

'Tell me why, then! And you're going to have to do better than, "they think they own the place".'

'How long have you got?' Georgie's face hardened. 'My dad did maintenance at the hotel for twenty years. A couple of years ago, he fell off a ladder at work and injured his back. He hasn't worked since. Guess how much workers' comp he got?'

'How much?'

'Two weeks' pay.' Georgie paused for a long time. 'You know why?'

'Why?'

'Because the doctor who assessed him said he wasn't in pain. How the hell would they know if he's in pain?' Georgie's eyes flashed.

'I'm sorry, I didn't mean to bring all that up,' Meg said. 'I'm sorry about your dad.'

A regular raised his hand to catch Georgie's eye. She sighed and went to get them another round. Instead of coming straight back, she picked up a cloth. Meg watched her, hoping she hadn't upset her. As she wiped down the bar, Georgie looked up at someone entering. Something about her expression made Meg turn to follow her gaze.

The man was handsome in a predictable kind of way. Square jaw. Dark eyes. Designer stubble. His white linen shirt was open at the neck—a few too many buttons undone in Meg's opinion; it made him look sleazy—exposing his tanned chest. His eyes were on Georgie as he swaggered towards the bar. Meg looked away, pretending to scroll on her phone.

'It's my favourite barmaid!' he said.

Meg glanced up to see Georgie roll her eyes playfully. 'I bet you say that to all the girls.'

'Only the pretty ones,' he said. Meg shuddered. This guy had to be mid-forties at least.

Georgie leaned forward, resting her elbows on the bar, which had the effect of accentuating her cleavage. Definitely intentional.

'Can I get you something? Or did you just come in here to flirt with me?'

'I'll have a Peroni.'

She got a beer from the fridge, then reached for a glass.

'I'll have it from the bottle,' he said, passing the glass back to her. He held on to it a moment too long, so that their hands touched. When he let go, he took a long swig from the bottle.

'Nine bucks,' she said.

He handed her a note. 'Keep the change.' Meg thought she saw the flash of a yellow fifty. Some tip. He turned his back to Georgie and leaned against the bar, assessing the room.

Georgie walked back to Meg. 'You want another beer?'

'Thanks.' Meg nodded. 'Who's that?' she asked, as Georgie put a glass in front of her and took the empty.

'Who?'

Meg nodded in his direction. 'Casanova over there.'

'Oh, that's Hugh Thorburn.'

Meg nearly choked on her sip of beer. Of course. She thought of the photo in the Sunday paper, when she'd seen him standing beside Isobel Ashworth.

'How do you know him?' she asked.

'He used to live around here.' Georgie shrugged. 'He follows me on Instagram.' Not the only platform he followed her on, Meg suspected. 'And I know Daisy.'

'Daisy?'

'Daisy Ashworth, Spencer's daughter. He's Isobel's oldest brother.'

'How do you know her?'

'We used to ride horses together. I'd muck out the stables in return for rides.'

Meg frowned. 'I thought you hated the Ashworths.'

'I do.' Georgie's eyes flicked to the door. 'Holy shit.'

Meg turned to see a horde of men with sweat-stained faces and dirty boots streaming into the bar. In the midst of them was Isobel Ashworth.

Chapter 26

'There's money on the bar,' Issy announced to the crowd assembled in the small annex reserved for them off the main bar. It was fine, although the whole place smelt of stale beer, which no one else seemed to notice. The turnout was strong, twenty-five or thirty she supposed, including Warwick, Cathy and most of the subcontractors who'd been on site that day. 'Grab yourselves a drink, then I'd like to say a few words.'

Warwick gave her a strange look as most of the subbies headed to the bar.

'What?' she said.

'I don't think you need to make a speech.'

'I won't make a *speech*, Warwick,' Issy said. 'I'll literally just say a few words.'

He sighed. 'Righto. What can I get you?'

'I'd love a glass of bubbles, thanks, Warwick.'

'Same for me,' Cathy added.

Once everyone had drinks, Issy stepped up onto a raised platform in front of the fireplace so she could be seen above the crowd. 'Okay, thanks all,' she called out, waiting for attention. The voices fell as the eyes of the room turned to her. 'I'll keep this brief so you can get back to your conversations. I want to say thank you to each and every one of you. We're all under a lot of pressure. It's a busy time of year with Christmas just around the corner. When everyone else is winding down, we need you to work harder than ever. Every single one of us needs to pull together if we're going to get this done, but I have total confidence we can do it.'

As she scanned their faces—pleased to see some nods and a few smiles—her eyes were drawn to a man beyond the group in the main bar. Hugh! What? When did he arrive in town? Frowning, she looked back at the group, who were waiting for her to go on.

'So thanks again.' She raised her glass. 'Here's to getting it done together!'

Glasses clinked and voices rose, the small space instantly humming again with conversation.

'Good speech.' Warwick gave her a wink. 'Everything okay?'

'Yeah, fine, I just saw Hugh in the bar. He didn't tell me he was coming.'

'He must've got down early. Stopped in for a quick one.'

Issy looked out to the main room again, straining to see between the subbies.

'Didn't you see him as we came in?' Cathy asked. 'I thought you knew he was here.'

Issy shook her head, feeling her face flush. 'He must have forgotten to tell me. He's been working on a big deal.'

She excused herself and went to the main bar, looking for Hugh, finding him in a corner, deep in conversation with a man with a long, dark ponytail and a full-sleeve tattoo covering his arm.

When he saw her approaching, Hugh's brief frown was replaced with a broad smile. 'Issy, babe!' He pulled her towards him and kissed her. 'What are you doing here?'

'Me? I'm having drinks with the construction team.'

Hugh gestured to the man sitting with him. 'Issy, this is Deano.'

'G'day,' Deano said, unsmiling.

'Hello,' she said, trying not to look at his repulsive earlobes, which had large holes in them created by those black circles that stretched the skin.

'Deano used to live up the road from me,' Hugh said. He prided himself on his strong network, although he took it a little far sometimes, in Issy's opinion.

Issy nodded as Deano looked at his phone. 'I didn't know you were coming,' she said quietly to Hugh.

'You didn't? I thought I told you.'

'No, pretty sure you didn't tell me.'

He shrugged as though it was of little importance.

'When did you get here?' she asked.

He waved a vague hand. 'I don't know. Half an hour ago?'

'Were you going to call me? Or just hope to bump into me at the pub?'

'Babe, settle down. I'm here. It's all good.'

Issy sighed. 'I've got to get back to the team. I'll stay for an hour or so, then we'll go, okay?'

Hugh gave her a nod and turned back to Deano.

Issy went back to work the room. If there was one thing her mother had taught her, it was how to make small talk. This was her chance to get these guys onside. Over the next couple of hours, she had an animated conversation about the cricket, put a young sparky in touch with the right person to get his beautician wife a job at the Ashworth Park Hotel spa, listened as one of the head carpenters talked about losing custody of his kids after his ex told lies at the family court, and even tried to make rudimentary conversation with Cathy, who was just about the only person she couldn't talk to. When she heard herself say, 'Who's looking after your cats while you're away?' she realised she'd hit a low point and managed to move on gracefully.

At around seven, she decided it was time to go.

'You're a lucky man, Warwick. Dani sounds delightful,' she said, putting a hand on his forearm. He'd just told her the very romantic story about meeting his wife at their one and only meditation class. 'You've just made me remember I have a fiancé in town who I've barely spoken to, so I'm going to head off.'

She slipped out into the main bar, but Hugh wasn't at the table by the window. She glanced around, locating him at the bar, and slotted in beside him. 'Are you ready to go?'

He looked up, with heavy-lidded eyes. 'Now? I'm getting a round.'

'Who for?' she asked.

'Deano and a few other guys I haven't seen in a while.'

'Can we go after that one?'

'I reckon I'll stay for a bit.'

Issy swallowed, trying to remain composed. 'But you just got here. We haven't seen each other.'

'We've got the whole weekend, baby.' He tucked a lock of her hair behind her ear and pulled her in close. 'We've got our whole lives.'

'I guess,' she said. 'I just … I'm tired.'

'Go home and get some sleep, babe. I'll head over in a little bit.'

'You don't even know where to go.'

'Oh, yeah.' Hugh laughed. 'Where do I go?'

'You go up the stairs on the right side of the—' She stopped. There was no chance he'd find it. 'Actually it might be easier if you just call me when you're leaving and I'll meet you outside the entrance to the jail.'

Chapter 27

Meg kicked open the door of her room, then locked it behind her and slumped onto the bed. The ceiling spun above her, the pendant light moving in a slow circle. She blinked a few times, then sat up, trying to calculate how many drinks she'd had. She'd stayed longer than she intended, watching Isobel Ashworth and Hugh Thorburn from a distance, wondering if she knew how he flirted with eighteen-year-old barmaids.

She woke with a start sometime later to a moaning sound coming from the room next door. Then another. Was that ...? Oh, no. A rhythmic banging started as something—a bed?—hit the shared wall. A second voice joined in, the pace speeding up, the banging louder now. Then one last moan, longer.

After a moment of silence there was a bang and some shuffling sounds, then a voice, sharp-edged. Meg froze, sensing conflict. She strained to hear, but couldn't make out the words.

Her heart pounded. What should she do? Lie still. That's what her instincts said. The voices rose again. She could hear her own breathing, shallow and fast. But what if someone was in trouble? Could she really do nothing? She covered her face with her hands, took a steadying breath. She could walk past—pretend she was going to the bathroom—just to check everything was okay.

She opened the door quietly and slipped into the hall, but all she could hear were muffled voices, quieter now. She kept walking to the bathroom. Just as she was about to step back into the hallway to return to her room, she heard voices again and looked up to see Georgie standing at the door, talking to someone inside the room, out of sight.

Meg's heart pounded. She quickly retreated into the bathroom again, behind the wall, listening. There was a man's voice, but she couldn't make out the words. After a moment, the door closed with a thud and Georgie hurried up the hall. Meg held her breath as she passed just inches away and disappeared down the stairs.

Meg exhaled, waited for her heart rate to settle, before she looked out into the hallway again. It was quiet. She slipped out of the bathroom and tiptoed up the corridor to her room, locking the door behind her.

*

There was a roar as Georgie heaved up the rusty garage door. Meg stood by her side, surveying the sight in front of them. She'd been expecting a car, or at least a space where one would fit. Maybe some shelves and a few bikes.

Not this garage. The whole space was packed full. From where she stood, she could see an old treadmill, a couple of fishing rods, at least five rusty bikes and countless cardboard boxes.

'Oh my God,' Meg whispered, under her breath.

'It's actually not as bad as it looks,' Georgie said. 'All the packing boxes came from Nan and Pop's place. Anna's box is probably in there somewhere.' She squeezed her way to a tallboy in the back corner and started rummaging through a drawer. She pulled out a Stanley knife and held it up. 'I'll slice 'em, you check 'em.' She looked at the time on her phone. 'I've got an hour, then I've got some work to do.'

'At the pub?' Meg asked.

'Nah, my other job,' she said, yawning. She pierced the tape on the top of a box.

Meg nodded, thinking about Georgie's OnlyFans profile. How much was she making? At five bucks a month, it couldn't be much.

Her mind flicked back to the night before, when she'd watched Georgie creep down the hallway. She'd been having sex with whoever was staying in that room. Was it recreational? Or another income stream? Hugh Thorburn had been talking to Sue at the bar that morning, around nine o'clock, when Meg was on her way out. Was it him in that room? The way he'd been flirting with Georgie the night before, she wouldn't put it past him.

Meg sighed, deciding it was none of her business, and flipped open the top of the closest box, dust tickling her nose. She sneezed, then rummaged through the contents. Cookbooks, mostly. She moved on to the next one. Quilting materials.

Once Georgie had opened all the boxes, she started checking them too.

After an hour, they'd found nothing.

Georgie sat down on one of the smaller boxes. 'Looks like it's not here.'

'Thanks, anyway.' Meg reached for her bag and handed Georgie four fifties. Georgie tucked the notes into her bra top. What a waste of money.

'Can I ask you for a favour?' Meg said.

'Another favour, you mean.'

Meg bit her tongue, thinking about the two hundred bucks she'd just parted with. Georgie was hardly doing this out of the goodness of her heart. 'Would you do a DNA test? It's really easy, just spitting into a tube. It'll confirm one way or another if Anna is my mother.'

'Ah, I dunno,' Georgie said, hesitant. 'Mum doesn't seem too keen on all this Anna stuff.'

'I'd pay you, obviously.'

'How much?'

'Fifty bucks?'

'A hundred.'

'Done.'

Georgie stood up. 'Alright, I've gotta—' She stopped abruptly, frowning. 'I wonder what that is.'

Meg followed her gaze to an archive box that sat high up on the shelves on the other side of the garage. It was dark brown cardboard with a wood-grain print and the lid was torn at one corner. Someone had reinforced the bottom with masking tape that came halfway up the sides of the box. As they got closer, they could see that someone had written *Anna Mitchell* on the side in texta, barely legible on the dark background.

'How the hell are we going to reach it?' Georgie said.

Meg pulled on the metal shelving to see if it was secured to the wall. It seemed solid enough. She stepped up onto the first shelf.

'Spot me from behind, in case I fall.'

She managed to get up to the third shelf. Her fingertips brushed the box, but how was she going to grab hold of it without letting go? She jumped back down.

'I'll go get a stool from inside,' Georgie said.

A few minutes later, she reappeared holding a kitchen stool. 'Dad asked me what I was doing. I told him I was cleaning out the garage.' She snorted. 'As if.'

Meg climbed onto the stool and reached for the box. It felt fragile in her hands, as though the bottom might collapse. She passed it down to Georgie, who put it on the floor. She waited until Meg had her feet back on the ground before she took off the lid.

At first glance, it didn't look too different from Georgie's grandparents' belongings. Random objects. Nothing special. Meg picked up a hairbrush, turning it over in her hand.

Georgie reached for a woollen jumper, embroidered with tiny roses, and held it up, modelling it. 'Mmm, nice,' she said, her voice dripping with sarcasm.

It wouldn't have been fashionable even thirty years ago. Meg couldn't imagine her mother wearing it. Underneath where the jumper sat there was a notebook with a gold embossed cover. Meg's heart fluttered. A diary? She opened it and read the name written inside the cover. Anna Elizabeth Mitchell. The writer had a heavy hand so that the letters made indentations in the page. Meg ran a finger gently over the words as though it was Braille. She could feel Georgie watching her.

'Does it look like your mum's writing?'

'I don't know,' Meg said. 'Kind of.'

She turned the page. A quote from Tolstoy. *Everyone thinks of changing the world. No one thinks of changing himself.* Anna had written *'or herself'* in brackets on the next line.

She turned the page again.

There was fog on the lake this morning. Sunlight beamed through the branches of the red gums and it was so beautiful I felt like I might cry. I took a photo of it in my mind so that I'll remember it forever. There were no quotation marks, no name. Anna's own words, Meg supposed.

She flicked ahead, skimming the next few pages, then stopped abruptly when she saw words she recognised.

A wave of emotion swelled in Meg's chest as she heard Stevie Nick's soulful voice singing 'Landslide'. She knew it well. Sometimes, Jenny would play it on repeat as silent tears ran over her cheeks.

'Why do you listen to it, if it makes you so sad?' Meg had asked her once.

'Not all pain is bad pain,' Jenny had said, a faraway look in her eyes. Meg had added the moment to the list of things she didn't understand about her mother.

Her thoughts raced as she ran her finger over the lyrics. What did this mean? Could it be a coincidence? What were the chances?

Georgie had stopped checking boxes. 'What is it? Did you find something?'

'This …' Meg said. 'These words, they're lyrics from "Landslide". Fleetwood Mac. You know it?'

'Yeah, my mum loves it.'

'She does?'

Georgie nodded.

'So does mine,' Meg whispered.

'You think …'

'I don't know.' Meg shrugged, struggling to judge where coincidence ended and truth began. 'It doesn't prove anything.'

She flipped the page, but there was nothing else.

'That's pretty.' Georgie reached for something Meg couldn't see. She held up a gold locket on a fine chain. She studied the engraving. 'Scales. That's the symbol for Libra, I think?'

'Don't know.' Meg wasn't into star signs. 'Is there anything inside?'

Georgie opened it, but it was empty. 'Sorry.' Her phone beeped. She passed the locket to Meg and reached for the phone. 'I really do have to go.'

'Do you mind if I stay a bit longer?' Meg asked. 'I just want to look through the rest of this.'

'Sure.' Georgie smiled. 'Pull the door down when you go. Dad will just think it's me.'

'What if he comes out?'

'He won't come out. Sorry it wasn't ...' Georgie shrugged.

Better? Useful? The answer? It all hung in the air between them.

'Thanks.' She was a sweet girl. Even if she was an extortionist.

Once Georgie was gone, Meg lay the locket flat on her palm and studied it. The scales of justice were embossed on the yellow gold. She ran her finger over them. Libra. What month was Libra? Jenny's birthday was in June, June seventeenth, although it struck her now that if Jenny was once Anna, even the date of her birthday was probably a lie. Meg shook her head. Even the little she knew about her mother was likely to be wrong.

But this, this locket, was real. Was it Jenny's once? On an impulse, she put the chain around her neck, fumbling with the delicate clasp a few times before she fastened it. Once she'd done it, she placed a flat hand on her décolletage, pressing the locket to her skin, waiting to feel something. Some sense of clarity or connection, as though, if it had belonged to her mother, she should feel it. But there was nothing. It just felt cold on her skin.

She looked into the box again. At first glance she thought it was empty, but something caught her eye. A pen, lying against the side of the box where the cardboard folded. She reached for it. There was something written on it in an old-fashioned, curly script.

The Ashworth Park Hotel.

Heart racing, Meg slipped it into her pocket, then flicked back through the notebook to check she hadn't missed anything. She hadn't. She took a photo of each page of the notebook. Once she'd put everything back, she climbed up and placed it on the highest shelf, exactly where it was before.

She thought she heard something then, a call from inside the house perhaps, but she wasn't sure. After a moment it came again, louder.

'Georgie!'

Meg grabbed her bag and rushed out, heaving the heavy door down behind her.

She was heading up Barton Drive when Pete rang.

'The same buyer's agent has bought six houses on that street in the last twelve months,' he said, without bothering with a greeting, 'but he's signed an NDA so he won't talk. There's definitely something going on there, and all my spidey senses say the Ashworths are involved.'

'Interesting,' Meg said, her mind still on the pen.

'I'll keep digging,' Pete said. 'See what you can find out down there.'

A few minutes later, she reached Chrissy's café. The bells tinkled as she entered, announcing her arrival. Chrissy looked over from where she stood taking an order from a young family. She narrowed her eyes and picked up the menus, ignoring Meg as she walked to the counter.

'Sorry to bother you again.' Meg felt like a broken record. 'I just have one last question.'

'I really don't want to talk about this again.'

'You said Anna was working while she studied nursing,' Meg said. 'Was she working for the Ashworths?'

She saw a flicker of something on Chrissy's face. 'She was, wasn't she? She worked at the hotel.'

Chrissy shook her head. 'Not at the hotel. She was working as a baby nurse at their home.'

Meg's mind raced. 'When Isobel was a baby?'

Chrissy nodded. 'Heather was sick. Anna was employed to look after the baby overnight.'

There was a tinkle from the door and Chrissy smiled at a customer.

'She was living with them?' Meg asked.

'She spent most nights there, if that's what you mean.' Chrissy reached for a menu. 'I'm not sure how relevant this is, though. I told you about the boyfriend.'

'I guess so,' Meg said. 'Thanks.'

She sat in her car outside the café, pen in hand, studying the ornate writing.

The Ashworth Park Hotel.

If Jenny was the riddle, she was starting to suspect the Ashworths had something to do with the answer.

Chapter 28

Hugh didn't call Issy when he was leaving.

She'd waited up, watching a reality series about bitchy LA real estate agents, but he'd texted at ten to say he'd bumped into Warwick, who it turned out was another old mate. Issy's emotions had swung between quiet fury—how dare he treat her like this!—and resignation. Hugh was an extrovert. It was one of the things she found so attractive about him. And he'd grown up in this town, so perhaps it wasn't surprising that there were friends he wanted to see. Maybe she was being needy.

By ten thirty, she was asleep on the couch. When she woke at eleven thirty, she rang him but got no answer. *Screw you then*, she'd thought, and hung up without leaving a message.

Just after midnight she woke again and checked her phone, but there was still nothing. Not even a text. It occurred to her then that maybe something had happened to him. An accident, possibly. Should she call the police? And tell them what, though? My fiancé hasn't come home from the pub? They'd laugh at her. Anyway, what could possibly have happened to him? He'd probably kicked on with his mates. It wasn't even particularly out of character, if she was honest. There had been a couple of nights out when she'd gone home before him, when the trips to the bathroom started. He was probably just back at someone's place, she'd told herself, then she'd put her phone on silent and gone back to sleep.

When she woke the following morning, bright rays of sunlight were shining through the gaps in the curtains. What time was it? She rolled over to look at the clock radio. Ten sixteen! Remembering Hugh, she sat up and reached for her phone, checking the notifications. Two missed calls, a voicemail message and four texts.

She read the messages first.

12:23am I ended up getting a room at the pub.
8:29am Call me when you're up.
9:17am Issy I'm waiting around for you. Call me.

And half an hour ago:

9:49am WTF Issy? Are you still asleep? Or are you punishing me? If I don't hear from you soon I'm going back to Sydney.

Crap. She quickly tapped a reply.
Sorry. Coming down now. I'll meet you in front of the jail.

'About fricking time,' Hugh said when he saw her. He hitched his overnight bag higher on his shoulder, as though to point out it was getting heavy.

'Sorry, I slept in. I didn't realise my phone was on silent.'

'Five more minutes and I would have left town.'

'I was asleep, Hugh.' A beat. 'I tried to call you last night and you didn't answer. How am I meant to know—'

'It's after ten, Issy. You knew I didn't know where you were staying.'

'But ...' She was lost for words. How was she the one in the wrong here? All week she'd been waiting for him to come, then he turns up without so much as a simple text to let her know and chooses to drink with random mates instead of going home with her! *She* was the one who should be angry! Wasn't she?

Hugh huffed. 'Can we go upstairs now? I've been in these clothes since yesterday. I need a shower.'

She nodded and turned back to the stairs. Tears threatened, but she forced them back. *No one likes a crybaby*, her mother's voice said in her head as she opened the apartment door.

Hugh dropped his bag and glanced around, the corners of his mouth turned down. 'It's certainly not the Ashworth Park.'

She swallowed. Best just to apologise, try to get things back on track. Maybe he'd meet her halfway. 'Sorry things got off to a bad start.'

He shrugged. 'It's fine,' he said, still sulky.

She reached out and touched his arm, but he flinched. 'I need a shower.'

She let her arm drop. 'Bathroom's down the hall.'

He picked up his bag. A moment later the shower started. Issy felt a surge of self-loathing and went into the bedroom to lie down. The weekend was wrecked. Was Hugh right to be annoyed? She tried to see it from his perspective. He'd come down to see her and she'd been more concerned about getting a decent night's sleep than being there for him when he needed her. She shouldn't have put her phone on silent. It was juvenile. It was her fault she didn't hear him call.

She thought of the missed call. Curious to hear what he'd said in his voicemail message, she tapped on it, playing it on speaker, but his voice didn't come.

Instead, there were shuffling sounds, then footsteps. She looked at the screen. The message was six minutes long. A pocket dial? There was a low voice, Hugh's, but it was muffled. She turned the volume up further, held it close to her ear, but it was no use. She couldn't make out the words. She put the phone down and lay back, staring at the ceiling while the message continued to play a whole lot of nothing.

Just as she was about to stop listening, there was a second voice. Higher pitched. Female. Issy's chest tightened as Hugh said something else, followed by a giggle. 'Shit,' his voice said, then the message ended.

She pressed play again, nausea churning in her stomach, trying to think of a reasonable explanation for what she was hearing. He wasn't at the bar. There was no background noise. They were in a quiet room. Were others there? Or just Hugh and whoever's baby voice she could hear?

The sound of the running water ceased. Her heart raced as she paused the message, closed the app and put the phone on the bedside table.

Chapter 29

'Name?' asked the tuxedoed host as Meg arrived at the entrance of the Grand Ballroom. The room beyond the door was already humming with conversation. She inhaled sharply, taking in the sheer opulence of the space. It was like stepping back in time. Gilded wallpaper covered the walls, and overhead, a soaring ceiling rose to a spectacular glass dome.

She'd driven through the imposing gates of the Ashworth Park Hotel half an hour earlier, catching her breath at the sight of the old sandstone mansion, nestled into rolling lawns between towering oaks and pine trees.

Instead of going inside, she'd sat in her car, debating whether she should have come. When she'd accepted the invitation a couple of days before, she wasn't sure she would actually go, but then she found the pen in Anna's box and discovered she'd worked for the Ashworths, and it just seemed like fate that she'd been invited. Not that she believed in fate.

Stalling, she'd opened Instagram and searched for Isobel's profile. Her eyes had landed on a photo of her, radiant in gold, posing in the empty ballroom. *Let's raise some money and have some fun!* the caption read. *#AshworthGala @theashworthparkhotel.* Meg swallowed, looking down at her old Zimmermann dress, then out the window at the guests arriving. Self-assured men in tuxedos and shiny shoes, leading wives teetering on bejewelled stilettos.

Eventually, she'd stepped out of the car. There was a refined stillness in the air, broken only by the rhythmic pop of a tennis ball on racquets somewhere nearby but out of sight and the crunch of pebbles under her op-shop Valentinos.

'Megan Hunter-Bainbridge,' she said, half-expecting (hoping?) for the host to say she wasn't on the guest list and turn her away.

'Lovely.' He passed her a name tag.

She pinned it to her dress, then entered the room. It twinkled with thousands of tiny fairy lights and gold balloons. A large banner emblazoned with CRDF WORKING TOGETHER FOR A BRIGHTER FUTURE! hung above a podium. The air hummed with the giddy voices and laughter of guests standing in tight clusters. The women sparkled like Christmas baubles. The men wore bowties, tight around fat necks.

Meg found herself wishing she had a plus one. Someone like Pete. He moved through rooms like this like he belonged there, which was probably because he'd been to a posh private school, where she suspected they must hold lessons in how to handle such situations.

She took a deep breath, relieved at the sight of a waiter with a tray of drinks. She took a glass of Champagne, even though she actually wanted a beer, and stood against a wall where she had a good view of the room.

Her eye was drawn to Isobel, who stood with a circle of blonde women. They all looked somehow similar; the cumulative impact of their expensive haircuts, botoxed foreheads and flawless skin. None shared the magical, ethereal quality of Isobel though, who shimmered like a goddess, radiant in gold silk wide-leg pants with a matching blazer.

Meg felt a sudden surge of self-consciousness and reached for her phone, pretending to be attending to something important that couldn't wait. What was she doing here? She didn't fit in with these people. Maybe she should go, before someone worked out she wasn't who she said she was.

At that moment there was a hand on her shoulder and she looked up to find herself face to face with Isobel.

'Megan! I'm so glad you could make it.'

Too late. 'Oh, yes … please, call me Meg. Thanks for the invitation,' Meg said, impressed that Issy remembered her. 'What a great cause,' she added, although she still had no idea what the cause actually was.

'It's my mother's pet project,' Isobel said. 'She asked me to step in to host at the last minute because she wasn't feeling well.' She lowered her voice, as though she was sharing her darkest secret. 'She's over there—' Issy glanced pointedly at a glamorous woman with an impeccable blow dry, '—currently on her third glass of Bollinger, so it seems she's made a speedy recovery.' She raised a provocative eyebrow.

Meg felt herself smile, warming to Isobel's charismatic cocktail of sophistication and irreverence.

'I'll introduce you.' Issy waved to Heather, who excused herself from her conversation and joined them. 'Mum, this is Megan Hunter-Bainbridge. She's doing a PhD on historical buildings. She really likes what we're doing with the Hartwell Gaol development.'

Another guest stepped up to greet Issy and she turned away, leaving Meg with Heather.

'Bainbridge?' Heather said, over-enunciating her words as though she was an actor in a play. 'I think I know your father. Does he sail?'

Meg started to mumble a response, but Heather interjected.

'Don't you have extraordinary eyes? So pretty.'

'Thank you,' Meg said, pleased to be on firmer ground. 'It's called heterochromia. I inherited it from my mum.'

'It's quite striking,' Heather said.

'Some people see it as a flaw, but I'm quite fond of it myself.'

'Good for you!' Heather nodded. 'Ah, here's Cathy. Cathy, this is—'

'Megan, yes, we met yesterday.'

'Hello again,' Meg said.

Cathy gave her a tight-lipped smile in response. 'How lovely you could come. Do you have connections to Hartwell, Megan, or is it just your research that brings you here?'

'Just my research.' Meg swallowed, feeling like this woman could see right through her.

'And where's your family based?'

'I don't have much family. It was just me and Mum growing up. She's in a home now,' Meg added, immediately wishing she hadn't.

'Oh, I'm sorry to hear that.' Heather winced and shook her head. 'Is she sick?'

'Okay, Mum, that's enough,' said Issy, as she joined them again. 'Sorry, Meg.'

'It's okay, really,' Meg said. 'She has dementia.'

'Terrible disease,' Heather said. 'My father died from it.' She reached out and took Meg's hands. 'If there's anything we can do to help, you let us know.'

Meg smiled. 'Thank you.'

'I mean it. Anything at all.' Heather's eyes flashed as she gave Meg's hands a squeeze.

The conversation was interrupted by an imposing man with a bushy moustache hovering nearby. He looked familiar.

'Excuse me, girls,' Heather said, turning to greet him.

'That's the mayor,' Issy said, dropping her voice.

Of course. Meg recognised him from the council website.

'He's a big supporter of the development too. You should have a chat to him while you're here.' Issy hesitated. 'This might seem a little out of left field, and please say no if you're not interested, but I wondered if you might like to write some articles about the Entertainment Precinct? There's been some negative press around the development and I don't want that to overshadow the opening. Our PR team will be able to use their contacts to get them published. I'm not sure if that's something you do, but I don't really trust journalists, to be honest, so I thought of you. What do you think?'

'Oh, ah … I have a lot on my plate, with my doctorate …'

'Why don't you have a think about it and let me know.' Issy took out her phone. 'What's your number? I'll text you so you have mine.'

Meg recited her number and felt her phone vibrate in her bag with Issy's message. A waiter approached, asking people to sit down for dinner.

'I'll show you to your table.' Issy lowered her voice. 'You were sitting next to my niece Daisy originally, but I swapped your name with someone else to save you from a truly excruciating conversational experience. All she can talk about is TikTok.'

'Thanks,' Meg said, still considering doing a runner.

'Pen, this is Meg,' Issy said when they reached the table. A curvy brunette looked up from the seat next to Meg's. 'Penny and I went to Beecham together.' Issy looked at her tiny gold watch. 'Oh, it's time for my speech.'

Meg sat down as Issy floated through the crowd to a lectern on the podium. Entrée plates of kingfish carpaccio were placed on the tables as she made a speech about children with rare diseases, which explained what CRDF meant. As they ate, a slide show of intubated babies and pale toddlers rotated on an enormous screen.

'Poor kids,' Penny whispered. 'Such a good cause.'

Meg nodded earnestly and looked around. Did no one else think it was strange to eat raw fish while viewing photos of dying babies?

Once the entrées were finished, she looked for the mayor and found him seated on a table near the ladies' toilets. Perfect. She excused herself and walked in that direction.

'Excuse me, Tony,' she said when she reached the table. She'd checked his name on the Lindsay Shire Council website to make sure she got it right. 'Sorry to interrupt. I just wanted to commend you on your persistence with the Hartwell Gaol redevelopment in the face of some very vocal objections. Lindsay's lucky to have such a visionary leader.'

He smiled and turned to face her. 'Thank you. It's been a long road.' Meg pretended not to notice as his eyes travelled down her body then back up to her face. 'Are you a resident of Lindsay?'

'I wish I was, but I live in Sydney at the moment.' She told him the PhD story. 'The Ashworths are amazing, aren't they? Their investment in this town is extraordinary.'

'Outstanding people. I've known Malcolm my whole life. We started at Hartwell Public on the same day in 1950.'

'Is that right?'

The mayor nodded and took a large sip of red wine. 'A very community-minded man. With all that he's gone on to achieve, he's never forgotten where he came from.'

Meg nodded, noticing a woman sitting a few seats away who seemed to be listening to their conversation, a frown on her face. She was one of the two female councillors Meg had seen on the webpage. When Meg's eye met hers, the woman got up abruptly and went into the bathroom.

'Well, lovely to talk to you,' Meg said to Tony, then followed her.

The bathroom was empty, except for one stall with a closed

door. Meg took her lip gloss out of her bag and reapplied, waiting for the woman to come out. When she did, she looked at Meg in the mirror. Meg gave her a quick smile.

She seemed to hesitate, then spoke quietly. 'You don't actually believe that, do you? What you were saying about the Ashworths.'

'I'm not quite sure what I think.' Meg spoke slowly, trying to walk a fine line. 'What do *you* think?'

'I got elected to council last year and some of what I'm seeing is—' she paused, choosing her words carefully, '—concerning, to say the least.'

'Like what?' Meg asked, as the door swung open and an elderly woman entered.

Once she was in the far cubicle, the councillor lowered her voice to a whisper. 'I just couldn't stand the sight of Tony Skelton singing the praises of Malcolm Ashworth. Community-minded, my arse. The reason he likes the Ashworths is because they paid for his twenty-five acres on the Old Lindsay Road.'

'They did?'

The woman scoffed. 'Look, I don't know that for sure, but the maths doesn't add up to me. You know how much a regional mayor makes a year?' She reached for a piece of paper towel. 'Personally, I think there's a lot of truth in that Harry Truman quote, about getting rich in politics.'

Meg nodded, although she didn't know what she was referring to. She would google it later.

The toilet flushed.

'Can I talk to you more about this, tomorrow maybe?' Meg asked.

The woman clicked her tongue and shook her head. 'I've probably said too much already,' she replied, as the elderly woman came out of the stall. 'Too much Champagne! Have a good night.'

She disappeared out the door.

*

Sue was calling last drinks when Meg got back to the Red Lion. Meg gave her a quick nod as she moved between the tables to the stairs, impatient to get to her room and transcribe the conversations she'd had with Tony Skelton and the councillor while they were still fresh in her mind.

But as she rounded the top of the staircase, she stopped dead in her tracks.

The door of her room was wide open. A shaft of white light fell across the hall from the streetlight outside her window. She stood motionless, holding her breath, trying to recall if she'd locked it. She would have, wouldn't she? She must have.

Heart racing, she walked slowly towards the room. A floorboard creaked underfoot, making her heart pound harder. She stopped at the doorway and looked inside. Empty. A gust of warm wind blew in through the open window, rustling the curtain.

That was strange. The door unlocked *and* a window open. One or the other, and she could believe she'd made the error, but both? No way. She was careful. Her mother's paranoia had seeped into her.

She flicked on the light and went to the window. A corrugated-iron roof ran along the wall below. Someone tall enough could get in or out that way. She pushed the window shut, locking it carefully, and turned back to the room.

Her suitcase, which she'd never bothered to unpack, was still on the floor, open. The denim shorts and T-shirt she'd worn that day were still draped over the chair. Her white trainers sat beneath them, side by side. Her laptop was on the desk, right where she left it, beside her tote bag. She exhaled a shaky breath.

Everything was exactly where she'd left it.

Chapter 30

It was almost one in the morning by the time Issy pulled into the car park at the jail. Two storeys above, she could see there was still a light on in the main bedroom of the apartment. Hugh must have waited up for her. An olive branch perhaps, or the closest she was likely to get to one. Things had gone from bad to worse that morning when she'd mentioned the fundraiser. She'd suggested he attend as her plus one but he'd declined, muttering something under his breath which she didn't quite catch.

Heels in hand, she tiptoed up the dusty stairs. She could hear Hugh's voice as she pushed open the front door. When she reached the bedroom, she stopped, listening. He sat on the edge of the bed, his back to the door.

'This is the last time,' he said, one hand on his forehead, a strange intensity in his tone. His head snapped around, sensing her presence, and he gave her a nod. 'Okay, mate, yep. I gotta go. Issy's just arrived home.'

A long pause.

'Get some sleep, mate.'

He hung up and tossed his phone aside. 'Marshall's having girl problems again.' He lay back on the pillows, massaging his forehead.

'I didn't know they were back together,' Issy said, dropping her shoes and dumping her bag on the armchair in the corner of the room. Marshall was Hugh's younger brother. He'd broken up with his girlfriend twice this year already. It was getting tedious.

'They're not anymore.'

She went into the ensuite and squeezed cleanser onto a cotton pad.

'How was the fundraiser? Did you raise lots of funds?'

'Of course we did,' Issy said, patting her face dry.

'Who was there?'

'All the usual suspects. Mum was in fine form. So much for the long covid.' She unzipped her pants and let them fall to the bathroom floor in a gold puddle. 'Helen was a no-show, although Daisy was there, which was a nice surprise. I suspect it was for the content, rather than the sick babies, but whatever.'

She went into the bedroom and reached under her pillow for her pyjamas. Hugh was scrolling on his phone. He glanced up at her naked body and smiled appreciatively.

'There was also a woman there who's in town to research the Hartwell Gaol development.'

Hugh's head snapped up. 'Research it?'

'She's an academic, very supportive of what we're doing which is a nice change.' She pulled the cami over her head.

Hugh frowned. 'What's her name?'

'Megan Hunter-Bainbridge,' she said.

'Warwick told me about her. Said she was asking all sorts of questions.'

Issy rolled her eyes. 'She's just a PhD student. Hardly cause for alarm. She's quite intriguing, actually.'

'Intriguing, how?'

Issy thought for a moment, then shrugged. 'I don't know, really.' She stepped into her pyjama shorts and went back into the bathroom to finish her skincare routine. Maybe intriguing wasn't the right word. Unusual, perhaps. She was nothing like the rest of the people in that room, who seemed airbrushed in comparison. There was something so self-possessed about her. Even her style was unique. Vintage Zimmermann and Valentinos. Issy's own outfit had felt predictable and unimaginative in comparison.

As she applied a retinol serum, she replayed the conversation they'd had as Meg was leaving. She was staying at the Red Lion pub, of all places! Issy had failed to mask her horror—if the smell of beer in the bar was any indication, the accommodation must be utterly dreadful. Meg had just laughed and said it was fine, politely declining Issy's offer to arrange a room for her at the Ashworth Park.

As she applied her eye cream, she thought of Meg's eyes, the golden-brown circling the iris, surrounded by the larger blue ring. She'd never seen eyes like that before.

Hugh was asleep when she returned to the bedroom. His phone was lying where he'd tossed it onto the quilt after he'd finished speaking to Marshall. She reached for it, intending to put it on the bedside table, but instead she paused, thinking of the weird call from the night before. The muffled voices. The girly giggle.

Had it really been Marshall on the phone just now? What was Hugh saying as she stood at the door? 'This is the last time.' Why would he say that to Marshall? *What* was the last time? Did he mean this was the last time Marshall could break up with his girlfriend? What an odd thing to say. It was Marshall's life, after all.

She looked back at the phone, tempted to check it, but decided against it. That was desperate, paranoid behaviour.

Although ... She swallowed. Maybe one quick look would reassure her that there was nothing to worry about. She'd seen Hugh enter his passcode a thousand times. Three taps with his left index finger, three taps with his right. Top left, then top right. 111333. She looked at him to check he was really asleep, then tapped in the code.

She checked his recent calls, expecting to see Marshall's name. It was there, they'd spoken just after ten, but it wasn't the most recent call. That was from *George Mobile*.

Who the hell was George?

DNA Sleuths Facebook Group

Stephen Lee: According to my parents, I was donor conceived due to fertility issues. I did a test recently because I'm studying medicine and I want to know more about my medical history on my biological father's side. Anyway, I have a few matches with the last name Langford. This name rang a bell for me. At first I couldn't work out where I knew it from, then I realised it was the name of our next-door neighbours when I was a little kid. My parents bought the house just after they were married. So I reached out to one of the people I matched with and they confirmed they have a cousin who lived in Castle Hill in the early 2000s. I have my own theory about what might have happened, but I'm interested in what others make of this?

Top comments

Karen Finn: I think your mum might have borrowed more than a cup of sugar from your next-door neighbour.

Sara Power: It's highly inappropriate to joke about something like this IMO

Patricia Pine: It's possible the name is a coincidence. I advise against jumping to conclusions. Have you spoken to your mother about any of this?

Karen Finn: A coincidence??? The match he spoke to said his cousin lived the same suburb at the same time!!!

Stephen Lee: Not yet **Patricia**. My mother is a very conservative person. I'm really struggling to believe she did what I think she did.

Mary Louise: Don't be fooled by that **Stephen**. My mother volunteered at the church for forty-five years and also had a long-term affair with my father's best friend.

Wendy Turner: I know the thought of talking to your mum about it is daunting. Just go into the conversation with an open mind.

Chapter 31

Meg spent the dark night trying not to think about the unlocked door, the open window, but every time she started drifting off, she woke with a jolt. In the darkness, the room felt sinister, with strange shadows dancing on the ceiling. She tossed and turned on the clammy mattress, the air thick and hot with the window closed, but she wasn't game to open it.

She woke up craving home. Her own bed. Her bathtub. Her cosy sofa and her fluffy, red mohair blanket.

She got every red light on her way back into Sydney. The roads were full of people doing last-minute shopping or leaving town for Christmas in SUVs laden with surfboards and bikes.

When Meg arrived at Rosedale, Jenny was in bed.

'They've taken our video, Meg!' she said, sitting up, deep creases between her eyes. 'They've stolen it!'

'What video?' Meg asked, but she knew Jenny was thinking of their old rental copy of *The Princess Bride*, which they'd never returned to Blockbuster before leaving whatever town that was. They must have watched it a hundred times, lying together in Jenny's double bed.

'It's that young one with the dark hair,' Jenny said. 'She's always coming in here and fussing with my things.'

'Mum, the video's at my house.'

Jenny frowned, eyeing Meg suspiciously. 'It is?'

Meg nodded. 'I'll bring it in next time, so you can see it.'

Jenny slumped back against the pillows and closed her eyes.

By the time Meg reached her building it was late afternoon. The apartment was dark. Her eyes struggled to adjust as she stepped inside and banged her foot on something sitting in the middle of the hallway. 'Bloody hell!' she yelled, clutching her foot as a spasm of pain shot up through her big toe.

Once it subsided, she fumbled for the light switch and flicked it on. A case of Carlton Draught had been thoughtfully placed in the middle of the hall. She pushed it aside and looked around. The peace lily on the hall table drooped sadly. Beside it was a stack of mail. She picked it up and flipped through it. Mostly junk.

A pungent smell intensified as she walked up the hall: a mixture of pot and cigarette smoke. She stood at the entrance to the lounge room, staring at the state of it in disbelief. The coffee table was covered in empty bottles. A pizza box and an enormous black bong sat among the bottles next to a decorative bowl Meg had taken from her mum's house when they'd packed up her flat. It was full of cigarette butts.

'Are you kidding me?' she whispered, rage building in her chest. 'Hello?'

Silence. Gav's bedroom door was ajar, his immaculate room empty. Jay's door was closed. She knocked and waited. Nothing. She pushed it open and looked in disgust at the mess that filled the tiny space. The carpet was hidden beneath clothes, shoes and bath towels. The bedsheets hung off the side of the bed, the bare mattress exposed, and the bedside table was piled up with dirty plates and empty beer bottles.

Hot rage bubbled up inside her. He could afford an endless supply of pot and beer, but he hadn't paid her a cent for almost two months! She stormed down the hallway to the kitchen, ripped a page from a notebook and scribbled a note: CLEAN UP AND PAY ME YOUR RENT OR GET THE HELL OUT!! Her hands were shaking as she stuck it on his door.

She took a long, slow breath and rang Pete's number.

'Hunter!' he said. 'I was just thinking about you. I've got intel.'

'Are you at home?'

'Yeah, why?'

'I hope you don't think this is weird,' she said. 'Any chance I can crash at your place?'

'Sure, of course, but I'm painting the spare room, so you'll have to sleep on the sofa. Hopefully you don't mind sharing it with Maggie.'

'Who's Maggie?'

'My kelpie.'

'That'll be fine. I could do with the cuddles, to be honest. Text me your address.'

She went into her bedroom, opened cupboards and drawers and chucked stuff into a blue Ikea bag. Remembering the video, she pulled down the box of random stuff she'd taken from Jenny's apartment and rummaged through until she saw a baby-faced Robin Wright staring back at her, a faded pink weekly rental sticker adorning the plastic cover. She chucked it into the bag, then hauled it up over her shoulder and slammed the front door behind her.

Meg could smell the barbecue when she arrived at the open door of Pete's old terrace, up the road in Newtown.

'Hello!' she called out as she let herself in.

A long-legged kelpie came bounding down the hallway. 'Hey, girl,' she said, crouching down to greet her. 'You must be Maggie.'

Meg walked down the long hall with Maggie by her side, until she reached the kitchen and lounge room at the back. She dropped the bag from her shoulder and looked around, admiring the modern, light-filled living space. Pete had shown her photos when he'd bought the fixer-upper years ago—before real estate prices in the Inner West had gone through the roof—and talked of his plans to do most of the renovation work himself. She'd found his optimism endearing, but inwardly thought it would take more than a DIY job to rescue the dark, rundown dump she saw in the photos. How wrong she was, she thought now, looking towards the glass doors that opened onto a tiny courtyard.

She wandered outside to see a table set for two beneath a frangipani tree adorned with coloured Christmas lights. Pete was wearing a butcher's apron, tongs in hand, intently inspecting the lamb cutlets that sizzled on the barbecue.

'You haven't gone to all this effort for me, have you?' Meg asked.

He glanced up, his summer-tanned face breaking into a wide grin. 'Hunter! I didn't hear you.'

She gestured to the house. 'This is gorgeous, Pete.'

'It's getting there.' He shrugged, but a slight smile revealed that he appreciated the compliment. 'Drink?'

'I'll have one of those, thanks,' she said, pointing to the Corona in his hand.

He took one from the bar fridge and popped the top.

'Thanks for letting me crash at the last minute,' she said.

'Everything okay?'

She sighed. 'Just flatmate problems.'

Pete frowned. 'I thought you got on well. Haven't you been living together for years?'

'Not Gav, he's fine.' She sat down at the table and took a sip. 'I rented out the third bedroom when I lost my job. Turns out the quality of applicants for a room the size of a shoebox is not high, so now we have an pothead gamer living in our midst. The place was such a filthy mess when I got back there that I couldn't stay. And he doesn't even pay his rent!'

'Might be time to kick him out,' Pete said, pressing one of the lamb cutlets to test it.

'I can't believe I'm almost thirty and I'm still dealing with this crap.' She sighed, weary at the prospect of confronting Jay then going through the whole process of finding someone new.

'How's your mum?' Pete asked, transferring the lamb to a plate.

'Not great.' She blew out heavily. 'She thinks the nurses are stealing from her.'

Pete shook his head. 'It must be awful, don't you think? Being confused all the time. Not knowing who people are and whether she can trust them.'

Meg nodded and swallowed a lump in her throat. 'You said you have intel?' she said, keen to change the subject. 'I'm intrigued.'

His face lit up. 'Yeah, so all of the properties on Barton Drive, seven at last count, have been bought in trusts, rather than by individual people.'

'What does that mean?' Meg asked, taking a crouton from the salad bowl and feeding it to Maggie.

'It's what people do when they don't want the media or the public finding out they own a particular asset.' He put the plate on the table. 'The trust company is in a different name with no official link to the owner of the asset. They'll have a contract that sits behind that, which legally identifies the asset as belonging to the owner, but that part isn't subject to the Freedom of Information Act.'

'So how do we find out?'

'I already have.'

Meg laughed. 'Of course you have.'

'Three of the trust companies—Goodwin Investments, Greenhill Family Trust and Apollo Ventures—link back to a law firm called Purcell Partners. Goodwin Investments is also listed as the owner of a derelict hotel in the Blue Mountains, which was sold a few years ago and is now in development by Ashworth Property.' Pete sat down and reached for his phone, finding something to show her. 'Check this out.'

It was a photo of a group of men on a yacht, the white sails of the Sydney Opera House in the background.

'What am I looking at?' Meg asked. It was a long shot, the shadows dark from the bright sun directly overhead, and most of the men wore caps, obscuring their faces. She leaned in closer. 'Is that Hugh Thorburn?'

'It sure is, with his arm around the shoulder of Evan Purcell, the Managing Partner of Purcell Partners. See anyone else there you recognise?'

Pete waited while she studied the photo.

'Spencer Ashworth,' she said, slowly.

'Yep.'

She tapped on the photo to see if they were tagged, but nothing came up. 'How'd you find this?'

'That's the Instagram profile of a guy I used to play rugby with. The boat belonged to a friend of his.'

'Interesting. It doesn't definitively prove anything, though, does it?'

'No, but there are too many touch points for it to be random. The likelihood that this *isn't* linked to the Ashworths is slim to none. This story could be big, Meg.'

'What do you reckon they're planning?'

'I haven't worked that out yet.' He poured the wine, then lifted his glass. 'What shall we drink to?'

She looked around at the little paradise Pete had created at the back of his tiny terrace in the middle of the city. The coloured lights reflected red and gold off the glasses on the table. Overhead, the sky was an inky blue. The festive sounds of a nearby Christmas party travelled over the fence. The rise and fall of voices. Laughter. The clinking of glasses. The beat of a song. The air was warm on her bare arms.

'Impromptu barbecues on summer nights,' she said, clinking her glass against his. 'Let's not talk about Mum or flatmates or the bloody Ashworths. I need a night off.'

Chapter 32

Issy pressed the brass doorbell at Kilmore and checked her lipstick in the opaque glass pane in the front door. Rouge Allure, by Chanel. She always wore a red lip on Christmas Day. Hugh put a hand on the small of her back and she felt herself stiffen.

'Are you pissed off about something?' he said, dropping his hand.

'No, sorry.' She gave him a tight smile and smoothed the brocade folds of her gold dress. She'd been trying to put aside her suspicions about Hugh's phone call, but it seemed her subconscious hadn't got the memo. Footsteps approached and the front door swung open.

'Come in! Merry Christmas!' They were ushered inside by a pretty, blonde teenager wearing a white shirt and a black apron longer than the skirt she wore under it. Who knew where Heather recruited staff willing to work on Christmas Day, but she always managed to find them.

They followed the waitress down the wide hallway, lined on either side by enormous artworks no one ever stopped to look at, to the kitchen, where Spencer and Helen stood with Heather and Cathy by the marble island bench. The steel doors behind them were open, white linen curtains billowing gently in the light breeze. On the terrace beyond, Olivia was photographing Daisy, who posed in front of the turquoise pool in a string bikini.

Heather greeted Issy with her characteristic aloofness. 'Merry Christmas. Don't you look lovely.'

'Thanks, Mum.'

'Merry Christmas, Heather.' Hugh kissed her on both cheeks. 'Stunning as always.'

'Oh, stop it,' Heather said, coyly, then dropped her voice. 'Have you heard? Felix is bringing a girlfriend.' She pulled a face, as though she would be less surprised if he was bringing a unicorn to Christmas lunch. 'A handbag designer, apparently,' she added, raising an eyebrow.

Hugh and Spencer slapped backs. Helen gave them a pained smile.

'There she is!' Malcolm boomed, as he entered the room. 'Merry Christmas, princess.'

Issy flashed her best smile. 'Hi, Daddy.' She kissed him, leaving a bright red mark on his rough cheek. 'Oops, I've marked you!'

'Better my cheek than my collar!' he said with a grin, rubbing at the mark. He beckoned the waitress. 'Sweetheart, could you get this gorgeous creature a drink? Champagne, Issy?'

'Bubbles would be lovely, thank you.'

'Hugh, what'll you have?'

He ordered a beer and the waitress disappeared.

The doorbell rang and moments later, Felix stepped into the kitchen with a waifish woman by his side.

'Sorry we're late.'

Heather glanced at her Cartier watch. 'Only half an hour. We consider that on time for you, Felix.'

He ignored the barbed comment. 'This is Polly. Polly, this is … everyone.'

Issy extended a hand, admiring her effortless style. Even in flats, Polly was at least half a foot taller than her. 'I'm Isobel,' she said. 'Pleasure to meet you.'

'So nice to meet you in person,' Polly said. 'I'm a big fan. I follow you on Instagram.'

'Oh, lovely,' Issy said.

'We'll do the presents now that everyone's here.' Heather's voice bounced off the marble. 'Everyone into the lounge!'

Issy took the bag with their gifts from Hugh and went through an archway to the formal lounge, which was dominated by an enormous tree twinkling with thousands of tiny lights. The star on top almost touched the ornate three-metre ceiling. She snapped a photo to post later, then surveyed the paltry collection of gifts. It looked quite pathetic this year, due to Heather's environmentally friendly secret Santa initiative.

Issy placed the two gifts she'd ordered online—one from her, one from Hugh—with the others and sat down beside Hugh.

'My goodness!' Polly exclaimed as she sat down opposite, next to Felix. 'What a stunning tree!'

'Thank you, sweetheart,' Heather said. 'Sweetheart' was a term she reserved exclusively for Felix's girlfriends—a deliberate strategy, Issy suspected, to avoid mixing up their names. Or learning them in the first place. 'I had to have it shipped here from America! It takes two men to erect it!'

Felix looked at Issy, raising his eyebrows. Last year, he'd shared his theory that their mother's obsession with her enormous Christmas tree was some warped version of penis envy. Issy stifled a giggle and looked away, draining the rest of her Champagne. Beside her, Hugh looked around until he located the waitress, who stood discreetly by the door.

'Can we get the glasses topped up?' There was a hint of irritation in his voice, as though the waitress should have noticed the need for another round without him having to ask. He raised his empty Peroni bottle. 'And another one of these?'

'Please,' Issy added, feeling like the apologetic mother of a rude child.

Once everyone was assembled, Heather reached for the first gift and read the tag. 'Merry Christmas, Hugh!'

She passed him a gold box and he unwrapped a bottle of whisky.

He let out a low whistle. 'Glenfiddich Grande single malt whisky.'

Heather clicked her tongue. 'I take it someone broke the spending limit.'

'Have you tried cheap whisky?' Malcolm said.

'I'm not much of a whisky drinker myself, but I take your point.'

'Well, thank you, whoever you are,' Hugh said. 'You know me well!'

'Now you deliver the next one, Hugh,' Heather directed.

He selected the largest one, which turned out to be a cold press juicer for Spencer. Issy suspected it was from Heather, who was always criticising his diet. She'd clearly also exceeded her own hundred-dollar limit.

On and on it went. Eventually Issy's gift was selected, a voucher for the spa at the Ashworth Park Hotel, something she could already use anytime she wanted to without charge. She looked at Felix, who grinned back at her. He'd made an artform out of using charm to compensate for a breathtaking lack of effort. She shook her head, but couldn't help smiling.

When Issy got up to deliver the next gift, there was only one left. A large, shiny, gold giftbag. She glanced around to see who was still without one. Daisy and Olivia both had Mecca gift cards, Heather had an Oroton makeup bag, Helen a Diptyque candle, Malcolm two hardback autobiographies, Felix two polo shirts (in very unfashionable pastels) and Polly had a restaurant voucher which Heather must have purchased at the last minute. Cathy's massage gun sat on her lap, Hugh was still cradling his bottle of whisky and Spencer's juicer sat on the floor by his side. No one was without a gift.

She read the tag, frowning. The names had been typed, rather than handwritten. 'For Spencer, Felix and Isobel Ashworth,' she said slowly. The formality struck her as strange. Inside were three identical boxes wrapped in brown paper. 'Who's this from?' she asked.

Spencer leaned forward. 'What is it?'

'I don't know. There's one for each of us.' She passed one to Spencer, one to Felix and took the last one out for herself.

'It must be from Santa,' Felix said.

Issy pulled at the tape on one end, ripping the paper to reveal a white box wrapped in plastic. She turned it over to read the front.

'Heritage DNA.' She looked up to see her brothers each holding an identical box.

'What is this?' Felix asked.

'It's a DNA kit,' she said, reading the back of the box, which boasted about the speed of their results and the size of their database. 'You know, those tests people do to trace their family history.' She'd seen them advertised on TV. 'This Christmas, give the gift of family,' the melodious voiceover said. They were marketed as a simple way to learn more about your ancestry and ethnicity.

'Who's it from?' Spencer asked. 'Mum?'

'They're certainly not from me!' Heather said. 'My tennis friend Rhonda did one of those things. She was doing her family tree and she wanted to track down the Greek side of the family. It turned out the Greek side was actually Turkish, and she hates the Turks so it was a disaster!'

Felix reached for a piece of smoked salmon from the enormous platter on the coffee table. 'Wow, Rhonda sounds racist.'

'I don't think she's *racist* necessarily, Felix. I think she just found it … disconcerting … to suddenly realise that she isn't who she thinks she is.'

Polly leaned forward. 'They can reveal all sorts of things, those tests.' Everyone turned to look at her. 'I read an article in *Vanity Fair* about people who discovered some long-hidden family secret when they did a DNA test. It was fascinating, actually.'

'Like what?' Issy asked.

Polly shrugged. 'One woman found out that her older sister was really her mother!'

An awkward silence.

Issy laughed. 'Well, I don't have an older sister, so that's one thing I don't have to worry about.'

'Not that we know of, at least,' Felix said.

'Someone must know where they came from,' Spencer said.

Heather gestured to the gold gift bag. 'That bag arrived yesterday by courier. I assumed it was from one of you and asked Rosa to put it under the tree.'

'So no one knows anything about them?' Spencer said.

They all looked at one another, blank-faced.

Malcolm shook his head and leaned forward in his chair. 'Only an absolute fool would do one of those tests.' There was a sharp edge in his tone.

Was Issy imagining it, or did her father seem angry? A strange feeling took hold in her stomach. Slowly, she placed the white box on the coffee table as though it was a bomb which required delicate handling.

Malcolm stood abruptly. 'Are we going to be fed at some stage?' he barked at the waitress, who snapped to attention.

'Please tell the caterers we're ready for lunch,' Heather said. 'Thank you, Georgie.'

'Were you expecting a football team?' Issy asked her mother, surveying the buffet table, which was laden with a roast turkey, a glazed ham, a side of salmon, golden potatoes and at least four festive-looking salads containing pomegranate seeds.

'The caterers always go overboard at Christmas,' Heather said with a wave of her hand, watching Felix add more potatoes to his already over-loaded plate.

Once they were seated, Malcolm raised his glass of red and made a toast 'to family', which seemed loaded somehow in light of the DNA tests.

'Where did you two meet, Felix?' Heather asked, once they'd cracked the bonbons she ordered every year from Harrods, gesturing to him and Polly.

Felix launched into story-telling mode, regaling them with the story of how he'd met Polly at a café in Paddington. 'We'd both ordered the same takeaway order. Smashed avo on sourdough and an almond latte,' he said, but he pronounced it 'shmashed'. He must be quite drunk. 'Pol thought I'd taken hers by mistake. She was quite feisty about it. It was very attractive.'

'I mean, what are the chances?' Polly added rhetorically, her hand a little too far up Felix's inner thigh. 'We decided it meant we were made for each other, and the rest is history!'

'The *rest*?' Heather asked. 'How long ago was this star-crossed meeting?'

'Almost a month ago.' Polly looked at Felix, doe-eyed.

Heather scoffed, not even trying to conceal her cynicism about the longevity of the relationship.

Polly looked hurt, momentarily, then regained her composure. 'How did you and Malcolm meet?'

Issy had heard the story a hundred times. She studied her father's face as he told them about the day fifty years before, when he'd seen Heather for the first time at Bondi Beach. Maybe it was the DNA tests, but Issy listened differently this time. How faithful had he been during those fifty years? There was at least one indiscretion that she knew of. She'd discovered that one day in year nine, when she walked into the locker room to find her best friend Claudia whispering something to a wide-eyed Melody. When they saw her, they'd leapt apart.

'What?' Issy had asked.

'Nothing,' they said in unison.

Eventually Claudia had told her the truth. 'Your dad's having an affair with my dad's friend's wife's sister. It's common knowledge. Everyone knows.'

Issy's brain had felt like it was going in slow motion, trying to compute the information, to make sense of it, while Claudia waited for her to say something.

Eventually, Issy had shaken her head. 'My dad wouldn't do that.'

'It's true, Issy. Your dad even bought an apartment for her at Circular Quay. He stays there with her while he's in Sydney.'

Issy's eyes felt hot with tears. 'How do you know?'

'My dad told me.' Claudia shrugged. 'At least your parents are still together. My mum's on to her third husband and my dad's girlfriend just had a baby.'

Bile had risen in Issy's throat, picturing her father with a new baby, and she'd run for the toilets. Claudia had followed and stood beside her, rubbing her back.

That night, Issy had called home. Heather answered.

'Is Dad there?' What was she planning to say if he was?

'He's in Sydney, darling. He's working on a big transaction. Everything okay?'

'Yep, fine. I just wanted to ask him something.'

She'd decided it was a good thing he wasn't there. Best to pretend she knew nothing about it.

When lunch was finished, they moved back to the lounge. The waitress brought out a platter of mince pies and took coffee orders.

Issy sat herself next to Polly, a strategic move to avoid talking about the Hartwell Gaol development with Spencer or Malcolm. She and Polly discussed handbags for fifteen minutes, before Issy looked around for Hugh. She hadn't seen him since they were at the dining table.

Just as she was about to go and look for him, Heather approached. 'Swap seats,' she said to Polly, who did as she was told.

Issy looked at her mother expectantly.

'You're not going to do that test, are you?' Heather murmured, glancing at Cathy, who was collecting discarded wrapping paper nearby. 'Sit down, Cathy, for God's sake. I'll have someone do that later.'

Cathy joined Felix and Polly, and reached for a mince pie. There was still no sign of Hugh.

'Isobel?' Heather said, her voice still low but firmer now. 'Listen here. I have no idea where they came from, but it would be *beyond* stupid to do that test.'

Issy frowned. 'Why?'

'For God's sake, Isobel. Don't be daft. It might be a fun Christmas gift in most families, but in a family like ours …'

'What?' Issy asked, playing dumb, trying to make her mother come out and say what she was thinking.

'A lot of people want what we've got, Isobel—' her mother let out a little laugh, '—and you just never know …' She sighed heavily. 'You've always been naive about the way the world works.'

'Bloody hell,' Issy muttered under her breath.

Her gaze landed on the box, which still sat on the coffee table. Someone must know something, something about their family, about their relationships to one another. What other explanation could there be?

She looked from Felix to Spencer. They both seemed distracted, slightly outside of the conversations they were having. Were they also thinking about the mysterious DNA tests, thoughts travelling backwards and forwards in time, wondering who had planted them under the tree and what they might reveal? Spencer had a deep crease between his brows. He looked up and caught her eye, then looked quickly away again.

She noticed Hugh slip into the room, head down, and join the larger conversation. She checked her watch. They'd left the dining room twenty minutes ago. Where had he been? On the phone again? Then someone else slipped quietly into the room.

The waitress.

Issy's chest tightened.

'Isobel,' Heather murmured.

Issy looked back at her mother. 'What?'

'Promise me you won't do the test.'

Issy exhaled. 'You've made your point, loud and clear. Thanks, Mum.' She needed to get out of there. She stood up. 'Hugh, it's time for us to go.'

The conversation stopped abruptly. 'Oh, okay,' he stammered.

Helen looked grateful for the interruption. 'Spence, we should go too. I'll round up the girls.'

Heather looked at Felix, whose eyelids were droopy, then at Polly. 'It's time to take Felix home too, sweetheart.'

Polly leapt to action. 'Come on, Felix.'

'But I just opened another beer,' he said, holding up his bottle, which was almost full.

'You've had enough,' Malcolm said. 'I assume you're driving, Poppy.'

Polly nodded, ignoring his error.

'It's Polly, Dad. Jesus Christ,' Felix said.

Malcolm shrugged vaguely, as though her name was immaterial. Polly extended a hand to pull Felix up from the sofa. He leaned heavily against her, steadying himself on his feet.

Issy picked up the DNA test from the coffee table and turned to follow the others.

As they stood on the cobblestone driveway, saying their goodbyes, it struck her that she didn't trust any of them. She was surrounded by liars. She closed her eyes and took a deep breath, suddenly queasy. Slightly off balance, as though everything she thought was solid and real was a flimsy illusion.

Daisy put a hand on her arm. 'Are you okay, Auntie Issy?'

Issy nodded, but she felt overwhelmed and weary, worn down by her own suspicion and speculation. She couldn't live like this, always sensing there was something she wasn't being told.

She tightened her grip on the box in her left hand. It wouldn't lie. It couldn't. It didn't have an agenda. It didn't stand to gain anything. It had nothing to lose.

It would tell the truth, no matter what.

She would do it, she decided. She would do the test as soon as she got home.

Chapter 33

The staff at Rosedale were doing their best to create a festive vibe, despite the depressing circumstances for the patients and their visitors. Michael Bublé crooned 'Jingle Bells' from the tinny intercom speakers. Red tinsel adorned the doorways and hung limply over the insipid watercolour paintings that lined the walls. Doreen, who sat in the office talking on the phone, wore Christmas tree earrings and an elf hat, although her facial expression still suggested she would rather be somewhere else. Meg put a box of Cadbury's Favourites on the desk—a Christmas gift to share with the other staff—which elicited a jaded smile.

A fake Christmas tree stood in one corner of the lounge area beside a long table set with supermarket bonbons. The adjacent sitting area was scattered with small family groups. Elderly relatives in wheelchairs sat with middle-aged sons and daughters, while grandchildren played hide and seek in the corridors. Meg side-stepped a toddler on a plastic motorbike and felt a pang in her chest. They didn't know how lucky they were, not having to do this alone.

Her mum's door was slightly ajar. Meg steadied herself with a deep breath then pushed the door open. Jenny, who was sitting in the armchair by the window, turned towards her. There was a long pause as Meg waited for her to speak first. Who would Jenny think she was today?

'Yes?' Jenny said, brows knitted. 'Can I help you?'

Meg sighed. Please let this not all be too late. 'Mum, it's me. Meg.' She pulled up the spare chair and took the video from her bag. 'I brought you the video.'

Jenny took it tentatively, her eyes travelling over the image on the box like it was a puzzle to solve. 'What's this for?'

'You were asking about it the other day. We used to watch it together in your bed. When I was little.' She studied her mum's face for some flicker of recognition. 'Remember?'

Nothing.

'Mum?'

'Oh. Yes.' Jenny nodded, but there was still distance in her eyes. 'Is Tina here to pick me up?'

'No, Mum.' Meg swallowed. She knew the truth now. It was time to stop pretending. 'Tina's not coming. She's in Hartwell, having Christmas Day with her family.'

Jenny's face flickered with something Meg couldn't read. Surprise? Confusion? Longing? Then it cleared and she looked out the window. 'It's Christmas Day today?' she asked when she turned back to Meg.

'Yes. They've set up a table in the lounge area. Shall we go out there?'

They chose a spot at one end of the table. Gradually other residents joined them, pulling crackers and donning paper hats.

'I'm Henry,' the man sitting opposite said. He was tall with bushy eyebrows.

'Meg.'

Jenny looked at her, frowning. Meg suspected she saw Tina.

'What did you get for Christmas, Jenny?' Henry asked.

She shook her head, unsure.

'I haven't given you your gifts yet, Mum,' Meg said, taking them from her bag. She passed the square one first. 'Merry Christmas.'

Meg's heart raced as she watched her mother unwrap the gift. She pulled the ribbon to untie the bow then teased at the knot Meg had tied, instead of just stretching it and pulling it off. Once she'd removed the ribbon, she painstakingly ran her finger under the tape, trying not to tear the paper.

'Just rip it, Mum,' Meg said, as someone filled her glass with prosecco.

Jenny shook her head. 'It's such pretty paper. Shame to spoil it,' she said, as though she was planning to reuse it. A frugal habit. Once necessary, now pointless.

Jenny frowned as she folded back the paper to reveal a small black giftbox. She slipped the lid off the box and inhaled sharply. Wide-eyed, she stared at the pendant, which sat on white tissue paper. She placed it on her palm to see it more clearly. Fluorescent light bounced off the chain.

'Very nice,' Henry said, eyes glistening.

'It's beautiful.' Jenny's voice was a whisper. She ran her finger over the design. 'The scales of justice.'

'Do you remember it?' Meg asked softly.

Jenny's face was hard to read. 'Remember it?'

Meg sighed. 'Do you want to put it on?'

Jenny shook her head and lay the necklace on the table, next to the box. Meg passed her the second gift.

Again, Jenny was slow and deliberate as she removed the wrapping. Meg felt a surge of impatience and took a deep breath, resisting the urge to take it from her mother and unwrap it herself.

Jenny frowned and picked up the pen. She squinted at the engraving on the side and reached for her glasses. A hand went up to her mouth as she read the words. *The Ashworth Park Hotel.*

When she looked back at Meg, there were tears in her eyes.

'You haven't opened the card.'

Jenny ripped the envelope, opened the card and whispered the words as she read. 'Merry Christmas, Anna.' She shook her head. Her eyes met Meg's. 'I don't understand …'

'I know the truth, Mum.'

Tears pooled in Jenny's eyes, but she said nothing.

'You were working for the Ashworths.'

'Shh,' Jenny said, the hissing sound slicing the air.

Conversations around the long table stopped. Eyes looked in their direction, sensing the tension. Her mother had always been intensely private, but Meg didn't care.

'You were their baby nurse. You were—'

'Stop,' Jenny ordered through gritted teeth, eyes glancing at the watching faces, as if to remind Meg they had an audience. 'I'm warning you.'

A strong wave of fury rose up in Meg. 'You stop! Stop lying to me!'

Jenny looked around at the other residents then back at Meg, eyes wide. 'You don't know what you're saying,' she whispered, shaking.

'Now, listen,' Henry said. 'I can see your mother is getting—'

'I know the truth, Mum!' Meg said. 'You grew up in Hartwell. You have a sister called Christina. Your parents are still alive, for Christ's sake! They live in a retirement village in Queensland!'

Jenny was bent over, her hands covering her face, shaking from side to side. Meg should stop—she knew that, it was too much for her mother to cope with—but she couldn't. Her anger was like a wild horse, galloping ahead. She was powerless to stop it. Henry stood up, looking around for a nurse to step in.

'You were working for the Ashworths, looking after their baby because Heather was sick.'

'That's enough!' Jenny stood up, her chair falling backwards. She glared at Meg. 'I won't stand for this!'

Meg stood, trembling, meeting her mother's gaze. Their faces were so close she could feel her mother's breath, see the tiny flare of her nostrils, the pulsing of her temples. Meg swallowed. Why stop now? She'd said this much. She held Jenny's gaze as she asked the question that had been on her mind since she'd discovered her mother had worked for the Ashworths.

'Is Malcolm Ashworth my father?'

'Stop!' Jenny shrieked, shoving Meg's chest. Caught off guard, Meg stumbled and fell backwards, just missing the Christmas tree. Blinking, she looked up at her mother, who stood above her.

'We need help in here!' Henry called out. He put two hands on Jenny's shoulders and moved her away.

'I told you to stop,' Jenny said.

An orderly appeared, picking up Jenny's chair and positioning it behind her.

Meg clutched for words, still reeling from the shock of the blow, but none came.

'You wouldn't stop,' Jenny said, slumping down into the chair, tears running down her cheeks. 'You wouldn't stop.'

Meg got to her feet, staring at her mother in shock. The locket, which lay on the table, caught her eye and she picked it up. She glanced around at the disbelieving faces of the other residents and guests, then back at her mother.

'Merry bloody Christmas,' she said, then walked down the corridor and out the front door.

Chapter 34

Issy always thought Boxing Day should be plan-free, a chance to relax after the silliness of the festive season, but instead she was plumping cushions and straightening coffee table books in an effort to make the display apartment presentable for Hugh's brother, who would be arriving any minute. It was the last thing she felt like, if she was honest, but he was her future brother-in-law and the poor man had found himself suddenly single, at Christmas no less.

She was slicing cucumbers for gin cocktails when the doorbell rang.

'Hugh, can you please get the door?'

She waited.

'Hugh?' She bit her lip. His phone had rung ten minutes before and he'd disappeared into the spare bedroom, shutting the door behind him.

'Hugh!'

Still nothing. A ripple of suspicion ran through her.

The doorbell rang again. She took a deep breath and went to open the door. 'Marshall!' she said. Oh. Carmen was standing by his side. 'And Carmen! How lovely! Come on in.' What were they doing here together? Hadn't they broken up? Clearly not. Hugh must have forgotten to fill her in on their speedy reunion. Where *was* he?

'Issy, lovely to see you again.' Carmen held out an enormous bunch of flowers wrapped in garish yellow cellophane. 'These are for you. Thank you for inviting us.'

Carmen, a psychologist, was one of those serious women who spoke in a deep tone and held eye contact for too long. They'd only met twice before, briefly, and both times her company had the effect of making Issy feel like a silly little girl.

They followed Issy through to the kitchen, where she put the flowers in the sink.

'Mate!' Hugh entered and gave his brother a rough hug. 'Carmen, looking lovely!' He leaned in and kissed her cheek. Issy thought he seemed twitchy beneath the amiable facade.

'Drinks?' he offered.

'Beer, mate,' Marshall said.

'Just something soft for me,' Carmen said. 'Thanks, Hugh.'

Hugh disappeared into the little laundry room where he'd put drinks on ice in the sink.

'Please, have a seat.' Issy gestured towards the lounges, where a grazing platter sat on the coffee table. She'd had her mother's caterers deliver it earlier.

'Much traffic on the way down?' Issy asked.

Marshall gave a detailed rundown of the route he'd taken out of Sydney, but when he'd finished, Hugh still wasn't back.

'I might see if Hugh needs a hand with the drinks,' Issy said.

When she entered the dark laundry, Hugh was standing at the bench, doubled over, his head in his hands. She put a gentle hand on his back, but he startled. She stepped back, shocked at the sudden movement.

He rubbed his forehead. 'Sorry, I didn't hear you come in.'

'Are you okay?'

'Yeah, I just have a headache.'

She frowned. He'd seemed fine before he'd received the phone call.

'Who was on the phone?' she asked, trying to keep her tone light.

'What? Oh, just Spencer.'

'On Boxing Day?' Issy kept her face neutral. 'What was he calling for?'

Hugh pressed his thumb and forefinger against his closed eyes. 'A property deal he wants to close before New Year's.'

Was that true? Was it really Spencer on the phone just now? If it was a lie, it came easily. She bit her lip. 'Is there something going on, Hugh?'

He opened his eyes. 'What do you mean?'

'I don't know, you seem …' She swallowed. 'Stressed.'

He shook his head. 'It's just the deal. Spencer's worried it's going to fall through.'

She scrutinised his face for evidence he was lying, but found nothing. She sighed. 'I'll get you a Panadol.'

'Not for me, thanks,' Carmen said, when Issy offered her a gin spritz once she'd finished her lemonade. 'I'm the designated driver today.'

It was only then that Issy started to suspect there was a reason she wasn't drinking. As the conversation flowed around her, Issy wondered. Had Carmen put on a little weight? Possibly, although it was hard to tell under the shapeless chiffon kaftan she wore. She did seem a little fuller in the face. She also hadn't touched the soft cheeses or the prosciutto. And then there were the little glances Issy had noticed between Marshall and Carmen. Surreptitious glances between people who shared a secret.

Marshall was on to his fourth beer when he cleared his throat. 'We have some news,' he said, taking Carmen's hand. He paused for effect with a dopey smile on his face, a less handsome version of his brother's.

'Well?' Issy prompted, although she knew what was coming. 'Don't keep us in suspense!'

Hugh looked clueless.

'Carmen's pregnant!' Marshall said, beaming.

Carmen nodded and put a hand on her belly. 'We're having a baby.'

'I knew it!' Issy said. 'How exciting!' She reached out and squeezed Carmen's hand, her mind racing with questions she wanted to ask—none of them appropriate. Was this why they'd got back together? What a disaster! 'How far along are you?' she asked instead as Hugh pulled his brother into a hug.

Once the excitement subsided, Hugh and Marshall went out onto the balcony, beers in hand, leaving Issy and Carmen alone.

'This calls for bubbles!' Issy said, already opening a bottle of Veuve.

'Pour me a tiny one so I can pretend,' Carmen said.

Issy poured two glasses and sat back down on the sofa next to Carmen.

'Cheers!' Issy clinked her glass against Carmen's. 'To your little one! And to you and Marshall, who will make wonderful parents!' She wasn't actually sure what sort of parents they'd make. She'd never heard them mention having children before. Clearly this whole situation was an unfortunate accident.

Carmen took an imaginary sip. 'Thank you, Issy. We're just thrilled.'

'You guys are good now, then?' Issy asked.

'Me and Marshall?'

'All the problems are behind you now. That's great news.'

Carmen narrowed her eyes. 'Problems?'

Crap. She'd put her foot in it. She obviously wasn't supposed to let on that she knew about their recent relationship dramas, but she had a nice buzz from the gin and, what the hell, they were going to be sisters-in-law. Carmen wasn't exactly Issy's first choice, but she would have to do.

'Oh, you know,' Issy said, keeping her voice light, as though it was no big deal. Every relationship has its rough spots! 'Hugh mentioned things were a bit rocky for a while there between you two.'

Carmen cocked her head to one side, as though she was still confused. It was very convincing. If Issy didn't know the truth, she would probably have believed her. She obviously wasn't ready to go there, which was fine.

Issy sighed and changed the subject. 'Are you and Marshall going away over summer?'

'Why didn't you tell me they were back together?' Issy asked as Hugh closed the door behind them.

'Who?' he asked, walking back up the hall. She followed him.

'Marshall and Carmen!'

He took another beer from the fridge, popped the top and took a long swig, then looked blankly at Issy, who was still waiting for an answer.

'Hugh?'

'I never said they'd broken up,' he said, but he was frowning slightly, as though he suspected he'd been caught in a lie.

Issy frowned. 'Yes, you did.' Didn't he?

'I just said they had an argument.'

Issy rifled back through her memory of the night she'd arrived home from the fundraiser, when Hugh had said he was on the phone to Marshall. She knew he'd lied. It wasn't Marshall on the phone when Issy arrived home, but he *had* spoken to his brother earlier that night. The dialled numbers log had confirmed that. She'd assumed the relationship dramas were legit.

'When I asked Carmen about it, she denied it.'

'Why the hell were you talking to Carmen about it?'

'Sorry, I was just trying to have a proper conversation!'

'Don't go telling Carmen stuff Marshall says to me.' He held her gaze for a moment too long, then shook his head, as though she'd disappointed him. 'I'm going to take a shower.'

She rubbed her face. Was anything Hugh said true? He was constantly slipping out of rooms to take calls. Like earlier: one minute he'd been sitting on a barstool at the island bench making a Spotify playlist, the next his phone rang and he'd disappeared.

Her head was throbbing now. This was why she hated day drinking—it always left her feeling groggy and slightly depressed. She needed to rehydrate.

As she filled a glass with water, she noticed Hugh's phone sitting on the bench and considered checking it again.

And then it lit up, flashing silently.

George Mobile.

Her heart raced as she swiped to answer. She said nothing.

'Hugh?' a husky voice said.

Issy's heart pounded. George was a woman. A very young woman, from the inflection in her voice.

'Hello?' the voice said. 'Hugh?'

Something stirred in Issy's subconscious. Thinking of the waitress at Kilmore yesterday, she closed her eyes, summoning the scene in the lounge room right before they sat down for lunch. Her mother's words echoed in her mind: *'Tell the caterers we're ready for lunch. Thank you, Georgie.'*

Issy inhaled sharply, stunned by the clarity of the revelation. 'George' was the waitress.

'Are you there, Hugh?' the voice on the phone said, as the sound of running water in the bathroom stopped.

Issy hung up, carefully placing the phone back where it was, then she spun around and opened the fridge, pretending to search for something.

Hugh appeared, his hair wet from the shower, a towel around his waist. 'Have you seen my phone anywhere?'

'I saw it on the bench,' she said, without turning around.

'Thanks.' He left the room again, phone in hand.

Chapter 35

'I didn't think you were coming back,' Georgie said, a Coke in each hand. She put them on the table and sat down opposite Meg in a dark corner of the Red Lion. Georgie was on her lunch break.

Meg shrugged. 'Just have a few loose ends I need to follow up,' she said vaguely. She didn't want to tell Georgie what Pete had discovered about the houses on Barton Drive. Instead, Meg told her about the confrontation with Jenny on Christmas Day as Georgie sipped her Coke through a paper straw.

'So, we're cousins?'

'Until we get the DNA results, we can't say for sure. But, yeah, Mum's reaction makes me think we are.'

'When will we get the results back?'

'Don't know,' Meg said. Georgie had done the test before Christmas. 'A week or so?'

A waitress delivered hamburgers.

'Do you think we should tell your mum?' Meg asked.

'Nah.' Georgie picked up the burger, barbecue sauce running down her hand. 'Not yet.'

'Why not?'

'You need to find out what happened before you tell her. You know Jenny is Anna, but you don't know anything else. You don't

223

know who your father is. You still have too many questions and not enough answers.'

Meg looked at her towering burger, considering Georgie's point. Maybe she was right. If there were too many gaps in the story, Chrissy might put her walls up even further. That was the last thing Meg wanted. But the urge to tell Chrissy what they knew was strong.

'Maybe Chrissy can help me find the answers I'm missing,' she said.

Georgie shook her head.

'Why not?' Meg picked up a knife to cut the burger in half.

'I don't want you ambushing her with all this.' Georgie pulled a piece of beetroot out of her burger, putting it on the side of her plate. She looked up at Meg. 'I dunno how much more she can handle.'

'What do you mean?'

'She's a wreck, Meg. She's working seven days a week at the café, but by the time she's paid the rent, the staff, the suppliers, there's nothing left.' Her eyes flashed with emotion. 'And Dad's not getting any better. He's in constant pain.'

'Can something be done to help him with the pain?' Meg asked.

Georgie abandoned the burger and slumped back in her chair. 'He's on oxycontin. It was prescribed by the doctor the Ashworths sent him to and now he's addicted. Mum's been trying to wean him off it, but when he stops, he moans most of the night in agony. She's basically working to pay for his medication at this point. That's why I'm working so much. I was going to study beauty therapy at TAFE, but we can't afford it right now. I'm giving most of my pay to her, but it's still not enough.'

Meg thought of the older girl in the Facebook photos. 'Do you have any siblings?'

Georgie nodded. 'An older sister, but she lives in London. She bailed when things got tough. Can't say I blame her, to be honest. It's not much fun around our place.'

'Chrissy's lucky to have you,' Meg said, feeling a wave of admiration for this young woman. And maybe just a tinge of jealousy. 'You really love her, don't you?'

Georgie shrugged. 'She'd do anything for us.'

'Is that why …' Meg hesitated, hoping she wasn't overstepping. 'Is that why you're doing OnlyFans?'

Georgie's face hardened.

'I saw the link on your Instagram,' Meg explained.

'I don't want your judgment, Meg.'

'I'm not judging.'

'It's just nudes,' Georgie said. 'Half the boys in this town have seen my nudes already after Charlie Cook sent them around when I was in year ten.'

'Do you make much money out of it?'

'Not yet. I'm still building my profile. Beats working here, though.' Her face brightened. 'Oh! I forgot to tell you, I worked at the Ashworths' place on Christmas Day. Heather and Malcolm's place.'

'What? You're just mentioning this now? How did that come about?'

'Heather was so desperate for a drinks waiter, she rang the pub to ask if anyone would be able to work on Christmas Day. I was happy not to spend it with Mum and Dad, to be honest.'

'I thought you hated the Ashworths.'

'I do, but I'd do just about anything for a hundred bucks an hour. Anyway, someone gave them DNA kits. The same as that one you bought for me.' Georgie told her about the gift bag addressed to the three Ashworth siblings and the awkward conversation that had followed. 'No one knew who put them there. They were all weirded out by it.' She popped a piece of gum in her mouth. 'I thought it might have been you.'

'Me? No. How would I have got them there?'

Georgie shrugged.

Meg frowned, thinking. 'Someone must know something. Do you think it could be to do with me and Mum?'

'Maybe. They're total pricks, though. If I were you, I'd run a freaking mile.'

'Even with all that money?' Meg said.

Georgie stirred the melting ice in her glass. 'I wouldn't be one of them for all the money in the world.' Her eyes widened and she leaned in. 'Speaking of the Ashworths …'

Meg turned to see Isobel walking towards the bar.

Chapter 36

'She's on a break,' the ponytailed bartender said, when Issy asked for Georgie at the bar.

After the realisation had struck her—that *George Mobile* was Georgie-the-waitress—Issy had called her mother to ask her about the lovely waitress who'd looked after them on Christmas Day. She'd made something up about wanting to contact her regarding an upcoming event she was organising for the staff ('You know how it is, Mum! It's impossible to find good people!') and Heather had told her she would find Georgie at the Red Lion Hotel.

So here she was. Issy wasn't sure what she was planning to say when she came face to face with Georgie, but she strongly suspected Hugh was cheating with her, so she wanted to suss her out.

She followed the bartender's pointed finger and saw Georgie sitting at a high table in the corner with Meg, the academic. It struck her as an unlikely pairing.

'Issy! Hi!' Meg said, frowning, when Issy reached the table. 'Ah, this is—'

'Georgie. Yes, hello.' Issy gave Georgie a tight-lipped smile, then turned to Meg. 'We met on Christmas Day.'

'Hi,' Georgie said, flipping her long, tousled hair from one side to the other. Issy shuddered, picturing Hugh's hands in that hair.

There was an awkward silence. 'Do you want to have a seat?' Meg offered.

'Thanks.' Issy sat down. 'How was your Christmas, Meg?'

'It was …—' she searched for a word, '—eventful.'

Issy let out a little laugh, thinking of her own eventful Christmas Day. Meg and Georgie looked at Issy as though they were waiting for her to explain what she was doing there.

She cleared her throat, wishing she'd given more thought to how she would approach the conversation. 'Thanks for helping out the other day,' she said to Georgie.

'All good,' Georgie said, chewing gum.

'I didn't know you knew my fiancé, Hugh.'

Georgie frowned. 'Hugh?'

'Yes. You were talking to him after lunch.'

'Oh, he just came looking for another beer. I just know him from around here, you know,' Georgie said vaguely.

'So you grew up around here, then?' Issy asked.

Georgie nodded.

'Georgie's dad worked at the Ashworth Park,' Meg said.

'Really?' Issy replied.

Georgie nodded, unsmiling. 'For twenty years.'

'Wow, he must be one of our longest-serving employees. Did he retire?'

'Not exactly.' Georgie bit her lip, brow furrowed.

'Tell her, Georgie,' Meg said.

Georgie shot her a look.

Issy glanced from one to the other. 'Tell me what?'

'Georgie's father had an accident at work—'

'Meg—' Georgie interjected.

Issy frowned. 'An accident? At the hotel?'

'She doesn't want to know—' Georgie said to Meg.

'I *do* want to know,' Issy said. 'Please tell me, Georgie. I'm listening.'

Chapter 37

The sun was orange in the western sky as Meg pulled into the driveway of thirty-seven Barton Drive. Georgie sat in the passenger seat, looking pensive.

'You okay?' Meg asked, the conversation with Issy still front of mind. Issy had listened quietly as Georgie recounted the events surrounding her father's accident. The pitiful workers' compensation. His ongoing pain. The addiction that followed.

'Yeah, fine.' Georgie rubbed her face. She stared through the windscreen at the garage door. 'Did I tell you Mum and Dad got an offer for the house?'

Meg frowned. 'They did? Who from?'

Georgie shrugged. 'Dunno.'

'I didn't know it was on the market.'

'It wasn't.'

'Are they going to take it?'

'Nah, they won't be able to afford anything else in Hartwell and Mum's business is here so …'

'How much was the offer?'

'Two hundred and fifty thousand. Mum reckons that's low.'

'Interesting.' Meg made a mental note to tell Pete when she called him later.

Something was still bothering Meg about their conversation with Issy at the pub. There'd been a coldness in her demeanour at first when she'd asked Georgie about Hugh. Did Issy suspect he was cheating with Georgie? The sight of Georgie creeping away from that hotel room flashed in Meg's mind.

She cleared her throat. 'Can I ask you something?'

'Sure.'

'Is there something going on between you and Hugh Thorburn?'

Georgie looked at her, eyes narrow. 'What?'

Meg chose her words carefully. 'It's just … I think maybe Issy, you know, maybe that's what Issy thinks.'

Georgie scoffed. 'As if I would go anywhere near her sleazy boyfriend. He's older than my dad!'

Meg remained silent, feeling like there was something Georgie wasn't saying.

'Don't you believe me?' Georgie asked.

'I want to.' Meg's voice was gentle. 'But I saw something, Georgie, which left me wondering if there is something going on with you and Hugh. I wasn't going to mention it …'

'What?'

'I think you were with Hugh at the Red Lion—'

'I work there! Of course I've seen him there!'

'But you were upstairs where the hotel rooms are.'

Georgie glared at her.

'Georgie?'

She shook her head.

'What were you doing there?'

'I don't want to get in the middle of this.'

'In the middle of what?'

Georgie ran her hand through her hair. 'Look, Hugh *is* cheating on Issy, but not with me.'

Meg frowned. 'Who with then?'

Georgie shook her head again and reached for her bag. 'I can't say.'

'What? How am I meant to believe you if you won't tell me anything?'

'Okay.' Georgie sighed heavily. She stared out the windscreen as she spoke. 'I'm not having sex with him, Meg. I'm blackmailing him.'

'Blackmailing him? What the hell?'

'I ... found out he's been sleeping with someone. Someone he definitely shouldn't be sleeping with. I saw them go upstairs at the pub, that night when you saw me, so I confronted them. He offered me money to keep quiet. That's how it started.'

'How it started? So it's still going on? You're still blackmailing him?'

'I figured if he paid up once, he'd pay again,' Georgie said quietly.

'Georgie! What the—'

'I knew I shouldn't tell you!' Georgie opened the car door. 'Just pretend you don't know.'

What the hell was she thinking, Meg wondered, as she watched Georgie disappear inside the house. Blackmailing the General Counsel of Ashworth Property! She closed her eyes as her mind raced, thinking of all the ways it could backfire.

A wave of tiredness washed over her. After the break-in and her fight with Jenny and finding out now about Georgie's blackmail situation, she felt utterly exhausted. What a relief that there was a deluxe king room waiting for her just down the road at the Ashworth Park Hotel. Issy had booked it earlier after Meg told her about the break-in. She would order room service for dinner, she decided, followed by a long hot bath.

As she drove up Barton Drive, she studied the houses on her left. Most of them were empty now. It was easy to tell which ones had sold first, their front gardens were overrun by waist-high weeds. The houses which had sold more recently looked like they might still be occupied, but the junk-filled letterboxes and cobwebs around the eaves suggested otherwise. And now the Baxters had an offer too. What were the Ashworths planning?

Georgie had mentioned a dairy factory. Noticing a pathway running between two houses, Meg pulled over to have a look around. As she passed through the narrow corridor, a chill ran through her, despite the heat of the day—the strange sensation that someone was watching her. She rubbed her bare arms and looked around to see a bony, ginger cat crouching on top of the graffitied fence, eyeing her suspiciously.

She laughed at her paranoia as she emerged into the large concrete space that separated the residential area from two rows of towering steel tanks behind a tall wire fence. Heat radiated off the concrete beneath her feet. She wiped sweat from her forehead.

So, this was the factory. She turned back to face the way she'd come, looking at the row of mostly empty houses. What could the Ashworths possibly want with these properties? It was hardly an ideal site for a new housing development.

She followed the fence until she reached the HIGHLAND DAIRY sign at the entrance, where imposing boom gates blocked the driveway. Red signs warned there was no unauthorised access. Just as she was about to turn away, she noticed a man sitting in a small booth.

'Excuse me,' she said. 'I think I'm lost.'

He looked at her quizzically.

'Can you point me towards Barton Drive? I left my phone in the car and my sense of direction is terrible!'

'You want to go that way,' he said, pointing. 'You'll see an alley between two houses, follow the path and you'll end up on the street.'

'Great, thanks. What is this place? A factory of some sort?'

'Yep, dairy. Not for much longer though.'

'Is it closing?'

'Decommissioned from December thirty-first. We just got the email this morning,' he said. 'Nice of them to let us know. Put me out of a job.'

Meg looked towards the towering tanks and warehouses beyond the boom gate. What were the Ashworths up to? Did they own the industrial estate? That would explain why they were buying up undesirable houses on the south side of Barton Drive. Were they planning to bulldoze them, along with the factory, to make way for a flashy new development?

Could they do that? The land would be zoned as industrial. The rezoning process was arduous: applications to local council, community consultation. Unless … She thought of Tony Skelton, Hartwell Mayor and Malcolm Ashworth's mate. What had Tony done to fund his twenty-five acres?

When she reached her car, she called Pete. It rang once, twice, three times.

'Come on, Pete,' she muttered. Voicemail.

'Pete, it's Meg. I've just thought of something. Call me back ASAP.' She hung up.

She was still standing by the car, trying to decide what to do, when her phone rang. She was expecting Pete, but it was Rosedale. Her stomach churned with guilt. She hadn't seen her mum since Christmas Day.

'Is that Meg Hunter?'

'Yes.'

'Meg, my name's Michelle. I'm the new manager at Rosedale. I'm calling about your mum, Jenny.'

'Why? What's happened?'

'Look, she's fine. She's just been very agitated since your brother visited this morning. She's trying to tell us something but we're not sure what it is. She got quite upset—'

'Sorry, did you say brother? I don't have a brother.'

There was a pause. 'Yes, I'm sure that's—'

Meg felt a surge of irritation. 'Well, I don't have a brother.'

Michelle started back-pedalling. 'Right, sorry, I must have my wires crossed. He was here earlier today, before I started my shift. I thought Brooke said he was Jenny's son, but—'

'So someone visited her today and pretended to be her son?' Meg's voice trembled. 'Can you please find out who it was?'

'Of course, I'll call Brooke and check. Are you able to come, though? She's very upset.'

Ninety minutes later, Meg stood at the door of Jenny's room. Jenny had been sedated.

'What happened?' Meg asked Michelle, who stood by her side.

'She was trying to tell Brooke something.' Michelle's voice was a low monotone. 'When Brooke didn't understand, Jenny got angry and hit her.'

'Oh my God. I'm sorry,' Meg said. 'Is Brooke okay?'

'She's fine. Occupational hazard, I'm afraid. It's not uncommon in dementia patients. Has she been violent before?'

Meg nodded, recalling the visceral jolt of her mother's hands hitting her chest on Christmas Day.

'I haven't seen you here before,' Michelle said. 'Do you not visit often?'

'I've been away.' Meg prickled at the judgment in the woman's tone. 'Have you spoken to Brooke yet? We need to know who came to see her.'

'I left her a message.' The nurse checked her phone, shook her head. 'I'll try her again.' She slipped into the corridor.

Meg stepped closer to the bed. Jenny's face was loose, her pale lips slightly open, her soft breathing gently rhythmic. She seemed like a different person altogether from the one who had knocked Meg to the ground on Christmas Day.

A moment later, Michelle returned, brow furrowed. 'Ah, I'm not sure what's going on here. Brooke is absolutely certain that he introduced himself as Jenny's son.'

'What did he look like?'

'She said he was a tall, skinny guy with tattoos. Late thirties.'

Meg's frustration gave way to confusion. She shook her head. 'I can't think of anyone it could be. It's just me and Mum. We don't have any other family.'

Michelle shrugged. 'A cousin perhaps? Someone she knew before you were born? All sorts of people come out of the woodwork when people get sick.'

'Was Brooke in the room when this man was here? Does she know what they talked about?'

'She was finishing her round when he appeared at the door. She left them to it. We like to give families privacy.'

'Did Brooke tell you what Mum was saying to her, before she hit her?'

'Yes, it was something about money. "I took the money." Something like that. Brooke said she wrote it down. That can help sometimes, when patients are confused or agitated, it makes them feel like we're really listening.' Michelle went over to the side table by the armchair at the window and picked up a notepad. '"I should never have taken their money",' she read. She tore off the page and passed it to Meg.

'I should never have taken their money …' Meg repeated the words, trying to make sense of them. Had Jenny stolen money? Was that what all this was about? Was that what she'd been running from, all this time?

'It probably means nothing, love,' Michelle said. 'Dementia patients get very confused.'

Meg nodded, but something told her the nurse was wrong about that. She remembered the cameras at the front entrance. 'You have security cameras, don't you? CCTV? Out the front?'

Michelle nodded.

'I need to see the footage.'

Chapter 38

'Issy! My darling!' Rosa said as she opened the door at Kilmore. She pulled Issy into a warm embrace, just like she would when Issy was a girl. She still smelt the same, like bread and soap. When Issy was packed off to boarding school, Rosa became Heather's housekeeper.

'Hello, Rowie,' Issy said, feeling strangely emotional at the warm welcome. When she was a toddler she couldn't say Rosa, so she called her Rowie, which everyone thought was delightful. The nickname had stuck.

'My goodness, look at you! So beautiful!' Rosa stood back, smiling like a proud parent. 'Come in, come in. I'll make you a cool drink.'

Heather was flicking through a magazine at the kitchen table, immaculate in a white linen dress and a full face of makeup.

'Isobel,' she said. 'What an unexpected surprise.'

It was impossible to tell from her tone whether it was a welcome surprise or an unwelcome one. Maybe coming here was a mistake, Issy thought, but she needed to talk to someone about Hugh. She'd spent the morning lying in bed, her thoughts ricocheting between Hugh's cheating and Georgie's poor dad.

Still, she did wonder if maybe Georgie had all that a bit wrong. The more Issy thought about it, the less sense it made. Why would her parents abandon a loyal, long-term employee who'd had an accident at work? They had insurance for workers' compensation claims and her parents prided themselves on taking care of their people! They were generous with their time and money, unlike some wealthy families, who never gave a second thought to the people who worked for them. Just look at Rosa! Heather had pulled strings to get her three boys into Dalton Grammar and paid the fees—she'd mentioned it once, years ago. And Cathy! Issy had stumbled across her salary in a remuneration report once and nearly choked on a grape.

The more pressing issue, though, was what to do about Hugh's cheating. Her conversation with Georgie had done nothing to alleviate her concerns. Just the opposite, in fact. Georgie had definitely seemed uncomfortable when she asked about Hugh. But she still had no actual proof and she was dreading the inevitable confrontation. Hugh would just deny it all and make her feel crazy.

After going around in circles in her head all morning, she'd decided maybe Heather could help her make sense of things.

'Is this a good time? I need to talk to you about something.'

'Of course.' Heather rose from the table. 'We'll have tea please, Rosa, in the formal lounge.' Heather was disappearing through the archway on the other side of the kitchen before she'd finished speaking.

'Thank you, Rowie,' Issy mouthed, following her mother.

'What's this all about, then?' Heather asked, sitting down on the plump cream sofa. They weren't the kind of family who dropped over uninvited.

Issy sat down opposite, wondering where to start.

'I think Hugh's cheating on me,' she said as tears welled in her eyes, much to her horror. Heather hated tears.

The hint of a frown played on her mother's taut forehead. 'What makes you think that?'

Issy ran through the story, outlining all the reasons she felt Hugh was up to something: the night he spent at the pub and the pocket-dial voicemail with a giggly girl's voice; the suspicious phone calls and the lies about who he'd been speaking to; and the call from 'George', who turned out to be a young woman with a husky voice. It felt good to talk to her mother like this. She would know what to do.

When she finished, Heather moved to sit beside Issy on the sofa and took her hand. Her fingers were cold. Issy blinked back tears.

'Isobel,' her mother said. 'You've always been an idealist. It's a lovely quality, but it's your Achilles heel.'

Issy frowned. Where was Heather going with this?

'Marriage is not all candlelight dinners and walks on the beach. It's a union between two people to build a life together. There are choices involved. Every day.'

Issy felt herself stiffen. 'What are you saying? That I should marry someone who's cheating on me?'

'There's that idealism again.' Heather sighed and pursed her lips. 'There are many ways to make a successful marriage. For some, fidelity is very important. Others take a more … pragmatic approach and do what works for them. This doesn't have to be a deal breaker.'

Issy couldn't believe what she was hearing. 'Is that what you and Dad have done? Taken a pragmatic approach?' She thought of her schoolfriend Claudia's story about the woman Malcolm kept in the harbourside apartment.

Heather let out a little laugh. 'Darling, we wouldn't have stayed married for forty-nine years if we were idealists.'

Issy glared at her mother, a lump in her throat. 'Is that why you're so worried about the DNA tests?'

Heather held her gaze, eyes shining. Just as she was about to answer, Rosa came in with the tea tray.

'Sorry for the hold up,' she said, apparently oblivious to the crackling tension in the air between mother and daughter.

Chapter 39

It took a series of strongly worded emails and two phone calls—in which Meg mentioned her media credentials and implied she might write an exposé about unsatisfactory security at Rosedale—before she was granted permission to review the footage.

The security company had a small office two suburbs away from Rosedale. In the fifteen minutes since she arrived there, she'd discovered that the two cameras inside the facility—in the entrance foyer and the main corridor—were not in working order.

'So let me get this straight,' Meg had said, pointedly. 'The cameras are there to create the *illusion* of security, rather than to provide *actual* security?'

The manager had shifted from one foot to the other. 'They're being fixed this week.'

'I'm sure they are,' Meg replied.

He'd excused himself in a hurry.

Now, Meg sat beside a sweaty security officer who had been tasked with taking her through the grainy footage from the camera above the main entrance. The officer, who was clearly irritated by the disruption to his standard duties, sped through the blurry footage, communicating mainly in grunts.

Meg watched the time stamp in the corner of the screen. Brooke, the nurse who had been working in Jenny's wing on Thursday, had narrowed down the time of the visit to the hour between three and four.

'Slow it down, please,' Meg said, when the time flipped over to 2:50. An extra ten minutes on either side made sense. Each time a person appeared on the screen, approaching the front door in jerky movements, the officer would pause the grainy footage to give Meg a better look.

A middle-aged woman with three kids in tow.

A slight, wiry man pushing an elderly woman in a wheelchair.

A young couple, hand in hand.

Meg sighed and waved him on, watching the minutes elapse, devoid of activity, until the clock flicked over to four.

The officer hit stop. 'Nothing there,' he said, as though he knew the exercise was a waste of his time.

'Please,' Meg said. 'Please, can we just watch a bit more?'

'I don't have all day to sit here looking for someone who might not exist.' He stood.

'The nurse may have been mistaken! She said she *thought* it was between three and four. She didn't say she was certain. Please can we just watch until four thirty?' She paused, waiting for him to cave. 'Rosedale management won't be happy if they find out two of their cameras are broken.'

He said nothing.

'Did I mention I'm a journalist? I write for *News Day Online*.'

He glared at her, sniffed loudly and sat back down. Without a word, he pressed play, then sped through the footage and picked up where they left off.

The timestamp said 4:26 when a man walked into the frame, head down, hands in pockets.

'Stop!' Meg leaned forward, straining to make sense of the image, trying to create detail where there was none. 'That's him.'

The officer paused the tape. The man was tall and thin with hunched shoulders, like someone who was trying to make themselves smaller. His face was obscured, but there was something about his lanky build that felt familiar. Meg searched her mind but came up blank. 'Can you move through the frames, please, one at a time? I need to see his face.'

He moved the tape forward, frame by frame.

Come on. Look up. She held her breath, hope sinking. Then, just as he was about to step through the door and disappear, he glanced up, making eye contact with the camera.

She inhaled sharply, leaned in closer. Even the officer seemed to sit up straighter in his chair.

The footage was blurry, but one feature was clear: the black earrings which encircled large holes in the man's lobes. Ear tunnels, Meg recalled, not sure where she'd heard the term.

'I've seen that guy before,' she whispered. Where, though? 'Is it possible to print that?'

The officer hit a button and a printer whirred to life behind them. Meg searched her mind. Was he a friend of Jay's? She tried to picture some of the losers she'd found asleep on her couch. No, that wasn't it. The officer reached for the page and put it on the desk in front of her. The image was even grainier in print than it was on the monitor. She leaned forward and took a photo of the screen with her mobile phone.

'At least you found something,' the officer said, standing up. 'I really gotta go.'

'Thanks,' Meg said.

She looked back at the printed page and inhaled sharply.

She knew where she'd seen him.

Meg drove towards Rosedale, thoughts reeling. Hopefully her mum would be awake now. Maybe she could shed some light on what had happened—if today was a good day. As Meg waited for a break in the seemingly endless traffic on Parramatta Road, she thought of the strange man. The shady way he held himself, lurking rather than walking, glancing surreptitiously at the camera overhead. What had he said to Jenny? Meg said a silent prayer for her mother to be lucid when she reached Rosedale, even though she didn't believe in God.

Her stomach churned. She had a bad feeling about this. Something must have scared Jenny. She put a hand to her chest, where her mother's hands had struck her on Christmas Day. Jenny was scared. That's why she'd hit out at her. Something in that Pandora's box of past secrets Meg had wrenched open had terrified her. That's why she'd gone to such extreme lengths to escape it. She must have been scared again, after the man had left, and frustrated as she tried to tell the nurse.

I should never have taken their money. Those were Jenny's words, written down by the nurse. What did it mean? If Jenny had robbed the Ashworths, why would they send someone here, now? Why would they care about something that happened such a long time ago? The poor woman was losing her mind, literally, in a care facility. She was no threat to them.

Meg exhaled loudly. First, her room was broken into. Now this. She couldn't make sense of it. The only thing she was sure of was that it had something to do with her presence in Hartwell.

Someone didn't want her there.

Jenny was sleeping. Meg sat by the bed for half an hour, wishing she could erase the last few weeks and go back to the time before she knew Hartwell existed. She wanted to curl up under her fluffy red blanket and hide from it all. From her mother's illness, from the Ashworths, from the lies Jenny had told her throughout her whole life.

'Mum,' Meg whispered, when Jenny stirred. She observed Meg with a faraway look in her eyes. 'Do you remember the man who visited you?'

Jenny glanced at the door, then back to Meg. 'Who?'

Meg showed her the printed page. 'This man. You don't remember?'

Jenny squinted at the grainy image. 'No,' she said, and closed her eyes again.

Chapter 40

Issy was still reeling from her visit to Kilmore when Malcolm's email arrived.

She'd been replaying the conversation with her mother over and over since she'd left the day before, dumbfounded by Heather's advice. Confiding in her had been a mistake. The visit had done nothing to reassure Issy that everything would be okay. Was her mother really suggesting she should overlook the cheating? It's one thing to forgive a minor indiscretion after fifteen years of marriage and three children, but to knowingly marry someone who isn't even faithful to start with? That wouldn't be pragmatic. It would be insane.

To make matters worse, that morning there was an article about Spencer and Hugh in the *Financial Review*. Hugh! Felix had sent her a photo of the article. She opened the image on her phone again and zoomed in. Her fiancé and her brother were seated side by side on a velvet sofa in an industrial warehouse with exposed beams and professional lighting. When had this photo shoot taken place? She bit her lip as she read the article.

Since joining Ashworth Property as a young lawyer with a
background in corporate property law, this rising star has enjoyed

a meteoric journey through the ranks to the most senior levels of
the business. His recent engagement to TAG heiress, Isobel, only
cements his central role in the family business.

Heiress! The rest was even worse.

She was reading the article for the third time when she got another text from Felix.

Check your email.

She swiped to her inbox.

Sender: Malcolm Ashworth
Subject: Succession Plans

With a sense of doom, she clicked on the message.

Given I'll be eighty this year, I've decided the time has come for me to step back. None of us is invincible, after all. Even me.

I've made some key decisions regarding the future of the business. There's a lot of detail involved, but the long and short of it is that Spencer will take over from me as CEO of the Ashworth Group, effective immediately. Felix, you will have access to a line of credit to be used for start-up ventures and investments, once approved by the TAG board. Isobel, you will be Head of Marketing & Communications for the corporate office, effective immediately. Spencer will be appointed to the board, obviously, in his capacity as CEO.

Issy's heart pounded in her ears. What the hell was going on? How had all this been decided? When? There must have been numerous conversations between Malcolm and Spencer. Malcolm and the lawyers. Spencer and the lawyers.

Her phone rang. It was Felix.

She swiped to answer. 'What the actual hell is happening?'

'Dad's lost his mind.' He let out a cynical laugh. 'So I'll have to go to Spencer to ask for capital? How the hell will that arrangement work?'

'And he's sticking me in the corporate office with a fancy title but no actual impact on anything!'

'What a joke,' Felix scoffed. 'No prizes for guessing who'll take over from Spencer at Ashworth Property.'

Oh, she hadn't thought about that. The top job in the property arm of the business would now be open. 'Who?' she asked, not following.

'You think that article this morning was an accident?'

'Hugh?' she whispered.

'If I was a betting man, which I am, that's where my money would be.'

'But wouldn't he … wouldn't he have told me?'

Felix laughed again, a cynical snort. 'Guess not.'

Her thoughts spiralled. Felix was right. Now the article made sense! It was a strategic PR exercise designed to profile Hugh before announcing his new role to the market. How long had he known?

'You know what, Issy?' Felix added. 'Maybe you're better off outside of the business. Working with Spencer is a total nightmare. Why do you think I went out on my own? Some of the shonky shit I saw him do …'

But Issy wasn't listening. She thought of Heather. Had this come as a shock to her too? 'I wonder what Mum thinks? Maybe I should talk to her about it.'

'Go for it,' Felix said. 'Not that it'll make any difference—she'll just support Dad's decision. She always does.'

Chapter 41

Meg opened the door of her apartment, bracing herself for the sound of Jay's presence.

'Hello?'

Silence. She could smell him though. The stale smell from his room now permeated the hallway where the almost-dead peace lily had dropped leaves onto the floor.

It had been so late the night before, when Meg had finally arrived back at the flat, that she'd crept inside in the dark. She'd slipped out again this morning without seeing either of her flatmates, nor the true state of the place. She knew she'd need to face Jay soon, but right now, a confrontation was more than she could handle.

She hurried past his closed bedroom door, then past Gav's open one, towards her own room, when she stopped suddenly and retraced her steps. Gav's room was empty. Completely empty. There was no bed. No desk. No bike. Nothing at all, except some dust balls in the corners.

She fumbled for her phone.

Gav answered on the second ring. 'Meg, I was just about to call you—'

'What the hell, Gav?'

'A room came up at a mate's place—'

'Were you planning on letting me know?'

'It happened really fast—'

'A phone call, Gav! You couldn't find the time to make a phone call!'

'I was going to call you this arvo. I just moved out this morning. I'll pay you a month's rent, Meg. I just had to take it. I can't live with Jay anymore.'

She couldn't speak. Fury pulsed through her. Her head felt hot.

'Meg? I'm sorry, Meg. I'm really sorry.'

She took a steadying breath. 'Bloody Jay,' she muttered. It wasn't Gav she was angry at. It was Jay. And herself. She'd let this situation go on for far too long. What the hell was wrong with her? She exhaled loudly. 'What am I going to do, Gav? I need to kick him out, but he owes me a ton of rent.'

'I reckon he's got a stash of cash in his room somewhere. There's been constant randoms coming to the flat. I'm pretty sure he's been selling pot.'

It took Meg less than ten minutes to find a Quality Street chocolate tin on a high shelf in Jay's wardrobe. She counted the notes. Eighteen hundred and fifty bucks. It was less than he owed her, but she'd call it even. She would email the agent that afternoon to terminate the lease and sort out her own living situation later. She felt relieved at the thought.

She rolled the notes up and put them in her pocket, then she put the tin back on the top shelf and started back down the hall. A ripple of delight ran through her as she imagined the moment he discovered the tin was empty.

She barely dared to breathe until she reached Pete's place.

'Hunter, where the hell have you been?' Pete asked when he opened the door, relief in his voice.

She hadn't spoken to him since before she'd visited the factory. She'd sent him a long, garbled voice memo while she drove to Rosedale after getting the call from Michelle, explaining her theory. Since then, she'd been so busy she hadn't returned his calls.

'The Ashworths sent someone to visit Mum.'

'What?'

He opened a Corona for her as she told him about the ear tunnels guy on the security footage, who she'd seen in Hartwell with Hugh Thorburn.

'Bloody hell,' he said when she finished the story.

'Do you think Mum committed some sort of crime when she worked for the Ashworths?' She'd told him all about Anna and Chrissy and the box of belongings with the locket and the pen after her disastrous Christmas Day.

He frowned, trying to make sense of it. 'How would they know you have any connection to Anna?'

'I don't know.' Meg sighed. 'And even if they did, why would they care about something that happened so long ago? It makes no sense.'

Meg thought of all those years her mum had spent uprooting their lives every six months or so, paranoid, running from something. 'Maybe Mum *thinks* it has something to do with her own past, but really it doesn't. Maybe it's about us, Pete. A way to scare us off the story.'

'You think they know you've been poking around at the industrial estate? They could be trying to scare you off so they can get on with their dodgy deals.' Pete rubbed his stubbly chin. 'It's a classic standover man tactic, I guess. Threaten a vulnerable family member—'

Maggie sat up suddenly and let out a low growl.

'What's up, girl?' Meg stroked her, calming her again. 'You're okay.' She looked back at Pete. 'Did you find out anything more about the factory?'

Pete nodded. 'I was just working on that. The industrial estate changed hands a couple of years ago, on the quiet. It was purchased in a trust—'

'Any of the same names as the Barton Drive properties?'

'No, I was hoping that too. It's called Argus Investments.'

'So we don't know who bought it?'

'Not at this stage, but it turns out that the Argus trust was set up by our friends at Purcell Partners.'

'You're kidding—'

There was a loud smash.

'What the hell?' Pete exclaimed.

Maggie ran down the hall, barking incessantly. They followed. Pete turned on the light as they went into his bedroom.

'Oh my God.' His voice was a low whisper.

The front window was smashed, jagged glass revealing the dark night outside. A brick sat on the carpet beneath the window, surrounded by shards of glass. He rushed to the window, head whipping one way then the other, looking up and down the street.

Meg's heart raced. 'It's them, Pete.'

Maggie paced, whining.

Meg pulled her back so she didn't step on the glass. 'It's them.' Her heart hammered in her chest. 'They must know we're on to them, Pete. We need to drop the story.'

'No.' He turned to face her, shaking his head. 'This means they're rattled, Meg. This must be bigger than we thought. This means we need to go harder.'

Chapter 42

'Did you know about this?' Issy asked, when her mother answered the door.

'Hello, darling, how lovely to see you again,' Heather said.

Issy pushed past her and charged up the hall to the kitchen. She turned to face her mother, who looked entirely unflustered. 'Well? Did you?'

'I assume you're talking about your father's email?'

'You assume correctly,' Issy said, trying not to roll her eyes at the charade. 'Were you aware that Spencer and Dad had been making succession plans?'

'Darling, you know how your father is with business. I try to stay right out of it.'

'This isn't business. This is your family's future. It's a bit different, don't you think?'

'Your father's an astute businessman, Isobel, with excellent judgment. He hasn't built this business from the three hotels he inherited to a multinational hotel and property group through luck alone. Who am I to question his judgment?'

Issy stiffened. 'Are you saying you agree? That Spencer should take over the entire Ashworth Group? And Felix and I should be in positions where we essentially report to him?'

'Don't be so melodramatic, Isobel. That's not what your father means. It's just a structural thing. Someone must head up the business. Spencer and Felix tried to work together years ago and look how that went! Can you imagine what a disaster it would be for the three of you to share the role? God help us. The Ashworth Group would be run into the ground in a matter of months! I think it's safe to say that none of us want that!'

'He led me to believe that I was next in line for the COO role. Instead, I'm stuck as Head of Marketing and Comms, which is basically a glorified way of saying event planner.'

'But you're so good at it, Isobel! One of the keys to a successful life—'

Issy braced herself for one of her mother's pearls of wisdom.

'—is knowing what you're good at and sticking to it. That's why I stay out of all this. I don't have a head for business.' Heather took Issy's hands. 'Focus on the wedding, darling. Before long, you'll be having a family. You won't want more responsibility than that. Family comes first.'

'But I've got ideas about the business, about its future and—'

'You'll still be able to contribute those in the marketing role.' Her mother's tone was placating, as though she was talking to a deluded child.

'But—'

Heather pressed her lips into a thin line. 'Look, Isobel, I wasn't going to say this, but you *are* still very young.'

'What do you mean by that?'

'Just that I can understand why he might not think you're ready for more responsibility.'

'What? Why?'

'Your judgment has always been a little … off.' Heather narrowed her eyes. 'Hasn't it?'

Issy inhaled deeply, steadying herself. 'What do you mean?'

'I know you'd prefer us all to pretend the accident never happened,' Heather said, 'but it did happen.' Her eyes flashed. 'Just ask Stella Austin.'

The mention of the name, unspoken between them in the decade since that terrible night, felt like a punch in the stomach.

'But, it wasn't … it wasn't my fault. It was the rain, the wet road—'

'Nonsense!' Heather's voice was sharp. 'I'm happy to pretend, Isobel, but don't think I don't know.' She glared at Issy, her cold blue eyes daring her daughter to argue.

As Issy stared at her, she was filled with a deep hatred, thrumming through her veins to every cell of her body. She imagined grabbing her mother by her hair, slapping her, clawing at her perfect face. She swallowed, then spoke instead.

'I did the DNA test.'

Heather's face twitched, then stilled. 'You didn't.'

Issy nodded, shocked by how much pleasure she was getting from watching her mother struggle to conceal her horror. 'Do you want to tell me what it's going to reveal? Or keep me in suspense until I get the results?'

Heather shook her head. 'You're a naive fool.'

Issy laughed.

'You were never very good at maths, Isobel, but even you won't be laughing if your inheritance ends up divided by more than three.'

Chapter 43

Someone followed me, Meg thought, as she opened her eyes, soft morning light illuminating the lounge room. It was the only explanation. They knew where her mother lived. They knew where Pete lived. How else could they know those things? She never posted anything personal on social media. She wasn't one of those morons who paraded her life online for anyone to see. Someone must have followed her. It was the only explanation that made sense.

She looked at Pete, who lay on a makeshift mattress on the floor, his chest rising and falling with the rhythm of sleep, dark hair just visible from beneath the quilt. After the brick incident, they'd agreed it was best for him to sleep in the lounge room. His DIY skills and building materials had come in handy to secure the house. He'd boarded up the window with plywood and put a lock on the outside of the bedroom door so they could lock it from the hall. It was a flimsy one he'd bought for the bathroom he was currently renovating—if someone wanted to get in, they probably could—but they told each other it would be fine. That the brick was just meant to scare them.

She got up and made coffee, hoping the sound of movement would wake Pete, but when she returned, a mug in each hand, he was still a stationary lump under the quilt.

'Pete,' she whispered. 'I made coffee.'

He stirred, a lazy hand scratching his messy hair, then sat up. 'D'you sleep okay?'

'Yeah, all things considered. You?'

'It'll take more than a brick through the window and a lumpy bed to keep me awake.' He yawned, scratching his bare chest. 'I'm an Olympic-level sleeper.'

'I noticed that.' She took a sip of her coffee. 'I've been thinking … someone must be following me.'

'You think?' he replied, reaching for the other mug.

'Ear tunnels guy. He must have followed me from Hartwell when I drove to Rosedale the day before Christmas Eve.'

'You reckon this guy is working for Ashworth Property?'

'Yep, I think they want to drive me out of Hartwell.' She thought of Dan James, the peace-loving yogi protester she'd found on Instagram. 'One of the protesters who was arrested at the jail said he left town because he was sick of having his tyres slashed.'

Pete raised his eyebrows, took a sip of coffee. 'But how would they know you're here?'

'That day before Christmas, I drove from Hartwell via Rosedale to my apartment. When I saw it was a cesspit, I came here. He must have tailed me the whole way.'

'But how would he know you were here last night?'

Meg thought about that. It was two days since she'd received the phone call about Jenny and driven back to Sydney. He couldn't have followed her all that time, could he? Issy Ashworth knew she was going back to Sydney. Meg had texted her to change the hotel booking. She might have told Hugh. Innocently perhaps. Or not.

'Maybe it was a coincidence,' she said, eventually. 'The brick could have been for you.'

Pete rubbed his chin stubble, looking unsatisfied with the explanation. 'Maybe.'

She finished her coffee. 'I need to get going.'

'Where to?'

'Back to Hartwell. I want to speak to Georgie about our mate.' Seeing Pete frown, she added, 'I saw her talking to ear tunnels guy at the pub. Maybe she can shed some light on what's going on.'

'Where will you stay? I don't like our chances of getting *The Times* to cover it.'

'I'll message Issy and see if she's still happy for me to stay at the Ashworth Park.'

As she drove towards Hartwell, Meg's mind travelled through the events of the last few weeks. So much had changed since she'd first made this trip. What if her mother had never mentioned Hartwell? Meg might have lived her whole life oblivious that the answers to the questions about her family lay just ninety minutes down this three-lane motorway. Would that have been better or worse?

The brick had left her rattled. It was so explicit, so brazen, so clearly intended to intimidate. She'd always regarded her mother's suspicious nature as slightly unhinged, but what if it wasn't? What if Jenny's fears were well founded? The memory of Christmas Day flashed in her mind, as it had so many times over the past few days, only this time it felt different. This time, Jenny was the victim. Meg's gifts were hand grenades she had lobbed carelessly into her mother's lap, unaware of the damage they could do.

Meg sighed. Had she been wrong to ambush her mum with the pen and the locket like that? Maybe. Actually, where *was* the locket? She hadn't seen it since she took it from the table on Christmas Day.

What had she done with it? She'd been so shaken, so furious about the never-ending lies, that she couldn't remember.

Dread settled in her stomach like a stone. Had she lost the only thing she had that was real?

She pulled onto the shoulder of the road and reached for her bag. She took out her laptop, then tipped the bag upside down, shaking it until her belongings covered the passenger seat, and clawed through the pile of crap. Her card wallet, old car-park tickets, keys, headphones, sunglasses, petrol receipts, Blistex, loose Tic Tacs that had spilled in her bag. Ah, there it was. Thank God. The chain was twisted into a tight knot, but at least it was—

She inhaled sharply, reaching for a black disc that sat among her belongings. She turned it over in her fingers. It was glossy black on one side, silver on the other. What the hell was it? She squinted to read some fine engraving on the silver side: *iTrack*. Was this ... was this a tracking tile?

Hand shaking, she reached for her phone to google it. An Amazon page came up: *iTrack GPS tracking device for vehicles, kids, dogs, motorcycles. 4G real-time. Smallest and lightest. Unlimited distance worldwide.*

Her heart hammered in her chest. They weren't *following* her, they were *tracking* her, and she'd led them right to her mother. She thought of the break-in at the Red Lion the night of the gala at the Ashworth Park Hotel. The open door. The breeze billowing in through the window. Was that when this stalking device had been planted in her bag? Or had someone casually dropped it into her bag as it hung over the back of her chair at the pub?

She didn't know, but she felt sick. She needed to get rid of it. She wound down the window, intending to throw it out, but stopped herself just in time. If she threw it away, they'd know that she knew. What would they do then?

Slowly, she put the tracker back in her bag.

*

Once she'd checked in at the Ashworth Park, Meg pulled out her laptop. Her thoughts had been spiralling ever since she'd found the tracker. Who *were* these people? If they would use a tracking tile to intimidate a journalist and threaten her sick mother, what else would they do? She thought about Georgie's dad's accident. Was it before or after Chrissy had started the *Save Hartwell* Facebook group?

She googled the *Highland Herald* and typed *Chris Baxter* to search the archives. There were pages of results, but when she read the list she realised it was picking up any articles that mentioned a 'Chris' and the surname 'Baxter'. There was no advanced search option, so she waded through the results to find the ones that referred to Chrissy.

There were more than she expected. She ignored one about a charity event at the Apple Tree, a story about the Hartwell Spring Festival that quoted Chrissy as a local business owner, and a couple of others that were more of the same, before she found one with the headline, FACEBOOK GROUP UNITES LOCALS OPPOSED TO HARTWELL GAOL DEVELOPMENT. Yes, that's what she was looking for. She clicked and checked the date. Two years ago.

She messaged Georgie. *When was your dad's accident?*

The reply came quickly: *It was the week before my birthday, so it will be two years in March*

Meg swallowed. That meant Chrissy had started the Facebook group before the accident and it was already galvanising local opposition by then.

She typed *how to see date Facebook group was created* into Google and watched a YouTube tutorial, then followed the simple instructions

on the Facebook app on her phone to access the group history. A
ripple of adrenalin ran through her as she saw the date: six months
before the accident in March.

Thinking of Dan James with his slashed tyres, and the other
protester, injured in a motorcycle accident, she opened Instagram
to send Dan another message.

Chapter 44

All afternoon, Issy's thoughts went round and round in circles. Rereading her father's email, outrage pulsated through her. How dare he! Replaying the conversation with her mother, contempt burned inside her. Patronising cow! But she kept coming back to Georgie's father and her sheer disbelief that her family would leave a man in this town injured and out of work.

She was on her second bottle of chardonnay when she decided she needed a mental image of this man, Georgie's father. He was listed on Facebook as Robbie—broad shouldered, leather-faced, a twinkle in his dark eyes that made him seem playful, the sort of father who would watch the footy with a beer and take pride in the quality of his dad jokes. Nothing like Malcolm.

That night, she dreamt about the accident. The slick road, the heart-thumping skid as the car spun out of control, slamming into a wall. In the dream, she wrenched at the limp figure slumped in the passenger seat, but instead of Stella, it was Robbie Baxter she saw, his eyes empty and cold.

She woke with a jolt, breathless, her silk pyjamas drenched in sweat.

Her head pounded as the room came into focus. Outside, currawongs made their strange guttural morning song. She went to the kitchen, ran the tap and drank out of her hand. The empty wine bottle sat by the sink. She flicked on the kettle, cursing herself for drinking so much.

Again, she thought of Robbie Baxter. It must be a mistake, surely. A simple oversight. Maybe if she brought it to her father's attention, he would rectify it so the family had the financial support they needed and deserved. Although, on second thoughts, he would probably tell her to speak to Spencer about it. And if she raised it with Spencer directly, he'd just accuse her of terrible idealism, which everyone considered a fatal flaw in her character.

She took her cup of tea and sat on the lounge. Her laptop was open on the coffee table. She clicked on Robbie's Facebook page again and noticed a photo she'd skimmed past last night, when she was looking for pictures of him. He stood with a dark-haired woman, sea cliffs in the distance. Was that …? She enlarged the photo as much as possible. It was! It was the woman from the café. The woman who had turned Issy away on her first day in Hartwell.

Issy pulled into a parking spot in front of the Apple Tree Café and cut the engine. Inside she could see Georgie's mum taking chairs down off tables, setting up for the day. When she flipped the sign on the door from closed to open, Issy took a few deep breaths and stepped out of the car. Hopefully she would get further than the front door this time. A quick chat was all she would need to confirm her suspicion that Georgie had exaggerated the situation.

The bells jingled as she pushed open the door. Chrissy looked up, smiling warmly, but when she saw Issy, the smile disappeared.

'I thought I'd been clear—'

'Please,' Issy said, raising her hands, open palmed. 'I just want to talk.'

Chrissy pressed her lips together and gave Issy a sharp-eyed stare, then picked up a cloth and started wiping down the coffee machine.

'Georgie told me about your husband.'

'So?'

Issy cleared her throat. 'She said … she said he's not well. I just wanted to know if he's … okay.'

'No, he isn't okay.' Chrissy turned her back again and picked up a milk jug. A piercing sound filled the room as she frothed the milk.

'Is there—' Issy stopped.

Chrissy turned to face her, jug in hand. 'Is there what? Is there anything you can do to help? Is that what you were about to say?'

Issy nodded.

'Actually.' Chrissy put down the jug. 'There is. You could visit him. Twenty years he worked for your family, and not one visit after his accident.'

'Oh!' Issy swallowed. 'Okay, sure, let's arrange that.'

'Now, I mean.' Chrissy took her handbag from a cupboard behind the counter. 'I want you to visit him now.'

Issy wound through unfamiliar streets on the west side of town, following Chrissy's battered Honda, until they reached Barton Drive. She'd never been over this side of Hartwell before, with its characterless, blond-brick homes on tiny blocks.

Chrissy pulled into a driveway that looked just like all the others. Issy parked her Mercedes on the street in front, wishing she drove something less conspicuous.

At the front door, Chrissy fumbled with a set of keys as Issy scanned her mind for small-talk topics and came up blank. It was a relief when Chrissy eventually opened the door and stepped inside. Halfway down the hall, she stopped and raised a hand, telling Issy to wait there, then slipped into a dark room.

'Robbie?' Chrissy whispered. 'There's someone here to see you.'

Issy pictured the man she'd seen in the photos, awaiting his reply, but instead there was a moan, a mumbled voice.

She felt an intense urge to leave. She'd been expecting something else. She'd pictured Georgie's father propped up comfortably in one of those hospital beds with a remote control to move up and down, watching Netflix in a room with sunlight streaming through a window, not moaning in the dungeon-like space that lay beyond this door. This was something else entirely. She didn't want to be here. She didn't *have* to be here. She shouldn't have come.

She glanced down the hall towards the front door. If she was quick, she could be gone before Chrissy came out.

She was almost at the front door when Chrissy emerged.

'Isobel?' Her voice was like a knife.

Issy swung around, reaching into her bag for her phone. She held it up. 'Sorry, something just … I need to…'

Chrissy's eyes bored into her, pinning her down. 'I told him that you're here to visit him on behalf of your family.'

'I just, I don't know if it's a good idea—'

'Isobel,' Chrissy said. 'Don't do this to him.'

Issy took a deep breath and blew it out loudly. The tension in her chest eased just a little.

She stepped into the room, blinking as her eyes adjusted to the darkness. The only light was a soft glow around the edge of the heavy blackout curtains. Robbie lay on a single bed under a dark sheet. A fan whirred quietly overhead. He propped himself up on his elbow as Chrissy rearranged the pillows so that he was sitting more upright.

He reached out a hand, wincing at the movement. 'Robbie Baxter,' he said, his voice weak. 'Pleased to meet you.' His cold, smooth hand squeezed hers weakly. The playful sparkle in his eyes she'd noticed in the photo was gone. Now they were flat, lifeless. His lined face had a sunken look. He'd aged twenty years since that picture was taken. It was hard to believe it was the same man.

'Hi Robbie, I'm Isobel,' she said.

'Thank you for coming. It means a lot to me.' He took a deep breath, as though the effort of talking was too much. 'I worked for your family for twenty-two years.'

'Yes, such a long time,' she said, scrambling for something else to say.

Chrissy picked up a chair and put it by the bed. 'Have a seat.'

Isobel took a backwards step. 'Oh, no, I'm fine, I can't stay.' She turned back to Robbie. 'I'm sorry about your accident.'

'Can't win 'em all, can I?' Robbie gave her an ironic wink, as though he knew there was no chance of that.

'I guess not.' Issy felt a pang in her heart. This hardworking man was a husband, a father. He didn't deserve this. Emotion rose in her throat and she felt like she might cry. Flustered, she looked at her watch. 'I'm sorry, I do have to go.'

She turned to Chrissy. 'Thanks for bringing me and—' she paused, knowing she shouldn't say the words that were about to come out of her mouth, but unable to stop herself '—let me know if there's anything I can do.'

Chrissy glared at her, then followed her out the bedroom door into the hall. 'Don't pretend to care about us,' she muttered through clenched teeth when they reached the front door. 'Now get out of my house.'

Chapter 45

Meg sat on a swing waiting for Georgie at the park on Barton Drive, kicking the dirt beneath her feet as a light breeze rustled the gum leaves overhead. It was one of those depressing suburban parks, wedged between brick houses on a vacant block. A swing set. A slide. A cold metal seat for a weary mum to sit on. Someone had dumped an old couch by the fence. Yellow stuffing spewed out of a rip in its brown checked fabric and half-a-dozen empty beer bottles lay in the long grass beside a VB box. Even around the play equipment the grass was knee high, dotted with dandelions and wild daisies.

She held the tracker in her hand, turning it over and over in her fingers.

There was a crunch of feet on gravel and she looked up to see Georgie exhaling a plume of white smoke.

'Hey.' Georgie sucked on her vape again, then sat on the swing beside her. 'What's going on?'

Meg looked towards the road, checking they weren't being watched, then passed Georgie the tracker.

She looked at it closely, then up at Meg, frowning. 'Is it a tracker? Like an AirTag?'

Meg nodded. 'Found it in my bag.'

'What the hell?' Georgie whispered. 'Why?'

'Because I dared to ask some questions about the jail redevelopment. And I'm getting close to working out what's going on around here.' Meg gestured towards the strip of houses to her right.

'What are you talking about?'

'Who do you think's buying all these places?' Meg waited for Georgie to connect the dots.

Georgie's eyes widened. 'The Ashworths?' Her voice was low.

Meg nodded.

'Why, though?'

Meg shared her theory that Ashworth Property owned the factory and was planning to bulldoze it, along with the houses, to make way for a development of some sort.

'Dodgy pricks,' Georgie said when Meg finished, hatred infused in the words.

Meg pulled up the photo she'd taken of the CCTV footage. 'Do you know this guy?'

Georgie squinted at the blurry image. 'Yeah, that's Dean Morgan.'

'Who's that?'

'Just a local dickhead. Why?'

'He visited my mum in the nursing home, pretended to be my brother. And last night, someone threw a brick through the window of the place where I was staying in Sydney.'

'What the hell?'

'I think he's working for them.'

'The Ashworths?'

'Yep. And there's more. You know Dan James, the protester?'

Georgie nodded.

'I spoke with him just now. He believes there was a systematic campaign against him, retribution for his public opposition to the

Hartwell Gaol development. The other protester, a guy called Joel Hardy, was driven off the road while he was riding his motorbike and had very serious injuries. Dan reckons it was someone working for Ashworth Property who did it, and that was when he decided to leave town.'

Georgie shook her head, stunned.

'Ashworth Property are clearly using these intimidation tactics to scare and silence anyone who publicly opposes their developments,' Meg said. 'And it's got me thinking about your dad's accident.'

Georgie's head snapped up, a deep crease between her eyes.

'Your mum started the Facebook group six months before your dad's accident. Two months before the accident, there was a story in the *Highland Herald* about the group, naming Chrissy as the founder.'

Georgie swallowed. 'So you think ... you think they didn't give Dad fair workers' comp because of Mum?'

'It's possible.'

Georgie sucked the vape, her eyes distant, a frown playing on her face. A crow flew overhead, its mournful cry piercing the thick, still air.

'I'm also wondering ...' Meg said, 'how much do you know about the accident? About what actually happened?'

Georgie looked at her. 'He fell off a ladder. That's it.' She held Meg's gaze, glassy-eyed. When she spoke again, her voice was a whisper. 'Do you think the accident was ... not really an accident?'

'I honestly don't know, but it's possible. If they drove a guy off the road for protesting, who knows what they're capable of?'

Georgie closed her eyes, sending tears down her cheeks.

'I need you to tell me who Hugh Thorburn is sleeping with,' Meg said.

Georgie wiped her tears away and shook her head.

'Please. I want to use it to force him to tell me what's going on.'

Georgie glanced sideways. 'I thought you didn't approve of blackmail.'

'I don't. Under normal circumstances.'

Georgie looked away.

'Georgie?'

'I'm already in over my head with the blackmail stuff. I'm not getting involved in a fight with the Ashworths.' She stood up and handed Meg the tracker. 'They always win.'

'Please, Georgie,' Meg pleaded.

She sighed. 'I can't.'

'Don't you want to find out what they did? To your father? To your family?' Meg's voice was sharper than intended. She took a breath and spoke softly. 'Please, just tell me the name. I won't say you told me.'

Georgie shook her head. 'They always win, Meg.' She looked at the time on her phone. 'I gotta go. You got something to do tonight?'

Meg frowned, then remembered it was New Year's Eve. 'I'm just going to order room service and watch telly in my king size bed.'

'By yourself?'

Meg nodded. 'I'll pick up a bottle of Champagne to make it feel a bit special.'

'You sure?'

'Yep. Honestly, I kind of love the idea of it.'

'Alright, have a good night then.'

Georgie stood up and walked away, but then she stopped and looked back at Meg. She seemed to be thinking. Then instead of walking to the path, she went to the slide and bent down. When she stood again, she held something in her hand. She walked back to Meg and gave it to her, a strange intensity in her eyes. Meg looked down at the flower in her hands. It was a daisy.

It took her a moment to understand, then she looked up, heart racing.

'Daisy?' she whispered. 'Daisy Ashworth?'

Georgie nodded, then turned and walked away.

Daisy Ashworth was on Meg's mind as she studied the Champagne range at the little bottle shop next door to the Red Lion. Meg had seen her across the room at the fundraiser, in a slinky white dress with cutouts in places only an eighteen-year-old could pull off. The moaning Meg had heard through the wall of her hotel room replayed in her mind and she shuddered at the thought that it was Daisy Ashworth with her aunt's fiancé, who was thirty years older than her.

No wonder Hugh had paid Georgie to keep his sordid secret. It was so callous, so cruel. Poor Issy. She deserved to know, but Meg had to keep the secret. For now, anyway. It was exactly the sort of leverage she needed. What else would he do, Meg wondered, to keep his betrayal from Issy? Would this information be enough to force a confession about the bribes?

She yawned, suddenly tired, and decided she wasn't in the mood for Champagne after all. A few beers and an early night was what she needed. Ideally, she would be asleep before the nine o'clock fireworks illuminated the Sydney Harbour Bridge.

She moved down the row of fridges to where the beer was stocked and reached for a six-pack, then weaved between shelves and stacks of wine boxes to the front of the store, catching her breath when she saw Issy standing at the register.

There was a beep as the attendant scanned Issy's bottle of expensive-looking Champagne.

'Got something fun planned for tonight?' the pimply guy behind the counter asked her.

'No, not really,' Issy said, flatly.

The attendant frowned at the unexpected admission. 'Oh, that's a shame.'

Meg turned away, pretending to peruse the vodka selection, listening.

'I was supposed to be going to Sydney with my fiancé, but I decided to stay here at the last minute,' Issy said, as though she wanted him to know she had options. 'So it'll just be me and my bottle of Bolly.' She laughed, an attempt to lighten the moment, but it sounded false.

Meg felt a pang in her chest and wished she didn't know about Daisy and Hugh. Before she had time to think things through, she turned around to catch Issy as she finished at the counter.

'Meg!' Issy smiled. 'Happy New Year!' She leaned in, kissing both cheeks.

'Happy New Year!' Meg said. 'Thanks for sorting out a room for me.'

'Happy to help,' Issy said, waving a hand. She glanced at the six-pack. 'Where are you off to tonight?'

'Nowhere, actually.' Meg hesitated. 'I'd love company, but Georgie's going to a party, and I don't really know anyone else …' She shrugged. 'If you're not busy, would you like to come around to the hotel? You probably have plans—'

'I don't actually,' Issy said. 'I'd love to join you.' She held up the bottle of Bollinger Meg had seen in the fridge for one hundred and nine dollars. 'I'll bring bubbles!'

'Great,' Meg said, feeling her Netflix-in-bed plans slipping away. 'Say six-ish?'

Issy's blue eyes sparkled. 'Perfect.'

DNA Sleuths Facebook Group

Natalia Gomez: Hi all, I've been contacted out of the blue by a man who matches me in the range of an uncle, and matches my mum in the range of a sibling. He's six years older than my mum. Could this be a mistake? We only did the tests for a bit of fun, now this!

Top comments

Mary Louise: DNA tests should come with a warning on the box! A bit of fun has a way of turning into something far more serious!

Fergus Schmidt: I dream of someone contacting me with news like this. One of your mum's parents must have had a child before they met.

> **Particia Pine:** Although the OP says a sibling, not half-sibling.

Wendy Turner: What lovely news **Natalia**! Whatever the story behind this match, you've found close family!!

Zelda Merlino: Does he match your mum as a full sibling or half **Natalia**?

> **Natalia Gomez:** Full sibling but she has never heard of him. Weird!

Zelda Merlino: How old would your grandparents have been when he was born?

Natalia Gomez: Both sixteen

Zelda Merlino: I have a theory about what might have happened here. I'll DM you now.

Chapter 46

As Issy walked through the dark carpeted corridors of the Ashworth Park Hotel, it occurred to her that Meg must have heard her talking to the shop attendant and taken pity on her. Why else would Meg invite her over on New Year's Eve? They barely knew each other. The realisation was mortifying—she wasn't used to people feeling sorry for her—but the truth was that Issy was so grateful for the kind offer that she didn't care.

Hopefully she hadn't appeared too desperate when she accepted the impromptu invitation—she was a little tipsy at the time. She'd had a drink (three) with Warwick and the subcontractors at the site earlier that afternoon to celebrate finishing the fit-outs. There were still some bits and pieces to do over the next few days—a minor plumbing issue here, a door handle there, and cleaning of course—but on the whole, it was finished. They'd made the deadline.

The mood had been jovial and she'd felt like kicking on, but the others were all heading off to New Year's Eve gatherings. The thought of spending the night alone had left her feeling strangely bereft and she'd momentarily contemplated going to Sydney, to one of the parties she'd turned down invitations to. Instead, here she was, standing outside room 114, holding a bottle of Bollinger.

'Happy New Year!' Issy said when Meg opened the door, handing her the bottle. 'Thanks for having me. I hope I'm not imposing.'

'Not at all!' Meg's response came a little too quickly. She popped the cork and poured the Champagne, passing Issy a glass and putting the bottle on the little bench above the mini bar.

'What shall we drink to?' Meg asked, holding her glass aloft.

'New friends?' Issy suggested.

They clinked their glasses.

Silence fell as they sipped their Champagne.

'I'll call for an ice bucket,' Issy said, picking up the phone by the bed. She made sure to mention her full name to the room service attendant who answered.

'Shall we sit?' Meg suggested, settling on the sofa.

Issy sat in an armchair and pulled her phone out of her bag, placing it face up on the coffee table in case she got a message from Hugh, who was spending the night on a yacht on the harbour. Or so he said.

'How's the room?' she asked.

'Perfect, thanks for sorting that out for me. It's very generous of you.'

'Happy I could help,' Issy said. She looked at the heavy curtains, which were pulled shut across the French doors to the garden. 'We should open the curtains. The view will be stunning at this time of the day.'

She went to stand, but Meg interjected.

'I'd prefer to keep them closed.'

Issy frowned at the odd intensity of Meg's tone.

'Sorry.' Meg bit her lip. 'After the break-in at the pub I'm just feeling a little … wary.'

'Fair enough,' Issy said, although it did seem a little paranoid. She took a long sip of her Champagne.

Another awkward silence was broken by the sound of the doorbell.

Meg got up and returned with an ice bucket and a cheese board loaded with brie, prosciutto, figs and crackers.

'Compliments of the hotel,' she said, putting it down on the table. She topped up the glasses, then reached for the cheese knife. 'This is a bit special. I'm not used to the VIP treatment.'

'Honestly, it's not all it's cracked up to be, cheese plates aside.'

'Really?'

Issy shrugged. 'It's ... complicated.'

'All families are complicated.' Meg wrapped a piece of prosciutto around a fig. 'What's that famous line? "All happy families are alike, but every unhappy family is unhappy in its own way"? Something like that. Chekhov or someone.'

'I'm not across my Russian writers, but it sounds accurate. How's your family unhappy, then?'

Meg let out a little laugh. 'I've recently discovered that everything my mother has ever told me about herself is a lie.'

'Wow, that's—' Issy searched for the right word, '—intense.'

'It was just the two of us, growing up. Just me and Mum. And now she's got dementia. I'm losing her and I don't even know her.' She stopped abruptly, her demeanour lightening again. 'I bet you can't beat that.'

'I'll give it a shot,' Issy said, galvanised by the frankness of the conversation. She had long-term friends who were never this honest about their lives. 'My oldest brother, Spencer, who is an absolute arsehole just between you and me, is taking over my father's company. If I want to keep working for the company, I'll be reporting to him. When I confronted my mother about it, she basically told me I'm a flake and that she understands why my father doesn't trust me. To make matters worse, I suspect my fiancé will be stepping up as the CEO of Ashworth Property, and now—' The words were tumbling out. How freeing it felt to tell someone all this! '—I'm starting to wonder if he even loves me or if he's just using me to embed himself in the family and the business.' She realised she was crying and wiped her eyes carefully, trying not to smudge her mascara.

Meg reached for a box of tissues and passed her one.

'Sorry, this must sound like a poor little rich girl sob story.'

'It doesn't, honestly.' Meg put a hand on her knee. 'It sounds awful.'

'I just … I just don't know who I can trust.' Issy took a shuddery breath. 'This is so embarrassing.' She wiped her eyes again, hearing her mother's voice in her head. *No one likes a crybaby.* She blew her nose and took a deep breath. 'I can't believe I'm crying. I never cry.'

Meg gave her a little smile. 'Sometimes it's just what you need.'

Issy sighed. 'I need to go to the bathroom.'

Chapter 47

Meg watched Issy close the bathroom door, feeling a little dumbfounded by the situation. She'd had some initial concerns about having Issy here in her hotel room—there was a tracking tile in her handbag, after all, placed there by someone working for the Ashworths, if her suspicions were correct. But any concerns she had were outweighed by the possibility that she might get some information out of Issy, about the plans for the dairy and Barton Drive. Now she suspected Issy was completely in the dark. Meg probably knew more than she did. It *was* interesting what Issy said about Hugh taking over Ashworth Property though—

Her thoughts were interrupted by the simultaneous flash of notifications on the two mobile phones sitting on the coffee table. She glanced at Issy's phone first, sticky-beaking.

It was a notification from Heritage DNA: *Click here to view your DNA profile.*

She looked at her own phone: *Heritage DNA: You have a new match.*

Meg looked at the bathroom door, which was still closed. With shaking hands, she tapped to open the link. It took her to a screen with two overlapping circles. In the left were her initials: MH. In the other: BA. Beneath that it said: *You and Bella Ash. Suggested relationship: Half-sibling. 23% shared DNA: 1865 Cm.*

Heart racing, she took a screenshot.

Bella Ash. Bella Ash. Bella Ash.

Bella. Isobel.

Ash. Ashworth.

They were Issy's results, under a fake name.

The toilet flushed and Issy returned, looking fresher. Seeing there was a notification, she reached for her phone.

Meg watched as the colour drained from her face.

Issy looked up, her eyes wide. 'I don't understand.'

'It's you, isn't it?' Meg whispered. 'Bella Ash?'

'Meg, please. Explain this to me.' Her voice trembled. 'What the hell is going on?'

'My mum was your night nurse when you were a baby,' Meg whispered. 'Anna. That's all I know. I only discovered this recently. Something must have happened while she was working for your parents.' Meg swallowed. 'Between her and your father.'

Issy shook her head. 'This can't be right.'

'DNA doesn't lie,' Meg said gently.

Issy slumped forward, her head in her hands. After a few moments, she looked up and frowned. 'Who are you? You're not an academic, are you? That story you told me about your PhD, that's not true, is it?'

'I'm … it's …'

Issy's eyes narrowed. 'Was it you who put the DNA tests there on Christmas Day? Under the tree?'

'Me? No! Georgie told me about them, but it wasn't me. Whoever did, though, they must know about this. They must want it to come out.'

Issy glared at her, blue eyes ice cold. 'This is about money, isn't it?'

'What—'

'I should have listened to my mother. You came here to set me up. You planted those DNA tests at my parents' house.'

'How would I—'

'Georgie was there. She could have—'

'I didn't—'

'You're a liar!' Issy rose to her feet, fury flashing in her eyes. 'Another freaking liar!'

Meg stood up. 'Issy, please, I can explain—' She put a hand on Issy's shoulder, but she hit it away.

'Stay away from me,' Issy warned through gritted teeth. She grabbed her bag and stormed out the door.

Chapter 48

Issy woke up on the first day of the new year with a splitting headache. She'd opened another bottle when she'd got back to the apartment and drank it alone, watching the fireworks on Sydney Harbour, wondering which of the yachts moored in front of the Opera House her cheating fiancé was on. And who he was with. When she'd tired of thinking about Hugh, her attention turned back to the DNA test results, the Venn diagram linking her and Meg. BA and MH. *Suggested relationship: Half-sibling. 23% shared DNA: 1865 Cm.*

To see her matches, her account had to be public, which was why Meg could see the result too. By now Issy had taken a screen shot and changed her settings to make the account private, but it was too late. Meg had seen the results. The damage was done.

Was it true, what Meg said? Had her father slept with the baby nurse hired to look after her? She knew Heather had struggled when she was a baby. She'd suffered so terribly from hyperemesis gravidarum while pregnant with Felix that she'd decided against having any more children. Heather had told her once that she was filled with dread when she'd discovered she was pregnant with Issy, which was a very confronting thing to hear your mother say. 'You take things so personally, Isobel,' Heather had said, when Issy was offended. When the difficult pregnancy ended, post-partum depression had begun, although her mother never called it that. It was 'a bout of the baby blues', which made it sound more like a bad mood than a mental illness.

If Issy was honest, she *could* believe that her father slept with the nurse. It was repugnant behaviour, with a sick wife and a tiny baby in the next room, but it was certainly possible. The thing she couldn't work out, though, was why Meg was here, in Hartwell. It all felt like a very unlikely coincidence and she couldn't shake the feeling that Meg had somehow set her up.

Eventually she'd gone to bed, hoping it would all be less confusing in the morning.

It wasn't. In fact, she only had more questions. She needed someone to help her make sense of it all. Not Heather, obviously. Or Malcolm. Who else might know what happened thirty years ago?

Rosa lived in a tiny stone cottage with a red tin roof and a pink magnolia in the front garden. When Issy arrived, she was sitting in a wicker chair on the front porch, sipping a cool drink. Issy watched her for a moment from the gate, second-guessing herself. Was she really doing this? Her questions would put Rosa in a terrible position—she knew that—but she was out of options. She pushed open the iron gate.

Rosa looked up. Seeing Issy, her face broke out into a warm smile. 'Issy, my bébé.'

Issy felt a warm glow inside. She loved it when Rosa called her that. It was like a little secret between them. She never said it in Heather's presence.

'Happy New Year, darling.'

'Happy New Year, Rowie,' Issy said. 'I hope you don't mind me stopping by.'

'Of course, of course. Have a sit with me.' She gestured to a spare chair. 'I'll get you a drink.'

'No, it's okay.'

'Darling, it's such a hot day. Let me get you a drink.'

'Okay.' Issy smiled. It was a joy to be cared for by Rosa. There was such confidence in the way she nurtured, every act infused with love. Issy breathed in the warm, sweet air.

Rosa returned, ice cubes clinking gently as she passed Issy a glass. Issy took a long drink, trying to decide where to start.

'I know about Anna,' she said, eventually.

'What do you know about Anna?' Rosa asked, quietly.

'She was my night nurse.'

Rosa nodded.

'She had a daughter,' Issy went on, 'after she left our home.'

'She did?' Rosa seemed genuinely surprised. Maybe she knew less than Issy thought.

'Her daughter is my half-sister.'

Rosa looked away, frowning, eyes distant. 'How do you know this?'

'She's here in Hartwell. We did DNA testing. We share twenty-three per cent of our DNA, which puts it in the range of a half-sibling.'

Rosa held her gaze, biting her lip, then she looked away, still frowning.

'What happened, Rowie?'

'I can't say.'

'Because you won't? Or because you don't know?'

Rosa closed her eyes and rubbed her forehead. 'All I will say is this.' She stared out at the street beyond the fence as she spoke. 'There was … an incident, which happened while Anna was living with the family.'

'An incident?' What did she mean by that? An incident? An incident which left a young woman pregnant? Issy swallowed, feeling suddenly off kilter. Did her father …? My God.

'Rosa?'

'I'm sorry, darling.' Rosa looked at her now, something vast and sorrowful in her dark eyes. She put a warm hand on Issy's bare arm. 'I can't talk about it. I've already said more than I should.'

'Why? Why can't you talk about it? I don't understand.'

'I can't talk about it anymore or my boy won't be able to stay in his school.'

'Your boy?' Rosa's boys weren't born then. How on earth could this impact them? What did it have to do with their schooling? 'Rosa, what does this have to do with your boys?'

Then it fell into place.

'Oh my God,' Issy said. Rosa's boys went to Dalton, the same prestigious private school Issy's father and brothers had attended. Heather had got them in, even though they weren't waitlisted as babies like all the sons of old boys whose enrolment was a birthright. Once Rosa's sons were accepted, Heather had paid the fees. The older two were at university now, but her youngest was still at school.

Thirty thousand dollars a year, times three boys, times six years.

Issy did a rough calculation. It was over half a million dollars.

'They did a deal with you, didn't they?' Issy met Rosa's eyes. 'They bought your silence.'

Chapter 49

New Year's Day usually made Meg feel hopeful. There was something so promising about the first day of a brand-new year, but today she could barely lift her head off the pillow. She lay in the oversized bed between the crisp cotton sheets, reliving the disastrous events of the night before.

After twenty-nine years, Meg had found a sister, only to lose her again. Issy hated her. And why wouldn't she? Meg had lied about who she was and what she was doing in Hartwell. She'd had no choice, obviously. She couldn't tell Issy she was investigating corrupt deals done by her family, but that didn't change the fact that as far as Issy was concerned, Meg was a liar.

Her phone flashed on the bedside table. *Pete.*

'Hey,' she said.

'Hey, yourself. Happy New Year, Hunter. You have a good night?'

'I drank Champagne in my hotel room with Isobel Ashworth.'

'Seriously?'

She told him about the DNA results, that Issy was her half-sister.

'Holy shit,' Pete said slowly, when she'd finished. 'What are you going to do?'

'What *can* I do? She hates me. She thinks I'm a liar. She wants nothing to do with me.'

'Could you confront Malcolm alone?'

'He'd just deny it. Bella Ash could be anyone. The results are useless without Issy's support.'

'Does this change anything?'

'What do you mean?'

'Well, if these people are your flesh and blood, are you still happy to blow the top off their corrupt property deals?'

Meg thought for a moment. 'It changes nothing. I'm more determined than ever.'

'Good, then listen to this.'

Meg ran through the plan in her head as she drove to the jail. It was time to come clean, to tell Issy the truth about Ashworth Property and hope she might believe her. But when she reached the spot by the towering jail wall where Issy's vintage Mercedes was usually parked, the space was empty.

The engine idled as Meg tried to decide what to do next. If she called her, Issy wouldn't answer. A text message would be pointless; Issy would ignore it. The only way Meg would be able to speak to her was to ambush her. She would drive the streets of Hartwell until she found that car.

She started working her way up and down the quiet streets, systematically moving from east to west. Fifteen minutes later, just as she was wondering if Issy might have left town, Meg caught her breath. There it was, parked outside a pretty sandstone cottage with a red tin roof. Issy was sitting on the front veranda with an older woman. Meg drove past, keeping her pace steady, and stopped far enough down the street that she wouldn't draw their attention. She adjusted her rear-vision mirror so she could watch them, and waited.

It was ten minutes before they stood, Issy towering over the tiny woman with dark curls and a kind face. Heart racing, Meg got out of the car and walked towards them. When they reached the gate, the older woman took Issy's hands, speaking intently, then pulled her into an embrace. They stood like that for a long time.

Meg stopped a few metres away, feeling like she was interrupting an intimate moment. When they parted, they both looked in her direction, sensing her presence. Issy's face was red, her eyes swollen.

Meg stepped forward, searching for words, but none came.

For a long moment, they all stood in silence, eyeing each other.

The older lady spoke first. 'This is the sister,' she said to Issy. A statement, not a question.

Meg and Issy both looked at her, confused.

'Yes,' Issy said. 'How do you know?'

The woman looked at Meg. 'You have your mother's eyes.'

Meg felt tears. She nodded, swallowing the lump in her throat. 'You knew her?'

'Yes. Anna. She was my friend.'

'Meg, this is Rosa,' Issy said. 'She was my nanny when I was a baby.'

'What happened?' Meg whispered.

Rosa shook her head. 'I've said too much already.'

'Please?' Meg begged.

'You tell her what I told you,' Rosa said to Issy. 'But I need you to go now.'

They watched as Rosa went inside and closed the front door.

Issy looked at Meg for a long time, then sighed. 'Come,' she said, opening the door of her car, motioning for Meg to get in.

They sat side by side as Issy told her what Rosa said. That there was 'an incident' while Anna was living at their home. Slow, silent tears ran down Issy's flawless cheeks as she spoke. The air between them felt heavy.

'An incident,' Issy said, softly. 'Do you think … do you think he … raped her?'

Meg recoiled at the word, nausea rising up in her throat. 'I don't know.' She took a breath. 'Issy, I need to tell you why I'm here in Hartwell.'

'It's because of this, isn't it? You knew.'

Meg shook her head. 'I'm a journalist.'

Issy frowned, still staring straight ahead. 'So the story you told me was a lie.'

'Yes. I stumbled across Hartwell because my mum mentioned it. It's true, what I said about her having dementia. She was confused. She thought I'd travelled from Hartwell to visit her. She called me Tina. When I tried to find out who she was talking about, who Tina was, I stumbled across the controversy about the Hartwell Gaol redevelopment. I pitched the story at work and they sent me down here to investigate.'

Issy turned to face her. 'But there *is* no story. We won the bid, did the redevelopment, and that's that.'

Meg bit her lip, wondering how much to tell her. There was something childlike about Issy, innocent, which made Meg want to protect her from the truth. She thought of what Issy had told her the night before, about Spencer being an arsehole, her father not trusting her and Hugh muscling his way into Ashworth Property, probably at her own expense. Maybe the only way she could make Issy trust her was to tell her the truth. The whole truth. It was a risk, but what else could she do?

'Well?' Issy prompted.

Meg swallowed. 'Issy, what I'm about to say will come as a shock but you need to listen.' Meg told her about the rumours that Lindsay councillors had been bribed to approve the Ashworth Property bid, about Mayor Skelton's twenty-five acres, which he bought shortly after the deal was done. She told her about the strip of houses on Barton Drive, which had been purchased through trusts they'd traced to Purcell Partners, run by Evan Purcell, who Hugh and Spencer seem to know. Meg showed her the photo on the yacht, and the tracking tile in her bag, and told her about Dean Morgan, who had visited her mother and possibly thrown a brick through Pete's window.

She ended with the final piece of the puzzle, which Pete had told her just an hour before. That the factory, which was now decommissioned, had been bought through a trust on behalf of Ashworth Property. Pete had spent New Year's Eve at a rooftop bar with Evan Purcell, who had loose lips after the three tequila shots Pete shouted him.

'According to Purcell, they're planning to bulldoze the lot and build a luxury golf resort,' Meg said. 'They've had it approved thanks to some help from friends in high places, even though it doesn't comply with the zoning laws.' Evan had mentioned the name of the State Government Minister for Planning. Turned out he went to university with Spencer and Hugh.

Meg waited for Issy to say something, anything, but she still stared out the windscreen.

'Issy?'

She turned to Meg, her face wet with tears.

'Do you believe me?'

Issy nodded. 'I left something out when I told you what Rosa said.'

'What?'

'My parents did a deal with her, bought her silence in exchange for putting her three boys through Dalton Grammar. Her youngest is in year eleven. That's why she won't talk.'

Meg looked at Issy. 'I'm the only one you can trust, Issy. We need to confront your father.' She swallowed. '*Our* father.'

Tears pooled in Issy's eyes. 'I don't think I can.'

'Why not?'

'You don't know what he's like.'

'You're right. I don't.'

The words hung in the air between them.

'Can I ask you something?' Meg said. 'Why did you do the DNA test?'

'Because I felt like everyone was lying to me and I wanted to know the truth.'

'You don't get to choose the truth, Issy, just because you don't like it. Please. Let's tell him about the DNA results, and what Spencer and Hugh have been up to. Let's tell him the truth.'

Meg waited.

Then Issy shook her head. 'If I do that, I'll lose everything.'

Chapter 50

Issy took a long sip of wine, enjoying the numbing effect as the alcohol infiltrated her bloodstream, anaesthetising her. She'd been waiting for Hugh for hours, dreading the inevitable confrontation, but impatient too.

Her head was spinning with all the things she'd learnt that day. Her thoughts kept circling back to Rosa. Why hadn't Issy asked the question? The most important question of all. *Did my father rape Anna?*

The words had formed themselves in her mind, but when she opened her mouth to speak them, she'd lost her nerve. Who was she protecting? Rosa? Maybe she didn't ask so that Rosa didn't have to admit that she'd concealed the rape of a young woman by a rich powerful man so that her boys could get an education she couldn't afford. Poor Rosa. She'd lived with the guilt of it for thirty years. The shame of knowing she'd made that choice.

But that wasn't *really* why Issy had avoided asking the question. If she was honest with herself—which she rarely was, it struck her now—she didn't want to know. What if the answer was yes? What then? What would she do with that? And what would it cost her? It was the same reason she couldn't bring herself to confront her father. When push came to shove, she was gutless.

Her phone lit up with a text message and she reached for it, glad to have a distraction from her self-loathing. It was from Nadia.

Babe! Can't believe it's taken me so long to send through this pic I took at your party. What a gorgeous family you have! Love to you and Hugh. Can't wait for the wedding!

Issy studied the accompanying photo. Hugh stood in the centre surrounded by Ashworths, his arms around Malcolm and Spencer. She was at one side of the group, severed from the rest of the family by the crack in her phone screen. The photo was a month and a lifetime ago. It felt like she was looking at a stranger. Someone who thought the ground beneath her feet was solid, blissfully unaware of the fault lines that ran beneath her, invisible but dangerous.

Her heartbeat picked up as she heard the growl of Hugh's 911 echo in the street below. She put the phone down and checked her reflection in the mirror by the door. The sound of his footsteps coming up the concrete staircase was followed by a knock.

'Honey, I'm home!'

He gave her an ironic, dimpled smile when she opened the door. There were lines around his eyes which made him look hungover.

'I thought you were coming back after lunch.'

'I was, but I saw a mate and had a few beers at Icebergs.' He pulled her towards him, pushing the strap off her shoulder and kissing her collarbone.

She moved away, straightening the strap, and went to the fridge. 'Beer?'

'Thanks.'

'How was last night?' she asked, taking the top off a Peroni.

Hugh shrugged. 'Yeah, awesome.' She passed him the beer and they sat on the sofa. He laughed. 'Marshall went home with one of the waitresses.'

'What about Carmen?'

'Carmen?' he replied, as though he didn't understand the question. He took a swig of his beer. 'Poor bloke, his life'll be over once that bloody baby arrives.'

Issy felt herself frown.

He saw it. 'What? You're not going to tell Carmen, are you?'

She regained her composure and shrugged, hoping it came off as blasé and disinterested. Cool. 'Of course not.'

She'd always been a cool girl—she'd inherited that trait from her mother. The kind of girl who didn't hassle her boyfriend. Who didn't make demands. The kind of girl who took things in her stride. She didn't get psycho about things. If you were a girl, you had two choices. She'd learnt that early. You could be a cool girl or you could be a psycho. That was the phrase Hugh used to describe his ex-girlfriends when he'd spoken about them, early in the relationship. Calculated, cautionary tales, Issy suspected now, designed to inform her what sort of girl she needed to be. 'You're so damn cool,' he'd say, when she waved away a change of plan, a late arrival, another boys' weekend. New Year's Eve in Sydney with your brother? Sure, whatever.

Hugh was saying something about getting his car towed after he parked it in a clearway, but she wasn't listening. She was watching him as he spoke, seeing him clearly for the first time.

'... I ended up slinging the guy three hundred bucks to take the car off the tow truck.' He drained the rest of his beer.

'Good one,' she said, sensing that was the desired response. 'Another beer?'

'Thanks.' He handed her his empty bottle. She checked the time on the oven clock as she took another beer from the fridge. He'd been home for half an hour, and he hadn't asked her a single question. Not one. Not, 'How have you been?' Not, 'Did you have a good night?' Not even, 'Have you missed me?'

She walked back over to the lounge and put the beer down in front of him. When she sat down she watched him, studying him. He didn't give a damn about her, it struck her now.

He met her gaze, frowned ever so slightly and lifted his beer towards her wine glass, which sat empty on the coffee table. 'Cheers,' he said.

She picked up the glass and clinked it against his, but said nothing.

'What?' he asked.

'I did that DNA test.' She watched his face, enjoying seeing his confusion at her defiance. He'd warned her against it.

He shook his head, raising his eyebrows. 'What the hell did you do that for?'

'Maybe I'm sick of lies. You want to know what the results told me?' She held his gaze, daring him to ask.

'What?'

'Turns out I'm not an Ashworth.' She didn't know where the lie came from, but it came to her fully formed. 'Mum must have had an affair, because my father's a panel beater from Canberra. I spoke to him. He worked here in Hartwell at the hotel for a while, thirty-one years ago.'

He scowled. 'What are you talking about?'

Issy just shrugged. Cool.

'It has to be a mistake, it can't be right.'

'It's not a mistake.' She swallowed hard. 'And I know about the cheating.'

His head snapped up. 'What cheating? You mean Marshall?'

'No.' She met his small, dark eyes. 'I mean you.'

Hugh's expression was indignant disbelief. 'I have no idea what you're talking about.'

'Don't lie to me, Hugh, you'll just make yourself look stupid.'

His face hardened. An accusation of stupidity was his Achilles heel. He'd told her that once as they lay naked in bed, in a rare moment of vulnerability. His father had been convinced Hugh was stupid, a fact confirmed when he missed out on law at Sydney by a couple of marks. According to his father, nowhere else was good enough for a Thorburn. He'd pulled some strings and after a year of engineering, Hugh had been offered a place in a Bachelor of Laws and a room at St Paul's College. But his father had never let him forget that he didn't get the marks to get in.

Issy couldn't read his face. At first, she thought he was about to cry, but then the set of his jaw tightened.

'I don't know what you're talking about,' he said again.

She slid the enormous solitaire off her ring finger and placed it on the coffee table.

He looked from her face to the diamond, then back again. 'I don't understand.'

'I want you to leave.'

'What? Issy, I don't know what's happened, I don't know why you're doing this. I love you!'

'No, you don't. You love Isobel Ashworth.'

'You *are* Isobel Ashworth! What the hell are you talking about?' Any softness in his eyes was gone now. She could feel the fury coursing through his body. He stretched his fingers, open and closed, making a fist. 'What the actual hell are you talking about? I'm too tired for this crap—'

'You can stay at the hotel until you've found somewhere else to live. I'll let Jeffrey know to expect you.'

'Please, Issy, please.' Tears spilled down his cheeks now.

She felt a twinge of embarrassment at seeing him like this. He reached out to touch her leg, but she flinched.

'Don't touch me.' Her voice sounded cold, even to her own ears.

He pulled his hand away and stood up, simmering with rage. As he walked past the door, he slammed his fist into the mirror, glass fragments smashing across the floor.

Chapter 51

That night, Meg decided she didn't need Issy or the DNA results. She'd lived almost thirty years without a sister or a father, and she was just fine. Georgie was right. They were arseholes. Entitled, spineless, greedy arseholes.

All that DNA stuff was a distraction from the reason she'd come down here in the first place. The story. It was bigger than sour grapes about privatising an old building. Much bigger. She and Pete were close, so close, to exposing years' worth of corruption at the expense of locals in this town. Their story would incriminate Spencer Ashworth, Hugh Thorburn and Lindsay Council, and probably uncover systemic corruption at Ashworth Property and at the highest levels of the state government.

But how could they prove what they knew? Pete had played Evan Purcell, plying him with shots and appealing to his ego to make him talk more than he should, but it wasn't enough to publish. They needed more.

She would call Pete tomorrow and come up with a plan, but first, she needed to speak to Chrissy. She was family. Real family. It was only right to tell her the truth.

*

The Closed sign was still up when Meg arrived at the Apple Tree the following morning. The day was already warm, the air thick with humidity. She knocked on the glass pane, looking to see if Georgie was there yet, but it was just Chrissy. She looked up, a slight frown on her forehead as she unlatched the door.

'I didn't know you were still here,' Chrissy said.

'Yeah, I'm … I'm still working on my …' She let the sentence hang there, unfinished, not wanting to lie anymore.

'You want a coffee?'

'Cappuccino would be great, thanks.'

Meg sat at a table close to the counter, watching Chrissy, admiring her fluid movements as she worked the coffee machine. There was some flicking and tapping, then the squealing sound of frothing milk.

There were footsteps outside and Georgie appeared. 'Morning,' she said.

Chrissy looked out from behind the machine and frowned. 'If you're up at this hour, Georgie, something funny's going on.' She looked from Georgie to Meg, then back at her daughter. 'What's the story?'

Meg looked at Georgie, who took her phone out of her back pocket and opened the Heritage DNA app. She tapped twice and put the phone on the counter, where Chrissy could see the Venn diagram, interlocking circles linking Meg and Georgie. *You and Megan Hunter,* read the text beneath. *Suggested relationship: Cousins. 12.8% shared DNA: 656 Cm.*

They watched Chrissy as she read the diagram. She looked up, dark eyes shining. 'You did a DNA test?'

Georgie nodded. 'I got the result a few days ago. Meg is your niece.'

Chrissy let out a loud sob, then another, resting her elbows on the counter and holding her head in her hands, her body shuddering with the power of the emotion.

Georgie put a hand on her back. 'It's okay, Mum, this is good news. This means Anna is alive.'

Meg sat quietly watching Chrissy cry, not sure what to do or say.

Eventually Chrissy looked up, studying Meg's face. 'I knew,' she said, taking a shaky breath. 'The first time I saw you, your eyes, I knew. They … I … And then you asked me about Anna and told me about your mother—Jenny, is it?'

Meg nodded.

'And you said she has dementia … I just … I couldn't bear the pain of it, losing her again. It felt … it felt like too much, with Robbie sick, and the pain my parents went through …'

'I'm so sorry,' Meg said.

'It was easier to pretend and hope you would go away,' Chrissy whispered.

'I'm so sorry,' Meg said again, crying silent tears.

Chrissy sat down at the table and stared at the wood grain.

'I'll make tea,' Georgie said.

When Meg felt Chrissy was ready, she said, 'Anna got pregnant while she was working for the Ashworths. There was an incident, apparently, whatever that means. Isobel Ashworth did a DNA test too. It says we're half-siblings.'

Chrissy looked up. 'Malcolm?' she whispered, her eyes hard.

Meg nodded.

'Did he assault her?'

'We don't know exactly what happened.'

'I want to kill him,' Chrissy said.

'You know what's even better than that?' Meg put her hand in her pocket, feeling for the tracker. 'Bringing him down, along with the rest of them. And I think I know how.'

Chapter 52

With just twenty-four hours until the launch, the jail—now rebranded as Hartwell Entertainment Quarter—thrummed with activity. Event coordinators holding clipboards directed staging consultants, audio technicians fiddled with sound panels and blew into microphones, and people pushing trolleys charged left and right with huge potted palms and striped market umbrellas.

Issy stood in the middle of it all and allowed herself a moment of self-congratulation. Her job was done. Well, almost. One more day, then she could leave Hartwell and try to regain some sense of control over her life.

She was overseeing the placement of tables and chairs when her father's Bentley pulled into the drive. She inhaled sharply. She knew he was coming down for the launch but hadn't expected him to turn up a day early, unannounced. She wiped her sweaty brow and looked down at her grey T-shirt and denim shorts, wishing she was wearing something nicer.

A hush fell over the space as the Bentley rolled to a stop. Her father emerged from the back seat and stood up to his full imposing height.

'Isobel,' he barked, squinting in the bright sunshine as he looked in her direction.

Her chest tightened as she went to greet him. 'What do you think?' she asked. 'It's coming together.'

He surveyed the space, then looked at her and made an ambiguous huff. 'Is there somewhere we can talk?'

As soon as the apartment door closed behind them, Malcolm turned to face her.

'Hugh said you did that DNA test.' He shook his head, scowling at her. 'If he's right, your stupidity astounds me. But, unfortunately, I suspect he is.'

She should have known Hugh would run to her father. She nodded. 'Did he …' Her voice faltered. 'Did he tell you about the results?' she asked, remembering her lie.

Her father glared at her. 'He said I should hear it from you.'

There was a long pause.

'Well?' Malcolm scoffed. 'What the hell were you thinking?'

Rage simmered inside her. 'Me? How is this my fault? I'm not the one with something to hide!'

'This is why I can't trust you, Isobel! You don't bloody think!'

Her fury boiled over. 'No wonder *you* didn't want me to do it!' She spat the words at him in disgust.

'What's that supposed to mean?'

'I know about Anna. I know what you did to her.'

'Who the hell is Anna?'

'The baby nurse.'

There was a twitch of recognition on his face. He frowned. 'I didn't do anything to her.'

'Don't you dare lie to me.'

'I'm not lying. What has this got to do with Anna?'

'You had sex with her. She had a child, and that child is my half-sister. The DNA says so.'

'But—'

'Even now, you can't help lying!' Issy shook her head. How pathetic he was, denying something she could prove!

'Isobel, stop!' Malcolm's booming voice reverberated off the walls.

She took a step back, shocked by the force of it.

He inhaled deeply, exhaled loudly. When he spoke again his voice was low.

'What you're saying isn't possible.'

'DNA doesn't lie—'

'Stop!' He held up his hand. 'I had a vasectomy when your mother was pregnant with you.'

DNA Sleuths Facebook Group

Bella Ash: Hello, I'm new to all this and feeling very confused by my DNA results. Hopefully someone here can help make sense of them for me. I was given a Heritage DNA test for Christmas and it seems to have revealed a mystery. I have a strong match. The Heritage DNA results say the 'suggested relationship' is half-siblings. I've just had a very awkward and potentially damaging conversation with my father, accusing him of infidelity with a nanny, but he says he had a vasectomy as soon as my mother became pregnant with me. According to the results, I share 23% of my DNA with this woman (1865Cm, whatever that means …) How can this be? Can someone help? Thanks so much

Top comments

Mary Louise: This is why DNA tests shouldn't be handed out willy nilly at Christmas! Relationships can be damaged for good. My 92-year-old mother hasn't spoken to me since I did one last year. I'm no expert so I can't help with the results, sorry. All the best **Bella Ash**, I hope things work out with your dad.

> **Bella Ash:** Thanks, tbh I'm wishing now I never did it.

> **Mary Louise:** Me too …

Wendy Turner: Maybe it will turn out for the best. Sounds like you had reason to believe your father might have been unfaithful? If that's the case, perhaps getting it all into the open will be a good thing.

> **Mary Louise:** The reason she suspected him of being unfaithful was because of the DNA results, which seem to be wrong.

> **Karen Finn:** The DNA is NEVER wrong!! It's just that sometimes we don't understand what it's telling us.

Patricia Pine: Someone has lied **Bella**, but it might not be your father. The 'suggested relationship' in your results is just one of the possible relationships which fall in the right DNA range.

> **Bella Ash:** Sorry I don't follow

> **Patricia Pine:** It's a bit confusing. **Zelda Merlino** can you help **Bella**?

Zelda Merlino: Patricia is right. The amount of DNA you share with your half-sibling will be roughly the same as the amount you share with your nieces and nephews, aunts and uncles, and grandparents. All those relationships will share somewhere in the range of 1200 - 2200 Cms (which is the measurement used for DNA). Does that make sense?

Bella Ash: So this woman could be my niece?

Zelda Merlino: Correct. You need to use your knowledge of your family to work out which relationship it is from those I listed above. Based on age, it's usually not too difficult. Do you have a brother? If so, would he have been the right age to father a child?

Chapter 53

Hartwell Entertainment Quarter was buzzing as people arrived for the launch. Meg and Pete, who had travelled down that morning, looked on from an inconspicuous spot under a large umbrella as visitors from Sydney mixed with local families, who had obviously decided to abandon whatever remaining objections they had to the development in exchange for free food and entertainment. Even Georgie and Chrissy were there, with Robbie in a wheelchair. 'He wanted to come,' Chrissy had said, when Meg had asked her why, 'and I guess I'm curious to see the place myself.' Delta Goodrem would be taking the main stage later that afternoon, after some formalities, including a speech from Mayor Skelton. People had already started staking their claim to the seats directly in front of the stage.

Meg watched Issy as she welcomed guests, taking their hands and smiling warmly, then moved on seamlessly to the next group, silk skirt shimmering behind her. They'd been spotting Ashworths, accounting for them one by one. Hugh Thorburn and Spencer sat at a table to one side of the stage, heads bent towards each other as though they were plotting their next shady deal. Heather and Malcolm stood with the mayor and a few others, councillors perhaps. The other brother—Felix?—sat with a pretty, bored-looking

317

woman, both looking at their phones. Daisy Ashworth and her younger sister were lining up at an ice-cream van on the far side of the square.

'I think it's time,' Meg said.

'Got the tracker?' Pete asked.

She nodded, patting her pocket.

He gave her a nod. 'Text or call if you get in any trouble.'

The factory was deserted. Meg pulled up in the driveway in front of impenetrable steel security gates. The tall wire fence stretched out on either side. It was topped with barbed wire, which would tear her to shreds if she attempted to climb over. Red signs at regular intervals on the fence warned that trespassers would be prosecuted. She took a deep breath and reached for the wire cutters Pete had bought from Bunnings on his way down that morning.

She'd told him her idea the night before: Once the crowd had gathered for the launch, she would go to the dairy factory. Whoever was watching the tracker would be alarmed—no one was meant to know Ashworth Property's plans for the factory, so Meg's presence there would raise questions—and hopefully they would follow her. When they arrived at the factory, she would confront them with what she knew and film the interaction on her phone.

It wasn't a perfect plan, but it was the only way they could prove what they knew was true, that Hugh Thorburn and Ashworth Property used bribery to do their deals and intimidation to make people too scared to blow the whistle for fear of retribution. People like Robbie Baxter, Dan James, Joel Hardy and even gutless Adrian Gorecki at the council.

Pete didn't like it. He'd spent half an hour pointing out everything that could go wrong. Eventually, they'd agreed to sleep on it. That morning, she told him she was going ahead with the plan with or without him, so he'd agreed to help. He'd argued that he should be the one to go to the factory instead of Meg, but she'd objected. They were tracking Meg, not Pete, so they needed to believe it was her at the factory. It wouldn't work if they could look around and see that she was still at the launch.

She left her car in front of the gates—where no one could miss it if they came looking—and got out, patting her pocket again. Working quickly, she started on the fence, snipping the wire just to the left of where it met the gate pole. Once she'd made the final cut, she tossed the wire cutters on the grass, pulled out the section of wire to make a large hole and slipped through.

Heart racing, she hurried between towering tanks to a large open space surrounded by warehouses, looking for somewhere to plant the tracker. Somewhere open enough that she would see anyone who traced her there, but where she could conceal it from view. It was so sparse, though, just metal walls and concrete underfoot.

A rusty staircase flanked the building opposite. She checked if she could see under it. No. Good. She would hide there. But where could she put the tracker? There was a small metal awning over a door on a building nearby—maybe she could fasten it underneath. She reached up, but it was too high. And how would she attach it? She should have got Pete to buy gaffer tape.

She checked the time on her phone. Thirteen minutes had passed since she'd left Hartwell Gaol. If someone was monitoring the tracker, they would be here any minute. A hot gust of wind picked up the dust, swirling it around. A glint of red sunlight bounced off something lying in a corner where two walls met.

A Coke can. That was it! She ran back between the towers, heart pounding as she grabbed the wire cutters. The street was deserted. Thank God. She hurried back to the Coke can and cut the top, making the hole bigger. She shoved the tracker inside, slicing her thumb on the razor-sharp aluminium. Damn it. She sucked the blood, tangy and metallic, as she lay the can back on the ground with the tracker inside, then raced towards the rusty stairs and slipped into the pocket under the lowest steps.

Chapter 54

Issy stood by the stage where the audio engineer was setting up, pretending to be busy overseeing the final preparations. Actually, she was watching her mother make dazzling conversation with a vaguely familiar, pasty-faced man in a navy suit. He had the soulless look of a politician. A surge of disgust rippled through Issy as she watched Heather throw her head back, laughing at something he said, her hand on his forearm. Had they paid him off, too? Put his children through private school? Funded a beach house?

Near the entrance, Malcolm shook hands with Tony Skelton and a couple of other grey-haired men. Lindsay councillors, probably. He hadn't even glanced in her direction, still angry. She pictured him, the day before, red-faced, his words charged with fury. 'I had a vasectomy when your mother was pregnant with you!' She'd rarely seen him so uncontained, so incensed.

When she'd returned to the apartment, she'd replayed the conversation over and over, each time more convinced he was telling the truth. And then there was Rosa's response when Issy had told her she had a half-sister. The confused frown, the distant gaze, as though something wasn't making sense. Was her father's anger a result of being exposed? Or was it indignation, outrage, at being accused of something he didn't do? If what he said was true—if he did have a vasectomy—he couldn't possibly be Meg's father. The timing didn't work.

Since her post in the Facebook DNA group the night before, she'd been consumed by theories. Spencer was eighteen when she was born. She looked over to where he sat with Hugh, who was on the phone.

'Got you a coffee.'

She turned to see Felix, a takeaway cup in each hand. 'Thanks.' She took the cup.

'Everything okay?'

'Yeah, fine. Do you remember my night nurse when I was a baby? Anna?'

Felix looked away, squinting, as though he was trying to see her in his memory. 'Yeah, she was nice. What happened to her?'

'She left town and had a baby.'

Felix nodded, not understanding.

'She had a baby ... not long after she left our home,' Issy added.

His eyes widened. 'You mean, she ...'

'She was assaulted, Felix. I thought it must be Dad, but apparently he had a vasectomy when Mum got pregnant with me.'

'Assaulted?'

Issy nodded. 'It must have been Spencer.'

She looked over at Heather, who had moved on to a group of women who all looked exactly like her: Eastern Suburbs socialites with puffy faces and quilted Chanel bags and oversized diamonds on their manicured hands. There was something grotesque about them. How had she never noticed that before?

Felix followed her line of sight to their mother, then looked back at her. 'Are you sure you're right?'

Issy nodded. 'I bet she knows what happened, and I'm going to find out.'

Chapter 55

'There's no one here,' a voice said. Deep, male.

Meg waited for a reply, but none came. There was rattling—a door opening?—then a clunk. Meg moved her head, trying to see through a small gap, but the angle was wrong. Had he gone inside?

Moments later, she heard the voice again.

'I don't know where she is!'

She moved again, steady, slowly, and inhaled sharply, catching a glimpse of Dean Morgan with his phone to his ear.

'Dunno. Shit!'

There was a tinny sound. The Coke can against the concrete? Had he found the tracker?

'That bitch hid the—'

A pause.

'Someone's coming. I gotta go.'

Meg heard footsteps.

'What the hell are *you* doing here?' Dean said. She could see him now, through the gap, looking towards the newcomer, who was frustratingly out of sight. Was it Pete?

Dean walked towards whoever he was speaking to. She strained her neck and got a glimpse of Georgie. What the hell *was* she doing here? Meg had confided in her the night before, sharing her plan to bring the Ashworths down, and Georgie had warned her against it, but Meg didn't think for a second she'd follow her here. What was she thinking?

'Where's Meg?' Dean said.

Meg pulled her phone out and started filming, a tiny sliver of vision.

'You tell me,' Georgie answered. Her tone was sassy, but there was a subtle tremor in her voice.

He lunged towards her, grabbing her by the arm and pulling her in front of him so he had her in a lock, his forearm across her throat.

'Where the hell is she?' he said, again. 'She must be here somewhere.'

'I don't know,' Georgie whimpered.

He pulled his arm tighter. She let out a loud sob as he walked her back towards the building, out of Meg's line of sight. Then there was the clunk of the door.

Meg held her breath. A moment later, the door opened and Dean came out alone.

He put his phone up to his ear. 'It wasn't her. ... Georgie Baxter. ... I don't know! I locked her in a cupboard! ... I didn't sign up for this shit, Hugh. I'm out.'

He pushed his phone into his pocket and ran.

Chapter 56

'Two weeks in Aspen, then a week in the Caribbean on the yacht. We keep it moored in Turks and Caicos,' Heather was saying, when Issy tapped her on the shoulder. 'One moment.'

'I need a word,' Issy said.

Heather glanced around at the stage, the crowd. 'Now?'

'Yes. Now.'

'I hardly think this is the time or place, Isobel.' Her voice was a discreet murmur.

'It can't wait.'

'I assume this has to do with the conversation you had with your father, about—' She huffed, shaking her head, and glanced in the direction of the women she'd been talking to, who were suspiciously silent. She took Issy's arm a little too firmly and steered her to a quiet spot a safe distance away.

'You have a nerve, ambushing your father with unspeakable, unfounded accusations.'

'I know, I was wrong. It wasn't Dad.'

Heather paused, surprised by the admission. 'Yes. You were. I'm glad to see you're finally seeing sense—'

'It was Spencer.'

Heather glared at her, ice in her blue eyes. 'What?'

'It was Spencer who fathered Anna's child.'

Heather's face twitched and her jaw tensed. She swallowed, visibly, then put her hand on Issy's forearm, holding it tight. She leaned in so her face was just inches from her daughter's. Issy could smell coffee on her breath. 'Never. Ever. Say that again. Do you understand me?'

'You covered it up,' Issy whispered.

'You know what I covered up?'

'What?'

'Your positive blood alcohol test.'

The accident again. Issy frowned. 'I didn't do a blood alcohol test—'

Heather let out a mean, cynical laugh. 'Your blood alcohol was taken when you were in hospital, Isobel. You crashed your car into a wall, critically injuring your passenger. Do you think they just *forgot* to test you? That you just *happened* to get off scot-free? The blood alcohol limit is zero for P-platers.' Heather narrowed her eyes. 'Yours was 0.08. That's mid-range if you're on a full licence.'

Issy felt her chest tighten, her breath shallow. 'But—'

'But nothing!' Heather hissed. She shook her head, as though Issy was a stupid joke. 'That poor friend of yours had half her face sliced open! Have you ever wondered why they moved away after the accident? It cost us a fortune, avoiding that lawsuit, but we did it to spare you the public humiliation. And you barely gave the whole escapade a second thought. Too busy thinking about Isobel Ashworth. Flitting from one party to another in your beautiful, charmed life, which you owe entirely, *entirely*, to your father and me.'

Chapter 57

'Georgie!' Meg yelled, rattling the heavy door. 'Can you hear me, Georgie?'

She stopped, straining to hear something from inside the building, but there was nothing. 'Georgie!'

She shook the door again, but it was stuck. She froze at the sound of voices in the distance.

Heart pounding, she raced back to her hiding spot under the stairs and fumbled with her phone as she dialled triple zero.

'Police,' she said, breathless, when the operator answered.

When she was put through, she spoke steadily, quietly. 'I'm at the Highland Dairy factory in Hartwell. A man has locked my cousin in a building. She's—'

There were footsteps now.

'Someone's coming. I can't stay on the phone. They might hear me. Please. You need to hurry!'

She hung up and squinted through the gap as the footsteps grew louder. Then Hugh Thorburn came into sight.

'I think she's in here,' he said. Who was he talking to? Was Dean back?

'*Who's* in here?' a second voice said.

Meg moved her head from side to side, up and down, trying to see who it was. Hugh didn't answer.

'You've dragged me here, now tell me what the hell's going on!'

'Dean locked some chick in a cupboard and took off.'

'What the fuck? Jesus Christ. We need to get the hell out of here!'

'Mate, we can't leave her locked up! The place is deserted! How's it going to look if she's found dead in a goddam cupboard?'

Hugh rattled the door, yanking it, then kicked it with his foot and it swung open. As they stepped inside, Meg glimpsed the back of a bald head. She gasped. Spencer Ashworth? Getting Hugh *and* Spencer here was even better than she'd hoped, but none of this would be worth it if something happened to Georgie.

There was a shout from inside the building. Hugh? She pictured her cousin, trembling with fear. She needed to do something. What though? Physically, she didn't stand a chance. She was five-foot-three, no match for two men.

She looked at her phone, inhaling sharply as she had an idea. She tried to slow her thoughts, think it through properly. Would it work? Maybe. Maybe not. But it was all she had. She tapped on the number, listened to it ring.

Come on. Pick up.

She checked the time—12:56. It might be too late.

It rang out.

She cursed under her breath and tapped the number again.

Answer the fucking phone.

Chapter 58

'I trust that's the end of all this nonsense,' Heather said, glaring at Issy, who was forcing back tears.

Issy said nothing.

'Good.' Heather gave her a tight smile and patted her forearm, then disappeared into the crowd.

Issy thought of Stella. Her tiny frame slumped against the dash. What did her mother say? That she'd had her face sliced open? Was that true? Issy had asked to see her after the accident, but Mrs Austin wouldn't allow it. That was what Heather had told her, wasn't it? Then they moved away shortly after, and that was that.

As Issy pictured Stella's face, bloody and disfigured, a ripple of shame ran through her. Issy had done that to her. It was her fault, but Heather was right. She'd barely given Stella a second thought. She'd thought she was different, but she wasn't. She'd inherited her mother's carelessness, along with her blonde hair and ice-blue eyes. She was just as bad as the rest of them.

She blinked a few times and took a deep breath. She needed to pull herself together. She checked the time on her phone—12:56. The formalities were due to start in a couple of minutes. Kelly, the event manager, would be losing her mind, wondering where Issy was.

As she made her way to the stage, her phone rang. *Meg.* She didn't have time for that. She switched it to silent.

'There you are!' Kelly said, exasperated, as Issy approached the stage, reaching for a walkie-talkie. 'She's here. Good to go in three minutes.'

Issy's phone vibrated in her hand. Meg again. She frowned and swiped to answer. Kelly shook her head as though she couldn't believe what she was seeing. Issy raised her finger to say, 'One minute.'

'Meg—'

'Issy.' She was whispering, breathless. 'I need you to—'

'Where are you? Why are you whispering?'

'Please, Issy, I need—'

'I can't talk now. I'm about to go on stage—'

'Listen to me!' There was fear in Meg's voice, a sharp edge of desperation that made Issy pay attention. 'Georgie's in trouble. I'm at the dairy factory. She's locked in a building here. Hugh and Spencer are in there with her.'

'What?' Issy looked around for Hugh and her brother but couldn't see them anywhere.

'I was trying to lure Hugh here using the tracker. I was hiding and this other guy turned up, then Georgie arrived, and he grabbed her and now she's trapped inside one of the buildings.'

'What?' None of this was making sense. 'Meg, you need to call the police.'

'I have, but it might be too late. I need you to text me your—' Meg stopped abruptly.

'What?'

'I just heard her cry out. I need you to text me your Instagram login.'

'What? Why? I don't—'

'I'll go live on your Instagram. You've got three hundred thousand followers. It'll go viral. They won't hurt her if they know the world can see.'

'But I—'

'Do it, Issy! Do it now!'

'But—'

Meg was gone. Issy looked at the phone, her mind reeling.

'Everything okay?' Kelly looked at her, frowning. 'You need to take your seat on the stage. You're on in thirty seconds.'

Issy gave her a nod. Mayor Skelton and Derek Palmer, the State Government Minister for Planning, were already seated on the stage, expressions smug with self-importance.

She searched the faces of the Hartwell locals standing at the back, hoping to see Hugh and Spencer somewhere there to disprove Meg's story. She saw Warwick and some of the subbies. Chrissy and Robbie, in his wheelchair. Sue, who had closed the Red Lion for the afternoon so she could come along. But there was no sign of Hugh or Spencer.

She looked back at the phone in her shaking hand.

Chapter 59

Meg stared at her phone, willing it to light up with a text from Issy. Nothing.

She looked out at the building opposite, where Hugh and Spencer were holding Georgie. There was silence now. Was that a good sign or a bad one? Meg didn't know. She felt sick.

She looked back at the phone. *Come on, Issy.*

Still nothing. Meg shook her head, disbelieving. She thought she'd seen something in Issy. Something that set her apart from the rest of them. Kindness. Empathy. Had she imagined it? Had she seen what she wanted to see? No. Issy had those qualities, but Meg had seen something else in her too. Fear. Cowardice, even. She'd seen it in Issy's eyes when she refused to confront her father with Meg. 'If I do that, I'll lose everything,' she'd said. When all was said and done, her inheritance mattered more than the truth.

Just as Meg was giving up hope, her phone lit up. *Issy.* Meg exhaled.

Username is Dizzy_Issy_Ashworth, password Trixie1234

Tears sprang to Meg's eyes as she felt a rush of relief—and something else too. Pride, maybe? Issy hadn't failed her. Or herself.

Meg wiped her eyes with the heel of her hand and flicked over to Instagram. She logged out of her own account and back in as Issy, fat-fingered as she typed with shaking hands.

Wrong username or password.

Shit. She took a breath, steadying herself, tried again.

Yes! She was in.

Heart hammering, she selected 'live', then flipped the camera so she could see her own face. She typed *Live abduction of Georgie Baxter by Spencer Ashworth and Hugh Thorburn* as a title, then started filming.

She was live. 'My name is Megan Hunter.' She kept her voice low, a steady murmur. 'I'm a journalist with *The Times.*' She moved out from under the stairs, still talking to the camera, her breath fast and shallow. 'I'm at the Highland Dairy factory in Hartwell, ninety minutes south of Sydney. Recently, I've discovered corruption at the highest levels of the state government—' she could hear the tremor in her voice, '—involving deals done with Ashworth Property, which is headed up by Spencer Ashworth.'

She drew in a laboured breath, trying to ease the tightness in her chest. 'But someone has been trying to scare me away from this story. They planted a tracking device in my bag and they've been following me. Today I used it to lure them here, to the site of their next corrupt deal. It worked. Spencer Ashworth and Hugh Thorburn followed me here, and now they have my cousin Georgie Baxter trapped in this building.' She angled the camera to show the door.

'I'm going to knock on that door and get them to come out.' She positioned the camera on the ground, leaning it against the leg of a metal bench seat so it had a good view of the door and the space in front of the building, but far enough away that hopefully Hugh and Spencer wouldn't see it. Over 2800 people were already watching, with more joining every second. Good. She needed viewers. The more the better.

She leaned in close to the screen. 'Wish me luck.'

Chapter 60

Issy stepped up to the lectern and gazed out at the crowd. There was still no sign of Hugh or Spencer. She avoided looking at her parents. Instead, her eyes met Felix's. He sat beside Polly, who was still looking at her phone. Issy looked at Chrissy then, standing behind Robbie in a wheelchair, his weak torso leaning awkwardly to one side, both unaware that their daughter was in danger.

She took a breath and tapped the microphone. The crowd grew silent. She glanced down at the speaking notes on the lectern. Was she really going to carry on with the launch as though everything was fine?

To her side, Kelly hissed at her, 'Get on with it.'

Issy nodded, flustered. 'Hello, everyone, I'm Isobel Ashworth. On behalf of my—' the notes said family but she couldn't bring herself to say it, '—on behalf of everyone who has worked so hard to create this new space for residents of and visitors to Hartwell, I would like to welcome you all to Hartwell Entertainment Quarter.' She saw Polly lean towards Felix, holding her phone in front of him. Felix frowned, then looked up at Issy, attempting to convey something to her.

To one side of the crowd, a dark-haired guy was doing the same, holding his phone up. She'd seen him with Meg earlier. 'Watch

Isobel Ashworth's Instagram live!' he shouted. The people around him craned their necks to see his screen.

The rumble of voices grew as the news travelled through the crowd. People reached for their phones or jostled for a better view of someone else's. At the front table, Heather looked around, trying to make sense of the strange energy. Malcolm looked increasingly irate.

'What's going on?' Mayor Skelton said, blustery and irritated, from where he sat on the stage.

Issy shrugged. Derek Palmer, who was still looking over his speaking notes, oblivious, looked up. Kelly walked onto the stage, phone in hand.

'Someone's hacked your Instagram,' she whispered, her breath hot on Issy's ear.

Chapter 61

'Georgie? Georgie!'

Meg's voice reverberated off the metal walls, like a cry for help in a nightmare, distorted and desperate.

There was a muffled cry from inside the building.

'Georgie!'

Voices, then footsteps. The door opened.

'Look who's here,' Hugh said, smirking at Meg.

There was another cry from inside.

'You need to let her go!' Meg said, hoping he couldn't hear the shake in her voice.

Hugh laughed. 'What would I do that for?'

Meg took a deep breath. 'I know what you've done. I know about the bribes.'

'I have no idea what the hell you're talking about.'

'You've had someone tracking me. He threatened my mother. He threw a brick through my colleague's window.'

Hugh glared at her and shook his head.

'And there's one more thing I know.' She glanced sideways, checking the phone was still capturing the confrontation. Her heart thumped in her head as she prepared to play her ace. 'I know who you've been sleeping with.'

Hugh's face reddened, the veins in his forehead swollen with fury.

'I have two demands if you want to keep that quiet. One, release Georgie. Two, admit to the bribes.'

'We didn't—'

'You want Spencer Ashworth to know what you've been up to?'

Hugh lunged forward to grab her, but she ducked. He stumbled onto the ground as Spencer appeared in the doorway.

Chapter 62

'Show me,' Issy said, snatching Kelly's phone as Spencer appeared on the screen. He stood blocking the doorway of a rundown industrial building. Hugh was on his hands and knees. Meg stood between him and the phone, which was positioned on the ground, distorting the image, making Meg appear far taller than her slight frame. There was no sign of Georgie.

Kelly shook her head and went to do some crowd control. A siren sounded, quiet at first, then ear-splitting as it passed on the road outside. Voices in the crowd rose and fell.

Issy looked over to Chrissy again. She stood behind Robbie's wheelchair, her expression confused rather than fearful, still unaware it was their daughter that police car was speeding towards. Issy willed them to reach the factory before Meg or Georgie was hurt.

Heather muttered something to Malcolm, who shook his head and looked around, irritated at the interruption to proceedings, no hint of concern for whatever disaster was unfolding outside.

As the siren faded, Issy looked up at the huge screen that hung above the stage. What if …? Her parents would never forgive her, but she realised she didn't care. She'd spent her life trying to please them, but she never could. Nothing was enough for them. She was done with that.

She hurried down the steps to where the audio engineer stood at the side of the stage, watching his own phone with one of the roadies. She held out Kelly's phone.

'Play it on the big screen.'

'You sure you wanna do that?'

She nodded. 'Quick.'

'Um ... I don't know ...'

'Do it,' Issy hissed. 'Now!'

'If you say so,' he said under his breath as he fiddled with some settings on a laptop. After a moment, the image was projected onto the screen. Hugh's mouth moved, his face snarling and angry, but there was no sound. Block text at the top of the image read, *Live abduction of Georgie Baxter by Spencer Ashworth and Hugh Thorburn.*

There was a cry, tortured and desperate, from Robbie Baxter. Chrissy crouched beside him, holding his hand, her face etched with anguish.

Issy turned back to the audio guy. 'We need sound!'

'I'm working on it.'

The silent film continued overhead. Hugh was looking up at Meg as she spoke.

'Hurry up,' Issy said.

The ear-splitting sound of feedback came through the speakers, then it levelled out and Meg's fierce voice filled the space, reverberating off the high, stone walls.

'You're running out of time, Hugh! Admit the truth about the bribes or I'll tell everyone your disgusting secret. You're on camera. Thousands of people are watching this right now.'

Hugh's head swung around as he looked for the camera.

The crowd watched on, enthralled. Issy glanced at her parents. Heather glared at her, shaking her head. Malcolm made a throat-cutting gesture. Issy felt like she might be sick.

'You've got ten seconds!' Meg yelled, fierce.

'No!'

'Nine.'

'Please!'

'Eight'

'I can't—'

'Seven.'

'It wasn't me—'

'Six.'

'It was Spencer, he—'

'What the hell?' Spencer yelled, stepping forward.

'Five.'

'Okay!'

'Four.'

Hugh looked up, panting, silent. He was about to crack. Issy could sense it.

'Please? Please don't—'

'Three!'

'Okay, we did it! We offered bribes to get the Hartwell Gaol development approved.'

Tony Skelton stood up. 'How dare he—' He looked towards the audio guy. 'This needs to go off now!'

'And?' Meg yelled. 'What about this factory? The houses on Barton Drive?'

Hugh's hands were on his head. 'We got Derek Palmer to change the state government advice for the land usage to—'

'Shut up, Hugh!' Spencer yelled.

Derek Palmer stood up now, red-faced, gesturing desperately at the audio engineer. Another siren passed by outside.

On the screen, Spencer took another step towards Meg and Hugh.

Meg put a hand up to stop him. 'Now might be a good time to tell you, Hugh's been sleeping with your daughter, Daisy.'

'You bitch!' Hugh cried. 'You said if I admitted to the bribes you wouldn't—'

'I lied,' Meg said.

Spencer glared at her, grappling with this new information about his eighteen-year-old daughter and his lifelong friend. Hugh got to his feet and walked towards him, his hands raised in a gesture of surrender.

'Mate,' Hugh said, pleading, 'I can explain—'

Meg ran towards the building as Spencer's fist connected with Hugh's jaw. Hugh flew backwards at the force of the blow. The crowd inhaled as one. Time seemed to slow down, his body suspended in midair, then his head hit the concrete with a harrowing crack.

Chapter 63

Meg shuddered at the crack of Hugh's skull connecting with the unforgiving concrete, but she didn't stop. She needed to find Georgie while Spencer and Hugh were distracted. Her heart hammered as she raced towards the open door.

Once she got inside, she looked around, trying to catch her breath. It appeared to be a staff room.

'Georgie?' she called.

Nothing.

'Georgie!' Louder this time.

There was a soft whimpering. Meg tried to slow her breathing, unable to hear properly over her panting and the pounding of her heart. She walked towards the kitchen, listening carefully.

'Georgie? It's Meg. It's okay, I'm here.'

She opened the doors of a tall pantry cupboard. Nothing.

'Georgie?'

She heard whimpering coming from a cupboard under the sink. Hot tears flooded her eyes as she opened the doors and saw her cousin, folded up around the s-bend of the sink pipes.

Georgie's eyes were obscured by the sink, but Meg could see her mouth. Her bottom lip was bulging and bloody.

'Are they gone?' Georgie whispered.

'Not yet, but it's okay. They won't hurt you now,' Meg said, the sound of Hugh's head hitting the concrete replaying in her ears. 'You can come out.'

Georgie didn't move, her eyes full of fear.

'It's okay, Georgie. I promise.'

As her cousin shifted out of the cavity, Meg gasped at the sight of her face. Red capillaries filled the white of her left eye and a dark, mulberry bruise had formed under her lower lashes.

'Oh my God, George—'

Georgie put a finger up to her bloody lip and looked towards the door.

Meg held her breath. At first she couldn't hear it, but then, there it was. The faint but unmistakable sound of a siren.

'Thank God,' Meg whispered.

Georgie slumped onto the ground, sobbing, as though everything she'd held inside was flowing out of her. Meg crouched beside her, holding her, as the sirens grew louder.

'Noooooooooo!' Spencer's desperate voice reverberated off the courtyard walls.

Georgie looked towards the door.

'Come on. The cops are nearly here.' Meg pulled Georgie up, linking their arms, and walked her towards the door.

They stopped in the doorway, looking at the scene in front of them. Hugh lay motionless, his head resting in a pool of dark blood. Spencer leaned over him, shaking him by the shoulders.

The piercing sirens were louder still. Red and blue lights bounced off the walls before the police car came into view, stopping with a screech of tyres. Two officers got out as an ambulance pulled in behind it. Meg exhaled with relief. It was over.

She and Georgie sat side by side on the bench seat, dazed, watching the activity around them.

Within minutes, Spencer was handcuffed in the back of the police car. His usually confident posture was gone as he sat, forlorn, staring out the window, watching the paramedics load Hugh onto a stretcher. Meg almost felt sorry for him. Almost.

The younger cop came over. 'Another ambulance is on the way to get you checked out, Georgie. We'll need to take statements from you both. I know it's the last thing you'll want to do right now, but ...'

Georgie nodded.

'It's fine,' Meg said.

He gave them a nod and walked back to the car to talk to his partner.

There was a gentle touch on Meg's back. She looked up to see Pete slip onto the seat by her side.

'You did it,' he whispered. 'You got them. It was incredible.'

He put his arms around her. They sat like that for a long time.

Chapter 64

'I'm not sure if your mother will see you,' Cathy said when she opened the door at Kilmore.

Issy ignored her and stepped inside. Felix followed. Neither of them had spoken to Heather since the chaos had unfolded the day before. Steady drizzle fell beyond the kitchen windows.

'Where is she?' Issy asked.

Cathy gestured towards the formal lounge.

Heather lay flat on the sofa like a corpse. She didn't move when they entered. Newspapers covered the coffee table, bold front-page headlines telling of corruption, intimidation, abduction. And death.

'Mum?' Issy said softly.

Heather didn't stir.

'Is she asleep?' Felix asked Cathy.

She shook her head.

'Where's Dad?' Issy asked.

Cathy glanced at Heather, who didn't speak.

'He went to Sydney to meet with his lawyers,' Cathy said.

They sat down. Issy reached for *The Times*. Oversized black letters dominated the page. ASHWORTH EXECUTIVE HUGH THORBURN DEAD: Spencer Ashworth arrested following live-streamed altercation.

By Megan Hunter, it said underneath. She must have written all night, after she left the police station where they'd both been interviewed for hours, along with Georgie and Pete. Issy skimmed the article, then a second one at the bottom of the page. ASHWORTH SHAME: PROPERTY BUSINESS CORRUPTION EXPOSED.

'I hope you're happy, Isobel.' Heather's voice was flat, low.

Issy looked up. Her mother's eyes were still closed, as though she couldn't bear to face this new world, one where the Ashworths no longer reigned supreme.

Happy? Issy frowned, tears filling her eyes. Hugh was dead. She didn't know how she felt about that, if she was honest, but she wasn't happy.

'You've destroyed this family,' Heather said.

Issy shook her head. 'No, I haven't. I've set this family free.'

Her mother let out a strange, unhinged laugh. 'Tell that to Spencer.'

There was a moment of silence, then the doorbell rang.

Heather sat up. 'Who's that?'

Chapter 65

Meg wiped raindrops from her face with the sleeve of her shirt as she followed Issy down a long hallway to a formal lounge room where Heather, Felix and the prickly woman from the building site sat on plump sofas.

'You remember Meg?' Issy said to her mother.

Instead of the immaculate socialite Meg had met at the gala, dark circles lay under Heather's puffy eyes and her blonde hair sat up at a strange angle. Her face, bare of makeup, was sallow and lined.

'This is my brother Felix'—Issy gestured to the man Meg had seen from a distance at the launch—'and you know Cathy.'

'Hello,' Meg said.

Felix nodded, giving her a small smile. Heather glared back at her, the set of her jaw hard, then turned to Issy. 'What's she doing here?'

Issy swallowed, visibly nervous. 'You need to tell us what happened, Mum.'

Heather looked from Issy to Meg, then out the arched window, where the world was distorted by raindrops on the glass.

Meg cleared her throat. 'Thirty years ago, my mother worked here in this house. Then she left Hartwell abruptly. Left her family, her friends, her whole life. Not long after that, she had a baby. Me. You need to tell me what happened.'

Heather was unmoved.

'Heather?' Meg said. 'DNA results show I'm related to this family.'

Heather shook her head, a tiny, almost imperceptible movement.

'You can't just ignore me!' Meg's voice was sharper now, louder.

There was a long silence, then Cathy leaned forward. 'If you don't tell them, I will,' she said to Heather, her voice low and firm.

Heather turned to her, frowning. 'What?'

Cathy exhaled sharply. Almost a laugh, but not quite. 'I was there, remember?'

'I don't know what you're talking about.'

'Heather,' Cathy said. It was a warning of sorts, like a school principal encouraging a confession from a guilty student. 'You knew who she was the moment you saw her—' a quick glance at Meg, before pinning Heather down again, '—just like I did. We would recognise those eyes anywhere.'

Heather held her stare, then sighed heavily and looked at the plush carpet, biting the inside of her cheek as she found the words. 'I had ... I'd had a very difficult pregnancy, even worse than when I was pregnant with Felix. I swore I'd never have another child, but—' She turned her hand up. 'They called it morning sickness, but it was relentless. Morning, noon and night. I was hospitalised twice with dehydration from the vomiting. When the baby came, I was very ... It was like I blamed the baby for making me so sick. I couldn't forgive her.'

Issy shook her head. 'I was a baby!'

Heather clicked her tongue. 'I know it makes no sense, Isobel. You said you wanted to know the truth, so I'm telling you.' She exhaled loudly, then went on. 'I had Rosa during the day, but at night I was on my own. The baby would cry and cry and I just couldn't get myself up, so after the first few weeks, Malcolm hired a local girl. Anna. Do you remember her, Felix?'

He nodded.

'She was studying nursing. She would stay overnight and get up with the baby to do the night feeds.'

Heather paused for a long time. Cathy cleared her throat, a reminder that Heather had no choice but to go on. She took a deep breath.

'Something happened between Anna and Spencer when he came home during his school holidays.'

'Spencer?' Meg whispered, thoughts reeling.

'I found him … in her room. He was … It was …'

'Rape?' Issy said, when it was clear Heather wasn't going to say anything more.

The word felt like a punch, violent and visceral. Meg took a deep breath.

Heather grimaced, looked up at the ceiling rose. 'It was … I don't know.' A beat. 'That word seems a little … extreme.'

'If he had sex with her and it wasn't consensual, it was rape,' Issy said.

'It wasn't aggressive, though,' Heather spoke quietly. 'She wasn't saying no or fighting him off. She was just lying there.'

Meg looked at Felix, sitting opposite. He looked back at her, sadness and regret in his eyes, then he turned to his mother.

'What happened next?'

'A couple of months later, Anna told me she was pregnant. I thought it would be best for everyone concerned if she terminated the pregnancy. I paid her for her trouble—' her eyes flashed, '—but it seems she took the money and disappeared, without upholding her end of the deal.'

Meg bristled. Was Heather really insinuating that her mother was in the wrong? She thought of arguing Anna's case, but what was the point?

'I don't know how you can live with yourself,' she said, instead.

Heather scoffed, incredulous.

Meg got up to go. She'd heard enough. She might have inherited DNA from these people, but she wanted nothing else from them. And nothing else to do with them.

As she stood by her car, fumbling in her bag for her keys, there was a voice.

'Meg! Wait!'

She looked up to see Felix jogging down the stairs and closed her eyes, summoning the energy for another conversation. She wasn't sure she could handle any more today.

'I …' He hesitated, rubbing his chin. 'I just …'

'Yes?' she said, frowning.

'I know what you must think of us. I just want you to know that we're not all like that.'

'I know, it's fine, it's just … a lot.'

Felix nodded. 'Your mum was really nice to me. When I came back from school for the holidays, she'd let me watch *Friends* with her on the little TV in her room.' A pause. 'I'm really sorry about what happened to her, Meg. What Spencer did. And Mum.'

Meg felt tears threaten.

'She didn't deserve that,' he said.

As Meg drove up the freeway towards Sydney, she replayed the conversation with Heather, trying to work out how to feel. At long last, she had an answer. She knew the truth. She was the product of a sexual assault. An act of violence, regardless of what Heather said. Spencer Ashworth was her father. A man who had gone through the world taking whatever he wanted. An entitled, selfish, pathetic man who was currently sitting in a prison cell. But he was nothing to her. Meg had inherited his DNA and nothing else. Every single thing about her that mattered, she had inherited from her mum.

She felt a pang of deep love. All these years, Meg had been so angry with her—about the isolation, the constant moving, the drinking, the emotional detachment—so resentful for what she lacked. Meg had considered her selfish and weak, but now she knew otherwise. Jenny was fierce, determined and loyal, sacrificing everything for her unborn child. She'd fought back against a wealthy, powerful family and made an impossible choice.

And she'd done it all for Meg.

Chapter 66

Issy arrived back at her Point Piper apartment to find a note from Hugh on the kitchen bench. *Issy, I'm staying with Marshall for a few days. Let's talk when you're back in town. I want to work things out. H x*

She stared at the words. How strange life was. Just days ago, Hugh was ripping a page from a notepad, writing these words to her. Now he was gone. She hadn't cried yet. Not about Hugh, anyway. It was Anna she'd cried for on the drive home. A young girl, sexually assaulted by her employer's son and paid to have an abortion. She'd barely been able to look at her mother once she'd told them the truth.

Issy crumpled the note into a ball in her fist and put it down on the bench. Her apartment felt foreign and unfamiliar. As she looked around the open space, her eye was drawn to a stack of her old Beecham Ladies College yearbooks on the tall bookshelves at the far side of the room. She reached for one.

It fell open on the page with Issy's own year twelve photo. Her pretty face beamed off the page, head tipped coyly to one side, high blonde ponytail tied with a white satin ribbon. Beneath her photo was Stella Austin, fresh-faced, eyes sparkling, just as Issy remembered her. She touched the image, as though somehow it would bridge the years between them, the chasm that had formed that summer night, the day she'd finished her last HSC exam.

For the first time in twelve years, she let her mind travel back there, but the memories were vague, fragmented, a series of vignettes that unfurled from the deep recess in her mind where they'd been lying dormant all this time.

The steep bush track that led them towards giddy voices and a bass beat, the last traces of daylight lingering in the luminous blue sky overhead. The pop of a Champagne cork, bubbles spilling onto the dirt beneath their feet. A shot of something that tasted of licorice. Dancing. Sweaty bodies. Another shot. And another. Distant lightning flashing like a strobe light. The low rumble of thunder. Slow, fat raindrops gathering pace until it was hammering rain. Squeals of laughter as the crowd dispersed, running towards the dark path. Issy and Stella hand in hand, barely able to see the ground beneath their feet.

Then a sudden jolt on Issy's arm as Stella slipped off the side of the path. Her friend's face wincing in pain through gritted teeth, hands clutching her fat ankle. The distant voices of the others. The struggle to hold Stella, torrential rain still hammering down.

The car park was deserted except for Issy's silver BMW, an early eighteenth birthday present, sparkling new in the rain under a lone streetlight. A cold white glow on Stella's face as they sat in the car, sheltering from the storm, her cheeks wet with rain and tears. The recorded message of the cab company, over and over.

Issy closed her eyes and forced herself to face what happened next. Headlights glistening on asphalt, the air impossibly clear after the storm had passed. A Pink song on the radio. Then Stella's face distorted as the car spun into a skid. Terror on the face of a taxi driver coming the other way, swerving to miss them. The sickening crunch of metal as they hit a brick wall. An airbag hitting Issy's face like a punch.

Then everything stopped.

Silent. Still.

'Stella?'

Nothing.

A siren pierced the silence.

Then everything went black.

Deep shame settled over Issy now like a heavy blanket. She'd known she was too drunk to drive, but when her parents picked her up from the hospital, there was no mention of it. And now she knew that they'd managed things so that it was like it had never happened. Her parents had paid the Austins to make a lawsuit go away, just as they'd paid Anna to abort her baby.

She looked back at the photo of Stella. Why had she abandoned her friend so easily? She tried to recall those holidays before uni started, but it was a blur. An endless stream of parties and party drugs, one night blending into the next.

She felt sick in her stomach now, the nauseous churn of self-hatred. She thought of the Peloton. A sweat session was her usual cure for feelings like this. Instead, she opened her laptop.

Stella Austin she typed in the search bar on Facebook.

There she was. Tears prickled Issy's eyes as she studied the photo of her friend, holding a chubby baby, a shiny scar stretching from her temple to her chin.

She clicked on *Message* and started to type.

DNA Sleuths Facebook Group

Natalia Gomez: Hi all, I thought I'd post an update on my situation for those who like a happy ending. As some of you will remember, I was contacted by a man who seemed to be my mother's brother according to his DNA results. Mum and I worked up the courage to speak to her parents about it, and **Zelda Merlino** you were right! It turns out my nan and pop had a baby boy when they were just sixteen and were forced to give him up for adoption. They stayed together, marrying at 20 and having my mum at 22, then my two aunties. My grandmother says she still dreams about her baby boy all these years later. He came to our house for dinner last night and she cried the whole time. Amazing to think that we didn't even know he existed until a few weeks ago. Anyway, to those of you who are looking for answers, keep the faith. You never know what's just around the corner.

Top comments

Fergus Schmidt: Thank you **Natalia**. I needed to hear this

Karen Finn: How sad that he has spent so much of his life without his parents, when they ended up together anyway! I would feel so ripped off if I were him!!

>**Natalia Gomez:** Yes, but so great they have been reunited now!

Wendy Turner: What a beautiful outcome. I shed a little tear reading this just now. It must feel like a miracle for your grandparents.

Natalia Gomez: It really does. Miracles do happen!

Chapter 67

Christmas Day, One Year Later

Meg stood at the kitchen bench, rereading the Jamie Oliver recipe for the sixth time to make sure she had the timing right. She didn't even like turkey, it was always so dry. A roast chicken was nicer, but it was Christmas, after all. The first step in the method was a little pep talk about the recipe being 'nice and simple', which she'd found strangely comforting. It was the reason she'd chosen this recipe over a similar Neil Perry one, which was a little irrational, obviously, but she'd always had a soft spot for Jamie.

According to her calculations—based on the size of the turkey and her knowledge of the oven, which was on the hotter side—it was time to pull it out.

There were footsteps in the hall and Pete appeared. 'How's my little Nigella going?' he asked, a light hand on her back as she studied the turkey through the oven door.

She pulled a face. 'It'll be a Christmas miracle if this turkey is edible. Can you help me get it out?'

Once the enormous bird was on the bench, they shrugged.

'Looks okay,' Pete said.

She reached for a knife and stuck it into the thigh, as directed by Jamie. Clear juice ran out. Pete literally hooted. Meg laughed.

There was a knock at the door. 'Show time,' he said, going to answer it.

Excited voices filled the hall, exchanging kisses and Christmas greetings. Meg wiped her hands on a tea towel and looked up to see Georgie, followed by Chrissy and Robbie, and Shirley and Bruce, her grandparents, who had travelled down from Queensland to share their first Christmas as a family. She forced back tears as she hugged them, one by one, and led them out the back.

'Everyone's here, Mum,' Meg said to Jenny, who was resting on a sun lounge in the shade of the frangipani tree.

Jenny's head moved ever so slightly to see them, and she smiled weakly, glassy-eyed. She was non-verbal since the stroke a few months before.

Shirley pulled a chair over to sit beside her eldest daughter and took her hand.

'Drinks!' Pete said. 'Beer, Robbie?'

Meg smiled watching the interaction. Robbie's progress since receiving proper treatment for his back injury had been swift. The wheelchair was gone. Movement in his back was still limited, but he was pain free and off the oxycontin, and even working a few hours a week. Issy had got him into the best specialists and covered the costs. 'Please, let me do this,' she'd said, when Robbie objected.

'Hello?' a voice called from down the hall.

Meg jumped up to see Issy and Felix at the screen door.

'Merry Christmas!' Issy said smiling, her lips impossibly red.

'G'day, Meggsie,' Felix said, ruffling her hair. It was the nickname he'd chosen for her and, strangely, she didn't hate it.

That was almost everyone. Just as she was about to follow Issy and Felix up the long hallway, the last guest arrived at the gate, her face obscured by the enormous pile of presents she held in front of her. All Meg could see were her soft grey curls.

'Is that you behind there, Cathy?' Meg asked, opening the gate.

'Yes, it's me,' Cathy said, peeking out from behind the giftboxes. She looked so much younger since she'd grown her hair out. 'Merry Christmas!'

'Merry Christmas!' Meg said, reaching for a couple of the top boxes. 'No DNA tests this year, I assume?'

Cathy laughed. 'Not this year, sweetheart. My work is done.'

Once the turkey was carved, glasses refilled and everyone was seated at the table, Meg looked around at the faces of her family.

She felt like she needed to pinch herself. Last year, she and Jenny had dined at Rosedale. This year, they were sharing Christmas Day with so many people that she'd had to join two tables together to accommodate them all. Her lip quivered as she watched Jenny in her wheelchair at the far end, flanked by her sister and her mother. Shirley was cutting Jenny's turkey into small pieces.

Shirley and Bruce had come down to Sydney as soon as Chrissy told them about Jenny. It had been painful, knowing they'd lost so many years, but they were making up for it with frequent trips. When Jenny had the stroke, Shirley had stayed for more than a month, visiting her daughter every day. The doctors had warned them that improvement was unlikely based on the brain scans, but Shirley had said, 'We'll see about that,' and taken Jenny through the therapy exercises every day. Meg wasn't sure how much difference it had made, but it was something Shirley could do for the daughter she'd lost at twenty-two and found again thirty years later.

Jenny smiled as her eyes met Meg's across the long table. She was different since the stroke. Along with the loss of speech, she'd lost her wary detachment. The wall she'd hidden behind—ever since that day when she drove straight past the medical clinic and never looked back—had tumbled down, leaving her raw and unprotected, as though the stroke, and the truth, had cracked her open. Just last week, Meg had downloaded *The Princess Bride* and they'd watched it together, lying side by side in Jenny's bed. As the end credits rolled, Meg had seen that Jenny's cheeks were wet with tears. 'Are you crying?' Meg had asked, laughing, expecting her mother to hastily wipe her cheeks. But Jenny had nodded and taken Meg's hand, giving it a little squeeze, a statement of love as clear as if she'd said, 'I love you.'

Feeling tears threaten her own eyes, Meg looked over at Issy and Felix, who were talking with Georgie. The fallout from that day at the Highland Dairy factory had changed their family for good. Spencer had been charged with manslaughter in January and granted bail, a shock to no one given his access to the best criminal defence team money could buy and the funds to pay the million-dollar bond. In addition to the criminal proceedings, the State Corruption Commission was investigating the role of Derek Palmer and Tony Skelton, among others, in the rise and rise of Ashworth Property while Spencer was at the helm.

How much Malcolm knew about his son's criminal activity was still unclear—it looked like he'd managed to keep his own hands clean—but Meg suspected he'd been turning a blind eye for years. According to Felix, Malcolm was hoping to sell off the property business once 'all this nonsense' was done with, but creditors had repossessed a number of Ashworth assets, including Hartwell Gaol, and a recent column in the *Financial Review* speculated that insolvency was likely. Regardless of the future of the company, his retirement plans were on hold for now. Meg had had no contact with Heather or Malcolm since the truth came out, which was fine with her. Technically they were family, but she'd come to believe that blood wasn't necessarily thicker than water, after all.

There was a ripple of laughter as Issy and Georgie pulled a Christmas cracker, sending the trinkets flying across the table. Meg smiled. It was good to see Issy looking so happy. It had been a hard year for her. After what happened in Hartwell, she'd been unable to slot back into her Sydney life as though nothing had changed. 'I can see through it all now,' she'd said, when Meg asked her why she never went out anymore. Once the administrators running Ashworth Property no longer needed her help, she'd struggled to know what to do with herself. The family business had always been her only plan, trading on her family name her only strategy, so it felt scary, Meg imagined, to suddenly have to forge her own path. But after many interviews and a few disappointments, Issy had found out a week ago that she was the successful applicant for a marketing role with a global hotel chain. 'It's the first thing I've ever really done on my own,' she'd said to Meg with pride in her voice, as they'd celebrated with Champagne. She was flying out to Dubai in a couple of weeks.

And then there was Cathy. Meg looked over to see her laughing with Chrissy, their faces already flushed with Champagne. For over thirty years, Cathy had devoted herself to the Ashworths. She'd been loyal to a fault. Keeper of their darkest secrets. So when Malcolm forced her to retire, it felt like a betrayal by the man she'd secretly loved for so long. When she'd seen Meg that first day in Hartwell and guessed who she was when she saw her unusual eyes, it had been the final straw. She'd been filled with quiet fury for what she'd seen over the years, and a little shame too, she admitted to Meg, for her own role in keeping things quiet.

'But how did you know I would have done a DNA test?' Meg had asked her, once the truth came out.

'I didn't,' Cathy admitted. 'To be honest, I didn't think any of the Ashworth kids would do the test, either. I just wanted to see the look on Heather's and Malcolm's faces on Christmas Day.'

Since then, Cathy had redirected her deep loyalty and outstanding organisational skills to Meg, who'd been ridiculously busy since she won the award for Best True Crime Podcast earlier that year. *Out of the Ashes*, which told the story of her time in Hartwell, was still in the top charts every week as more and more people listened to her extraordinary account of uncovering corruption and finding a family. Because of the viral Instagram video, the podcast went global. She was interviewed on *USA Today*, *Good Morning Britain* and countless other programs across the world. In April, she'd given up freelance writing to focus on podcasting, which meant she wasn't working with Pete anymore.

That was probably for the best. They'd agreed to take things slowly at first, but then she'd stayed over one night and never left. As she looked at him now, pulling a cracker with Issy, warmth flooded her body. Love. She was surrounded by it.

She dinged her glass with her knife, swallowed the lump of emotion that sat in her throat, and stood up.

Everyone looked at her, waiting for her to speak.

'To family,' she said.

Book Club Questions

1. Have you ever done a DNA test?

2. The novel explores many different types of inheritance: behavioural, genetic, financial. What have Meg, Issy and Georgie inherited?

3. How does Meg's idea of family change by the end of the novel?

4. Issy has grown up with extreme wealth, surrounded by people who act with entitlement. How did you feel towards her at the start of the book? Did this change throughout the story?

5. Why do you think Rosa accepted the deal offered by Heather?

6. Who did you suspect of planting the DNA tests under the Christmas tree? What did you think when the truth was revealed?

7. What do you think of Chrissy's decision to pretend she didn't know Meg was her niece?

8. The novel ends with Meg and Pete together as a couple. Did you see this coming?

9. The two mother–daughter relationships depicted in the book are both complicated. What do you think makes mother–daughter relationships often fraught?

Acknowledgements

While writing this book, I developed a superstitious belief that to even *think* that I *may*, one day, need to write acknowledgements would be so utterly presumptuous that it would ensure the manuscript never saw the light of day. This meant I steadfastly avoided any activity which would, in retrospect, have been helpful at a moment like this, such as keeping a simple list of people to thank. But guess what? It worked! You are now holding my book in your hands so clearly my suspicions were correct! Obviously, I'm now terrified I'll forget someone, but I'll do my best.

Firstly, to the dream team at HQ HarperCollins Australia. That day when I met you all over coffee and fancy cakes in the HQ office was an absolute 'pinch me' moment. Rachael Donovan, I'm so glad you loved my manuscript and snapped it up so quickly. It's been enormously reassuring, as a debut author, for my beloved book to be in such safe hands. To Laurie Ormond, thank you for getting the manuscript into tip top shape, with the help of Kylie Mason and Pam Dunne. Stuart Henshall, your creativity and commitment to marketing this book has been above and beyond – thank you. Hazel Lam, your cover design is sheer genius. I know we're not meant to judge books by their covers, but I have no problem with it in this case. Judge away, I say!

To the HQ Sales team—Caroline Johnson, Kerry Armstrong, Hillary Albertson, Anne Walsh and Sean Cotcher—you are brilliant at what you do and I'm so grateful for all your hard work to get this book onto shelves. To the wonderful HQ Field Sales reps, thank you for working tirelessly to get my book out there into the bookshops. And of course, to the booksellers! Your love of books and commitment to readers is the cornerstone of the industry. Sincere thanks for all you do.

To Clare Forster. Thank you for believing in this story. I'm so thankful that I snuck onto your list at Curtis Brown Australia just in the nick of time. I was so grateful to have your wisdom and experience on my side as we worked to find a publishing home for this story. Pippa Mason, I appreciate your support in recent months. Alexandra Christie, I look forward to working together on all the future has in store.

Kathryn Heyman, thank you for helping me bring this story into the world through your mentorship. You always approached our conversations as though I knew the answers, and it turns out I mostly did. For any aspiring authors out there, I highly recommend Kathryn's *Australian Writers Mentoring Program*.

Di Blacklock, your feedback on my manuscript was invaluable. You don't pull any punches, but somehow you are wonderfully supportive at the same time. Thank you for guidance and advice.

To the wonderful community of Australian authors and writers, you are such a warm, welcoming bunch and I'm chuffed that I get to hang out with you all. To Ber Carroll, Cassie Hamer, Ali Lowe and Vanessa McCausland, thank you for the wonderful endorsements on the cover of this book — it is so thrilling to hear such glowing reviews from writers I admire so much — and to the other amazing authors who generously gave their time to read advance copies of this book: Anna Downes, Karina May and Jessica Dettmann. Ali, thank you also for your support and friendship since very early in my writing journey. Jess Kirkness, thank you for being one of my first readers. I wonder how many authors can say they taught one of their beta readers at high school? To the 2025 Debut Crew, it's been such a comfort and joy to navigate the lead-up to publication with you all. Thanks also to the many other authors and writers who have been a great support to me.

I'm indebted to the late writer-activist Wendy Mitchell, a tireless advocate for those living with dementia, for generously sharing her first-hand experience of the disease so that others could learn from it. Her book, *Somebody I Used to Know*, was invaluable in my representation of Jenny's illness. The bookshelf analogy used in *The Inheritance* to explain how memory is affected by dementia (by the doctor who gave Jenny her diagnosis) is borrowed from Wendy.

To my friends with very useful niche expertise who helped me with various aspects of this story: Dave Parsell, Simone Constant, Steve Mordue, Luke O'Neill and Kim Arlington. Special thanks to Wendy O'Donnell—I am so grateful for your help with medical matters over the years I've been writing. Any mistakes (or latitude taken) are entirely mine.

To my gorgeous friends, thank you for letting me talk about my story (often at great length) when I'm either very excited or very perplexed by it. This is invaluable for someone like me, who does her best thinking when talking (a somewhat inconvenient personality quirk for a writer). There are too many of you to name, but you know who you are. Special thanks to MVPs Lisa Harrington and Fi Poole.

This is a book about the things we inherit from our parents, and I'm so grateful to have two of the best. To my Mum, Jackie, you are one of a kind. Your sense of humour, pragmatic optimism, and all-round no-nonsense approach to life has shaped me. To my Dad, Brian, who was a brilliant story-teller, I wish you were here to see this. I think you would have been really proud.

To my sister-friends Brigid McKensey and Lucy Messara. Briddie, our conversation as we walked from Caves to Catho was when these characters first started to emerge into existence and the story began to take shape. Luce, you are my unofficial publicist. I'm touched by your evangelistic enthusiasm for this story. (Also, thank you for enlightening me that Issy couldn't, in fact, order a Prada dress from Net-a-Porter and have it by lunch time—stylist to the rescue!). To my brothers-in-law, Bob and Mike. Bobby, thanks for always making me think more deeply about my characters and why they are the way they are—it is very useful having a psychiatrist in the family—and Mike, please keep sending me those weird and wacky news articles.

To my three boys. Eddy and Ben, being your mum means more to me than anything else in the world. I'm so proud of you. Thank you for being proud of me. To my husband Craig, who has always considered my success in this writing caper inevitable, even (especially) when I had moments of doubt. You are my writers' room when I have plot problems, my counsellor when things go wrong, my adviser with the business side of writing, and always, you are my rock, the solid ground beneath my feet, always there, always supporting me. I couldn't have done this without you.

And finally, to you, the readers (and extremely committed ones too, if you are still reading). Writing a debut novel is an act of faith. There's no guarantee that it will ever be published, which can mess with a writer's head from time to time. Whenever I had moments of doubt, I would think of you and keep on going. Thank you for picking up this book. Your support means the world to me.

*

This book was written on the unceded lands of the Gadigal people, the traditional owners of the land where I live, write and read.

talk about it

Let's talk about books.

Join the conversation:

@harlequinaustralia

@hqanz

@harlequinaus

harpercollins.com.au/hq

If you love reading and want to know about our
authors and titles, then let's talk about it.